Brothers

An Immanu'El Novel

D. L. Maynard

ISBN 1482308053
ISBN-13 978-1482308051

This story is dedicated to Theresa,
who kept me going.

A Note about the Names and Dates

The Hebrew calendar is different from the Gregorian calendar commonly in use today. Years given throughout the novel are Hebraic years, which are measured from Creation (as calculated by adding up the ages of the people mentioned in Torah). The calendar uses a system of lunar months, as follows:

Spring months: Nisan, Iyyar, Sivan

Summer months: Tammuz, Ab, Elul

Autumn months: Tishri, Cheshvan, Kislev

Winter months: Tebeth, Shebat, Adar

Each month is 29 or 30 days long. In ancient times, the beginning of each month was determined by observation: the Sanhedrin would proclaim the start of a new month based upon its sighting of the first visible crescent ("new") moon. The first day of Nisan marks the beginning of the year for sacred purposes, but the first day of Tishri is the "head" of the year (Rosh Hashanah) and this is when the date officially changes and the new year begins, just as a new day begins at sunset. In order to keep the lunar year in sync with the solar year, an extra month of Adar is added every two or three years. These "pregnant" years, as they are called, serve the same function as the "leap" years in use with the Gregorian calendar today.

With few exceptions, the Hebrew/Aramaic names are to be pronounced in the "Sephardic" fashion, with the accent on the last syllable. Vowels are the European vowels: *a* as in father, *e* as in net or weigh, *i* as in pit or piece, *o* as in ocean, *u* as in cruel. *Ch* is always pronounced as in Bach (not as in church).

To avoid mispronunciation of the *J*, which should always be pronounced in the German fashion (like the English consonant *y*), I have used the letter *Y* as often as I could (hence Yaakob rather than Jacob). However, to make certain place-names easier for readers to identify, I have kept the traditional spellings for Jerusalem, Jordan, Jericho, and other well-known names rather than using the more-accurately transliterated Yerushalayim, Yarden, Yerichoh, etc.

Sicae, which is Latin, is pronounced see-CHAY.

A glossary of terms can be found at the back of the book.

Prologue

10 Elul 3778

The five young men walk slowly, sharing the weight of their burden as brothers ought. Though the day is already growing oppressively hot, none of them are in a hurry to be done with this task, for that means rolling the final stone over their hope and fully accepting their loss, and the shock is still too fresh, the grief too new, to be so quickly and casually embraced.

Abba, the eldest cries in the depths of his heart, *are you really gone?* Yisu hasn't wept yet, has been too busy tending to the needs of others to give expression to his own hurt, release his own tears to flow, allow his own anguish to escape. *What will I do without you?* He pushes that thought aside, not ready yet to surrender to the pain.

Despite their deliberate pace, the brothers reach the cave all too soon and hesitate outside. Yisu is the first to stoop and enter, and the others have little choice but to follow. The interior of the tomb is cool and dry, but the odor of corruption lingers as if to remind them of their purpose here. Carefully, they lay their father's body on the bare stone of the niche where it will lie until his flesh has returned to dust and all that remains is bone. Yisu looks at the ossuaries lining the wall at the back of the cave, his eye stopping on one that bears the inscription YAAKOB BAR MATTHAN. He helped Yosef transfer Yaakob's bones from this very shelf two years ago; he will return next year carrying a stone box carved with the name YOSEF BAR YAAKOB to do the same service for the man who raised him.

Beside him, his brother Yaakob-Katan lays a hand briefly on the linen wrappings that tightly wind Yosef's body. Katan's hand trembles slightly as he lifts his fingers to his lips and kisses them—as if Yosef's corpse were a *mezuzah* or Torah scroll, as if contact with it has somehow purified Katan. The

Law, Yisu knows, states just the opposite—all of the brothers have become defiled by their contact with the dead—but he says nothing, understanding and sympathizing with the impulse that came over his younger brother.

Squeezing Yosei's shoulder gently and kissing the top of Yehudah's head, Yisu takes Shimeon by the hand and leads his brothers out into the glare of the late-morning sun. Just to the left of the cave's opening is a large stone standing on edge, chiseled to the shape of a mill wheel and as big around as Yehudah is tall. A smaller stone has been lodged beneath it to hold it in place, and an iron bar lies on the ground nearby. As Yisu reaches for the pry-bar, Katan shoves him aside—not roughly, but with determination. "No," the younger man whispers. "I'll do it." With unshed tears blurring his vision, Yisu nods and steps back out of the way. Katan wedges the bar under the block that holds the huge stone in place and, with a grunt, pries it loose. At the same time, Yosei puts his shoulder to the stone and shoves hard, and it rolls smoothly down the carved channel to land with a soft *thud* in the groove before the tomb's mouth.

Maryam, who is standing just a short distance away, lets out a choked sob and falls to her knees, doubling over in her grief and wailing loudly. Her daughters gather around her, Rachel murmuring words of comfort while little Rebekah clings tightly to her mother and cries. Hannah wraps her arms around the three of them, weeping softly; eleven-year-old Sarah stands blank-faced and dry-eyed but throws herself into Yisu's embrace when he joins them, and refuses to let go. He holds his sister tightly, letting his tears fall at last into her hair, crying for both of them as an obscure scripture replays itself endlessly in his mind: *Put my tears in Your bottle; are they not in Your book? When I cry to You, my enemies will fall back; I know You are for me. Put my tears in Your bottle...*

Katan stands and stares at the tombstone, the iron pry-bar still clenched in his hand, his back turned toward his family and friends, alone in his grief and rage. Grief and rage. His knuckles are white from the force with which he grips the rod, but otherwise he manages to hide what he is feeling. The grief is socially acceptable—expected, even obligatory—but the rage is not. Even Katan finds the rage hard to accept. He doesn't know where to direct his anger; his vehemence has no target. It overflows in hot, thick tears and splatters into the dust at his feet as he hurls the iron rod at his father's grave. The pry-bar strikes the stone with a loud ringing clash, knocking loose some chips as it rebounds and misses his feet by scant inches. One of the limestone chips does not miss; flying through the air, it slices open his cheek, mixing blood with his tears and causing him to cry out at last. "Father!" He never even got a chance to say goodbye; Yisu was the one who held Yosef as he lay dying; Yisu was the one who heard Yosef's last words and closed Yosef's eyes. Yisu was always the one. Even when they were children...

Part One

When We Were Children

*How good and pleasant it is when
brothers live together in unity!*

—*Psalm 133:1 (NIV)*

1

KATAN

1 Tishri 3769
(The Days of Awe)

T he first trumpets sounded in Sepphoris, faint and far off and easily ignored, but almost immediately they were echoed loudly and clearly right in Nazareth. I could picture Rabbi Zephanyah standing on the roof of the synagogue with the *shofar* held high, his cheeks puffing out and his eyes squinting as he blew the long blast at the end. He didn't manage to hold it as long as he should have, and it ragged-off like a drunkard staggering down the street after a really good wedding. I laughed. Grabbing a hammer from the bench nearby, I held it up to my lips and blew a loud and wet *ppffffff*. "Maybe it's time for Abner to take over the *teruah*!" I suggested to no one in particular.

"For shame, Katan," Father scolded. "Have some respect."

The sharpness of his tone surprised me. True, Rabbi Zephanyah was one of the chief elders of our town, *hazzan* of the synagogue, and my teacher for the last seven years—but I knew better than most people just how little my father respected the man, and I didn't see why he was leaping to Zephanyah's defense all of a sudden. "But, Father—"

"No *buts*, Katan." Yosef bar Yaakob got out his serious look and turned it full force on me. I knew better than to argue with that look. That look was just like the angels who came to warn Lot to flee from Sodom—fire wasn't about to fall from heaven, but there was a thick rod in the corner that would fall on my butt if I kept going in this direction. It was time to get out of town, so to speak. Lowering my eyes and my voice, I did my best to appear humble.

"I'm sorry, Father. I didn't mean it the way it sounded."

Without waiting to be told, I put my hammer down and began to clean up the work area. That *shofar* blast was just the first of many that would be sounding over the course of the next day: one hundred in all, announcing the start of the new year and the approach of Yom Kippur. This first one, though, was a warning—we had just a few hours to get ready for the special Sabbath, for once the sun went down, all work was outlawed.

Yisu, of course, was already putting his tools away, and Saba had begun to sweep the shavings from the benches onto the floor as he did every evening. Usually we just let them pile up until the end of the week, but since this was a holiday, Father got out his broom and started pushing the sawdust into the fuel pile near the door. It should have been my job—mine or Yisu's—but Father had been doing it since he was just a boy and didn't want to give it up. So my job was to hang up all the tools and then muck out the donkey's stall and feed her. After that, I was free to wash up and put on clean clothes. I hurried through my chores without giving them much thought, focused on the idea of a day off from school and the sweets that would be on the supper table tonight.

With the arrival of sunset, the trumpets blew like crazy, some nearby and some far away. Everywhere in the land of Israel and all around the world, wherever our people had been dispersed, the *shofarot* were calling us to turn our hearts toward God. We ate our supper that evening with lots of extra blessings and prayers. Saba Yoachim said most of them, and he took his time about it, too, while the last hot meal we'd eat for a while (no cooking allowed on a holiday!) got colder and colder. "We will celebrate the solemn holiness of this day, how awesome and fearsome it is. On this day Your rulership is lifted up, Your throne is established in mercy, and You sit upon it in truth. Truly You alone are judge, arbiter, discerner, witness, recorder, sealer, inscriber..."

Blah blah blah. I stifled a yawn as he continued, "The great *shofar* is sounded, the still small voice is heard, and the angels tremble with fear..." My stomach growled, and I looked wistfully at the sweets piled on the table in front of me. "Like a shepherd seeking out his flock and causing them to pass under his staff, You cause every living soul to pass before You; You count, reckon and review every creature, determining its lifetime and inscribing its destiny. On Rosh HaShanah it is inscribed…" I listened halfheartedly as Saba launched into a recitation of all the possible destinies God could write in His book for us this year, including some pretty brutal ways to die—savaged by wild beasts, stoned, starved—the latter, most likely, while waiting for the supper prayers to end. Just when I thought I could take no more, Saba Yoachim wound it up. Then, picking up a loaf of *challah* from the table, he finally spoke the grain blessing: "Blessed are You, O Lord our God, King of the universe, who brings forth bread from the earth."

"Amen," I said almost before he'd finished, digging in at last. The *challah* was stuffed with dates and raisins, sweetened up like everything else on the table tonight. I've never been sure why we eat so well on Rosh HaShanah. Some say the tradition was started by the prophet Nehemiah to celebrate the rebuilding of Jerusalem, that he was copying the Persian custom of eating sweet foods as a symbol of a sweet new year and a new start for the Jews; personally, though, I think the tradition began so the adults could fatten up a little before Yom Kippur.

Yisu came over to me about halfway through the meal, while I was dipping an apple slice in honey. "*L'shanah tovah tikatevu*," he said, smiling. *May a good year be inscribed for you.*

"*L'shanah tovah*," I replied, stuffing the fruit into my mouth. It was just the customary greeting, but in his case it was probably a given. Except for two years ago, when Abner bar Zephanyah had beat him senseless, my brother always had a good year. And why not? He was practically perfect, after all. That rod in Father's shop, the one that so closely followed Yosef's serious look, had only visited Yisu's backside once— and that was for something *I'd* done. Even now, when any normal kid would be eating, he was making the rounds of the table with good wishes and blessings. Sometimes I just couldn't figure him out. "Sit down and eat, why don't you?" I said between bites.

"Sure, okay," he said and plopped down beside me, helping himself to some honeyed chicken. He took a few bites and then stared at me while I ate, as if he was waiting for something.

"What is it?" I asked after a while.

"I can wait 'til you're finished."

"I can't eat with you staring at me that way, Yisu. It's creepy. Just tell me what you want."

"Not here."

I sighed. He was in one of his weird moods. If I didn't go along with it, I'd never get rid of him. I balled up my napkin and dropped it on the table, then started to get up.

"Where do you think you're going, Katan?" My father. The Look.

"Nowhere, sir." I flopped back down, making a face at Yisu. *Thanks a lot.*

"Excuse me, Abba," my brother said. "May Katan and I go outside for a few minutes, please? I need to talk with him. It's a matter of *teshuvah.*"

"Certainly, in that case. Don't be too long. Come back in for grace."

"Yes, sir." Yisu turned back to me, getting to his feet and holding out a hand to help me up. "Come on, let's go." Ignoring his outstretched hand, I stood and followed him out the door, through the workshop, and out into the courtyard. "Not here," he insisted. "Up top." We climbed the stair that led to the roof, and then scrambled up the short ladder to the top of the escarpment against which our house had been built.

"Father said not to go too far," I reminded him.

"Just up the path a little ways."

"Why so private? And what did you mean, a matter of *teshuvah*?"

"What I said."

Teshuvah—repentance—is a big deal this time of year. According to the *rabbim*, on Rosh HaShanah God looks at all our actions for the past year and makes a judgment, but that judgment isn't actually sealed into His book until Yom Kippur. That gives us ten days to convince Him to change whatever He's written. *Teshuvah* is one of the ways to get on God's good side, as I understand it—the other two are prayer and good deeds. Part of *teshuvah* is going to the people you've hurt and getting their forgiveness. I racked my brain, trying to figure out what I'd done to Yisu lately that I needed to apologize for. It must have been pretty bad, for him to drag me out here, but try as I might I couldn't think of a thing. Stalling for time, I said, "I don't get it. What's so important that it couldn't wait until after supper?"

Yisu climbed to the top of a boulder that looked out over the pasture where Saba Yoachim grazed his sheep during the daytime. The moonless sky was clear, and the evening star shone out brightly near the horizon. Climbing up beside my brother, I waited for him to confront me with my crime. Instead, he pointed toward the cluster of houses a quarter-mile away that was the heart of Nazareth. "Think of it, Katan! Everyone is eating the same foods tonight, saying the same prayers, singing the same songs, even thinking the same thoughts as we are. Isn't that amazing? That so many different people can come so close to like-mindedness?" He started to sing one of the psalms:

"Behold, how good and how pleasant it is
For brothers to dwell together in unity!
Like the precious oil upon the head,
Running down on the beard, the beard of Aaron,
Running down on the edge of his garments.
Like the dew of Hermon—"

I left the supper table for this? "Get to the point, Yisu!" I interrupted.

"That *is* the point, don't you see?"

"No, I don't."

He sighed and turned to face me. "What have I done to offend you, brother?"

"Nothing.'"

"No, really. Tell me, please."

And here I'd thought he wanted *me* to apologize to *him*. I should have known. Yisu was worried that he'd somehow sinned against me. I heaved a huge sigh and slid down from the rock. "I'll tell you what you did—you dragged me away from the best meal I'm going to get all year, that's what you did. Do you have any idea how annoying you can be, Yisu?"

He jumped down beside me. "No."

"Fine, then. You really want me to tell you? You're like an itch on my back that I can't reach to scratch. Look, you've never taken anything that belongs to me, you've never talked bad about me, you're never mean to me. You don't have anything to 'teshuvah' over, okay? But you're still the most annoying person in the whole universe!" *Never taken anything from me...* Well, that wasn't exactly true. He'd taken almost all of Father's attention. It wasn't stealing, since Father gave it to him freely and before I was even born. Yisu got more than his fair share, though, even if you figure he was entitled to double because he was the firstborn. I tried to think of a way to explain my frustration, but I couldn't. Besides, there wasn't anything Yisu could do about it. The fact is, *Father* owed me an apology, but I knew I wasn't ever going to get one, so what was the point in bringing it up?

Instead, I lit into Yisu about the things that *were* his fault. "You're too *perfect*, Yisu. It isn't natural. You—you make everyone else look bad. You make *me* look bad! You get me into trouble almost every day, do you even realize that? You've—you've *spoiled* Father, and he expects the rest of us to be as perfect as you are, and we can't. We *can't!* Don't you see? Yosei and Shammai are only eight, so it's not as bad for them, but I'm just a year younger than you. You're—you're—" I couldn't think of the right words.

Yisu stared at me, biting his lower lip. "I'm who I am, Katan."

He sounded sorry. Sorry! That only made it worse. "Why don't you just get mad at me, yell at me, tell me I'm wrong? No, not you—you have to actually *listen* to what I'm saying! You have to *care* that I'm upset and frustrated! You can't even give me the satisfaction of being self-centered about it! What's *wrong* with you?" Every word that came out of my mouth made me feel worse, but I couldn't stop myself. "You're a *freak*, Yisu, and I wish I'd been born anywhere else! You're all but impossible to live with! I hate being your brother, and I hate *you!*" My tongue had run on with a will of its own, and now my eyes decided to betray me, too, filling with tears that blurred my vision and made my feet stumble as I turned to leave.

"Katan, wait. Please."

"No! Leave me alone, will you?" Ignoring the pain in his voice, I ran along the path back toward home. Instead of climbing down the ladder to the roof, though, I took the sheep trail; it was steep and rocky, and we weren't supposed to use it after dark, but I didn't care. Actually, I *did* care—since the path was forbidden at this hour of the night, I knew Yisu wouldn't follow me. *Stupid kiss-up.* I slid down the trail on my heels at breakneck speed, steadying myself against the cliff with one hand as I waved the other for balance. I hit the bottom so fast I had to run a few paces to keep from pitching forward on my face, but I recovered my balance quickly and skidded to a stop just short of slamming into the stable wall. Then I brushed myself off and wiped my face with my sleeve so no one would see that I'd been crying, turned around, and walked calmly into the house while Yisu was still at the top of the stairs.

By the time he walked in, I was already seated at the table and finishing my supper. I refused to look up even though I could practically feel his eyes burning a hole in the back of my head. I did glance up at Father, who looked first at Yisu and then at me with a puzzled frown, but neither of us said anything and Father didn't ask. After Yisu went and sat beside Saba Yoachim, I peeked up over the rim of my cup just long enough to see that his eyes were red and puffy—I wasn't the only one who'd been crying. In my head I replayed the end of our conversation over and over again, listening to myself scream *I hate you,* and hating myself for having said it. I hadn't meant it, not really, but there was no way to take back the words that had flown out of my mouth with a life and fury of their own. One thing I was sure of—I hadn't exactly swayed God's judgment in my favor tonight. So much for *teshuvah.* As usual, Yisu had gotten me in trouble just by being himself.

I did what I could over the next week to get myself in good graces; I was especially obedient and made a point of saying "yes, sir" and "yes, ma'am" whenever I was told to do anything. I tried to keep what Father called "a good attitude," but it was hard. I wasn't really sure that my actions would change God's mind one way or another—I mean, He was God. I didn't see how a few days of good behavior on my part would make Him do anything He didn't already want to do. I made the mistake of saying as much to Rabbi Zephanyah in school one day.

"Remember, Yaakob," he began (he always called me by my given name), "how Abraham bargained with the Lord for the people of Sodom. For Abraham's sake, Adonai agreed to spare the city if only ten righteous men could be found there."

"Yes, Rabbi," I said, "but did Abraham actually change God's mind? Or was that His plan all along?"

"A good question, bar-Yosef!" He smiled at me. "Tell me, then, what of this? When the Israelites bowed down to the calf of gold, Adonai said to Moses, 'Leave Me alone with this stiff-necked people so that My anger may burn against them and I may destroy them.' What was Moses' response to God's judgment?"

I thought quickly, trying to recall the exact words. "Um, he said, 'Turn from Your fierce anger; relent and do not bring disaster on Your people. Remember Abraham and Isaac and Israel to whom You swore by Your own self...' " I trailed off uncertainly.

"That's right, Moses turned to the Lord in prayer. In *tefillah*. And what did Adonai do?"

"He relented, Rabbi. He spared the people."

"Yes. So you see, Yaakob, that the works of *Yamim Noraim* are not in vain—the Lord's judgment can be softened if his people turn to him in *teshuvah*, *tefillah*, and *tzedakah*." In order to be spared another long lesson, I bit my tongue to keep from speaking my thoughts aloud: *But that was Moses and Abraham—not an eleven-year old boy from Nazareth!* But Zephanyah wasn't finished. "I don't expect you to see the connection, child. But the Days of Awe aren't simply about behaving well. They are about returning to God, to our roots in him. In *teshuvah*, we do not simply turn from sin; we turn to the One who is without sin, the One in whose image we are created, and we seek to reflect that image more perfectly. In *tefillah*, we do not merely ask for what we need, but we seek to connect with the One who provides for all our needs, both physical and spiritual. In *tzedakah* we do not merely give out of our own generosity, but we acknowledge that all we have and all we are belongs to Him who sustains us, and we seek to reflect His righteousness by treating others as generously as He has treated us. In connecting with the Most High and reflecting His glory, we move toward Him. And has He not promised that if we seek Him, we will find Him?"

" 'But if from there you seek Adonai your God, you will find Him if you look for Him with all your heart and with all your soul,' " Yisu murmured to himself, quoting from the

Torah.

Zephanyah hadn't been speaking to Yisu, nor had he given my brother permission to speak. With a frown, he turned and brought his rod sharply across Yisu's hand. "Hold your tongue, boy, and don't interrupt me again," he said brusquely.

"I apologize, Rabbi."

"As you ought." Zephanyah turned back toward me and continued his lesson, but I barely heard a word of it. My attention was focused on my brother, who sat with his eyes downcast and his cheeks flushed as red as the back of his hand where the rod had landed. He hadn't deserved that blow; but then, he almost never deserved the blows he received from our teacher. While Zephanyah's discipline was a daily occurrence and every boy in the room felt the rod at least once each week, the Rabbi punished Yisu for things he pretty much ignored in the rest of us. That whisper hadn't even carried across the room; it was hardly an 'interruption' at all, just a student remembering a scripture in answer to the teacher's question. If I'd been the one to blurt it out, I would have been praised, not punished. I clenched my jaw and looked down at my feet, seething with anger at Zephanyah's double standard. *We seek to reflect His righteousness by treating others as generously as He has treated us.* Well, maybe God should take a rod to Zephanyah, then. *Tzedakah* indeed!

After school the rabbi told Yisu to stay behind, so I waited for him outside the bet-sefer while Yosei and Shammai ran on ahead. My brother was only inside for a few minutes, but when he joined me he was pale and his voice shook slightly. "Come on, let's go home."

"What's wrong? What did Rabbi do now?"

He didn't answer.

"Yisu, I'm telling Father when we get home that Rabbi hit you for no reason again."

"No, please don't do that. It has nothing to do with that." Over the past year, Yisu had asked me again and again not to tell Father about Zephanyah's injustice. *It'll just upset Abba and in the long run it'll make things worse, not better.* "Besides, it wasn't for no reason—I was talking out of turn. I didn't obey his rule. Rabbi Zephanyah has the right to enforce his rules."

"Not when he only picks on you!"

"Don't worry about it, Katan. Really, in a couple of weeks it won't make any difference. He won't be striking me any more. He said as much just now." That sounded like good news to me, but Yisu didn't seem very happy about it. In fact, his eyes filled up with tears and he choked back a sob. "I don't want to talk about it any more, okay? Let's just go home."

2

YISU

4 Tishri 3769
(The Days of Awe)

I didn't mean to be brusque with Katan. I just didn't trust myself to discuss what had happened. Katan shrugged and walked on a few paces ahead of me, giving me the privacy I so desperately needed. *Thank you, Father, for giving me a brother who loves me so fiercely that he's willing to fight for me.* Since the assault two years ago, Katan had appointed himself my protector—he never let me walk to or from school alone, and he was quick to leap to my defense at the slightest provocation. (I'd had to work hard to convince him not to protest every time the rabbi disciplined me.) At home, I was the elder brother, but at school it was as if our roles were reversed. Not only was he popular with the other boys, but he was also, without a doubt, Rabbi Zephanyah's favorite student, the one most often called upon to read, recite, or answer difficult questions. At home, Katan was just a middle child who fell through the cracks and got swept up with the sawdust, but at school he was a shining star. I didn't grudge him his success, not one bit. He needed it.

My brother's remarks to me on Yom Teruah had been enlightening though hard to accept: *You're like an itch I can't scratch. You're the most annoying person in the whole universe. You make everyone look bad.* Was it true? Was that really how my brothers saw me? I'd tried to put myself in Katan's place, tried to imagine the hurt that had provoked his angry tirade.

Until that moment, I'd always thought Katan's troubles stemmed from a conscious decision to behave well for Zephanyah and badly for Yosef—that he simply wasn't trying very hard to please Abba, for whatever reason—but I'd suddenly found myself thinking, *What if this is truly the best he can do?* It was a sobering thought. What if sin was not just a choice—this had never occurred to me before, and it was almost impossible to really get my mind around the idea—but what if sin were my *only* choice? How would I feel? How would I feel if my best was *never* good enough? How would I feel if God were to judge me the same way Zephanyah did, punishing me for the circumstances of my birth, for something I was powerless to change?

The tears had come then, tears at the unfairness of it all, hot, angry tears of frustration. I'd wanted to lash out at someone as Katan had lashed out at me, to blame someone for the trap I was in, to scream out against God for allowing such injustice. Before I could run too far down that path, though, I'd gotten control of myself. *Poor Katan.* His words had stung me like a slap in the face, but the pain that had spawned them was a knife in the gut, twisting and remorseless. For the first time, I understood the words of the Psalmist:

> Adonai, don't withhold Your mercy from me.
> Let Your grace and truth preserve me always.
> For numberless evils surround me;
> my iniquities engulf me—I can't even see;
> there are more of them than hairs on my head,
> so that my courage fails me.
> Be pleased, Adonai, to rescue me!
> Adonai, hurry and help me!

I'd clung to that thought with all my might. *Be pleased, Adonai, to rescue me!* If all men were truly caught in a trap from which they could not escape, no matter how hard they tried—this thought was still so new to me as to be almost unbelievable, but I sensed the truth of it—then it would be unfair indeed for God to hold men accountable for their sins. But God's goodness, His justice—His love—was not something I could deny on a whim. Surely He had also offered men a way out, a salvation that was not dependent on them, something like Noah's ark. Somewhere, a door stood wide open, just waiting for men to pass through it into safety. If I could help my brother to see that....

We hadn't spoken about that night again, except once the next day, briefly, when Katan had come up to me to apologize.

"I'm sorry I said I hated you, Yisu," he'd mumbled, red-faced. "I don't, not really."

"I know," I'd answered with a smile. "I forgive you, Yaakob."

"Yeah, I knew you would," he'd replied with a sigh. Then he'd walked away shaking his head, and I'd decided it probably wasn't the best time to preach a sermon about Noah and God's rescue plan.

Now, however, walking home from one of the worst days I'd ever had at school and thinking again about the insight Katan's confession had sparked, I determined to talk to him about the open door. Anything was better than stewing over Zephanyah's remarks. It would help me to talk about God's grace, and it wouldn't hurt Katan to listen. I ran a little to catch up with him. "Hey, I'm really sorry I was short with you back there."

"It's okay."

"No, not really. You were trying to help. Thanks."

"So, what happened?"

"I'll tell you later, but I need to talk with Father about it first."

"More of the usual?"

I nodded, which satisfied his curiosity for the time being. While I was pretty sure Katan was unaware of the origin and more important details of Yosef's battle with Zephanyah over my education, my brother wasn't blind or stupid. He'd even given testimony before the judge in the hearing that followed the assault, and of course he witnessed "the usual," as he put it, nearly every day. "But that's not what I wanted to talk to you about."

"What, then?" He sounded suspicious.

"I wanted to thank you for what you said the other night."

"Huh? *Thank* me?"

His confusion was understandable. "Well, maybe not for your exact words—" I laughed. "But for taking a chance sharing them with me. What you said—well, I know it wasn't easy for you, but it really helped me see some things in a new light."

"Like what a jerk I am?"

"No. Like how hard you try to do what's right. And how

frustrated you must feel when Father doesn't notice. And how easy it is to let frustration turn into anger and get the best of you. And—and how close I am to falling off that same cliff." I hadn't planned the confession, but I was glad that it had slipped out; Katan perked up and I felt like we'd connected for a change.

"The way Rabbi treats you," he said, "always jumping on every mistake as if that's all you ever do…that's how I feel around Father most of the time, like nothing I do is right."

"I was thinking about that, and it made me think, what if it's true, that feeling?"

"You mean, nothing I do *is* right? What, that I'm just one big *wrong* walking around?"

He was getting defensive, taking it personally. "Not just you, Katan. Everyone," I explained quickly. "It made me think of the days of Noah. Remember? 'Adonai saw that the people on earth were very wicked—'"

"'—that all the imaginings of their hearts were always of evil only,'" Katan finished with me, and then concluded: "'Adonai regretted that He had made humankind on the earth; it grieved His heart.' What does that have to do with me, Yisu?"

"Tell me first what God did about the evil in the world."

"Oh, come on, you know as well as I do. He sent the Flood and wiped out everyone except Noah and his family."

"Why not them too?"

"They were the good ones, remember?"

I started to laugh again. "That's what I used to think, before our little talk on Yom Teruah! But go over the verse again: who was wicked?"

He frowned, and then his eyes got big and his mouth dropped open. "Everyone," he said, adding another verse: "'God saw the earth, and, yes, it was corrupt; for all living beings had corrupted their ways on the earth.' *All* living beings. I guess that would include Noah."

"Right!" Zephanyah had never bothered to point this out. It had taken Katan to get me to see it for myself. "So why didn't God destroy Noah too? Come on, you know as well as I do," I teased.

He did. "'Noah found grace in the sight of Adonai,'" he quoted.

"Exactly."

"Wait a minute, Yisu, are you implying that Noah was just as bad as the rest of them?"

"Implying? No, just accepting. Moses is the one who implied it."

"But in the next passage, Moses states clearly that Noah was righteous: 'Adonai said to Noah, "Come into the ark, you and all your household; for I have seen that you alone in this generation are righteous before Me."' How do you explain *that*?" He sounded smug.

"By taking the events in the order they occurred. When did God call Noah righteous?"

He thought about it for a minute, running through the entire chapter in his mind. "Um, it was after Noah built the ark." I opened my mouth to explain, but Katan had already arrived at the conclusion on his own, like the strong student he was. "God didn't warn Noah about the Flood because Noah was righteous—God called Noah righteous because Noah believed God's warning and took action."

I nodded. "But deep down inside, Noah was still just as wicked as the rest of them."

"Can you prove it?" my brother challenged with a grin.

"You need more? Okay. What's one of the first things Noah did after the Flood?"

"He built an altar and sacrificed a burnt offering to Adonai. Righteous."

"Granted. But after that?"

My brother laughed. "Oh, I see where you're going! After that, Noah planted a vineyard, got drunk on the wine, and passed out butt naked! Excuse me, I meant to say 'shamefully exposed.'"

"Yes, the action of a righteous man," I observed with a grin. "And then he cursed his own grandson, who was probably just a baby at the time. Another very righteous act. As to the legacy he passed on to his sons, in just three generations they forgot Adonai and built Babel."

"Then why did God spare him?" Katan asked with a frown.

"Good question. But I have a better one. If God spared Noah—if God warned him to build an ark and then kept that ark safe and then gave Noah everything he would need not only to survive but to prosper—if God did all of that for wicked Noah, then doesn't it stand to reason that he'd do the same for anyone?"

"But, Yisu, He didn't. He wiped everyone else off the face of the earth."

"But Yaakob," I countered as gently as I could, "how long did the door of the ark stand open? Did Noah turn anyone away? Or did they simply choose not to come?"

My brother walked in silence, pondering the questions.

Just before we reached home, I turned and led him off the path a short way to one of my favorite thinking spots, a large, sun-warmed boulder that overlooked the pastures to the east. We climbed up on the rock and stretched out side by side, watching the clouds pass by.

"You still haven't told me what all this about Noah has to do with the conversation we had the other night," Katan said after a while.

I breathed a prayer for the right words, not wanting to spoil the camaraderie we'd built. "It didn't go at all the way I'd hoped. Can we try again?" Without sitting up, I turned my head to look at him. He just stared up at the clouds, but his jaw was tense. "I love you, Yaakob. I thank God you're my brother—"

"Don't rub it in, Yisu. I already told you I was sorry for what I said."

He'd thrown the wall up so quickly that I was left standing on the other side of it with my mouth hanging open. "Yaakob—"

"Not another word, okay? I get it. You have me figured out. I'm just like Noah—everything I think or say or do is somehow wrong, and I better hope and pray for God's mercy because what I really deserve is to be wiped off the face of the earth. Worse, God's offered me mercy but I'm simply choosing not to accept it. Is that what you wanted to tell me, Yisu?" He rolled off the rock and stomped down the path without a backward glance.

The trouble was, he'd summed it up perfectly.

3

KATAN

10 Tishri 3769
(The Days of Awe)

Yisu decided to fast on Yom Kippur along with the adults. When I heard, I about went through the roof. "You can't! It's not fair!"

He looked genuinely puzzled. "What do you mean, it's not fair? I'm only a few days from adulthood. It's practically a *mitzvah* for me."

"But not for me!"

"No, of course not. What does one have to do with the other?"

"Oh come on, Yisu. You don't *have* to fast this year, but if you do it anyway, then I'll have to, too. I might not be as old as you, but I'm just as big. If you're strong enough to go the whole day without food and water, then so am I. That's what everyone will say."

"No they won't."

"Well, they'll be thinking it, anyway. So if I'm eating and drinking, I'll look bad."

"If it bothers you that much, what people might be thinking, then fast."

I felt like hitting him. "You just don't get it, do you?"

He laughed. "No, I guess I don't. You don't want to do what I do, but you feel like you have to do what I do, and somehow you blame me for that. Am I right?" I didn't answer. When he put it that way, it did seem unreasonable, but he was entirely missing the point. "So rather than doing what you want to do, or what you feel you ought to do, you want *me* to do something I don't want to do and oughtn't do. I think you're right, Katan. It isn't fair." He laughed again.

Part of me wanted to join in his laughter, but most of me was too angry. I stomped out of the room. *Fine, then, have it your way.* I would fast, too, would show him that I was just as good as he was. I went and told Father of my decision.

"Commendable, Katan, but you know you don't have to do this. If you change your mind, just tell your mother and she'll get you something to eat."

"Yes, sir. But I won't change my mind. I swear—"

"Don't," he interrupted. "No vows. No oaths. Just give it your best, and if you aren't ready yet, there's no shame in that."

"May I fast, too, Abba?" Yosei asked.

"Absolutely not. Eight is far too young. Now, go wash up. Dinner will be ready soon, and there'll be lots of food for everyone." He swatted Yosei out the door, turned to me, and laid his hand across my shoulder warmly. Putting two fingers under my chin, he tipped my head back so our eyes met. "Eat slowly and chew your food well, and drink as much as you can before sundown tonight. It's not the hunger that breaks your resolve—it's the thirst. And don't even think about staying up for the vigil tonight. Go to bed early and sleep late; the fast will go much easier."

"Is that what you told Yisu?"

"Yes, and what my father told me the first time I tried it. Remember, there's no shame if you change your mind—you are still just a child. But try to make it to the morning, at least. The experience will be good for you."

I made it to the morning without any trouble at all. But I woke up thirsty and it was all I could do to pass up a bowl of milk when I saw all of my younger brothers and sisters eating breakfast. Walking outside and some distance away from the house to relieve myself, I heard a voice murmuring indistinctly and looked around to see who it was. Yisu was on his hands and knees under a big juniper, crying. I started to go to him, but then I heard what he was saying and I backed off. "Father, oh Father, please don't let him take Your word from me. More precious than silver, sweeter than honey! How can I keep my way pure? A lamp to my feet, a light to my path..." His eyes were scrunched tight, and black streaks smeared his cheeks and forehead as if he'd had his face pressed into the dirt for a while. "Help me, Father. I'm so tempted to tell him off—help me to respect him. 'Gray hair is a crown of splendor; it is attained by a righteous life. Better a patient man than a warrior, a man who controls his temper than one who takes a city.' Teach me patience, Father. But please, please, don't take Your word away from me!" He began to sing in a broken voice, tears pouring down his face:

> "May Your unfailing love come to me, Adonai,
> Your salvation according to Your promise;
> then I will answer the one who taunts me,
> for I trust in Your word.
> Do not snatch the word of truth from my mouth,
> for I have put my hope in Your laws.
> I will always obey Your law,
> for ever and ever…"

What had Zephanyah done to Yisu? (I assumed that's who "him" was. If I were Yisu, I'd have told him off a long time ago—it would have been worth the beating.) I'd never seen my brother this upset, not about anything. As quietly as I could, I backed away, leaving him alone with God.

4

YISU

10 Tishri 3769
(The Days of Awe)

Father had advised skipping the all-night prayer vigil, and I'd followed his advice to the point of going to bed and closing my eyes. Sleep, however, refused to come, though I waited hours for it. Too many things were warring in my mind: hunger and thirst, for starters, but also my repeated failure to make peace with Katan and, overlaying everything else like a poorly-applied coat of varnish, the words Rabbi Zephanyah had spoken to me a week ago. I'd done my best to put them out of my mind, realizing that there was nothing I could do—myself—to change the situation, but in the darkness of the night they clamored for attention.

Unless I am mistaken, you will soon turn thirteen.

Yes, Rabbi. On Erev Sukkoth.

You understand what it means, to be a bar mitzvah?

Yes, Rabbi, I think so.

Think so? You'd best be sure, boy. Up until now, the guilt of your sins has rested upon your father's head. Once you turn thirteen, you will be responsible for your own choices, be they good or bad. You will be a man in God's sight, bound by His Law. I have done my best to teach you that Law, so you are without excuse. He had looked at me for just a moment without his usual hostility, and I knew his next words were going to be painful but that he was delivering them out of concern for me, for my wellbeing. *I can no longer participate in this deception, Yeshua.* It was the first time I'd ever heard him speak my name, and I steeled myself for what was to follow. *I cannot have your blood on my head. Young man, I have compromised my integrity for eight years. I have allowed others to convince me to do what I knew to be wrong, but the Law is clear....*

The internal warfare had begun at that moment. Rabbi

Zephanyah was speaking what he believed to be true, but it was *not* the truth, and the truth cried out to be told. I'd opened my mouth to release the truth that burned in the depths of my being and ran through my veins like blood, the truth that would get me what I so desperately wanted, but just before it could leap from me, another thought had clamped my mouth shut again: *Honor your father and your mother*. Yosef had chosen to keep this truth secret from Zephanyah, and without his consent I could not do otherwise—to contradict Yosef here, now, would be to brand him a liar, and that I would not do. To place my desire above his judgment was an act of disrespect so great as to be almost inconceivable, and the fact that I was even able to consider such an act had appalled me. I'd stood and listened to the rest of Zephanyah's admonition without a word, fighting back the tears that would surely have washed away my resolve if they'd been allowed to escape. Only later, when I was well out of his presence, did I at last give voice to my grief.

Now, lying awake on my pallet listening to the murmured prayers of the older men of the family, who had gathered together downstairs in the common room for their vigil, I took the only righteous course of action available to me: I, too, prayed. Silently at first, letting the words form in my heart, I brought my struggle to my Father and asked Him for the wisdom to know the right path and the strength to stay on it. *I need Your help, Father.* Tired and hungry as I was, however, I couldn't keep my thoughts focused while lying on a comfortable bed in a darkened room; all at once, the sleep that had eluded me all night was wrapping me in its arms and crooning enticements, trying to drag me into oblivion and chaotic, half-formed dreams. I roused myself and tried whispering my prayer aloud, but the sound of my voice caused Katan, who was sleeping beside me, to stir restlessly. Not wanting to wake him—not wanting anyone to listen in on my prayers or witness my distress—I got up as carefully as I could and made my way outside.

The gibbous moon threw enough light on the stairway for me to descend safely. I headed down the path that led toward Saba's pastures, seeking a spot far enough from the house that I could speak softly without being overheard. Stopping near a large juniper, I tipped my head back and stared into the black vastness of the heavens, wondering (not for the first time) how many stars there were and if Abraham had ever tried to count them. Beautiful as they were, however, the stars were not my reason for coming out here, and so I closed my eyes against their distraction and began to pray aloud. "Oh my Father..." Recalling the psalmist's call to worship—*Enter His gates with thanksgiving, enter His courtyards with praise; give thanks to Him and bless His name*—I whispered the rest of the song: "You are good, Father, and Your love continues forever; Your faithfulness lasts through all generations. *Baruch atah Adonai Eloheinu.* Blessed are You, oh Lord our God. *Baruch HaShem Adonai.* Blessed be the name of the Lord."

Though every word was heartfelt, the formulaic prayer was inadequate. My soul cried out for more. I opened my eyes again, and the stars seemed to shine even more brightly after my brief, self-imposed darkness. One shot, flaming, across the sky, and all I could think in that moment was, *When I consider Your heavens, the work of Your fingers, the moon and stars that You set in place—what is man, that You are mindful of him, the son of man, that You care for him?* "Who am I—what am I— that You care for me?" I murmured, still staring up into the vault of the sky. "Do You? Truly?" All week, I had restrained myself, held myself back from asking the one question to which I most wanted an answer, the same question Job had asked again and again without ever getting the answer he so craved. Perhaps it was a question that should never be asked, but I could hold it in no longer. "Then why, Father? Why?" My voice broke and I fell to my knees. "I don't understand! Why are You letting him do this to me?" *Have I somehow displeased you?* "Search me! Father, You know my heart! If there is any offensive way in me, turn me around and lead me the right way, Your way, that You set up in the beginning. You *are* the way, Father; You are truth and life. Please don't let this...this...*thing* cause me to stumble off the path, away from You."

A breeze caressed my face and I inhaled deeply, as if I could draw closer to God simply by breathing Him in; and, though I knew that idea was nonsense—the *Ru'ach* Spirit of Adonai was infinitely greater than the *ru'ach* wind He had created—I still drew comfort from the truth that my Father was there with me, surrounding me and filling me and bearing me up with His presence. Somewhere in His word, I was sure, was a promise to that effect, and I tried to bring the scripture to mind but was unable to recall it. *It's probably somewhere in the Prophets, the books I haven't studied yet, the books I'm now forbidden to touch...*

The thought was a fist in my gut. Tears welled up, selfish tears perhaps, but beyond my ability to contain any longer. Alone in the night, I gave release to all of the anguish that had been building in my heart day after day, weeping uncontrollably over my loss. Having so recently found my Father, was I now to be separated from Him, unable to hear His voice, unable to read the words He had penned especially for me? "Please, Father, please don't take Your word from me." I leaned forward, burying my hands in the loose, dry dirt beneath the juniper, bending down to press my forehead, also, into the dust. As I lay there, snatches of Torah and phrases from the psalms ran through my mind, forming a bizarre conversation:

I have been so bold as to speak to Adonai, though I am nothing but dust and ashes...

You are dust, and you will return to dust...

What gain is there in my destruction, in my going down to the pit? Will the dust praise you? Will it proclaim your faithfulness?

"I am dust, I am dust," I confessed, feeling the truth of it deep in my bones. "But I am also *ru'ach*, filled with Your breath, Father, formed in Your image!" I wasn't trying to claim any special privilege. On the contrary. "I am Your son, but I am also a son of Adam, a son of Abraham, a son of Israel, a son of David—I am the son of sinful men!—I *need* Your word, Your law, Your righteous *mitzvot*. I can't do this on my own! Oh my Father, if I have found favor in Your sight, teach me Your ways!

> "Wholeheartedly I am calling on You;
> answer me, Adonai; I will keep Your laws.
> I am calling on You; save me;
> and I will observe Your instruction.
> I rise before dawn and cry for help;
> I put my hope in Your word.
> My eyes are open before the night watches,

so that I can meditate on Your promise.
In Your grace, hear my voice;
Adonai, in keeping with Your justice, revive me..."

Be still, and know that I am God...
Abruptly, I stopped singing and lay silent with my face
pressed into the dirt, my tears mingling with the dust and
debris. A calm washed over me, and I relaxed my body,
stretching out under the juniper, cradling my head on my arm,
eyes closed. Again I inhaled deeply; again I felt as if God
himself were filling my lungs. *Be still and know...* The sounds
of the night enveloped me: close by, the music of a lone cricket;
above me, the sigh of the wind in the tree; at a distance, the
hoot of an owl. *Be still...* I drifted into sleep.

*When I wake up, the sun is shining into my eyes and the
cricket's song has been replaced by a chorus of cicadas. How
long did I sleep I wonder, for the pasture is dotted with grazing
sheep—it's not like Saba Yoachim to lead them out on such a
sacred day as Yom Kippur, but there they are, and so he must
be close by, for it is even less like him to leave his flocks
untended. It occurs to me for the first time that Saba Yoachim,
being of the same age as Rabbi Zephanyah, might be able to
offer me some new insights into my current situation, perhaps
advise me on how best to appeal to the rabbi to reconsider his
decision. Scrambling to my feet, I head out to the pasture,
where I can see the outline of a shepherd resting on a boulder
not too far away.*

*As I draw nearer, I realize it's not Saba but a boy about my
own age, one of the hired men I've never met before. He's
sprawled across the rock with his staff at his feet and his face
turned toward the sun, picking out a melody on a small* kinnor.
*I recognize the tune, one of King David's favorites, called
"Lilies." Something about the shepherd is vaguely familiar;
perhaps it's his coloring, which is the same as Katan's: he has a
ruddy complexion and auburn hair that falls in waves to his
shoulders. "Shalom aleikha," I greet him. "I'm Yeshua bar
Yosef. What's your name?"*

*He smiles up at me without stopping his playing. "Some
free advice, young man. It's unwise to give your name so*

quickly to a perfect stranger."

Young man? *I look again and wonder how I could possibly have mistaken him for a boy. Though his face is clean-shaven and unlined, his hair is shot through with silver and his voice is a rich baritone. Nor is this man one of my grandfather's shepherds—he wears a heavy gold signet ring on his right hand and the sun glints off the golden circlet that rests on his head. "My apologies, sir." I start to bow, but something stops me before I've moved so much as an inch.*

The stranger laughs, a sound at once attractive and repellent. "No rush, no rush. We've plenty of time for that. You know, I've been looking for you a long time. You're not an easy man to get close to. Even now, I've had to come in through the back gate. Hunger is a wonderful thing, don't you agree?" Without waiting for an answer, he begins to sing, but his tone seems to mock the words of David's psalm:

> *"Save me, God!*
> *For the water threatens my life.*
> *I am sinking down in the mud,*
> *and there is no foothold;*
> *I have come into deep water;*
> *the flood is sweeping over me.*
> *I am exhausted from crying,*
> *my throat is dry and sore,*
> *my eyes are worn out*
> *with looking for my God.*
> *Those who hate me for no reason*
> *outnumber the hairs on my head.*
> *My persecutors are powerful,*
> *my enemies accuse me falsely..."*

He stops playing then, for the first time, and stands to his feet. "Why do you weep, Yeshua?" he asks, but there is no compassion in his voice. "Why do you hunger so? Who is your enemy, this Zephanyah bar Uziyel?" His scorn is undisguised. "You seek guidance?" Again he laughs, and this time the laughter is a knife, slicing brutally through his words and the unspoken questions that hang like curtains in the air between us.

How does he know...?

"You agonize over the 'right' thing to do. Come now, boy, what is 'right,' after all? Does it not depend on who is involved? It seems to me that your 'right' choices are three, and which choice you make must ultimately depend on who you believe you are." Smiling warmly, he holds up one finger. "If you are, as Zephanyah maintains, a mamzer, *then the 'right' thing is for you to recuse yourself from the assembly and—if you're feeling particularly gracious—to thank the Rabbi for setting you straight.*

"If, on the other hand," he says, holding up a second finger, "you are the son of Yosef, then the 'right' thing to do is to follow in your father's footsteps and take Zephanyah to court. Demand what is yours by 'right.' You already have a judge sympathetic to your cause; victory is assured. Take refuge in the Law.

"However," he warns, and his smile drops away as if it had never been, replaced by a piercing gaze as he holds the third finger up before my eyes, "if you are the son of God, then tell Zephanyah to drop dead. Or, if you prefer to show him mercy, tell him to go hump a camel, but don't let him stand in your way! How dare he?" He spits with indignation. "How dare he!"

I feel the same indignation rising in my chest, burning away the tears that had been there earlier. Balling my hands into fists, I draw in a deep breath, inhaling air that reeks of sulfur, malice, and wrath. The foul stench chokes me, makes me gag, bends me double and drops me at the stranger's feet. He laughs in delight. "Yes! This would be a good time!"

Gagging and retching, I lurched upright with my eyes staring. The blackness of night had melted into dawn, but the sun had not yet cleared the horizon. Over my head, the dark branches of the juniper swayed gently in a clean autumn breeze, and birds greeted the morning with sweet trills. The smell of sulfur lingered only in my imagination, but the horror of my dream had left my heart racing and my body drenched with sweat.

Immediately I fell on my face. "Father, help me! Get this thing out of my heart, out of my mind, please! Vengeance is Yours, only Yours." I grasped for a scripture, but I was so shaken by the nightmare—the horribly *real* nightmare—the unimaginably, terrifyingly *real* nightmare—that for a moment, I was unable to bring a single relevant verse to mind. Instead, I spoke the first words that came to me, the ones I heard most often: "'Hear O Israel, Adonai our God, Adonai is one! And you shall love Adonai your God with all your heart and with all your soul and with all your strength.'" I drew in a shuddering breath, still caught in the grip of the dream's temptation—for, although I had faced the tempter only in a dream, the temptation itself was real enough to withstand the light of day. "'You are to fear Adonai your God, serve Him and swear by His name. You are not to follow other gods, chosen from the gods of the peoples around you; because Adonai, your God, who is here with you, is a jealous God.'"

The scriptures came to me then, from *D'varim*, of course. "'Vengeance and payback are mine,' You said, Father, 'for the time when their foot slips; for the day of their calamity is coming soon, their doom is rushing upon them. Yes, Adonai will judge His people, taking pity on His servants, when He sees that their strength is gone...'" This promise was for me, but not for me alone—Zephanyah, too, was a son of Israel, one of God's people, subject to His judgment and eligible for His pity. "Have mercy, Father," I whispered, not sure whether I was asking on behalf of Zephanyah or myself. I didn't want my teacher to suffer calamity and doom; neither did I want him to rob me of my place in the assembly. I wanted God to judge him, to repay him for his unkindness toward me...I wanted God to spare him, to reward him for opening Torah to me.

The conflict between the two extremes threatened to tear me apart.

I tried to pray for Zephanyah, but all that came out was prayer *about* him, pleading for myself. "Father, oh Father, please don't let him take Your word from me!" Listening to myself, I realized that until I could deal with my grief—my anger—any prayer I might force past my lips on Zephanyah's behalf would be, at best, insincere—mere words spoken out of a sense of obligation—not true prayer at all. I knew that such a sham would be displeasing to my Father, and I abandoned the attempt at once. Instead I focused on *my* hurt, *my* hunger, which was like a splinter—no, more like a log—jammed in my eye, irritating to such a point that I couldn't think clearly about anything else.

Letting my tears flow freely, I laid my grief at my Father's feet, not trying to feel any way other than how I really felt, not trying to be brave or selfless or humble or merciful—but simply admitting that I was in pain, afraid, betrayed, angry. Angry. Righteousness, I sensed, wasn't about how I *felt* so much as what I *did* with those feelings. Cursing Zephanyah, telling him to drop dead (or hump a camel) was out of the question. It was not my place. But the anger—it demanded release. "Help me, Father. I'm so tempted to tell him off—help me to respect him." I continued to pray, reciting every scripture that came into my heart, desperately searching for a weapon I could use to defeat this temptation. There must be a righteous way to express anger. There must be.

The words of a psalm I had quoted in the night came back to me in a rush: *Search me, God, and know my heart...* Beginning to understand, I sang the verse that came before that one.

"God, if only You would kill off the wicked!
Men of blood, get away from me!
They invoke Your name for their crafty schemes;
yes, Your enemies misuse it.
Adonai, how I hate those who hate You!
I feel such disgust with those who defy You!
I hate them with unlimited hatred!
They have become my enemies, too."

David had certainly had no problem expressing anger. Then again, he wasn't exactly the best role model a young man could have. On the other hand, God had referred to David as "a man after My own heart." Perhaps the answer to my dilemma lay in this psalm, but I couldn't quite see it. A teacher—I needed a teacher, someone to open the books of the Prophets and the other sacred writings to me as Rabbi Zephanyah had opened Torah.

I remained under the juniper, praying, until the sun had cleared the horizon and dried up the dew on the ground. By the time I reached home, my tears had also dried up, replaced by hope. It was, after all, a new year. As I passed between the doorposts, I reached out and caressed the sacred words I'd inscribed there years ago, and smiled. A new year. Who knew what my Father had inscribed in His book for me? I would just have to trust that it was good.

5

KATAN

14 Tishri 3769
(Feast of Tabernacles)

Dressed in my finest tunic and coat, I sat at Father's feet with my arms wrapped loosely around my knees, listening as Yisu read from Torah: "'The priests are to keep My requirements so that they do not become guilty and die for treating them with contempt. I am Adonai, who makes them holy…'" He was wearing a new woolen *tallit*, a gift from Saba Yoachim honoring his status as a *bar mitzvah*, and the leather *tefillin* were properly tied at his forehead and on his hand. The near-black of the leather matched his eyes and made his face look pale. His voice, however, was strong and clear as he pronounced each word with care, well aware that every eye in the synagogue was upon him.

As was traditional, Rabbi Zephanyah had called Yisu to the raised platform at the front of the hall to read the final portion of today's Torah section. What was not traditional was the way Zephanyah had called him. Instead of simply saying, "Yeshua bar Yosef," the *hazzan* had stepped down from the *bimah* and walked over to the bench where the men of our family sat, while all of our neighbors looked on curiously. "Since today is your thirteenth birthday," he'd said, looking down at Yisu, "I can no longer call you 'boy,' for you are now considered a man in the eyes of HaShem and this community. And so, as it is customary for a young man to be given *aliyah* on the Sabbath of his birth week, I invite you to come up and read for us." The words had been polite enough, except for Zephanyah's refusal to address Yeshua by his name. That was considered rude in the extreme, and I heard one or two people mutter. Had they also heard the animosity that edged his voice? I didn't think I had imagined it. Certainly Father's frown was an indication that he'd also noticed. But Yisu had stood without a word and had made his way to the *bimah*, and Father had held his peace.

Yisu had been born on the fourteenth day of Tishri, the day before Sukkot began, which meant that Father and the other men of our family were usually away in Jerusalem for the Ingathering. But because Yisu's thirteenth birthday had fallen on Sabbath this year, Father had made the decision to remain in Nazareth several days longer than usual. "Let Yisu take his rightful place in the assembly before heading south. We'll spend the first two nights of Sukkot at home, take the fast road through Samaria, and still arrive in the City in plenty of time for Yisu to fulfill the *mitzvah*."

"Just you and Yisu?" I'd asked, disappointed. After all, I'd been allowed to go up for Passover last spring, though Father had made us boys stay home on Shavuot. (That was Yisu's fault; he'd gotten separated from the rest of our family after Passover and Father had spent three whole days looking for him.)

"No, everyone," Father had replied with a grin. And so it was decided: instead of merely pretending to be wandering Israelites by sleeping in booths for a week, the entire family was going to camp out for real as we made the pilgrimage to Jerusalem.

"Even Sarah?" I'd asked in disbelief.

"Yes, even Sarah. She's almost as old as Yisu was when we traveled up from Egypt. She's a whole year older than you were, Katan, and you handled the trip just fine."

"But, Father, you never let any of us go up until just last Passover—"

"Yes, well, I've changed my mind about that, at least for this Feast."

"But why—"

"I hardly think I need to explain myself to an eleven-year-old boy. Enough." Even if I hadn't seen The Look, I would have recognized The Tone. I shut my mouth. Still, it wasn't fair. Yehudah was only three, Yosei eight—I'd begged year after year to be allowed to go up to the Feast with Father and had always been told that I was too young. This would be my very first Sukkot in the City—although, with our late start, we'd probably miss all the festivities except the last day or two—and now I'd have to spend it lumped in with the little kids. Great.

"This time, may I sleep on the roof with Yisu and Yonni?" I'd asked hopefully. My brother had attached himself to our cousin Yochanan during our last visit and the two of them had guarded their friendship like a fortress, keeping me at a distance the entire time.

"No. Have you forgotten? I told you, Yonni left home several months ago. Besides, I don't want to camp this entire brood on Aunt Elisheba—that would be imposing on the High Priest's hospitality, to say the least. We'll pitch our *sukkoth* somewhere outside the gate along with the rest of the latecomers."

"Will Yoshiah be there?"

"Yes, I think so." Well, then, at least there would be one friend for me. I hadn't seen my cousin Yoshi since just after Passover, when the two of us had traveled back from the feast with his father, my uncle Zebdi. Yoshiah and I were just a year apart in age and always had fun together—when we weren't getting into trouble. Before I could ask Father any more questions about our Sukkot plans, though, he'd interrupted me. "That's enough, now, Katan."

I thought about our plans for the upcoming week as I listened to Yisu finish his *aliyah*. "'Keep My commands and follow them. I am Adonai. Do not profane My holy name. I must be acknowledged as holy by the Israelites. I am Adonai, who makes you holy and who brought you out of Egypt to be your God. I am Adonai.'" He stood quiet for a long moment after he had finished reading, staring at the scroll with a strange expression, and then kissed his fingertips in reverence before returning to his seat.

Although I was not yet an adult in any recognized sense of the word, I was more than old enough to sit with the men in assembly; still, a spot on our family's bench would have to wait until either Saba Yoachim or Saba Yaakob died. We boys had to sit on the floor. Earlier, Yisu had been sitting beside me, but when he came down from the *bimah*, Father and Saba Yaakob scooted apart to make room for him on the bench. I looked over my shoulder as Yisu sat himself down between them. Father was beaming, even more than usual where Yisu was involved. Saba also looked pleased and whispered, "Well done, Yeshua."

My brother, on the other hand, was pale and drawn. His eyes looked huge in his face, like big black pools of ink, making his cheeks seem even whiter. He smiled briefly, but then his face collapsed again and he sat down with his head lowered and his lips moving soundlessly. From where they were sitting, the adults could probably only see the top of his head, but I could read his lips: *father, please, no.*

The thing about living in a *sukkah*—there is no privacy. None. The walls are thin, the roof full of holes. It's fun as long as you remember that every word you say can be overheard by everyone in your *sukkah and* outside of it. Apparently Yisu and Father forgot.

Our family built only three *sukkoth* this year, since we'd need to pack them with us all the way to Jerusalem. Mother, Aunt Mimah, and the girls slept in the biggest one; Father, Saba Yaakob, and Saba Yoachim slept in another; and we five boys slept in the third. I had a hard time falling asleep; there was a rock or a root or something poking me in the small of my back, and it took a while for me to find a comfortable position. After what seemed like hours, I dozed off briefly, but someone started snoring loudly in the next booth, and once I woke up I couldn't get back to sleep again. I lay on my back staring at the full moon shining through the loosely-woven palm mat that served as our roof. An owl *whoo-whooed* in the distance and then, closer, another cry broke the stillness—a human cry, muffled and wordless and filled with grief. It sounded like it had come from the plateau.

I rolled over to see if Yisu had heard it, too, and noticed that his half of the pallet was empty. At the same time, I heard footsteps crunching lightly on the gravel of the sheep trail, moving away from our camp as they climbed toward the crying on the plateau above. "Yisu, is that you?" Father's voice was low, as if he was trying to be quiet, but it carried clearly through the night.

Although I knew it was none of my business, my curiosity got the better of my manners. As soundlessly as I could, I crept barefoot out of the *sukkah* and made my way up the stairs to the roof of our empty house. A low wall of plastered-over mud bricks surrounded only three sides of the roof; the fourth side rested against the limestone of the cliff, which rose about three cubits higher than the house. I crouched in the shadow of the escarpment, not sure exactly where my father and brother were and not wanting to show myself. Just as I was about to peek over the ledge, I heard their voices practically on top of me, and I hunkered down against the stone of the cliff out of their sight.

"What's wrong, son?" Father said softly.

Yisu didn't answer him except to sniffle, as if he was sucking up his tears.

"Come, now, Yisu, you've been keeping something from me for nearly two weeks now. Do you think I haven't noticed? Whatever it is, it's tearing you up inside. Please, let me help."

Why couldn't Father ever take that tone of voice with *me*? He sounded like he was ready to take on the world if Yisu asked. But all my brother said was, "Thank you, Abba. I know you want to help. But I think…I think this is something I need to handle myself."

"Would you at least tell me what it is? Perhaps I could counsel you…"

There was a long silence. I heard a *snap*, and a moment later a thin piece of wood flew end-over-end past my head and bounced across the roof to land a short distance from where I sat. I knew at once what was going on: Yisu had this weird habit of snapping twigs and tossing the bits around absentmindedly whenever he wrestled with a problem. "'Plans fail for lack of counsel, but with many advisors they succeed,'" my brother murmured to himself before answering Father in a stronger voice. "All right. I'll tell you, sir. I won't be going back to school—"

"That's ridiculous!" Father interrupted. "Of course you're going back. You're a gifted student, Yisu, and you've worked so hard to come this far—"

"Abba. Please. I won't be going back because Zephanyah has made it plain to me that I'm not welcome anymore."

"But the judge ordered him—"

"To accept me in *bet-sefer*. *Bet-sefer*. I've graduated, Abba." My brother's voice was resigned, matter-of-fact. "But higher education? No one can force a rabbi to take a *talmid*. Even if the elders did order such a thing, do you really think Zephanyah could be compelled to teach me what I most need to know?" There wasn't even a hint of tears in his voice. In fact, I didn't think getting kicked out of school was the thing that had him upset at all. I guess Father came to the same conclusion.

"Then what were you crying about?" he asked.

Again, a long silence and a twig snapping. When Yisu spoke this time, his voice was hoarse. "My *aliyah* yesterday..."

Father waited, probably afraid to interrupt again, but Yisu said nothing else for a long time. Finally Father spoke up. "It was wonderful. You read well. I can't wait until next time you're called to the *bimah*."

"It *was* wonderful," Yisu whispered. "There won't be a next time."

"What?" Father voiced what I was thinking, and in the same tone of disbelief.

"The rabbi told me that he wouldn't be calling me up again. Ever." His voice broke.

"But Yisu, every man has a right to read from Torah—"

"And he also said that I will not be permitted to touch the books in his library."

Father was practically stammering with rage. "He can't do that! He can't forbid you access to the Law—"

"The Law is in my heart, Abba. He made sure of that." In a trembling voice, he said, "'In the beginning God created the heavens and the earth. The earth was unformed and void, darkness was on the face of the deep, and the spirit of God hovered over the surface of the water...'"

My brother continued to recite Genesis from memory until Father cut in, stopping him somewhere during the third day of Creation. "Enough!"

Yisu's recitation had calmed him down, and he continued in a steady, quiet voice. "Rabbi Zephanyah hasn't forbidden me access to the Law; he's just gotten between me and the Prophets. I'll still be able to hear the prophecies that others read out during assemblies, but I won't be able to study the books for myself."

"But why, Yisu? Did he give a reason?"

"Oh, yes. He has an excellent reason." Like any *talmid* worth his salt, my brother repeated Zephanyah's words in exactly the tone of voice that the Rabbi, no doubt, had first spoken them: "'Young man, I have compromised my integrity for eight years. I have allowed others to convince me to do what I knew to be wrong, but the Law is clear—you should not be allowed in the assembly. I cannot forbid you to enter the synagogue; I do not have the authority to ban you from the assembly, though HaShem is my witness that I have tried. Your blood be on your own head, and on the head of the man you call your father. What I can do, however, I will. As *hazzan* I have the authority to decide who will and who will not read from the books in my keeping. This one time and this one time only, I must again succumb to pressure and give you your *aliyah*. Savor the moment. But understand this—I have nothing against you personally, boy, really it's for your own good—I will not permit you to handle the sacred texts again.'" Yisu fell silent, probably reliving what he'd felt the first time he heard those words. I remembered the expression on his face when he'd come out of the synagogue that day. *I don't want to talk about it.* Poor Yisu. He ate and breathed scripture. Rabbi Zephanyah's insults and beatings were nothing compared with this latest injustice.

Father was seething. "I'll take him back to court, right after we return from the City. Abiyud has already ruled twice that you're legitimate, so Zephanyah doesn't have a leg to stand on. He can't single you out like this..." Father continued to rant, but I didn't pay attention.

Up until that moment, I'd been so focused on the fact that Yisu had been banned from the books—a fate worse than death for my studious brother—that I hadn't paid attention to the reason. But what did Father mean, the judge had ruled that Yisu was legitimate? Who said he wasn't? Zephanyah? *The Law is clear—you should not be allowed in the assembly.* Was Zephanyah implying that Yisu was illegitimate? That my brother was a *mamzer*? But that would mean...Mother...?

"Abba...please," Yisu was saying. I wrestled my attention back to him. My brother had put on his teaching voice, the one he used with me whenever he wanted to make a point. But he wasn't talking to me now; he was talking to Father. "How can I say this? I respect everything you've done for me, how you fought to get me into school, and how you want to fight for me now. All my life, you've loved and protected me."

"Not well enough."

"Forgive me if I disagree with you. God could not have given me a better father. I thank Him for you every day. Every day. But..." He drew in a deep breath and blew it out again, noisily. "I'm not a child anymore, Abba. This thing with Zephanyah—I need to handle it myself. As a man. Are you hearing me?"

"Yes, you're right," Father said. "I'm sorry. Of course, *you* should be the one who takes him to court this time."

"No, Abba," Yisu said quietly. "I'm not going to bring suit against him."

"But, son, he won't relent on this otherwise."

"Probably not, but I can't humiliate him further just for doing what he thinks is right. He's wrong, of course, but he doesn't know what he's doing—because no one has told him. How can I fault him for that? You yourself, before you understood, came to the same conclusion; you told me so yourself, remember? God set you on the right path, and if He wants to, He can do the same for Zephanyah. Face it, Abba, if the rabbi had all the facts, he'd probably beg me to be his *talmid*."

Father's tone became worried, urgent. "You're not going to tell him, are you?"

"No, no, it's not my place. If my father doesn't reveal it to him, he isn't meant to know."

"Good. On that, we're agreed."

"I *am* praying for him. I've been praying about this situation day and night since it happened. But that's all I'm going to do. No judge. No court. No demands. No opposition from me at all."

"But Yeshua..." Father's voice trailed off into a soft murmur and I had to strain to hear him at all. The only words I could make out clearly were his last ones: "How will you learn what you need to know?"

"God will provide. I don't know how. I don't know when. But He wasn't surprised by this, Abba. He's allowed it for His own purpose. Remember the Patriarch Yosef, what he said to his brothers? Zephanyah might mean this for evil, but God will use it for good. I keep coming back to that. I've been thrown into a pit, but I'm not alone. My father is with me. He hasn't forsaken me."

Of course Father was with him. What was Yisu talking about? He sounded like a fool, talking about Father as if Father weren't even there, but it was late and I was tired and all of his words were starting to melt together in my mind as I began to doze into a dream about Yisu falling into a pit. "You can't do this to me," he said, or perhaps it was "*for* me." I roused enough to realize he was still standing on the plateau above me, and caught the words,"battle belongs to Adonai," before slipping back into sleep.

I wandered around aimlessly for a while in a dark place, searching for something, hungry and cold. Very cold. Then I looked up and Yisu was standing over me, but he was older and dressed like a prince of Egypt. "Remember what I told you last year," he said in Father's voice, but it was strangely muted, as if he were standing much farther away. "I am Yosef bar Yaakob..." I knew the genealogy of the Patriarchs from school—*Yosef bar Yaakob, bar Isaac, bar Abraham, bar Terah*—but Yisu was getting them all wrong. "...bar Matthan, bar Eleazar, bar Eliud..." As he spoke, his voice changed, split in half; and the words began pouring out of his mouth in two streams, one high-pitched and one deep, running together like water, name after name after name after name in a meaningless murmur. Then his voice came into focus again, though still far off and hard to understand. "Don't forget," he warned me solemnly in Father's voice. "It's when they forgot their origins that our fathers sinned. They let themselves grow proud and fat and turned away from God; they made the mistake of thinking they'd raised themselves to the palace on Mount Zion, instead of humbling themselves before the One who had set them there." He crouched down beside me and stared into my eyes, his gaze intent and searching as he gripped my shoulders. "Don't trust your brothers with this. They're still too young to guard the secret." *What secret?* I tried to ask, but nothing came out. Yisu mumbled something I couldn't make sense of and then said more clearly, "Yaakob, have you been listening?" Again I tried to speak; again failed. "Yaakob?" my brother repeated, insistently. "Yaakob? Yaakob?" He reached out and pushed me, not too roughly at first, but then harder and harder.

"Yaakob! Katan! Wake up!" my father was saying as he shook my shoulder. I opened my eyes and shivered in the cold of the midnight air. "What are you doing on the roof, son?"

The moon had gone down a ways; I'd been up there for more than an hour from the looks of it. I didn't want Father to know I'd been deliberately eavesdropping, so I mumbled something incoherent and pretended to be still half asleep. I was vaguely aware of Yisu standing in the shadows behind Father, but my brother didn't say anything. Father half-led, half-carried me to the stairs and down to the courtyard, stopping outside the sukkah where my younger brothers were quietly snoring. "I'll help him to bed," Yisu murmured, taking my arm. I didn't want or need his help, but I couldn't say that without admitting that I was wide awake, so I hung my head and let my eyelids droop, allowing him to lead me to our pallet and tuck the blankets around me. "Katan?" he whispered. Quickly I rolled over so my back was to him, mumbling some nonsense syllables before pretending to fall back asleep. My pretense caught up with me, though, and before I knew it I was lost once again in my dreams.

6

YISU

15 Tishri 3769
(Feast of Tabernacles)

The sun rose earlier than it should have on the first day of Sukkot, or so it seemed, but that was probably due to the fact that I'd gotten so little sleep. I opened my eyes to find that my brothers had already vacated our *sukkah*; from the sounds, the family was gathered nearby eating breakfast. Though I wanted nothing more than to lie in bed and think about the things Abba had told me last night—*it's when they forgot their origins that our fathers sinned*—I instead whispered a quick prayer and rose to join them, staggering slightly as I yawned and blinked to clear my eyes. Abba was also just making his way to the table that the women had set up in their booth; my grandfathers and brothers were there already and, judging from the half-empty plates in front of them, had been up for quite some time.

"Yisu, where is your *tallit*? Surely you haven't forgotten the assembly?" Saba Yaakob greeted me in a tone of disbelief. "What, Yosef, you're not ready either? Were you two up so late that you've forgotten what day it is?"

"I'm sorry, Father; I didn't know we had plans this morning, other than to rest," Abba said in a weary tone. It was, after all, a holiday.

"If we were in the City, we'd be at the Temple right now. Since we're here, though, it's only right that we join the assembly. Hurry and get dressed, both of you. Sleepyheads!"

Each year, the men of Nazareth who were unable to make the pilgrimage to Jerusalem for whatever reason—most of them old or in poor health—gathered in the synagogue on the first and last days of Sukkot for worship, and those of our family who stayed at home usually joined them. Considering the *hazzan's* remarks to me over the past two weeks, I thought it would be best for everyone concerned if I was not among them this year. My grandfathers, however, who knew nothing of Zephanyah's decree, insisted that both Abba and I accompany them to this morning's service. I waited for Abba to give them some reason that would excuse the two of us, but he was silent, nor could I myself think of one good reason to skip the assembly—other than the fact that I knew how little my presence was welcome there.

Should I share that fact with my grandfathers?

Only in my dream on Yom Kippur had I thought of broaching the subject of my unusual birth with either of them, and even then only with Saba Yoachim. Despite the tainted nature of the dream—if *tainted* could even begin to describe the fester of evil permeating that nightmare—I wondered if it might indeed be wise to seek Yoachim's advice. There was something *different* about the way he interacted with me. Saba Yaakob treated me as a beloved grandson, but Saba Yoachim...well, it was nothing I could nail down, but I suspected that Yoachim already knew a lot more about my conception than he let on, perhaps more than anyone besides my parents.

Without my father's consent, however, I was unwilling to include Yoachim in my confidence. It would have looked odd in the extreme for me to pull Yosef aside now, so I simply nodded and acquiesced to my grandfather's request, rising to my feet without finishing my breakfast. Abba frowned at his breakfast plate but also nodded and stood. "Dress quickly, Yisu," he said. "If we're going, then we'll all go together. We can eat when we get back." I had little appetite anyway, envisioning the cold reception I was going to receive from Zephanyah upon my arrival. *Your blood be on your own head.* Abba saw the look on my face and drew me aside. "I know this isn't going to be easy for you, Yeshua, but it's the right thing to do. You belong in the assembly."

"Yes, sir." I turned and ran upstairs to change into my best clothes—during the Feast we are required to eat and sleep in *sukkoth*, but changing clothes within the privacy of solid walls is not only permitted, but encouraged. As I donned my new *tallit*, I tried also to put on a better attitude. *The purpose of the gathering is to glorify God. Whether or not Zephanyah wants me there is unimportant. My Father wants me there. I'm going to sing His praises and listen to His word.*

That last thought gave me the strength I needed to walk into the synagogue with my head held high and a smile on my face. I started to sit on the floor with my brothers, but Saba Yaakob stopped me, gesturing for me to sit beside him on the bench as I'd done yesterday. There was plenty of room—Saba Yoachim didn't take his usual place but crossed to the bench nearest the *bimah*, the bench reserved for those chosen to read. In astonishment, I looked up at Abba, who raised his eyebrows and shrugged, obviously as surprised as I.

In truth, the only thing that should have been surprising was the fact that I'd never seen Yoachim up there before. As an elder member of the community and a descendant of Aaron ha-Kohein, Yoachim should have been given *aliyah* on a regular basis. For reasons of his own, however, he had always declined the honor. Always. Apparently, something had happened to make him change his mind. "Did you tell him…?" I whispered to Abba, but he shook his head, leaving me none the wiser. The mystery would have to wait, however, for at that moment, Zephanyah sounded the *shofar*, calling the assembly to worship.

Because this was a special day, a *Yom Tov*, the usual prayers and blessings were only a small part of the service. Everyone present had also brought a *lulov* made from the four species listed in Torah—palm, myrtle, willow, and citron—and we waved our branches in all directions as we obeyed the commandment to "rejoice before Adonai." There were special readings from Torah—passages about God's establishment of the Feast and how it was to be kept—and a long and gruesome *haftarah* reading from the prophet Zechariah about the Day of Adonai, which included many dire warnings for those who failed to keep the festival of Sukkot. I wondered briefly at Zephanyah's choice for the *haftarah*—was I the only one who had difficulty rejoicing while listening to scriptures that promised "a plague in which their flesh rots away while they are standing on their feet, their eyes rot away in their sockets, and their tongues rot away in their mouths"? Perhaps if I could study the prophecy in more depth…

Then Saba Yoachim rose and went to the *bimah*, unrolling another scroll. He met my eyes and smiled before beginning. "The word of Adonai, spoken through His prophet Isaiah:

> "But a branch will emerge from the trunk of Jesse,
> a shoot will grow from his roots.
> The Spirit of Adonai will rest on him,
> the Spirit of wisdom and understanding,
> the Spirit of counsel and power,
> the Spirit of knowledge and fearing Adonai—
> he will be inspired by fearing Adonai.
> He will not judge by what his eyes see
> or decide by what his ears hear,
> but he will judge the impoverished justly;
> he will decide fairly for the humble of the land.
> He will strike the land with a rod from his mouth
> and slay the wicked with a breath from his lips.
> Justice will be the belt around his waist,
> faithfulness the sash around his hips.
> The wolf will live with the lamb;
> the leopard lie down with the kid;
> calf, young lion, and fattened lamb together,
> with a little child to lead them…"

It was not a traditional selection for Sukkot, I could tell that from the look on Zephanyah's face—apparently the *hazzan* had not chosen this passage and wasn't expecting Yoachim to read it—but I knew immediately who *had* chosen it: my Father. Not only did these words help me rejoice over the earlier passage from Zechariah—understanding more fully the nature of the justice that Adonai would mete out against those who opposed Him—but they answered the question that had nagged at me a week ago: was His Spirit truly with me?

Yes. Oh, yes.

We rose before the sun the next morning, disassembled the *sukkoth*, and loaded them onto our wagon along with the other provisions we'd need for the journey to Jerusalem. I say "our" wagon, but in reality it belonged to our neighbor Netzer bar Abiyud, as did the ox that pulled it; Abba had rented the wagon for the trip since our own cart was far too small for all the gear, and our donkey wouldn't have been able to handle the burden either. Netzer and his family (including Shofet Abiyud, the judge who had twice ordered Zephanyah to teach me) had already gone up to the Feast. Most of the pilgrims had left a week ago, in fact; the only one traveling with our family was a boy two or three years older than I, named Shimon, whose uncle had taken ill on the way up to the City.

"Shimon," Saba Yaakob said, after introducing the young man to the rest of us, "you're welcome to bunk in with us older men, but there's room for one more in the boys' *sukkah* if you don't object to sharing a pallet with Yisu."

"No, sir, that won't be a problem," Shimon replied.

"Fine, then. Katan, you'll move to Yehudah's bunk."

Katan heaved a great sigh before saying, "Yes, Saba." I understood the reason for his reluctance; Yehudah was only three, and sleeping too closely beside him could have unpleasant consequences, as I'd discovered myself on several occasions. I'd have volunteered to take the risk this time, but Saba had already invited Shimon to bunk with me, and I didn't want to appear inhospitable. Katan must have also realized there was no use protesting the swap; he turned to Yehudah, warning, "You'd better not wet the bed, Yudi."

While Yehudah squealed in protest, Saba finished the introductions and arrangements, and within the hour we were on our way. Yehudah rode in the wagon with Sarah, since both of them were too little to keep up, and Mother walked nearby with Aunt Mimah and the rest of the younger children. I'd expected to walk with Shimon—to help him feel welcome and get to know him a little—but Abba had other ideas, so the two of them went ahead of the party with thick staffs in their hands, scouting the road for potential problems.

The road through Samaria always had potential problems, but so far Abba had managed to travel it safely on many occasions. If we'd been journeying in the company of the Pharisees, the route would have been impossible—their concern for purity made Samaria off-limits. Abba was more worried about bandits. He laughed at the idea that simply passing through Samaria might defile a man. *Rocks are rocks, air is air, water is water. God gave all of this land to Abraham, and we are sons of Abraham—why should we go miles out of our way?*

I was assigned to the rearguard with Saba Yaakob, an easy task; we walked a few paces behind the wagon and made sure no one fell behind or wandered off. Katan was supposed to be leading the ox, but after an hour or two he got Yosei to take over that job and ran back to Saba and me. "Can I have a turn as guard?" he asked, obviously eager to do what he considered "man's work."

"I don't see why not," Saba Yaakob nodded with an indulgent smile. (He had a soft spot for his namesake, I'd noticed more than once.) "Yisu, give Katan your staff and take a break."

"Yes, sir." I'd have honored his request under any circumstances, of course, but in this instance his desire and mine were in perfect harmony. While I loved and respected Saba Yaakob, we had never really connected on a deeper level. I don't know why. Certainly I'd tried to get close to him, but he always held me off. It was as if…as if he'd already made up his mind about me, already decided who I was, and so felt no need to get to know me. We'd just spent over an hour marching side by side and had spoken barely a word to one another. At home, it was the same way: Yaakob's words were few; when they did come, they revolved around wood and stone, the proper use of a hammer, and other impersonal topics. I craved more, but my attempts to find out who lived beneath his skin were always turned aside with a gruff, "Not now, Yisu."

Since I had no duties at the moment, I was free to do as I pleased. Ordinarily, I would have enjoyed some alone time, but I'd already spent nearly two hours in relative silence and I was in the mood for conversation. Abba was still walking ahead of the party, and he'd made it clear that he wanted Shimon to himself, so I decided to walk with Saba Yoachim.

My two grandfathers were as alike as stone and grass. Where Saba Yaakob was a wall—*come this far and no further*—Saba Yoachim was a pasture: his soul was expansive, welcoming, holding out the promise of rest and refreshment to anyone who chose to come in. At the same time, however, he guarded secrets of his own, hidden behind knolls and under rocks. I determined to do a little digging around one of those rocks, to see if I couldn't unearth the reason he'd chosen to read in the *knesset* yesterday and why he'd chosen that particular passage from Isaiah.

Yoachim was strolling beside the wagon, chatting with Mother, although the two of them fell silent when I approached. "Yeshua," he said with a warm smile, "walk with me for a bit, son." Had he again intuited my desire? Wordlessly, I fell in at his side as he picked up his pace, putting some distance between us and the wagon, but not going so far as to catch up with Abba. Shammai started to follow us, but Saba shooed him away. "Go help Yosei with the ox," he ordered his son. Once we were alone, he asked, "So, what's going on? Why didn't you want to go to the service yesterday?"

My own question would have to wait. "Was it that obvious, sir?"

"Blatantly, to anyone with eyes to see. Oh, relax, most of them are as blind as Samson. I've been watching you, though, since you first came home from Egypt, and I like to think that I'm not completely stupid. Zephanyah's been giving you a hard time again, hasn't he?"

How should I answer him? Seeing my hesitation, Saba continued as if I'd said yes.

"I'm not surprised. I remember how it was just before you were born, and I knew Zephanyah would never let it rest. I'd like to believe that I'd be more generous in his place, but who am I to judge even myself?"

"You know then, Saba? What he says about me?"

"Of course I know. I hate to break the news, Yeshua, but half the town knows—or knew, at any rate: most of the rumors died out when Yosef and Maryam left for Bethlehem, and after the uprising nobody really cared any more. Except, apparently, Zephanyah. So, what has he done now?"

I told him.

"Well, I wish I could say I'm surprised, but I'm not. Still, the situation is intolerable. That he should dare to do such a thing to you, to *you*, of all people—" He caught himself, cut himself off in mid-sentence, but not before he'd answered my unspoken question, given me a glimpse of what lay beneath the rock: indeed, Yoachim knew much more about my origins than he'd let on. He saw the expression on my face and smiled sheepishly. "Ah, I gave myself away, didn't I?" He shook his head and sighed. "I never could keep a secret for long."

Glancing around once to make sure no one else was listening in on our conversation, I dropped my voice before asking, "How did you find out, Saba?"

"Maryam is my daughter. She told me."

"Oh. Of course." How simple. I should have known.

He laughed. "Don't give me too much credit, Yeshua. I didn't believe her."

"Then how...?"

"I believed Yosef. He had nothing to gain from such a story, and everything to lose. And once you came along— watching you over the years as I have—well, that erased the last of my doubts. You're quite an extraordinary young man, Yeshua."

I didn't know what to say. His praise brought tears to my eyes. "Thank you, Saba. You honor me."

"You honor me, son, every time you call me Saba. I've done nothing in my life to merit such favor. Your father...Yosef knows how little I deserve such favor. However—" He drew in a quick breath, pulled himself a bit straighter, and continued matter-of-factly. "As I was saying, the current situation is intolerable. Until another teacher can be found for you, I will have to suffice. The only problem is, I have no library. So, here's what we shall do, if it meets with your approval. You shall ask questions, I shall search the books, and then I will find opportunity to share the pertinent scriptures with you. Agreed?"

I smiled, blinking aside the tears, and shook my head. "As you did yesterday?"

He looked puzzled. "What do you mean?"

"Your *aliyah* yesterday. From Isaiah."

"Ah, you caught my mistake? I was supposed to read the section that corresponds to the Zechariah passage—the one that goes, 'On this mountain Adonai-Tzeva'ot will make for all peoples a feast'—but I opened the book to the wrong place, and once I'd started reading I thought I'd look a fool to stop and fumble around until I found the right spot, so I just went on."

I laughed. "I was looking for that very scripture, not one week ago."

"Are you telling me that it wasn't a mistake at all?"

"Not as far as I'm concerned. Adonai directed your hand."

Saba stopped walking and began to weep.

"Saba?"

He held up one hand, asking for my patience with a brusque shake of his head. I understood. For reasons of his own, he needed to be alone with his thoughts. I stayed by his side, loath to abandon him in his distress, but otherwise left him to himself. *Father, You know what's on his heart right now, the burden he's carrying. I don't. Please help him.*

We walked on in silence, while snatches of other conversations drifted through the air around us. Shammai and Yosei were arguing over whose turn it was to lead the ox; Yehudah was whining to get down from the wagon; my sisters Rachel and Hannah were giggling about something; and up ahead, Abba had stopped walking and was berating Shimon in a tone that was barely controlled. I caught the word "Zealot" and knew there was trouble brewing.

Few things provoked Yosef past the point of self-control, but the Zealots—even the mention of the Zealots and their Cause—brought out a side of him that he normally kept deeply buried. I didn't know the full story, though I'd pieced together a lot of it over the years; our family, like most of the families in Nazareth, had suffered greatly in the uprising led by Yudah bar Hezekyah, who had become the leader of the Zealots in the Galil around the time I was born. My uncles, father's younger brothers Yehudah and Matthanyah, had joined in the revolt and were killed. More than that, none of the adults would say— Yaakob had made it clear that the topic was off-limits, and Yoachim once told me the tale wasn't suitable for children—but Abba never spoke of the Zealots without clenching his jaw, his fists, and (I suspected) his heart. Two years ago, when there had been another revolt in the eastern parts of the Galil, Yosef had caught Katan and some of his friends playing a game, throwing rocks and sticks at targets, calling the targets "Romans" and themselves "Zealots," and he'd beaten Katan and forbidden him to see his friends for the rest of the month. The next day, he'd sat the two of us down and told us in no uncertain terms that we were to avoid the Zealots, avoid even speaking of them. *It's not a game*, he'd said. *They claim to be God's servants, but the*

Zealots are ruthless, seeking only to devour, and they will devour themselves in the end. Stay away from them, do you hear me? Stay away from them.

All of this ran through my head in an instant. I was close enough now to see the expression on Yosef's face as he lit into Shimon, and to hear his words clearly. "Is there already a price on your head? You're only fifteen!" he cried out, and then he must have noticed that the rest of the family was catching up to him, because he fell silent, shooting a warning glance at Shimon before composing himself. "Let's rest here for a while and have a bite to eat," he said once all of us had come together.

While the women prepared a simple meal, I unharnessed the ox and led it to a grassy patch by the side of the road to graze, then returned to the wagon to make myself useful. "Where's Yosei?" Mother asked. No one knew; Shammai was also missing.

Always the shepherd, Saba Yoachim put two fingers to his lips and let out a powerful whistle that brought the boys running. He scolded them. "Wandering sheep, the two of you. Stay close from now on. There are still bears in these hills."

Shammai unwound a strip of leather from his waist, bent and picked up a stone, and fitted it into the pocket of the sling. "Bears?" Grinning, he whirled the sling faster and faster over his head. "See that tree stump over there?" He released his shot and bits of rotted wood flew from the stump. Our guest, Shimon, applauded the shot.

"I can do it too!" Yosei shouted, and loaded his sling. "Watch!" His stone fell short of the target. "That one doesn't count. I was just warming up. Watch this one." He missed again, overshooting this time. "I can do it!" he protested. "One more try—"

Abba interrupted. "That's enough, Yosei. Sit down and rest, or you'll never make it to Gannim." I heard the warning in his voice and guessed the reason behind it, but my brother was too young to understand. He protested.

"But, Abba—"

"I said enough. We're not even halfway there yet." Taking the sling from Yosei, Abba then turned his attention on Shimon. "Don't encourage them." His words were neutral but everything about the way he said them was hostile, confirming my guess.

"N-no, sir," Shimon stammered.

Looking confused, Shimon crossed to the other side of the road, as far away from Yosef as he could decently get, and sat down on a large rock. I picked up a loaf of bread from the wagon and followed Shimon, half expecting Yosef to come after me and pull me away, but although he looked up sharply as I passed, Abba said nothing. I took his silence for permission and climbed up on the rock beside Shimon. "Here," I said, tearing the loaf roughly in half and holding the larger piece out to him. "You must be hungry."

"Thanks," he replied, accepting my offering, and reached into his satchel to pull out some smoked mutton, which he shared with me. Mumbling a hasty blessing, he began to eat.

I let him chew in silence for a while. It was a thick silence, though, filled with Yosef's warnings, his unspoken threats. I had to break it. "You're a Zealot, aren't you?"

My bluntness took him by surprise, and he coughed, spitting out a half-chewed bit of meat along with the words, "Why do you ask that?"

"That tone of voice Father used when he told you not to encourage Yosei and Shammai. It's his *stay-away-from-the-Zealots* voice. I heard it a lot two years ago, during the revolts." I fixed my gaze on him, trying to see him clearly, and failing. Like Saba Yaakob, he was closed, guarded, carved from granite. There was nothing outwardly soft about him: his build was lean and muscled, his features sharp and chiseled, his eyes hard like flint. His youth only accentuated his hardness—he didn't even have a beard to soften the angle of his jaw. *What have you gone through?* I wondered. *What happened to make you so...so...resolute?* I fumbled for words, not wanting to make him uncomfortable, but driven to know him better, to find the part of him that was made of flesh. "You don't look like I'd expect a Zealot to look, but there is something about you that's different from other boys I've known. You seem—I don't know—*older* than you are."

"Do I?" His tone, like the rest of him, was guarded.

I sensed that I'd have to proceed carefully; if he thought I posed a threat, he'd bolt like a frightened sheep. Nodding casually, I took a bite of the mutton and chewed it over slowly along with my thoughts. *Why do I care?* This stranger, I'd never seen him before and would probably never see him again once we reached Jerusalem. There must be hundreds like him, men and boys made hard by life, hearts turned to stone by the things they'd witnessed, the choices they'd made. *Why do I care?* This boy—no, this *man*—had chosen to involve himself with thieves and murderers; he might even be one himself. Why should I care about such a person? Yosef had warned me to stay away from people like Shimon.

As if in answer to my thoughts, a fragment of Torah rose up to confront me:

I will demand from every man an accounting for the life of his fellow man...for God made man in his image.

Cain had asked God, "Am I my brother's keeper?" *Yes!* my heart had cried when first I'd read the tragic story, and that cry echoed in my heart now. *Why do I care?* How could I not care? Was I to stand by and watch Shimon plunge headfirst off a cliff without even crying out a warning? He wasn't the only one who could be resolute. Perhaps he was bent on destruction, but my Father had named me Yeshua for a reason. If I could just get Shimon to talk to me...

Still chewing, I said, "I heard Father say you're only fifteen. You're the right size and all, but your eyes—they're older somehow, as if they've seen a lot." It was a clumsy invitation, but sincere.

He turned it down. "Did you also hear your father mention the price on my head?"

"Yes."

"It's true." He said it boldly, as if challenging me, watching to see how I'd react.

"You don't have to worry about it," I assured him. "He won't turn you in."

"Will you?"

This question was so unexpected that I laughed. "You're kidding, right?"

"No, I don't usually kid about matters of life and death. Especially my own."

He really thought I would hand him over to the Romans. What had he done that weighed so heavily on his soul that he would be afraid of an unarmed thirteen-year-old? I stared at him in wonder, having finally found a soft spot, a piece of flesh in this granite man—but the flesh was rotting and leprous with fear, and it broke my heart to think that this was all there was to Shimon Zealot: stone and fear.

"Well, will you turn me in?" he asked again.

"No, of course not. Why would you think such a thing of us?"

"It's pretty clear that your father hates everything the Zealots stand for."

"Only because he's seen the end result of those beliefs, Shimon. His brothers sided with the rebels and were hanged. Hundreds—thousands—of men have died horrible deaths because of the Zealots."

"See, that's where you and your father are wrong. Those men didn't die because of the Zealots; they died because of the Romans. Blaming the Zealots is like…well, it's like blaming a farmer for losing his crops to the drought, or blaming a physician for the death of a man who fell head-first off a roof, or blaming the shepherd boy when a bear steals a lamb."

Did he really see it that way? Had no one ever taught him that men are responsible for their choices, that actions have consequences? Did he truly think the Zealots were innocent victims? I challenged, "What if that shepherd led his flock to the bear's den? If the physician was the one who pushed the man off the roof? If the farmer planted his crops in the desert?"

"It's not the same."

"Are you sure?" I challenged him again. *Come on, Shimon, think about what you believe.*

"Of course I'm sure. What would you know about it? You're just a kid."

"Father says—"

"You can't believe everything your father tells you, you know."

It was true, although I'd never really stopped to consider the possibility before. Yosef was a man, and like all men, he had a capacity for falsehood. I knew he had told lies, but the thought had never once occurred that he might lie to *me*. For a second I pondered the revelation, feeling sick to my stomach. But then a second, more powerful truth rose up to take its place: Yosef might lie to me, but my Father never would, never could.

You can't believe everything your father tells you, you know.

All of a sudden, I knew why Shimon had joined the Zealots.

"Neither can you," I said gently. With that, I got up and left him alone with his thoughts.

7

KATAN

20 Tishri 3769
(Feast of Tabernacles)

Even though we didn't get there until the sixth day of the
festival, Sukkoth in Jerusalem was all I had hoped for.
We pitched our booths outside the city walls along with
thousands of other pilgrims, and it seemed like there was
always a celebration going on somewhere. We only got to
attend the evening service in the Temple one time, but it was
worth every bit of the four-day trip from Nazareth; the music,
the dancers, the lights—it was all so incredible! Never had I
seen anything like it. "Oh, they do that every night during the
Feast," Saba Yoachim told me when I asked him about the
torch dancers. "Of course, they spend most of the year
practicing."

"Were you one of the dancers, when you lived here?"

He laughed. "You honor me, Yaakob. Can you really
picture me doing a dozen back-flips with a lighted torch in my
hand?"

"Well, you were young once, Saba."

"I suppose so, but my talents lay elsewhere. No, I never
even aspired to be a musician, much less a torch dancer. Only
the very best young men of the City are chosen for such a
thing."

"Then you should have been chosen," I said solemnly.

He ruffled my hair. "Shame on you for such blatant flattery,
boy. Off with you."

All too soon Sukkoth was over and it was time to return
home. We didn't go back through Samaria, though—since there
was no rush, Father said, we'd take the usual pilgrim route up
the eastern bank of the Jordan—so we had lots of company on
the road and the celebration continued all the way to the Galil.

Better still, just before leaving Jerusalem we met up with our relatives from Bethsaida. Father decided to travel in the same caravan as Uncle Zebdi and Aunt Shelomith, and that meant I got to spend a whole extra week playing with my cousin Yoshiah. As if that wasn't enough to make my week perfect, that boy Shimon stayed behind in the city, so Yehudah bunked with Yisu for the rest of the trip.

Once we got home, I expected things to go back to normal, but they didn't. How could they? Yisu was no longer in school. Although I'd known for weeks now that Rabbi Zephanyah had kicked Yisu out, I hadn't really thought about how the change would affect *me*.

At first it was strange, walking to school without Yisu—walking into the synagogue without having to ignore the whispered insults and stifled laughter that always seemed to greet my brother's arrival. After a few days, though, I got used to the change…and I discovered that I liked it. I hadn't realized, before, how on edge I had been—always waiting for something to go wrong, always waiting for Rabbi to hit Yisu, always waiting for one of the boys to trip him or push him or insult him…always expecting trouble and always hoping, always praying, that Yisu would somehow manage to avoid it for just one day. Just *one* day.

Even on those rare days that my prayer was answered and nothing went wrong, I hadn't been able to relax. I was one of Rabbi's favorite students, but I hadn't been able to enjoy that favor because part of me always felt guilty whenever he praised me. As much as Yisu annoyed me, he was still my brother, and he didn't deserve the abuse that Rabbi heaped on him; accepting praise from my brother's enemy felt *wrong*, like I was somehow being disloyal. And, to be honest, part of me always wondered: *is Rabbi praising me because I deserve praise or just because he's trying to hurt Yisu?*

But now Yisu was gone, and Rabbi was still showing me favor on a daily basis. It felt good. It felt so good. *Oh please, God, don't let Rabbi change his mind*, I caught myself praying one day. *I'm tired of being my brother's keeper.*

At the thought, I cringed, waiting for guilt to wash over me. It didn't.

8

YISU

Winter 3769

For years, my daily schedule had been basically the same: up before dawn, prayers, chores, breakfast; three hours with Rabbi Zephanyah studying Torah; three hours working with Abba in the shop; dinner, prayers; three more hours with Abba or helping one of my grandfathers, or (once a week) preparing for Sabbath; then an hour or two for myself before supper, prayers, and bed.

With my graduation from *bet-sefer*, a huge hole had appeared in my day, but Saba Yoachim had come up with a plan to fill those hours, a plan that benefited both of us: I became one of his hired hands. I started getting up earlier, training myself to wake with the first cockcrow, grabbing the satchel Mother had filled for me the night before, and heading out to the far pasture with my flute, a staff, and a sling. I made my prayers there, alone except for the sheep I led out from the fold, and sang psalms as I watched the sun rise.

I say alone, but really I was never alone; my Father was always there with me, I knew, though I could neither see him nor hear him. Like David, I learned to find the gifts he had left in the pasture for me: the parables he had written in the stones and across the sky, the words he whispered on the breeze and in the nickering of the ewes to their lambs. Like David, I responded with stories of my own that I sang back to him—sometimes using my voice, but as often through my flute. *Adam* I named it, though it was shaped of wood, not clay; work of my hands, lifeless until I breathed into it, Adam took my breath—my *ru'ach*—and let it soar to heights I could not reach on my own. *Is this why you created men, Father? That you might play upon us a song otherwise impossible?*

At mid-day, when the sun had climbed high enough to

warm the air and the boulders of the pasture, Shammai relieved me of my watch and I joined Abba to practice my trade. Most of the time, that meant working in the shop; on occasion, however, it entailed a three-mile hike to Sepphoris. Abba, of course, would already be there, engaged on whatever building project he and Saba Yaakob had been hired to complete, so I made the outward journey with Katan and Yosei as soon as they finished school; we all returned together at the end of the day. Finally, after supper and devotions each night, Saba Yoachim drew me aside to give me my wages.

He didn't pay me in *denarii*, but in scriptures.

He'd quickly learned which ones would most delight me, and brought me a new treasure each day, a treasure I hurried to lock away in my heart. Throughout the day, as I sat guard over the sheep or worked the wood with my hands, I would take out my treasures and meditate upon them until they became part of me.

From the prophet Isaiah, a promise that my Father would strengthen me:

> Here is my servant, whom I support,
> My chosen one, in whom I take pleasure.
> I have put My Spirit on him;
> he will bring justice to the Gentiles...
> He will bring forth justice according to truth;
> he will not weaken or be crushed
> until he has established justice on the earth,
> and the coastlands wait for his Torah.

From the prophet Jeremiah, a promise that my Father would reveal himself to me:

> "For I know what plans I have
> in mind for you," says Adonai,
> "plans for well-being, not for bad things;
> so that you can have hope and a future.
> When you call to Me and pray to Me,
> I will listen to you.
> When you seek Me, you will find Me,
> provided you seek for Me whole-heartedly;

and I will let you find Me," says Adonai.

From the prophet Jonah, a promise that my Father would always heed my cries:

> Out of my distress I called to Adonai,
> and He answered me;
> from the belly of Sheol I cried,
> and You heard my voice.

From the prophet Zephaniah, a promise that my Father would always love me:

> Do not fear! don't let your hands droop down.
> Adonai your God is right there with you,
> as a mighty savior.
> He will rejoice over you and be glad,
> He will be silent in His love,
> He will shout over you with joy.

From the prophet Hosea, a promise that my Father would heal my wounds:

> Come, let us return to Adonai;
> for He has torn, and He will heal us;
> He has struck, and He will bind our wounds.
> After two days, He will revive us;
> on the third day, He will raise us up;
> and we will live in His presence.

Day after day throughout that long winter, Saba Yoachim fed me on the books of the Prophets, the words of promise that had been denied to me. Like a pregnant woman I craved the full text, but that was impossible right now, and so I learned to be content with my daily crumbs of bread, trusting that one day my Father would make a way for me to enter into a deeper study of His word. I was never filled, never satisfied, but neither was I starving, and for that I gave thanks.

One other person brought me scriptures that winter, though not as often, and with a different purpose in mind. Shimon

Zealot discovered me sitting in the pasture at daybreak one morning late in the month of Cheshvan and struck up a conversation with me. Perhaps it would be more accurate to say *I* discovered *him* in the pasture, since I had a legitimate reason to be there and he had none. However, since he was not actually stealing a sheep when we met, I saw no reason to make an issue of it. "*Shalom*, Shimon," I greeted him.

"*Yom tov*, Yisu," he replied.

"You look hungry," I observed casually. Indeed, although it had been only a month since I'd last seen him, he had lost several pounds off his already-lean frame and his chiseled features had become hawkish. I held up my satchel. "Would you join me for breakfast?"

"Gladly."

One thing I liked about Shimon—he was sincere. Some in his position would have been too proud to accept *tzedakah* from a shepherd boy, would have pretended they didn't need it, but not Shimon. As we ate, sitting side-by-side on the promontory overlooking the pasture, I wrestled with indecision, however. Yosef had been explicit: *Stay away from the Zealots.* At the same time, my Father had reminded me that Shimon, too, was created in the image of God and had value in his sight, and that I had a responsibility to him. I wouldn't listen to talk of revolution or join Shimon in his rebellion against Rome—that would be blatantly disobedient to Yosef and bring him dishonor and grief—but neither would I rebuff Shimon's friendship for no cause. I wasn't sharing my breakfast with a Zealot; I was sharing it with a hungry, fatherless boy not much older than I.

"Your trade is carpentry, right? You're a builder?" he asked out of the blue.

I nodded.

"Then why are you spending so much of your time in a sheep pasture day after day?" Day after day? Apparently he'd been watching me for a while. "Shouldn't you be practicing your trade, sharpening your woodworking skills, laying stones, that sort of thing?"

It was a valid question and one I was more than willing to answer, although I was by no means prepared to confide any secrets. "Saba's getting too old to be out here hour after hour, and Shammai's still too young," I said. "Saba has a few hired men, but they don't care about the sheep the way they would if they owned them—do you hear me?" He nodded, saving me the trouble of a long explanation. "So I help out as much as I can. Lately, I have a lot of extra time on my hands—what better way to spend it?"

He opened his mouth to reply, but at that moment my attention was caught by a young ram that had wandered away from the rest of the flock. I whistled sharply as the stray climbed to the top of the ridge. It paused, glanced at me, and then sprang up and over the top, toward Netzer's barley field. I leapt to my feet to give chase. "Keep an eye on the others!" I called back over my shoulder, figuring Shimon could handle the watch for a few minutes. "I'll be right back!"

Although there was nothing growing in Netzer's field at the moment, he and his sons had been sowing new seed all week. A few days ago the ram I was now chasing, while grazing on the slope that bordered the field, had happened on a pile of barley that had spilled unnoticed from one of the bags. Now he had a taste for the grain and kept running off to the newly-sown field in search of more, churning the soil into mud with his hooves and licking up whatever seed he could find.

By the time I crested the ridge, the ram had already covered half the distance to Netzer's field, but I had to watch my footing as I slid down the rocky slope chanting a treasure from the prophet Habakkuk: "Elohim Adonai is my strength! He makes me swift and sure-footed as a deer and enables me to stride over my high places." (Saba had said every shepherd needed to know that one.) I caught the ram at the edge of the field before he'd done too much damage, grabbing him by the horns and wrestling him to the ground. Then I hoisted him across my shoulders, grunting at his weight, which was probably more than half of my own. "Elohim Adonai is my strength," I panted again as I plodded back up the hill. The ram kicked a few times, but I managed to hold on to him all the way to the pasture.

Shimon was still sitting where I'd left him, examining my flute with a thoughtful expression, but he looked up and smiled when he saw me coming. "You caught him."

"This is the one I have to watch closest; he thinks he knows best," I said, laughing. "Five times this week he's gone over that hill!" I set the ram on its feet and gave it a swat on the rump, sending it leaping toward the flock with an angry *baah*. "There's nothing over there but some hungry farmers who'll be glad to butcher you!" I called after the retreating sheep.

Shimon laughed with me and then held out the flute. "Did you make this?"

"Yes. Do you play?"

He shook his head. "I was just admiring the workmanship."

"Thanks! It's nothing much compared with the one my father made," I admitted, "but I'm still learning."

He nodded and changed the topic, asking about this sheep and that, and commenting on the weather. After a few minutes, he went on his way.

Though we didn't speak much that first morning, the beginnings of a bond had formed, and Shimon came by two or three times a week after that—always while I was alone on my watch, but only to fill his stomach and, occasionally, to join me in song. It was in song that he first shared a scripture I'd never heard before. I arrived at the pasture on a cold and overcast morning in Tebeth to find him already seated in our usual spot with his eyes closed, singing to himself a hauntingly sad melody:

> "Remember, Adonai, what has happened to us;
> look, and see our disgrace.
> The land we possessed
> has been passed on to strangers,
> our homes to foreigners.
> We have become fatherless orphans,
> our mothers now are widows.
> We have to pay to drink our own water;
> we have to buy our own wood.
> The yoke is on our necks; we are persecuted;
> we toil to exhaustion but are given no rest…"

He opened his eyes and saw me standing there listening, and abruptly stopped in the middle of his song. "No, please," I said, "don't stop. It's beautiful. What is it?"

"Jeremiah's *eikhah*," he replied. "Why don't you play along? It's meant to be accompanied by a flute, you know."

"I'll try." I sat beside him, unwrapping Adam, and listened as Shimon began again. The melody was slow but complex, the fingering difficult but not impossible, and soon I was able to play a harmony of sorts; mostly, though, I just listened as Shimon poured his heart into the lament.

"They have raped the women of Zion,
virgins in the cities of Judah.
Princes are hung up by their hands,
leaders receive no respect.
Young men are compelled to grind at the mill,
boys stagger under loads of wood.
Joy has vanished from our hearts,
our dancing has turned into mourning.
The crown has fallen from our heads."

He didn't comment on the song; he didn't need to. We both knew why he had chosen the lament and its relevance to the current situation in our land, but he merely sat in silence for several minutes and then asked if I'd brought any meat this morning. And so it went. Over the next two months there were a few times when I thought he was about to say something of more significance than to comment on the weather or the quality of our food, but each time he seemed to reconsider. For that I was grateful; as long as Shimon avoided the topic of the Zealots, I didn't have to guard myself against him. To be truthful, I didn't want our friendship to end—for, by the middle of winter, our acquaintance had indeed grown into friendship—but end it must, if he determined to make a Zealot of me, to use me for his own ends.

A week or two later, I failed to rouse when the rooster sounded his morning alarm. Mother shook me awake as the sun was rising, only to discover that I was flushed with fever; every bone in my body ached and I was racked with chills. Katan skipped school and went out to the pasture in my stead, since it was far too cold and damp for Saba Yoachim to be out there, and Katan's studies could handle neglect better than the sheep could. I lay abed five days. On the sixth day I woke of my own accord long before dawn, feeling almost myself again, except for a lingering cough. Katan was already up and out; as quietly as I could, I grabbed a half-full skin of watered-down wine and a loaf of bread and headed out after him.

For the first two days of my illness, I hadn't been coherent enough to think of anything but the pain I was in, but after that my thoughts and prayers had been consumed with Katan— alone in the pasture with Shimon. I knew the two must have met up by now; not a week passed without at least two visits from my Zealot friend. Though I prayed their interactions had been harmless, I knew both of them too well to believe that the prayer would be answered according to my desires, and Katan was far too immature to know how to deal with someone like Shimon. In that, Abba had been right to forbid the contact. Katan hadn't spoken a word to confirm my suspicions, but I had noticed him looking at me strangely a few times over the past days, and I feared the worst.

Sure enough, by the time I got there the two of them were deep in conversation. They looked up when I coughed— Shimon with a smile and Katan with the staring eyes of one who'd been caught with his hand in his neighbor's purse. It was Shimon's smile that upset me. Although we'd had no spoken agreement, I felt betrayed.

"How could you?" I asked, and I felt my eyes burning with held-back tears.

Katan thought I was speaking to him. "I haven't done anything, Yisu, honest. Don't tell Abba."

I ignored him. "How could you?" I asked again, drilling a hole in Shimon with my stare. "He's not even twelve."

"Relax, Yisu. I haven't hurt your little brother. All I've done is give him a few things to think about, shared some scriptures with him, eaten a little of his food. As I've done with you. Nothing more. I swear it." I didn't want his oaths. I wanted him to leave Katan alone. He saw the anger in my eyes and stood up. "I'll go now."

"Yes, that's a good idea."

He left without a backward glance and for a few minutes there was silence on the hillside except for the bleating of the sheep and a few early birdsongs. Then Katan said again, "Please don't tell Abba about this, Yisu. I promise I'll cover for you—"

I wheeled on him. "There's nothing to cover, Katan. I haven't said anything to Shimon that I wouldn't have said if Abba had been standing right beside me. I haven't done anything that I need to keep secret. I hope you can say the same."

He took my warning as a threat. "You're going to tell?"

"You don't know me at all, do you?" A few years ago, I'd taken a beating for Katan rather than tell on him. "Brothers are supposed to look out for each other, Yaakob."

He closed his eyes and heaved a sigh of relief. "Thanks, Yisu."

"Don't make me regret my silence."

"Huh?"

"Abba promised his brothers that he wouldn't tell on them, either, and they ended up dead. Do you think he's ever—" A coughing spasm interrupted my speech. As soon as I could breathe, I took it up again. "Do you think he's ever forgiven himself for that? Could you? If all you did was share a few meals with Shimon, then there's nothing to tell, Yaakob. But if you're planning to follow him into Sheol, I won't keep quiet. I can't. I love you too much."

He nodded, meeting my gaze this time without flinching. "You won't be sorry."

"Good." I smiled at him for the first time. "Thanks for watching the sheep this week, Katan. Now go to school. I'll be fine here today."

Shimon came back the next morning as if nothing had happened. We caught and milked one of the ewes, savoring the warmth of the drink along with our breakfast; Katan's name never came up in our conversation, nor did the Zealots. The rest of Tebeth passed without incident, as did Shebat, and soon the weather was warming into early spring. The only time we even came close to discussing revolution was in our talks about God's word. Shimon knew that I was no longer in school—though not why—and I confided in him that I missed my studies.

"The men I was staying with, in Gamala, before I moved out here," he replied, "they taught me some from the *Sefer ha-Shofetim*. You've been generous with your food. If you want, I can share some of the scriptures with you. I committed a lot of them to memory." So we began to study the book of the Judges. It was easy enough to see why the Zealots studied this book. For one thing, it began with a lengthy indictment against the tribes of Israel who had failed to drive out the foreigners from their land. "'But when the people of Israel cried out to Adonai, Adonai raised up a savior for the people of Israel,'" Shimon recited again and again. He told me of Othniel, of Ehud and Shamgar, of Deborah and Barak. Once, he broke into song, the Song of Deborah:

> "You who ride white donkeys,
> sitting on soft saddle-blankets,
> and you walking on the road,
> talk about it!
> Louder than the sound
> of archers at the watering holes
> will they sound as they retell
> the righteous acts of Adonai,
> the righteous acts of his rulers in Israel!"

He told me of Gideon, of Tola and Ya'ir, of Yephtah and many others who had devoted their lives to driving the foreign oppressors from the land of Israel. Not once, however, did he mention the current situation in our land. Rome was not spoken of, nor was the name of Yudah bar Hezekyah. Shimon simply shared scriptures from the *Shofetim* and then left me to make my own applications. Of course, I knew where it was all leading, and he probably knew that I knew, but we never spoke of it.

9

KATAN

Adar Alef 3769
(Winter)

I was born in a "pregnant" year, in the month of Adar Alef,
exactly one month before Purim. In most years, though, this
month didn't exist, and so my birthday fell instead on
Purim. I loved that. Although we Jews didn't normally make a
big celebration of birthdays like the Gentiles did, I always
thought of Purim as belonging to me. Ema would whisper,
"Happy birthday, Yaakob," and then everybody in the whole
town—in the whole province!—would sing and dance and
laugh and tell stories and eat sweets and give gifts and get
drunk. Through a cruel quirk of the calendar, though, every
third year or so (the "pregnant years") Purim was celebrated in
Adar Bet, taking the festivities with it. As if to rub salt in my
wound, in those years the fourteenth day of Adar Alef—my
birthday—was called "Little Purim." *Purim Katan*. It was an
irony that I didn't understand for many years, and one I never
learned to appreciate.

I turned twelve on Purim Katan, which actually made me
happy—it guaranteed that my thirteenth birthday, the one that
would mark my entrance to adulthood, would be accompanied
by a huge party. But this year, I had to settle for Ema's
whispered blessing and a few extra sweets with dinner. After
dinner, as usual, Abba gathered the family for scripture reading
and worship. I waited for him to hand the book to Yisu, but he
surprised me. "Katan," he said, "you start us off tonight, since
it's a special day for you."

"Yes, sir." I stood and crossed the room to take the book
from his outstretched hand. "What would you like me to read,
Abba?"

"You choose," he said with a smile.

I wasn't expecting that, and for a moment I had no idea what passage to select. I didn't want to go for one that was too easy—the *Shema*, for instance—because I wanted to show my father that I had a strong knowledge of the Law. Yisu was generally considered the scholar in our family, but truth be told, I was one of the best students in the *bet-sefer*. A passage that spoke of events related to the day would be best—Purim was all about Queen Esther, and of course those events weren't told in *D'varim* (the only book our family owned), but the holiday was also about God's protection from enemies: outnumbered and outarmed, the Jews had nevertheless defended themselves in the face of annihilation and emerged victorious. Quickly I scrolled through the book, waiting for inspiration to strike. Suddenly I had it. Standing straight, I began to read in a clear voice:

"'When you go to war against your enemies and see horses and chariots and an army greater than yours, do not be afraid of them, because Adonai your God, who brought you up out of Egypt, will be with you. When you are about to go into battle, the priest shall come forward and address the army. He shall say: "Hear, O Israel, today you are going into battle against your enemies. Do not be fainthearted or afraid; do not be terrified or give way to panic before them. For Adonai your God is the one who goes with you to fight for you against your enemies to give you victory."'"

Father didn't stop me, so I kept on reading: "'The officers shall say to the army: "Has anyone built a new house and not dedicated it? Let him go home…"'" My attention was focused on the scroll, so I didn't immediately notice the expression on Father's face as I read the officers' instructions to their men. Just as I got to the end of the passage—"Is any man afraid or fainthearted? Let him go home so that his brothers will not become disheartened too"—I made the mistake of glancing up, and the look on Father's face turned my tongue to stone; whatever I had been about to say dried up in my mouth and I stood stock still.

He was furious.

That was my first thought, but as I stared into his eyes I noticed that he was fighting back tears. "Abba?" I whispered.

Without a word, he reached out his hand for the book. I

scrolled it up and handed it to him, still not sure what it was about my reading that had upset him so. Hanging my head, I turned to go back to my seat, but Father touched my shoulder. "Wait," he said softly. "You—you read well, Katan." He started to offer the scroll to Yisu, but Saba Yoachim reached over and took it from him.

"My turn, I think," he said gruffly, but then spoke from memory without even opening the book: "'And Moses recited the words of this song from beginning to end in the hearing of the whole assembly of Israel:

> "Listen, O heavens, and I will speak;
> hear, O earth, the words of my mouth.
> Let my teaching fall like rain
> and my words descend like dew,
> like showers on new grass,
> like abundant rain on tender plants.
> I will proclaim the name of Adonai.
> Oh, praise the greatness of our God—'"

Saba Yoachim paused in his recitation. "The song needs to be sung," he noted. "Get out your instruments." Father didn't move; he was sitting with his eyes closed and head down, still lost in whatever painful memory my reading had brought to his mind. Yisu, however, jumped right up and opened the box where we stored the instruments we'd made. Carefully, he took out two cloth-wrapped flutes and laid the larger one in Father's lap before sitting and unwrapping his own. I fetched my *kinnor* while Shammai and Yosei each picked up a drum. We were a musical family: even Rachel and Hannah had tambourines. The littlest ones—Yehudah and Sarah—just clapped along and made joyous noises as we sang, but one day they'd have instruments, too. Father would insist on it.

At the moment, however, Father's flute sat shrouded in his lap, so the melody was up to Yisu and me. Although I was no David, I was able to pick out simple tunes on the strings of the *kinnor*, and Yisu breathed a harmony that filled out the song almost as well as Father's would have. Except for the two of them, everyone else sang, Mother's clear voice taking the lead:

"I will proclaim the name of Adonai.
Oh, praise the greatness of our God!
He is the Rock, His works are perfect,
and all His ways are just.
A faithful God who does no wrong,
upright and just is He..."

About halfway through the song, where it turns into an angry lament, a second flute began to weep with passion and I realized that Father had joined us, though his playing was uneven. I looked up from my harp, letting my fingers find their own way among the strings, so that I could watch Father as he played. He didn't see me staring because his eyes were still closed, his brow furrowed in anger; but his tears began to flow when Mother sang:

"Adonai will judge His people
and have compassion on His servants
when He sees their strength is gone
and no one is left, slave or free..."

I missed some notes then and had to focus my attention on the *kinnor's* strings as the melody became more complex. The song—one of my favorites to play—went on and on but never got boring, as Moses told the whole story of God's relationship with His people, ending with His promise to avenge their mistreatment at the hands of the idolatrous nations that surrounded and oppressed them. A series of intricate chords announced that Adonai was now speaking:

"I put to death and I bring to life,
I have wounded and I will heal,
and no one can deliver out of My hand.
I lift My hand to heaven and declare:
As surely as I live forever,
when I sharpen My flashing sword
and My hand grasps it in judgment,
I will take vengeance on My adversaries
and repay those who hate Me.
I will make My arrows drunk with blood,

while My sword devours flesh:
the blood of the slain and the captives,
the heads of the enemy leaders.

We all sang the last verse loudly, and the boys went wild with the drums while the girls danced around the room shaking their tambourines and the little ones clapped and jumped:

"Rejoice, O nations, with His people,
for He will avenge the blood of His servants;
He will take vengeance on His enemies
and make atonement for His land and people."

Abba finished the last note of the song, stood up, and abruptly let his flute fall to the floor. In the shocked silence that followed, he left the room. A slamming door punctuated his exit. Saba Yaakob rose and went after him, gesturing for the rest of us to stay put. Yisu, who had already leapt to his feet, bent over and picked up Father's flute before sitting down again. Carefully he began wiping it clean.

"Mimah," Mother said quietly, "help me get the little ones to bed. Come, children—upstairs now." Aunt Mimah picked up Sarah while Rachel led Yehudah by the hand. Hannah, Yosei, and Shammai returned their instruments to the box and then followed Mother out the door and up the stairs. I remained behind with Yisu and Saba Yoachim; though technically I was still one of the children, I wasn't a "little one" and I certainly wasn't ready for bed. There were some questions I wanted the answers to before I'd be willing to call it a day. Saba Yoachim might have them.

"Saba," I asked as soon as we were alone, "do you know why my father's upset?"

"Know?" He shook his head. "But I can guess. All this talk of fighting and vengeance—it's probably reminded him of his brothers."

"Oh," I said. *That explains a lot.*

"I was hoping Moses' song would lift his spirits," he sighed. "I'm afraid my selection just made things worse." I moved to Saba's side and gave him a hug, knowing just how he felt. Certainly I hadn't intended my choice of scripture to cause such a disturbance, but the night was ruined all the same.

Yisu spoke without looking up from the flute. "Don't blame yourself, Saba. It was the right decision, to turn to the Lord for healing. Abba just wasn't ready, that's all." He wrapped the boxwood flute in its cloth, set it aside, and then began to clean his own instrument.

My harp still sat on my knee, and I strummed a light chord. *Healing. Lift his spirits.* Father wasn't in the room, but Saba was, and he was hurting too. Was there a song I could play to lift *his* spirits? King David, scripture taught, could drive demons away with his *kinnor* when he was no older than I was now. I ran my fingers over the strings and then plucked the bittersweet melody of "As the Deer." Instead of singing, though, I hummed softly while the words echoed in my mind:*As the deer pants for streams of water, so my soul pants for You, oh God...*

Yisu picked up the song:

> "Why are you downcast, oh my soul?
> Why so disturbed within me?
> Put your hope in God,
> for I will yet praise Him,
> my Savior and my God."

Yoachim joined in as well, and they sang it all the way to the end. "Another, Yaakob," my grandfather said to me. Rather than starting a different song, though, I played through that one again, singing aloud this time. I'd chosen the *maskil* for Saba, but as I sang the words I found myself drawn into worship.

> "Then will I go to the altar of God,
> to God, my joy and my delight.
> I will praise You with the harp,
> O God, my God."

As I plucked the strings of the *kinnor*, I forgot for just a moment where I was and why I had begun the song. The song became *my* song, my prayer, and when I sang the words *my God*, I truly meant them. In that brief moment—less than the space between one breath and the next—I reached toward my

Maker and it seemed for just an instant—again, in a space so fleeting that my heart didn't even have time to falter—that I touched Him. I gasped and my fingers froze on the strings, leaving Yisu and Yoachim to sing the final verse without accompaniment.

Desperate to understand what I was feeling, I tried to hold on to the moment, but I failed, unable to stop the dream from unraveling until all that remained was a memory of a memory; and then even that faded and I was just Yaakob-Katan again. "Oh!" I breathed, and then a tightness wrapped itself around my heart and worked its way upward, pressing and burning until I burst into tears. "O God, my God!" I cried again, but He was gone.

Both Yisu and Saba Yoachim had fallen silent, and as I came back to myself I was uncomfortably aware of their eyes upon me. Quickly I drew my sleeve across my face, blotting up my tears; as soon as I could see clearly, I began to pluck the shortest of the *Hallel* tunes, a fast-paced melody that was meant to be danced. Mother and Mimah returned to the room just then and started to clap and whirl amongst the furniture. As I'd hoped, Yisu and Saba got up, dragged the table aside, and joined them, leaving me alone.

While I was playing through the upbeat tune for the third or fourth time, I felt a gust of cold air on the back of my neck as the outside door opened and shut, and then a pat on my shoulder. I kept playing, but I glanced up long enough to see Father and Saba Yaakob joining in the dance. Soon both of them were smiling.

"Roni, Roni!" cried Mimah, requesting my favorite song of all. Grinning, I plucked the simple melody as the women sang, "*Roni, roni, bat Zion! Hariyu Israel...!*" *Rejoice, rejoice, daughter of Zion! Shout aloud, Israel!* As they sang and clapped, the men formed a circle and danced around them. The song started out fairly slow, but with each repetition I played faster and faster; the goal was to see if the dancers could keep up with the musicians, and it was a game I'd only won twice. I felt as if I could go on indefinitely tonight, but Father stopped me after only three verses.

He laid a hand on my shoulder, taking the *kinnor* from me and setting it on the floor. "I need to talk with you, Yaakob," he said. The fact that he'd used my given name alerted me that the talk we were about to have was a serious one. Hopefully it would provide me with the answers I was seeking, but I wasn't optimistic. More likely I was about to get a lecture about whatever it was I'd done wrong tonight. Expecting the worst, I followed him outside and up the trail to the plateau, taking a seat on his favorite "talk-with-you" rock.

He sat beside me.

"You're twelve now. That's a dangerous age, I know. You aren't quite an adult, but you don't think of yourself as a child either, and for good reason. When I was twelve, I realized that I knew more than both my father and my teacher, and I turned away from everything I'd believed up to that point. I don't know if you've come to the same conclusion yet. If you have, then I'm probably wasting my breath. If you haven't, then we probably don't even need to have this conversation. Still, wasted effort or not, I have to try."

He paused, perhaps waiting for some response from me. I wasn't sure what to say—I wasn't even sure what he was talking about—but I obviously needed to say something. "Yes, sir. I'm listening." I fixed my gaze on the full moon, hanging low on the eastern horizon, and swung my heels against the rock, waiting for my father to get to the point.

"That passage you read from *D'varim* tonight. Why did you choose it?"

"I was trying to impress you," I admitted. "I thought if I chose a scripture that related to Purim, you would see how well I've done with my studies."

"Is that the only reason?" He sounded surprised.

I nodded, still staring at the moon.

Father was silent.

"Why did it upset you?" I asked. When he didn't answer, I glanced at him. Now *he* was the one whose eyes were glued to the moon. "Abba?" I nudged. "Why did that scripture make you angry?"

"Because those words were used—misused—to lead many young men down the wrong path, Yaakob, including my brothers. You've heard part of the story, you know what happened to them, but you can't begin to imagine the horror of their deaths. When I heard those words coming out of your mouth, I thought…" He paused, swallowed hard, and then continued. "I thought that Shimon had been talking to you. I was afraid that he'd already begun to win you over to his cause. I told him to stay away from you, you and your brothers."

"Shimon? You mean that boy who went up to the Feast with us last fall?"

"I mean the Zealot who's been living in the hills outside of town. I mean the thief who's been raiding the local herds and gardens for six months now. Yes, that Shimon."

If I claimed that I hadn't spoken with him at all, I'd be lying and Father probably already knew that, so I decided to make a full confession. "Well, yes, he has talked to me a few times, me and Yisu both."

"Tell me what he said. All of it."

"Yisu probably remembers it better than—"

"I don't want to hear it from Yisu. I want to hear it from you."

"Yes, sir." I swallowed hard. Some of what Shimon had said was going to anger Father beyond reason, and I didn't want to share it with him. But if he'd spoken to Yisu—well, I didn't want to leave it out if Father already knew it. "He's come out to the pasture a few times when we were helping Saba with the sheep. He said he was hungry, so Yisu let him have some milk."

Father grunted. "And then?"

"I don't really remember how the conversation got started. But he said we shouldn't tell you about it. He said…well, he said you…" I couldn't do it. I just couldn't bring myself to say the words out loud. "I don't believe any of it, Father. If I did, I would have told you about it, but it's just a pack of lies so what difference does it make?"

"What did Shimon say about me?" When I didn't answer, he got up, moved to stand in front of me, and met my eyes. "He called me a coward, am I right? He told you that several years ago I refused to fight against the Romans, that I somehow collaborated with them, that I allowed good men to die without lifting a finger to help them, that I betrayed my people and my God. Am I close?" He spat on the ground. "Have you ever noticed, Yaakob, how few men there are of my age in Nazareth? Have you ever wondered why? It's because men like

Shimon managed to convince them that Rome was theirs for the taking, that a few Galileans with swords and faith could rise up and throw off the greatest army the world has ever known."

"But, Father, don't the scriptures promise—"

"That God would give His people victory over their enemies? Certainly. But read it in context, Yaakob! He was talking to Joshua about the conquest of Canaan. Later, there were other times when He gave the Israelites over to foreign rule, for His own good purposes. And then He warned them not to oppose the kings He set over them. When they rebelled, they died."

"But how are we to know, Father, if God wants us to submit to Rome or oppose it?"

"In the past, He sent prophets to tell His people what to do."

"In the past." This really bothered me. I wasn't trying to argue with Father. I wanted to understand. "But now?"

"Well, son, it seems to me that if God wanted us to rise up in arms against Rome, He would send a prophet to lead us into battle. It's not the sort of undertaking you should attempt on your own. I mean, even King David consulted the Lord before going to war."

"Shimon said that Yudah bar Hezekyah was a prophet, that God had sent him."

"Yes, I know. That's what Yudah believed. Some even saw him as Messiah. I think my brothers may have made that mistake. Time has proven him—and them—wrong, though." He clasped my shoulders and leaned toward me, speaking to me and not through me. "Don't be easily swayed, Yaakob. Trust me on this one, please. I truly believe that God will reveal His will if we genuinely want to know it, but if we're simply trying to justify our own plans we run the very real danger of seeing signs where there are none. Look how careful Gideon was—it wasn't *his* idea to attack Midian, and he demanded proof that it was truly God's will. Yudah saw himself as Gideon's heir, but he didn't follow Gideon's ways or practice Gideon's caution. I made the mistake of trying to reason with him, and for this I was branded a coward and a traitor. Now Yudah is dead, he and too many of those who trusted him. I live. Unfortunately, so does Yudah's dream. Don't get seduced by it."

My father was talking to me as if I were a man grown, with respect rather than scolding. I didn't know how to respond. "I'm only twelve, Abba."

"So was Shimon when he got dragged into the Zealots. Now he's fifteen and there's a price on his head. That's why he's forced to hide in the hills and beg milk from shepherd boys; did he tell you that?" He shook his head. "My heart breaks for that boy. He's just like Matti. I'm afraid he's going to end up in the same place. I feel sorry for him, but not so sorry that I'll allow him to drag you down too, Yaakob."

I had to ask. "Did you have this same talk with Yisu?"

"I don't need to. Do I?"

I'd already heard Yisu's response to Shimon. Shaking my head, I said, "Yisu isn't in any danger of being dragged anywhere by Shimon or anyone else."

"Are you?"

"No, sir." I meant it, too.

Father looked back up at the moon, biting his lower lip. After a long while he turned back to me and spoke. "I'm going to break with tradition tonight, Yaakob. There's something I want to tell you. Normally, I'd wait another year, but I think you're old enough to handle this now." He walked to the edge of the cliff, where the ladder led down to our roof, and peered over. Laughing, he said, "I should have done that before I spoke to your brother last autumn—who'd have guessed you were down there listening? But I think you slept through most of it."

"Most of what, sir?"

"Yaakob bar Yosef, do you have any idea who you are?"

"I'm your son, aren't I?"

"Indeed, in every sense of the word. And who am I?"

"You're Yosef bar Yaakob."

"Yes, I am, and when I turned thirteen my father told me who he was. But he warned me first that the knowledge was dangerous. You have to swear to keep this secret, Yaakob. Your life depends on it—yours, mine, and your brothers' lives as well. And no, I'm not joking." He riveted his eyes on mine; I'd never seen him more serious.

"Yes, sir. I promise. I won't tell anyone."

What he told me next caused my jaw to drop. Then I started

to laugh. I couldn't help it. Father was obviously not happy with my reaction, so I tried to explain. "It's the *kinnor*, sir. Just tonight, I was thinking about David and how he played for King Saul when he was my age. I was thinking, 'I'm no David, but...'" I started laughing again.

Father laughed with me this time and then gave me a big hug. "That's why I made it for you," he whispered. "Keep playing, son. There *is* healing in your fingers. And worship in your heart, Yaakob bar David."

Remembering the moment when I'd seemed to touch the hand of God, I nodded.

10

YISU

Adar Alef 3769
(Winter)

W hen at long last Shimon broached the subject of my own involvement in the fight for freedom, he did it in such a roundabout fashion that I was deep into the conversation before I realized where it was headed, and by then it was too late to extricate myself. Months had gone by since our first meeting; winter was fast fading into spring, and our friendship had sprouted and was growing as quickly as the barley that greened all the valleys of the Galil.

"Remember that first day we met out here, how I admired your flute?" he asked out of the blue a day or two after Purim Katan.

I nodded.

"I couldn't figure out why a carpenter was spending so much time herding sheep." He laughed. "I have a confession to make—I thought you were just lazy."

It was my turn to laugh. Since leaving school, I'd been working two jobs instead of one, and maintaining my studies as best I could at the same time. *Lazy* wasn't a word I'd ever thought to apply to myself.

Shimon picked up my staff, fingering the carvings I'd worked into it over the past few months: wheat stalks and pomegranates, along with one of the first scriptures Saba had given me in payment, a verse from Ezekiel: *I will place over them one shepherd, My servant David, and he will tend them; he will tend them and be their shepherd.* "You do good work for a lazy man," he smiled. "If Noah had been as lazy as you, he'd have finished the ark in a year. But you said you were still learning your trade." The laughter dropped out of his voice. "What else can you make?"

I shrugged. "Doorposts, boxes, cartwheels, toys...I've helped with lots of bigger things, but I'm not ready to build a house on my own yet—do you hear me?" He nodded, but the expression on his hawkish face was no longer neutral; his eyes had narrowed appraisingly, and the hint of a smile played about the corners of his mouth. Deep within my soul, I heard the cry of a distant raptor and a shadow passed over me, swift and fleeting. With dismay I realized that, not only had he heard me, but the hawk had sighted his prey. "Why?" I asked guardedly. "Did you have something specific in mind?"

"If I gave you something, do you think you could make copies of it?"

"What?" I asked again, afraid that I already knew the answer.

"A bow."

I'd guessed correctly, but too late. "No, I don't think Abba would let me do that."

"So don't tell him. I'll provide the wood, you provide the skill, and—"

"No. I'm sorry, Shimon, but I can't do it. I can't even discuss it with you." I rose to my feet.

"Come on, Yisu. We've been over this before. Your father's a good man, I'm sure, but he just doesn't understand what the Zealots are trying to accomplish. He's proved that again and again. Now, you told me to leave Katan alone, and I have—I've honored your wishes as I honor you. I've respected what you've said and what you've left unsaid, but the two of us have been dancing this dance for five months now, and you're not a child anymore. It's time for you to start making your own decisions. Can you honestly tell me that you believe in what Rome stands for, in the way they've treated our people?"

"No. Of course not."

"Then how can you approve of their occupation of our land?"

"I don't *approve*, Shimon."

"Good, then we're in agreement. Rome needs to go. If they won't go peacefully—and they won't, everyone knows that— then they have to be *driven* out."

"In God's time. In God's way."

"Yes! God's way!" He was determined to win me over.

"And what is God's way? Look at our history, Yisu. God has always used the Israelites to cleanse this land that He gave to Abraham. He used Joshua to destroy the Amalekites, didn't He? He could have just opened up the earth and swallowed them, but no, He chose to work through Joshua. He used Gideon's band of three hundred to drive out Midian; He used Samson and David to defeat the Philistines; by the hand of Elijah He slew the prophets of Ba'al; with the hammer of Yudah Maccabee He drove out the desecrator Antiochus. All of these men answered God's call to arms against the pagans and the oppressors, and God used them to work His will, to bring His deliverance. *That* is His way."

"Yes, what you say is true."

"Then join us now in answering His call once more. Join us in driving out Rome."

"*His* call? Or yours?" That was the whole point, wasn't it? I leaned on my staff, looking out at Saba's sheep. I knew what I wanted to say, but not how. *Father, would You please give me the right words?* No, not words. Shimon claimed to hear me, but his ears—like the rest of him—were of stone. He heard only what he wanted to hear. I needed to show him. "Watch this, Shimon," I said, and then let out a call, a high-pitched ululation I'd learned from Saba. It wasn't loud, but one group of sheep that were grazing nearby immediately raised their heads and began to walk toward me, as I'd known they would. "Now you try it," I invited.

As best he could, he copied my call. "Ha-yah-yi-yi-yi-yi-yi-yi-ah!"

The sheep stopped in their tracks, let loose with a few *baahs* and began to scatter in all directions except toward Shimon. Delighted at the success of my demonstration, I laughed and slapped Shimon on the shoulder. "That's what I mean. You need to learn to hear God's call and follow it; at the same time, you need to watch out for those pretending to speak for Him. Sheep may be stupid, but they recognize their shepherd's voice and they won't follow anyone else." I riveted my gaze on him, speaking with intensity. "Do you hear me?"

"I think you just called me stupid."

"Hardly." I stopped laughing. "Shimon, how old were you when you lost your father?"

"I didn't *lose* him. He was taken from me. There's a huge difference, you know."

His pain was tangible, and in that moment I realized something else about him: Shimon was carved of stone but he was not a statue, nor was he a building. He was a tomb. His father's tomb. He carried around his father's memory and his father's bones and his father's death—his father whom he never called by name—and these things had consumed his flesh (as all flesh is consumed in the grave) and turned him to stone. "I'm sorry."

"I was twelve."

"Katan's age." I frowned, imagining Katan without Yosef's influence—or worse, Katan *robbed* of Yosef's influence. My brother would not turn to stone, but to flame, burning up the world in his rage. "He's so impressionable. He hasn't trained his ears yet."

"Are you still talking about sheep?"

I shook my head. "I wish I were. Eyes and ears—it's all about eyes and ears. Do you hear me?"

"No," he said with a wry smile. "This time, I don't. You'll need to try again, Yisu."

I sighed. I'd spent so much time alone in prayer over the past months, sometimes it was impossible to put what I had learned into words that others could understand. I needed my Father's words to speak for me. "What did God say to Cain? 'Sin is crouching at your door. It desires to have you.' I feel like that. Sin is watching me, calling out to me, every hour of every day. If I listen to it, if I look back at it with that same desire, then it will have me. Eyes..at least they can be shut. But ears...they have to be trained. There are things it's best not to listen to."

"Let me guess—things the Zealots say."

"I'm not attacking you, Shimon."

"No, just everything I believe to be true." He got up and dusted himself off. "Thanks for breakfast." He turned to leave, but then looked back at me again, shaking his head. "I had hopes for you, Yisu, I admit it. I still believe you'd be an incredible asset to us—maybe when you're a little older and not so enamored of your father. I swear, if Yosef pointed to a pile of sheep droppings and told you it was silver, you'd try to pay your taxes with it."

"Will I see you tomorrow?" I didn't want our relationship to end on this note.

"What's the point?" he said, but before he could turn away again, the air was torn by an angry shout.

"You! Zealot!"

Abba appeared out of nowhere, grabbed the back of Shimon's tunic, and yanked him off balance, spinning him around and barking, "I told you to stay away from my sons!" In his free hand Abba held a hammer, which he brandished threateningly in Shimon's face. Dropping his voice so low that I could barely hear it, he said through clenched teeth, "You want to call me a coward, do it to my face. I welcome the chance to prove you wrong."

"That won't be necessary. I was just leaving." Shimon's voice, like the rest of him, was stone.

"Too late."

"Don't worry, Yosef, Yisu is your son through and through." The contempt in his voice was unmistakable, carrying with it the sound of a friendship breaking—no, being torn, ripped, shredded into countless bits. My heart ached as his claws slashed through it.

"Abba," I whispered, "please let him go. He hasn't done any harm here."

"I'm sure that's more to your credit than his," Yosef replied without turning around.

"Nevertheless. He isn't Yudah. He's Shimon."

Yosef heard me. He lowered the hammer and relaxed his grip on Shimon's tunic. "Go back to the hills, Zealot. Better still, go back to Gamala. And wherever you go, as you value your life, stay away from my sons—all of them. Do you hear me?"

"Oh, I hear you." He backed away several paces, too much the soldier to turn his back on Yosef.

I took a few steps toward him, still unwilling to accept that our friendship could end so suddenly, that it had meant nothing to him, but I stopped when Abba laid a warning hand on my shoulder. I sent my words after him instead. "Go with God, Shimon. Remember: eyes and ears. Learn to listen."

"Listen?" he spat at me. "To your father? Never. To God?

Who are you to say I don't?" He left. It would be a long time before I saw him again.

11

KATAN

Adar Alef 3769
(Winter)

After catching Yisu in the pasture with Shimon Zealot, Father whipped both of us. It wasn't fair. I mean, hadn't we already discussed it, worked it out? Besides, Father had tricked me. I wouldn't have said anything if he hadn't implied that Yisu had already told him everything. And then it turned out that the only reason he caught Yisu was because of what *I'd* said. Parents shouldn't be allowed to do that.

Of course, he warmed the rod on *my* backside before calling Yisu into the shop. As I'd gotten older, my visits with the rod had become fewer and further between, but those few…well, if the rod hadn't gotten thicker over the years, then my skin had become thinner, and this beating was worse than any that had come before. Ever.

"Father, please," I begged after the first blow. "I've learned my lesson. I won't talk to him again. I promise!"

"Not good enough." The second blow was harder than the first, and I couldn't talk any more even if I'd wanted to. All I could do was cry, thinking all the while:

It isn't fair. I didn't do anything. It isn't fair.

I lost count after five or six, though I'm pretty sure Father let up long before the forty strokes allowed under Torah. I wasn't going to be sitting down for a long time, of that much I was sure. My buttocks throbbed and burned under the thin layer of homespun that had been my only protection. It hurt to lie there, it hurt to stand, and it was agony to walk away.

"Yaakob," Father said as I made my way to the door.

I didn't want to talk to him, but I wasn't such a fool as to ignore him. "Yes, sir."

"Stay away from the Zealots."

"Yes, sir."

"Now send your brother in here."

"Yes, sir."

I wiped my face on my sleeve, gritted my teeth, and left the shop. I expected to find Yisu waiting in the next room, but he wasn't in the house. I limped across the room and out the back door, cursing my brother under my breath with every painful step. "Yisu!" I hollered. "Father wants you!"

"I'll be right down," his voice floated from above. I looked up. He was on the roof. Satisfied that he'd gotten the summons, I went back into the house and threw myself facedown on my pallet.

It was laundry day, so all of the women were down at the spring with the babies; Yosei had gone to the pasture with Shammai and Saba Yoachim, and Saba Yaakob was out working on someone's leaky roof; basically, I had the house to myself. The door to the shop was still open a few inches, so I could hear everything that went on in there.

"Here I am, Abba," Yisu said quietly.

Father's voice was equally quiet, but strained. "Here you are." I heard the outside door closing, the bolt sliding into place. "Lean over the bench there, Yeshua." He paused, cleared his throat. "You do understand why I'm doing this?"

"Yes, sir, and I'm sorry I've put you in this position. I've been thinking about what you said this morning, and you're absolutely right. I made some very poor choices."

I lifted my head off the pallet, seething. If Yisu talked his way out of this…

But Father wasn't stupid. "Yes, you did. I can't let you forget that, Yeshua, much as I'd like to think you'll remember and learn from this without my help. But this…you've never done anything like quite like this before, and it's my duty to make sure you never—*never*—do such a foolish thing again. Five months! You've been deceiving me for five *months*! Do you have anything to say for yourself, anything at all?"

"No, sir. I was more focused on building a relationship with Shimon than in honoring the relationship I have with you. Talking to Shimon seemed like the right thing to do, but I should have come to you with my dilemma the first time he approached me, and I didn't."

"If I let this go..."

"You can't, Abba. I know that."

"Fine, then. Let's get this over with."

Yisu cried out at the first blow, as much from surprise as from pain, I guessed. Judging from the sound, Father wasn't going any easier on my brother than he had on me; I counted thirteen strokes in all, and by the end of it Yisu was sobbing.

"Yeshua." Father's voice was gruff.

"Yes, Abba?"

"Don't ever shut me out again. You come to me, do you hear?"

"Yes, Abba."

"I love you, son."

"I love you, too, Abba."

I love you, son. Father's words stuck in my gut like a knife. What had I gotten from him? Just another warning to stay away from the Zealots. I pulled myself out of bed, across the room, and out the back door before either Yisu or Father could find me there.

Part Two

Rites of Passage

*Be happy, young man, while you are
young, and let your heart give you
joy in the days of your youth. Follow
the ways of your heart and whatever
your eyes see, but know that for all
these things God will bring you to
judgment.*

—Ecclesiastes 11:9 (NIV)

12

YISU

Adar Bet 3769
(Winter)

“**A**nd so Haman was impaled on his own gallows and the King's signet was given into the hand of Mordekai. And from this we can learn…what?” Looking up from the cabinet door I was hanging, I glanced over my shoulder to see the rabbi staring hopefully at the young faces surrounding him.

One brave child spoke up. “That the King didn't like Haman?”

It was the best answer he was likely to get from a five-year-old. He smiled encouragingly and asked, “Why not?”

“Because Haman was mean!”

The teacher cringed just a bit but was obviously trying not to let it show. “Well, yes, that is true.” Turning to one of the older students, a boy of ten or eleven, he asked, “Hevel, can you be a bit more specific than Matthyah here? Why did the King hang Haman and promote Mordekai in his place?”

“I don't know, Rabbi.”

“Take your best guess. Come, Hevel, you know the Purim story.”

As I listened to Hevel stammer his way through the facts of the story, I watched the teacher. He was somewhere between forty and sixty, his beard shot through with gray, his frame stocky but not fat. While he was very patient with his *bet-sefer* class, I could tell his patience was being worn thin at the moment. Hevel, though only two or three years from graduating, was having trouble finding any meaning in the story, although he knew the basics.

“Yes, Rabbi. Um, Haman was plotting to destroy the Jews,

and that would have included Queen Esther. She asked the King to spare her life and told him Haman was the one who had threatened her. The King had Haman executed because he'd dared to attack the queen. He promoted Mordekai because he was Esther's cousin."

"Better." The teacher sighed. It still wasn't the answer he was looking for.

"If it please the Rabbi?"

I'm not sure what came over me, why I spoke out as I did. I wasn't part of this class; I was just a workman fixing a storage cabinet at the back of the room. But the cabinet was designed to hold *megillot*—roll upon roll of beautiful books, Torah and Prophets and Writings—and the sight of all those sacred words, the sound of a teacher opening the scriptures to his students, the very smell of the parchment and ink had dragged me to the end of my self-control and pushed me over the cliff. Bowing my head in apology for the interruption, I stood and wiped my hands on my work apron.

"Yes?" The rabbi's voice was terse; he probably expected me to ask him something about the construction.

I cleared my throat. "Begging the Rabbi's pardon, but I couldn't help overhearing the lesson. Wasn't Mordekai of the tribe of Benjamin and a descendant of Kish?" As he nodded, I continued, "And Haman was descended from Agag of Amalek, whom King Saul—the son of Kish—spared in disobedience to God's command. In Purim, then, do we not find at last the fulfillment of God's decree that Amalek be utterly destroyed?"

"Indeed." He smiled and sat up straighter, as if a load had been lifted from his shoulders. "And so the lesson for us?"

"Obedience."

"Explain further." For the moment, at least, I had been adopted into his class.

It had been a long time since a teacher other than my Saba had questioned me, and I couldn't remember Rabbi Zephanyah ever addressing me with such delight. I hesitated, robbed of words for just a moment. *Thank you for this treat, Father.* Swallowing and drawing in a deep breath, I answered him. "Yes, Rabbi. Well, Saul disobeyed God and lost his position of authority—and eventually his very life. On the other hand, Mordekai was obedient to God and gained not only his life, but a position of high authority. In effect, Saul and Mordekai switched places."

"How can you say Mordekai was obedient to God, when HaShem does not even appear in this *megillah*? Granted, Mordekai was loyal to his people, but is it the same thing?"

I felt my face growing warm. It was true, the answer I'd given was of my own invention; I'd never actually studied Esther. I hadn't even known that God's name was missing from the book. "Forgive me, Rabbi, if I've spoken of matters beyond me. I haven't had the opportunity to study the *megillah* beyond what's read in the assembly. But it's my understanding that Mordekai earned the enmity of Haman by his refusal to worship Haman or kneel before him, and wasn't that in obedience to God's command? For it is written, 'Adonai will be at war against the Amalekites from generation to generation.' It was Mordekai's obedience to this decree, his refusal—at great personal risk—to bow down to a son of Amalek, that led directly to the demise of Haman."

The teacher's eyebrows rose and he motioned to me to come closer. "Have you any more insights into the lessons of Purim, young man?"

"If it please the Rabbi."

"It does."

"Purim is also a lesson in the paradox of humility."

"How so?"

This was a bit harder to put into words, being more of a stretch, but it was also more fun. I smiled as I answered him. "There are many examples, Rabbi, as I'm sure you know."

"Give me one."

I nodded. Since he'd just been telling his students about Haman's fall, I decided to go with that as my example. "Haman was high in the King's favor, but in his pride he sought to raise himself even higher. Didn't he get his wish? For though it is written, 'Pride goes before destruction and a haughty spirit before a fall,' in his fall Haman rose a full fifty cubits on the execution stake he'd built for Mordekai! Therefore in seeking to humble Mordekai, Haman exalted himself in the most painful way imaginable. Paradox."

He actually laughed out loud. "What is your name, son?"

"Yeshua bar Yosef, from Nazareth, sir."

"Well, Yeshua bar Yosef from Nazareth, why don't you come back in two hours, after I've dismissed these young students of mine, and we will discuss this further. That is, if your work permits."

"Thank you, Rabbi. I'll talk with my father and see if he can spare me."

"Good."

With a smile in my heart and, no doubt, on my face as well, I turned back to my cabinetmaking as the Rabbi returned to his *bet-sefer* students. "Now, boys, let's review..."

I'm not sure how I managed to finish the cabinet; my mind was no longer on the work of my hands, but on the incredible opportunity that was opening up before me. *Oh, Father, is this how You're going to answer my prayers?* Six months...it had been nearly six months since Zephanyah had exiled me. And now...

It suddenly occurred to me that I didn't even know this rabbi's name. All I knew is that he was somehow connected with this synagogue, one of several that had been built in Sepphoris over the past decade. His accent, like that of my grandfathers, was of the South—he was not a Galilean by birth, but a Judaean—and he was obviously a learned and respected man. The rest was a complete mystery. Perhaps Abba knew more of him.

It took me another hour to finish the cabinet and put away my tools, after which I raced outside to find Abba, who was working with the rest of the family on the synagogue's roof, patching and replastering it now that the rainy season was over, and replacing some tiles that had cracked in a hailstorm. I flew up the ladder, breathless with excitement.

"Cabinet all done?" Saba Yaakob asked.

"Yes, sir."

"Did you remember to oil the hinges?"

"Yes, sir. It's ready for your inspection." I glanced over at Yosef. "Abba, may I please speak with you when you have a moment?"

"Sure. Come give me a hand with this troweling and I'll be done in half the time. If you want, we can talk while we trowel."

I knelt beside him, stirring the plaster and doling it out as fast as Abba could spread it. "While I was working on the cabinet," I said softly, "there was a teacher in the room with his Torah class. He asked a question none of them could answer, and—"

"And you jumped into the conversation." Abba heaved a sigh. "Well, you don't seem upset, so I'm assuming the rabbi wasn't too angry."

"On the contrary, Abba. He asked me to come back an hour from now. He wants to talk with me some more. May I go, sir? Or do you need me here?"

He laughed. "Yeshua, the day I need you on a roof more than you need to be in school is the day I must fall on my face and beg God's forgiveness. Finish this patch with me and then go wash up. How dirty are you?" He stopped spreading plaster long enough to inspect me carefully. "The apron has to go, of course, but your tunic isn't too bad. Take it off and shake it out really well before you meet with the rabbi. Who is he, by the way?"

I described the man as best I could. Father nodded. "That's the *hazzan* here, Ezra bar Shimeon. If you find favor with him…" He left the rest of the thought unspoken, but it hung in the air like a promise of rain after a long drought.

As I washed off the worst of the day's grime and shook out my tunic, I thought about my situation and how it tied in with the "paradox of humility" I'd discovered in the Esther *megillah*. Of course I'd never actually read the scroll; but the story was told each year in the synagogue during Purim, and it had always touched me. From start to finish it was a story of pride and humility; those who exalted themselves were humbled, and those who humbled themselves were exalted. Like Esther, I was now in the position to rise or fall based on my choices. Like Esther, I resolved to move in humility. Let Rabbi Ezra decide for himself if I was worthy to sit at his feet. *May I find favor in his sight, Father, and in Yours.* I opened the door to his chamber. He had his back to me, bent over a table, reading.

"Rabbi Ezra?" I called in a hushed tone.

"Yeshua," he replied without looking up. "Come here, lad. Are your hands clean?"

"Yes, sir. I washed before coming in."

There were two stools at the table, and he gestured for me to take the other seat and then pushed the scroll closer to me. "My eyes are getting old before the rest of me, it would seem," he commented casually. "Read this to me."

Read this to me. Even though I'd been hoping for this, part of me hadn't dared to believe it would happen. At the words, my eyes filled with tears and I was suddenly unable to breathe. *Oh, my Father!* With effort, I got myself under control and blinked away the tears. "Th-thank you, Rabbi. I would be glad to read to you."

I looked down at the scroll he'd proffered. It was Esther, not surprisingly, and it was open to the most ironic example of the humility paradox, the scene where Haman is forced to honor Mordekai with the tribute he'd designed for himself. I began. ""Go at once, the king commanded Haman. "Get the robe and the horse and do just as you have suggested for Mordekai the Jew, who sits at the king's gate. Do not neglect anything you have recommended." So Haman got the robe and the horse. He robed Mordekai, and led him on horseback through the city streets, proclaiming before him, "This is what is done for the man the king delights to honor!" Afterward Mordekai returned to the king's gate. But Haman rushed home, with his head covered in grief, and told Zeresh his wife and all his friends everything that had happened to him...""

The words fell effortlessly from my lips, taking on a life of their own, as if I had read them many times before. I found myself swept up in their beauty, their power; I could almost taste their sweetness as they formed on my tongue. My eyes saw the letters, black upon the page, *het* and *mem* and *nun*, but in my mind I could see Haman hanging his head, humbled before his enemy in the city streets. I hadn't read far, however, before the Rabbi spoke up.

"Stop there." He took the Esther scroll from me, rolling it tight.

My first thought was that my reading had displeased him, but the expression on his face set my concerns to rest. He rose from his stool and crossed to the new cabinet where he'd already stored the other *megillot*. Muttering softly to himself, he ran his hands over the scrolls, lifting first this one and then that one before returning them to their cradles. "Ha!" he exclaimed at last, and removed one of the scrolls from the cabinet, carrying it back to the table where I sat. Without a word to tell me which book he'd selected, Rabbi Ezra laid out the scroll, opened it to the middle, and slid it in front of me, pointing to the place he wanted me to begin.

It was obviously a test of some sort.

I began reading. "'As I looked, thrones were set in place...'" What was this? I'd never heard it before, but as my eyes ran ahead to the next words, I knew it was nothing that should be read while seated. I slipped off my stool and stood in reverence as the rest of the words took shape in my mouth and then burst forth into the room, proclaiming God's glory. "'And the Ancient of Days took His seat. His clothing was as white as snow; the hair of His head was white like wool. His throne was flaming with fire, and its wheels were all ablaze. A river of fire was flowing, coming out from before Him. Thousands upon thousands attended Him; ten thousand times ten thousand stood before Him. The court was seated, and the books were opened...'"

It was as if I myself were having the vision the prophet described, so vividly did the words burn and blaze in my heart. I half-expected the parchment itself to burst into flame, but the letters remained there, subdued, tamed, unaware of the power they contained. I could feel the power like tongues of fire crawling over my skin; indeed, the hairs on my arms were standing up as if in awe. I couldn't stop reading, couldn't have stopped even if the Rabbi had ordered me to, but he didn't. Without pausing, I glanced up at him and saw that his eyes were shut, his head tilted back, his face filled with peace as he listened to the words pouring from my mouth like rain:

"'In my vision at night I looked, and there before me was one like a son of man, coming with the clouds of heaven. He approached the Ancient of Days and was led into His presence. He was given authority, glory and sovereign power; all peoples, nations and men of every language worshiped him. His dominion is an everlasting dominion that will not pass away, and his kingdom is one that will never be destroyed...'"

It suddenly hit me, all at once, what I was reading—this was a prophecy about me.

Me.

Talk about the paradox of humility.

My face flushed and my ears burned with embarrassment, though of course I was the only witness to my personal revelation and the discomfort it was causing me. Up until now, I'd been thrilled by the discovery that God was my Father in a very special and unique way, and I had longed to know Him better; but I'd been focusing on the *past* aspects of our relationship—my conception and birth—and the *present* aspects of our relationship—my struggle to live in a way that would be pleasing to Him. I'd never really thought about the *future*. These words...they described my future. *He approached the Ancient of Days and was led into His presence.* They took my breath away, and I had to fight to keep reading. All I wanted to do was fall on my face, but I commanded my legs to hold me up and forced my mouth to push out the rest of the words on the page, not pausing until I came to the bottom, where I read:

"'This is the end of the matter. I, Daniel, was deeply troubled by my thoughts, and my face turned pale, but I kept the matter to myself.'"

"Yes, let's stop here," Rabbi Ezra said, and this time I was grateful for his interruption. Like Daniel, I needed time to put myself back together, to draw a few breaths of air—ordinary, earthbound air. "You read well, Yeshua bar Yosef. Who is your teacher?"

That question brought me back to earth faster than anything else could have, like a slap across the face. Fortunately, I'd been expecting it sooner or later. "Zephanyah bar Uziyel, sir. He *was* my teacher. I'm no longer in school."

The Rabbi muttered something under his breath (it sounded like "criminal" but I couldn't be sure) before asking, "Would you like to be in school, Yeshua?"

Would I like to be in school? Ask a drowning man if he'd like to be pulled from the sea. I swallowed, but still my voice came out as a whisper. "Oh, yes, Rabbi. I would."

"Ask your father to come see me tomorrow, Yeshua. With no disrespect to Yosef—I've no doubt you're an excellent carpenter—but your talents are being wasted there. We'll see if an arrangement can't be made for you to join me in study of the

Prophets."

"You—you want me to join your *bet-midrash*, Rabbi?"

"You'd have to *be* my *bet-midrash*, Yeshua, since I don't have any other students at your level. No, I'm talking about taking you as my *talmid*. You're a bit young for it, but I think you can handle the responsibility. If that's agreeable to you and to your father."

"I—I—I'm speechless, Rabbi." I was stuttering like Moses. This was more than I'd ever dreamed. "Yes, yes, that would be most agreeable!" Listen to me, speaking for Yosef. "I'll ask Abba right away, sir. What time do you want to see him?"

"After dinner tomorrow, if that's convenient. Better yet, ask him if he will join me for dinner. Speaking of which, I haven't eaten yet and my wife is no doubt wondering what has kept me this long. Off with you now."

Abba was as ecstatic as I. "Of course I'll meet with the Rabbi! It will be a pleasure to talk to someone who actually *wants* to teach you."

That's when it hit me.

I couldn't fall asleep. I lay on my back, staring at the beams of the ceiling until the room was engulfed in darkness, and then staring into the darkness as if it held the answer I so desperately craved. The darkness stared back at me, but it said nothing. The only sound was Katan's snoring, soft and in my ear. Then, like a chorus of frogs, other snores: some soft, some loud, but none containing words of wisdom.

Father, give me wisdom.

The Rabbi's words kept repeating in my mind: *with no disrespect to Yosef...* He believed that I'd left school because Yosef had taken me out. If he knew the real reason, would he still be eager to have me as his disciple?

Silence would guarantee my acceptance. Silence would restore that which I'd lost. Silence would serve as a shield, defending me, protecting me.

Silence would serve as a cloak, hiding the truth.

I have to tell him.

At first cockcrow, I crept out of bed and donned my tunic and *tallit* as quietly as possible, not wanting to wake anyone—not wanting to wake Yosef. Feeling my way in the darkness as I did every morning, I crossed through the shop, sandals in hand, and swung the door open just wide enough to slip out, blessing the well oiled hinges for their silence.

I avoided the stairs; my footfalls on the roof would be heard by those sleeping below. Instead, I made my way up the narrow sheep path to the plateau. About halfway up, my foot slipped on the loose scree and sent a clatter of stones raining noisily down the side of the cliff, and I cringed at the sound. Only then did I realize what I was doing.

Are you mad, Yeshua?

I got up early every morning and, out of courtesy to the sleepers, I always made an effort to be quiet, but this was different—I wasn't being courteous; I was being sneaky. I was sneaking out. I didn't want Yosef to catch me.

Why not?

As if in answer to my unspoken question, my buttocks tightened. It had been barely a month since they'd tasted Yosef's rod, and here I was about to do the same thing all over again. No, not the same thing. Worse. My conversations with Shimon Zealot had been incidental, my silence an afterthought. My conversation with Rabbi Ezra—though it hadn't happened yet—was intentional, my silence deliberate.

Don't ever shut me out again. You come to me, do you hear?

I turned around and headed back the way I'd come.

"Abba?"

Yosef roused slightly, rolled over to face me. "Hmmm?" His eyes were still closed.

"Abba," I whispered again, "I need to speak with you."

He cracked one eye open.

"I'm sorry to wake you so early, sir, but it's important."

He blinked and sat up. "Come on outside." We tiptoed around Mother and baby Sarah, out the door, and up the stairs to the roof. "Is this okay?" he asked.

Our roof, like most roofs, served as another room of the house. Mother used it as workspace, drying clothes in the sun, sitting at her loom in the shade of the cliff; it was also a great place for conversation. But not for this conversation. I shook my head.

"The rock, then," Yosef said. He shivered slightly in the pre-dawn chill; he'd gotten out of bed half-naked at my summons. Beside me was a basket of clothes waiting to be washed; I pulled out a robe that wasn't too badly soiled and handed it to him. "Thanks." Wrapping himself in the robe, he led me up the ladder and to the rock we used for private talks. "Now, what has you bothered, Yisu?" He frowned, only now awake enough to really see me. Concern filled his voice. "Have you been up all night, son?"

Nodding, I said, "I have a problem, sir."

"Let me help."

I didn't think he could—part of the problem was of his making—but I'd promised to let him try. *Don't ever shut me out again.* Respect for him tied my tongue in knots; my love for him—and his for me—loosened the knots and let me speak. "Yesterday, I told Rabbi Ezra that I'd left school, but I didn't tell him why. He thinks it was your decision. I—I can't let him go on believing that. I've decided to go to him and tell him the truth."

"The truth." There was a hint of question in his voice.

"Yes, sir."

"Exactly what are you planning to say to him, Yeshua?"

I understood all too well the reason for the trepidation in Yosef's voice. "I'm going to tell him that Rabbi Zephanyah has refused to teach me any longer. That he's banned me from his library, and that he won't give me *aliyah*."

"And when he asks why?"

"The truth. Because Zephanyah believes me to be *mamzer*."

Yosef sighed and looked down, pondering. He shook his head but said nothing for a long while. When finally he spoke it was in a tightly controlled tone that I knew was causing him effort. "And when he asks the reason for that belief? And whether it has any merit?"

This was the hard part, the reason I hadn't wanted to face Yosef. "Abba, you know I love you. But I can't lie to him. I can't!"

"You can't tell him the truth, Yeshua! I forbid you to confide in this—this *stranger*, things that I haven't even told my own father!"

"What would you have me say?" I was on the verge of tears, torn between two impossibilities. "What would you have me say? That Zephanyah is deluded? That I am your son, your legitimate son? That's—that's—"

"That's the truth!"

"*Your* truth, Abba, the truth you want everyone to believe."

"God gave you to me, Yeshua."

"As He gave Moses to Pharaoh's daughter—"

"No! It's not the same!"

"—for a time, for a purpose—"

"You are my son! That's the truth!"

"But not the whole truth."

"No!" he snapped. "Not the whole truth." Abruptly he got very quiet. Drawing in a deep breath, he reached out and wrapped me in his arms, pulling me close. "Not the whole truth," he whispered into my hair. He held me there for a while, saying nothing, just holding me as he had when I was little. I closed my eyes, felt them fill with tears, knew if I opened them the tears would escape and run down my face.

Yosef stroked my back with one hand and then pulled away slightly, unfolding me from his embrace. Gently he lifted my chin. I blinked through my tears, trying to bring his face into focus. In the first light of the approaching dawn, I saw tears glimmering in his eyes as well. "Yeshua," he whispered. "My son. I wish all men were as honest as you, as faithful, as worthy of trust. But they aren't. You have goodness, but you lack the experience that builds wisdom—you simply haven't lived long enough to understand what men are capable of. Truth…truth is a two-edged sword. You have to wield it carefully. You can't hand it to just anyone; he might turn and run you through. Do you understand what I'm trying to say?"

I didn't answer him. I just stared into his eyes. *You see me. And I see you.* He was right. I didn't understand the evil that men committed. I didn't *want* to understand it, didn't want to believe that men such as Rabbi Zephanyah—good and learned men who professed to love God—could willfully, knowingly, deliberately choose to harm another human being. But they could. And they did. Even Yosef did it. Even Yosef.

"What should I do, Abba?"

"Tell Ezra what you must, son. But if you will, accept my advice—tell him no more than you must. That Zephanyah has questioned your legitimacy is a matter of record, and many are aware of it. Beyond that, I would ask you to remain silent."

"And if the Rabbi questions me?"

"Tell him the truth: I have forbidden you to discuss the matter. If he has questions, he may ask me, and I will answer them as I see fit." He grasped my shoulders firmly, holding me at arms length. "Honor me in this, Yeshua, by trusting my judgment."

Father, what should I do? I couldn't bear the thought that, whether by action or inaction, I was condoning Yosef's lie. He must have read my indecision on my face, because he spoke one last time.

"I promise you, son, I won't perjure myself. You needn't fret about that. Everything I say to the man will be true, just as I spoke only truth before Shofet Abiyud."

"But if you allow him to believe I'm your natural son—"

"If *I* allow him to believe? What power or authority do I have over men's thoughts? You yourself said that God will reveal the full truth as He pleases. If He pleases to reveal it to Rabbi Ezra, nothing would make me happier." Yosef stood up, took one step, and then turned. In a firm tone he said, "Yeshua, I want you to trust me. I'm only a man and I'm far from perfect, but I've never betrayed you. I believe I've earned the right to ask for your trust—and to receive it."

Indeed he had. My Father had trusted Yosef enough to place me in his care and under his authority. Who was I to question my Father's judgment? Or Yosef's? I slid off the rock and stood before him. "You have my trust, Abba, along with my love and respect. I'm still not sure I agree, but I'll do as you've said."

Two of my three problems had been resolved, two of my three burdens lifted. I was no longer going behind Yosef's back, and I knew what I was going to say to Rabbi Ezra. This should have lightened my step, but the third load I carried was heavier than a Roman pack and I had to bear it much farther than one mile. I bent under it, each step of the three-mile road toward Sepphoris harder to take than the one before. Again and again and again

and again—three thousand paces, three thousand temptations—
I thought, *Silence would serve me better.* Three thousand times
I almost turned back.

I'd been devastated back in Tishri when Zephanyah had
robbed me of my Father's word. It had taken every fiber of self-
control, days—weeks—of constant prayer, fasting from food,
fasting from water, fasting from sleep...I'd sat *shiva* for the
books I'd lost, mourned them as a brother who had died, wept
for the words of wisdom locked away in Zephanyah's cabinets
forever beyond my reach. I'd been a man without air, gasping
for breath, despairing of life.

Hands had reached out to me, fanning distant breezes, and
I'd survived. I'd survived. Day in, day out, just enough air to
keep me going, keep me gasping. And then, yesterday—
miraculously, it seemed to me—rescue! Rabbi Ezra had opened
the door and the wind had gusted—*ru'ach ha-Elohim*, breath of
God that gave Adam life—and restored me to myself. But
now...now...

The thought that I was about to lose the books all over
again—that Rabbi Ezra would slam the door in my face as
Zephanyah had—weighed down my steps and slowed my
progress. It was worse this time, far worse, for I'd now tasted
the mysteries that lay within the folds of parchment; I knew the
delights my Father had prepared for me. I wanted more. More.

The only book I owned was *D'varim*; I'd read it so many
times that its words had become part of me, as much a part of
me as my skin or my bones or my blood. *D'varim* spoke to me
now:

You shall not covet anything that is your neighbor's.

This wasn't my neighbor's! It was mine, mine by right! *My*
Father's words. Mine!

But *D'varim* was not finished speaking. *Be careful to follow
every command I am giving you today, so that you may live and
increase and may enter and possess the land that Adonai
promised on oath to your forefathers. Remember how Adonai
your God led you all the way in the desert these forty years, to
humble you and to test you in order to know what was in your
heart, whether or not you would keep His commands. He
humbled you, causing you to hunger and then feeding you with
manna, which neither you nor your fathers had known, to teach*

you that man does not live on bread alone but on every word that comes from the mouth of Adonai. Your clothes did not wear out and your feet did not swell during these forty years. Know then in your heart that as a man disciplines his son, so Adonai your God disciplines you.

The point was not lost upon me. The Israelites had complained about the manna and begged for other food, but they had learned over time to be content with God's provision. While I'd gone hungry for more of His word, I'd not starved. My Father had fed me. I wanted more, craved more—but I was not starving. Could it be—could it possibly be—that this, too, was part of His plan for me, His discipline? "Please, Father, not forty years," I whispered as the eastern sky shimmered with the first hues of dawn. Six months had already tested me to my limits, or so I felt. How much longer might Zephanyah rule over the synagogue in Nazareth? Ten years? Twenty? And who would follow after him—his son Abner? *Forty years...* To a thirteen-year-old, forty years is forever.

Silence would serve me better...

But these passages from *D'varim*—the only book I owned, the one that I knew best—they challenged me to persevere. I spoke them aloud, defying the silence that so tempted me, adding my favorite verse of all: "'And you shall love Adonai your God with all your heart and with all your soul and with all your strength.'" *All my strength.* It wasn't sufficient. *Forty years...* "Increase my strength, Father. My spirit is willing, but my flesh is so weak."

Silence would serve me better...

Six months, a year, ten years, forty years...Abraham lived a *hundred* years without ever receiving his inheritance; Isaac and Yaakob hundreds more; Moses never entered the Promised Land; yet all of them died praising God. How many words in all had God spoken to the Patriarchs? To Moses? I had every one of them memorized, and many psalms as well, plus the treasures Saba had smuggled out to me...why, compared with Abraham, I was rich! It should be enough. It should be more than enough. If not, if my Father wanted me to have more, then He would provide it. If He did not...

Silence would serve me better.

"Oh, my Father! Must I tell him? Truly? Is that what You

want?"

The sun lifted itself fully over the horizon at that moment and leaped into the sky, shedding its husk and bursting forth in blinding light. I had to turn my eyes away. But the light had not only burned my eyes, it had also burned away some of the fog shrouding my soul, bringing to my memory the words of a prophecy that my cousin Yochanan had shared with me a year ago: *The Dayspring from on High has visited us to give light to those who sit in darkness and the shadow of death.*

To give light. That was my purpose. Even if the light burned me, I had to bear it. I didn't have the luxury of sitting in darkness and I couldn't use darkness for my own gain. Though I would obey Yosef and remain silent on some matters, trusting him to say what was needed, I would also obey my Father and reject the dark silence that served only my own desires.

My desires...

Three thousand times I picked up my feet and pushed them toward Sepphoris.

When I arrived at the synagogue, Rabbi Ezra was just opening the doors.

"May I please come in, sir?" I asked quietly. "I need to tell you something."

He didn't answer but stepped aside to let me enter.

If I didn't speak quickly, I might not speak at all. Without waiting for his invitation, I blurted out the words that had been strangling me all night. "Rabbi Ezra, I owe you an apology. I wasn't completely honest with you yesterday. I told you that I wasn't in school anymore, but I—I didn't tell you why. That was wrong of me." I realized that I was staring at my feet and raised my eyes to his face, but I couldn't read his expression through the tears that blurred my vision. Silence rose up in me again, clamoring to be heard, but I swallowed it back down and continued, "Rabbi Zephanyah expelled me, sir. Not only from school, but from the library as well. I'm not supposed to touch the books or read from them, not even in the assembly. If he knew I was here, that I'd read for you yesterday, he'd be livid. He—" I cut myself off. *Tell him no more than you must.*

I waited for Ezra to ask for an explanation, but he just stood there like a wall.

Silence—now that it could no longer help me—swelled until it filled the room and then gave birth to a new temptation: the temptation to tell Ezra everything. I'd obeyed my Father and held up the lamp that exposed my disgrace; I'd obeyed Yosef and said no more than that; wasn't I even going to get a chance to defend myself against Ezra's unspoken accusations and suspicions? *Forty years...* Biting down on my lower lip, I forced myself to wait for Ezra's response.

A full minute passed before he broke the silence. "Had he good reason?"

It wasn't the question I'd been expecting—most men would simply have asked *why?*—and so I hesitated before replying,"Yes. Yes, he did." Before he could question me further, I said, "He believes I'm illegitimate."

"Are you?"

There it was, the question I couldn't dance around, the question I'd been dreading. Blinking back the tears and fighting to keep my voice level, I replied in the only way I could. "I'm not a *mamzer*, Rabbi. If I were, I wouldn't be here. For it is written, 'No one of illegitimate birth nor any of his descendants may enter the assembly of Adonai, even down to the tenth generation.' God forbid I should put myself above the Law." I closed my eyes and bowed my head, begging my Father to release me from this ordeal, but the world refused to come to an end. I was walking such a narrow path here—one step to either side would plunge me headfirst off the cliff. "But Zephanyah has reason to believe otherwise; I won't deny that." I would not slander my former teacher, whose only crime was zeal for the Law. "I wish I could tell you more, sir, but my father has forbidden me to talk about it." I would not dishonor Yosef by breaking my promise to him. "I'm sorry I didn't tell you sooner. I was so excited—I had hoped—" Having spoken all of the words I was allowed to speak, having thoroughly condemned myself to forty years in the wilderness, I choked back the rest of what I wanted to say and slipped through the door. Setting my face toward Nazareth, I began to walk. Briskly. My sheep were waiting.

Three thousand times I almost turned back.

Almost.

13

KATAN

Nisan 3769
(The Counting of Weeks)

"**P**lease, Abba."

My father looked at me, then at Yoshiah, then at Uncle Zebdi, and then back at me again. "I don't know, Katan. Two months…that's a long time to be away from home, work, school…" He shook his head.

"He can go to school with me, Uncle," Yoshiah offered.

"I'll make him work for his keep," Zebdi added.

"I'll work twice as hard when I get home," I promised.

Father smiled and shook his head again, but this time I could tell his answer had turned from a *no* to a *yes*."What can I say? I'm hopelessly outnumbered. All right, I surrender—on one condition." He turned to Uncle Zebdi. "You have to teach him to swim, Zebdi. Under no circumstance is he to set foot on a boat until he knows how to swim. Agreed?"

"I'm insulted, Yosef. As if I'd let him drown. Please."

Yoshiah and I were already doing a victory dance.

Just as had happened last year, Uncle Zebdi was in a hurry to get back to his fishing boats, while Mother wanted to stay in the city for the entire week of the Feast to visit with her Aunt Elisheba. Last year, Yisu and I were *supposed* to travel to Bethsaida with Uncle Zebdi—and indeed, *I* had, though Yisu had wandered off somewhere and thrown our parents into an uproar—but I'd only gotten to stay with Yoshiah for a couple of days before Father had shown up and claimed me. This time, however, it was agreed that Yisu would stay with our parents while I accompanied Yoshiah and his parents. For two months, I'd get to live the life of a fisherman.

Although there had been a few short family visits over the past year, I hadn't ever been allowed away from home on my own. Seven weeks. Seven whole weeks without anyone comparing me to Yisu! And if that wasn't cause enough for rejoicing, I'd be spending the time between Passover and Shavuot with my favorite relative of all. Yoshi and I shared the same age difference as Yisu and I, but in reverse: my cousin would turn eleven at the end of the summer. That meant he was old enough to do the things I enjoyed—and he was young enough to follow my lead most of the time.

"This is going to be great!" we said at almost the same instant, and then we dissolved in laughter. A few hours later, I said goodbye to my parents and Yisu, put Jerusalem behind me, and set out for Bethsaida.

"No! No!"

"Quit screaming, Yakob, and let go of me before you drown us both!" Yoshiah yelled. Fortunately, he wasn't talking to me but to his younger brother, who just happened to share my name. We were several boat lengths from the shore and the water was deep; although Yakob could swim better than I could, he had panicked when he fell overboard and was clinging to Yoshiah with all his might. The two of them were now tangled in the net, the fish had all escaped, and Yakob wouldn't stop fighting his brother's rescue attempt.

"I said st—" The rest of Yoshiah's admonition was lost as he went under and got a mouthful of water. I had better do something, and fast. I thought about jumping in myself, but if Yoshiah couldn't pull Yakob out of the water, I probably couldn't either. Three of us tangled in a net was worse than pointless. Thinking fast, I grabbed one of the oars and extended it toward the shrieking three-year-old.

"Here, Yakob, take the oar," I called.

He ignored me, but Yoshi managed to get a hand free long enough to grab on to the shaft. It was slippery, though, and he lost his purchase on it when I started to pull them in; to make matters worse, the boat started to drift and I had to lean far over the side to reach the oar out to them a second time. Even so, it fell short of Yoshi's reach by a full span.

"The net!" Yoshiah gasped before going under again.

"Yakob, let go of Yoshi!" I shouted. *The net?* Suddenly I understood what my cousin was trying to tell me. I shoved the oar down into the drifting net and began to pull it toward the boat. After three or four tries, I managed to get my hands on the ropes and haul in the net, which was full of half-drowned boys and two or three unlucky fish.

Yoshiah coughed and vomited over the side of the skiff, and then rounded on Yakob. I expected him to tear into his little brother, but instead all he said was, "Kobi, are you all right?" The poor kid was crying too hard to answer. "That means *yes*," Yoshiah said, smiling up at me. "Thanks, Katan. Boy! I never thought *you'd* be the one rescuing *me*!"

Ordinarily, I'd have laughed at that—just two weeks ago, Yoshiah was teaching me to swim—but I was still so shaken that the best I could manage was a feeble grin. "Yeah, well, hopefully you won't need to return the favor."

The wind had picked up a bit and was coming out of the south, so Yoshiah decided to sail back rather than row; we were about a mile from Seven Springs, and it wouldn't take us long at all to get home with the wind at our backs. "Do you want to steer?" he offered.

"No, I'll leave that to you." After all, it was Yoshiah's boat. He'd practically built it himself, my uncle had told me proudly, taking a simple rowboat and outfitting it with a mast, sail, and rudder that he'd paid for himself with his share of the fish he'd caught—and all this before his tenth birthday. My cousin hadn't yet finished the boat when I'd visited last year, but we'd taken it out practically every day since Uncle had pronounced me a fit swimmer a week ago.

"Okay, then you get to mend the net." Yoshi pointed to the tangled mess in the bilge.

"What about me? Do I get a job?" Yakob asked, sniffling.

"Sure, Kobi. You get to sort the fish."

"But there's only three!" he pouted.

"Well, whose fault is that? You're supposed to pull the net into the boat, not jump overboard into the net, little fisherman."

"I didn't jump. I falled. In the *water*. Not in the net. I'm not stupid!"

Yoshiah was the one who had jumped, the instant Yakob started screaming, leaving me in the boat all by myself. If I'd had the presence of mind to hang onto the net that he'd dropped, they probably wouldn't have gotten tangled in it, and Yakob would have more than three fish to sort, but there was no sense wasting my time in *what-ifs* now. No one had been hurt, and a torn net was a small price to pay for that.

"So, did you catch some good fish?" Yoshiah asked his little brother.

Yakob looked over his prizes, singing softly to himself:

"The fish with fins and scales, it's true,
God has made for me and you.
The fish without are unclean things;
Be careful of the catfish—he stings!

"They're all good fish, Yoshi!" he announced happily, throwing them into a basket.

"Well, that's something else to be thankful for." Yoshiah tipped his head back and shouted at the sky, "Thank You, Lord God!" Then he adjusted the sail, took a seat in the stern of the boat, and cried, "Hold on, everybody!" just as the wind gusted and the boat leaped forward.

Yakob, his chore finished, ran to the bow and knelt there, holding tightly to the side of the boat with one hand as he leaned over and dragged the other through the waves. "Quit that, Yakob!" I scolded. "Do you want to fall in again?" I sat down in the bilge just forward of the sail and tried to untangle the net. "Come here and help me with this." Since Yakob was three months younger than my brother Yehudah, I didn't expect him to be any help at all, but it was better than letting him lean over the bow as we raced across the lake.

"Okay, I'll help!"

"What was that song you were singing?" I asked as we fiddled with the net.

"The catfish song." He sang it again, but this time when he got to the end—*he stings!*—Yakob pinched me and giggled.

"Ow!" I exclaimed, playing along.

"Do you know any songs, Katan?"

"Sure. Lots."

"Sing one!" Yoshiah called out.

"Okay." I launched into "Roni" because we were moving so fast and because no one had been killed, and Yoshiah sang along with me while Yakob clapped enthusiastically.

The sun beat down on us, drying us off long before we reached Bethsaida, and we decided not to mention the fact that Yoshiah and Yakob had nearly drowned. Explaining the torn net and scanty haul was another matter, but Yoshi said he'd handle it. "I'll tell Father the truth, of course, that Kobi fell into the net and spoiled the catch. We just won't say anything about his screaming and flailing and trying to stand on my head. Okay?" He tickled Yakob until the boy squealed. "Unless, of course, you want Father to forbid you to come out with us again?"

"No, Yoshi, I won't tell."

"There's nothing to tell, really," I agreed. After all, nobody had been hurt, and the net was easily repaired.

There was no synagogue in Bethsaida, which was just a fishing village on the outskirts of Capernaum; we attended school in town, in the afternoon. "In Nazareth," I told Yoshiah and his friend Andrai, "we have school early in the morning."

"Here, we fish," Andrai explained. "Lots of the boys in bet-sefer do go earlier, but Rabbi Berekhiah has a special class just for us fishermen."

Other than the unusual hour, school was pretty much the same: reading, writing, and reciting, plus lessons from Torah. Our class included boys from five to twelve, so I was one of the oldest there, and I did my best to set a good example. "Yaakob bar Yosef, you are a credit to your father and to your teacher," Rabbi Berekhiah commented at the end of the first week, and I beamed at his praise. Andrai bar Yonah, who was the same age as Yoshiah—they actually shared a birthday—was a competent student, but my heart ached for my cousin. Try as he might, he could not read a passage from Torah without butchering it. His memory work was fine—as long as someone was patient to read the scriptures to him several times—and he could write passably well, but his reading was beyond atrocious.

After everyone else had taken a turn at the podium, the rabbi called, "Yoshiah bar Zebdi," wincing slightly as he added, "please read the Song of Miriam." The Song of Miriam was one of the shortest (and simplest) songs in the whole Tanakh; the rabbi was being gracious.

"Yes, Rabbi," Yoshi answered, stepping to the podium. He

began, "Sin...since the Lord—"

"Sing to the Lord," the rabbi corrected.

"Sing to the Lord, for he is h...huge and ex...extend...no, extolled—"

"Highly exalted," the rabbi sighed.

"Sing to the Lord, for he is highly exalted. The house of rid...ridder—"

"The horse and its rider! Yoshiah, please think about what you're saying!"

"Yes, Rabbi. I'm sorry. I really am trying, sir."

"Yes, yes, I know," he sighed again. "Go ahead, finish it up."

Yoshiah drew in a deep breath, and began again. "Sing to the Lord, for he is highly exalted. The horse and its rider he has hur...hurried...into the...sea?"

"Hurled into the sea. No, no, don't start over. That's fine. You're finished for the day."

I heaved a huge sigh of relief. Poor Yoshiah. I didn't understand—he was good at everything else he tried. Why couldn't he read? After school, on the way home, I asked him.

"I don't know," he admitted. "It's always been like that. The letters just won't stay still on the page. It's like they have so much joy in them, they just have to dance, know what I mean? I don't understand how everyone else manages to catch them. If only I had the right net, maybe I could, too."

I wasn't sure what he meant. "Yoshi, the words don't move unless you shake the book."

"They move for me."

"Is there something wrong with your eyes?"

"No, I don't think so. Stand still a minute." I froze in my tracks while Yoshiah stared at my face, frowning. "No, your face doesn't jump around; those rocks down by your feet aren't moving either. It's just words. Don't ask me to explain it, 'cause I can't."

Andrai laughed and swatted his friend across the back. "Who cares? So you'll never be a rabbi or a scribe. You don't want to be cooped up inside all day anyway, do you? I sure don't." He turned to me. "Fact is, Katan, your cousin Yoshiah is the best fisherman in Bethsaida, and I'm not kidding. You can ask anybody. Yoshi wins every contest we have! He even beat my brother, and Shimon's fifteen! Plus he's the youngest boat owner, and the youngest team captain, and—"

"That's enough, Andrai! Stop bragging on me, please. Katan doesn't care about that stuff, right?" He started to run toward the shore. "Hey! We still have time for a sail. Who wants to come?"

The weeks flew by too quickly. I wish I could say I missed my family and friends back home, but it simply wouldn't be true. Yoshiah had no idea how good he had it as the firstborn of only two sons. Most people would look at my home and say it was the more blessed because it had more children in it—it sure did!—but being one of eight is no fun at all unless you're either the oldest or the youngest. No one in Yoshiah's house was stuck in the middle.

And my trade…much as I enjoyed working with my hands to build things, it wasn't nearly as much fun as being outside all day sailing around the lake, jumping in whenever the sun got too hot, and knowing the thrill of pulling in a really good catch. Sure, the sorting and gutting that followed was smelly work, but it was fun sitting together and listening to stories as we worked, and then hanging around the marketplace for a little while before heading off to school.

School here was easier, too. Rabbi Berekhiah wasn't half as demanding as Rabbi Zephanyah, and Uncle Zebdi wasn't half as demanding as Father. I hadn't felt the rod even once since coming to Capernaum. Everyone agreed that I was the best student in the class. I didn't even have to study hard. It was the perfect end to the workday, and then Yoshi and I were free to play with Andrai until suppertime, which—along with bedtime—came early in Bethsaida.

We did have to get up in the middle of the night, but that was fun too—exciting and mysterious, all the hushed hustle and bustle by lamplight as the men and older boys ate a hasty breakfast and headed down to the lakeshore to pile into boats and shove off onto moonlit waters. The sound of voices muted by the darkness calling out to one another, the lapping of the waves against the sides of the boats, the *whoosh* of sails being raised and the *splash* of nets being cast—these things were all made sweeter because they filled an otherwise dark and silent world. I was captivated by them, and by the hush that fell as the first light of dawn appeared behind the eastern hills each morning. Sometimes I forgot to breathe.

No, life in Bethsaida was nothing like Nazareth.

Some things, of course, were the same, and would have been anywhere in the world—after all, we were Jews. Just as we would have done in Nazareth, we said the daily blessings, rested on Sabbath, and counted the days of the *omer* throughout the weeks between Passover and Pentecost. Still, there were a few surprises. On the forty-second day of the *omer*, had we been at my home in Nazareth, Father would have begun making preparations to travel to Jerusalem for Pentecost, which was the last day of Shavuot and one of the three required ingatherings. Uncle Zebdi, however, ignored the day entirely.

"Uncle," I asked him that evening as we made ready for bed, "aren't we going up for Shavuot?"

He looked at me as if I were crazy. "What, and miss two weeks of fishing?"

"But the Law says—"

"I know what the Law says, Katan. But Herod's law says that if I don't pay my fishing lease on the due date, my whole family starves to death. I can't afford to shut down operations every two months, especially at this time of year. Passover is a huge sacrifice. Shavuot on top of that—well, it would be suicide. Maybe if God had blessed me with more sons, as he has your father, more hands to share the workload, maybe then I could afford the pilgrimage. But as it is, well, the Law also makes provision for those living far away, doesn't it?" He patted me on the shoulder and sent me to bed, leaving me alone with my thoughts.

Three times a year all your men must appear before Adonai your God at the place he will choose: at the Feast of Unleavened Bread, the Feast of Weeks and the Feast of Tabernacles. All your men, Rabbi Zephanyah said, meant *all.* The Law did make a special exception for those who were too far away, but Uncle Zebdi had it wrong. It didn't excuse him from the gathering; it just said he could sell his tithe in his hometown and bring the silver to the Temple instead of lugging baskets of fish a hundred miles. That's what Father did. I had to admit, though, that my father, in keeping all three feasts, was in

the minority. So instead of begging to go up for Shavuot—
which I'd still never done with success—I dropped the matter,
knowing with certainty that Father would not only *allow* me to
go next year, but he'd *insist* upon it as a *mitzvah*.

The next day passed pretty much the same as had the thirty
before it, with one notable exception: I actually caught the
biggest fish! Unlike carpentry, the fishing trade was highly
competitive, and the men of Bethsaida vied with one another to
see which boat could bring in the most fish each day and which
fisherman could bring in the biggest fish using a hook and line.
The game was fun, but I hadn't thought to ever stand a chance
of winning it. This fish, though, was the father of all biny, two
full cubits from head to tail, and it nearly pulled me overboard
when I hooked it. "Hold fast, Katan!" Uncle Zebdi shouted, but
he didn't help me other than to offer advice and
encouragement—to do so would have disqualified me from the
contest. By the time I finally landed the monster fish, my hands
were raw and sliced open by the pull of the line, but I didn't
care. I'd bested Yoshiah!

I heard him whooping from Uncle Sheth's boat on the far
side of the trammel net as I lifted my prize into the air with
both hands. Andrai, who was working with his father and
brother in the third boat, also congratulated me. "I told you
we'd make a fisherman out of you!" his cry floated across the
water. "Too bad you're leaving in less than two weeks!"

Too bad, indeed.

After hauling in the trammel, we headed to shore, my prize
fish swimming along on a stringer tied to the stern of the boat.
"Salt the rest," Zebdi declared, "but this one we keep alive as
long as possible. If we can sell him still swimming, he'll bring
in a small fortune. I'd wager Herod himself would be happy to
see this biny on the table!" He turned to me. "Speaking of
wagers, of course you'll enter him in the pool."

"What pool?" I asked.

"Each fisherman wagers his best catch. Winner takes all.
You'll have to keep this biny out of sight, though. If anyone
else sees it, there won't *be* a pool."

"My father doesn't approve of gambling."

"What gambling? You can't lose. It's a sure thing."

"He says a sure thing is just a fancy way of stealing from

your neighbor."

"Trust me, Katan, these neighbors have 'stolen' a few of my fish. Go ahead, enter him."

Oh, why not? After all, it was just fish, not money. They were all fishermen; they could always catch more to replace the ones they lost. "All right, Uncle. If you say so." I grinned.

"Leave everything to me."

Everything turned out to include a side bet with one of the neighbors, a man named Yaakob (wasn't everyone?) whose son, Yehudah, went by the nickname "Thaddai." Thaddai was about the same age as Yisu and was also entering a fish in the contest.

"Ha!" Uncle Zebdi said to Yaakob. "That will be the day, when Thaddai outfishes Yoshiah!" Yoshiah? I didn't know he was entering. He hadn't caught anything even close to the size of my fish. But my cousin stood beside his boat with his arms folded and a grin on his face, as if daring the world to do better than he had. When he saw me gaping at him, he winked and yelled out, "I've got my catch right here! Count me in!"

"Your son's a good fisherman," Yaakob admitted, "but he isn't the *only* good fisherman in Bethsaida. My Thaddai—"

"Your Thaddai!" Zebdi scoffed. "My land-locked nephew here could outfish your Thaddai!"

"You talk big, Zebdi!"

"So do you, Yaakob!"

"An insult like that demands more than hot air behind it."

"Are you proposing a wager?"

"Yes, I'm proposing a wager. Everyone here is my witness—you claim this boy from Nazareth can outfish my Yehudah. Don't try to deny it now."

"I always stand by my words." He sounded reluctant.

"Do you stand by them to a copper minim?" Yaakob sneered.

"I stand by them to a silver denarius. I'm a businessman. My word is my life."

"Is your life worth no more than a denarius?"

"I'm not a rich man, Yaakob."

"Five denarii. Five denarii for the insult to my son. Perhaps next time you will choose your words more carefully, since you value them so highly."

"All right," my uncle sighed. "Five denarii it is." Then he

turned to me, no longer able to keep the smile off his face. "Katan, bring out your fish."

My head was still reeling from the wager. To take a few fish was one thing, but five denarii? That was a week's wages for most men. It was more than double the annual Temple tax. It was—it was a "sure thing." Between the denarii and the value of the fish, I'd just earned my keep for the whole month, which was bound to make my uncle happy. I knew one more "sure thing," though: Father better not find out about this or I wouldn't be allowed to visit again.

There were two other handsome fish entered besides Thaddai's, Yoshiah's, and mine. The first was a big carp that fell short of winning by only a span or so. Nothing else even came close to my biny. Thaddai's fish—another biny—was respectable but not extraordinary, and the musht Yoshiah entered was a joke, far less than a cubit in length, but he had nothing to lose by venturing it and everything to gain in his father's ruthless scheme. Yoshiah had been the bait, I the hook, and Zebdi the master fisherman who set it in Yaakob's mouth so firmly there was no way he could squirm loose.

He tried nevertheless. "This boy did not catch that fish!"

"Yes, I did," I said.

"We all watched him do it," Yonah added. Uncle Sheth and Shimon nodded agreement.

"With help!" Yaakob insisted.

"As HaShem is my witness, I didn't lift one finger to help Katan," Zebdi swore. "No one did."

"Then he used a net. There is no way that boy pulled in a fish that big on a line—"

"Show him your hands, boy," my uncle said. I held them up, and the cuts from the line witnessed to the truth of Zebdi's claim more than anything that had been said. And so my uncle collected his silver and I collected my fish. He rejoiced and lavished praise on me the rest of the day. I tried to feel guilty about my part in the scheme, but honestly, I didn't. Yaakob was a grown man. No one had forced him to make the wager. One thing, however, I vowed to myself as I watched him hand over his hard-earned silver: never would I make a wager I couldn't afford to lose.

* * *

The second surprise of the week came the very next day as we were mending the nets. While Yonah and Sheth—the senior partners in the business—took the day's catch to the market, Yonah's son Shimon worked on the big trammel with Uncle Zebdi; and Yoshiah, Andrai, and I repaired the cast nets and replaced the weights that had fallen off. Since I knew how to use a drill better than either of them, I was given the task of boring holes through suitable stones, and then Yoshiah, whose fingers were the nimblest, tied them to the edges of the net. Andrai crawled around the middle of the spread-out net, looking for holes and repairing them with bits of flax. As we finished each net, we washed it clean and then hung it out to dry.

The going was slower than usual today because my cut-up hands slowed my efficiency with the drill, but we managed with a little extra help from cousin Yakob, whom I enlisted to gather stones. He ran happily to and fro picking up rocks that he thought might please me and piling them at my feet. We had just begun on the third net when I heard the last voice I would have expected. "Yaakob-Katan bar Yosef, have you finally come to your senses and run away from home?"

Holding the drill in one hand and the stone in the other, I looked up, torn between obedience and curiosity. Sure enough, there stood Shimon Zealot. My first thought was that he'd followed me here, but that was crazy. What *had* brought him to Bethsaida? Not fishing, that much was obvious at first glance. He had a ragged and rugged look about him, as if he'd been sleeping out in the open for weeks, hunting for his food likely as not, or stealing it. I thought about some of the stories my father had shared with me over the past two years, about the lawlessness of the Zealots and how they'd stolen sheep from Saba Yoachim—how they'd even manipulated my uncles Yehudah and Matthanyah into stealing from family and neighbors! I was to have nothing to do with such men, Father had told me over and over; and the one time I'd disobeyed him, the one time I'd let Shimon talk to me, I'd received the worst beating of my life along with another stern warning: *Stay away from the Zealots.*

At the same time, Father had confessed to feeling sorry for Shimon, who had been living without a father's care or guidance since he was my age. I tried to imagine such a thing, imagine myself in Shimon's place, hiding in a cave, never knowing where my next meal would come from, alone and hunted...

"*Shalom aleikha*, Shimon," I finally said. "Do you need something?" I hoped he'd say *no* and move on, but I wasn't too optimistic. He stood with one hand on his dagger—his customary pose—and looked around at the fishermen spread out along the coastline.

"Yes," he said after a few moments. "Yes, I do, and I think I might find it here."

14

YISU

Sivan 3769
(The Counting of Weeks)

"Would you lead grace today, Yeshua?"

"You honor me, Rabbi." I folded my napkin and stood with my head bowed, murmuring the first words of the *Birkhat Hamazon*, the grace after meals. "Blessed are You, Adonai our God, king of the universe, who nourishes the whole world in goodness, with grace, kindness, and compassion."

Compassion. With my head still bowed, I smiled, filled with joy and gratitude for the compassion my Father had shown me over the past two months. "Let us thank God, whose food we have eaten and through whose goodness we live. He gives bread to all flesh, for His mercy endures forever. And through His great goodness we have never lacked, nor will we lack food forever, for the sake of His great Name. For He is God, who nourishes and sustains all, and does good to all, and prepares food for all His creatures which He created." Lifting my face and my hands, I concluded the first prayer: "Blessed are You, Adonai, who nourishes all. Amen."

Amen. I couldn't stop grinning. Indeed it *was* true—my Father had provided bread for me, a feast beyond my hopes, better even than the taste I'd gotten in Jerusalem one year ago. Lately I'd come to think of Zephanyah's school as Egypt— when I'd been forced to leave, I had lamented the loss of my cucumbers and melons, believing that God had abandoned me and I would starve in the wilderness. Instead, he had opened springs of fresh water and rained down manna—food I'd never before tasted, but oh! how sweet it was in my mouth, how it filled my stomach and my soul as nothing else could. And the freedom! I hadn't realized how cumbersome my bonds were, how heavy the chains I wore day in and day out as I labored to please my taskmaster, never daring to open my mouth for fear of his whip. Now each morning I sang the Song of Miriam as I danced up the road to Sepphoris: *Sing to the Lord, for he is highly exalted; the horse and its rider he has hurled into the sea!* Sometimes I even turned cartwheels.

I looked across the table at the man who had led me out of Egypt—my Moses.

Rabbi Ezra stood with his eyes closed and a smile on his face; his right hand rested on the head of his daughter, Leah, in blessing. When I fell silent, he opened his eyes and met mine, nodding his approval and giving me permission to continue. I was in the mood for a song, so I began to sing the next blessing, and the others—Ezra, Leah, and Ezra's wife Talyah—added their voices to mine without hesitation.

> "We thank Adonai our God for having given
> a lovely and spacious land
> to our fathers and mothers;
> for having liberated us from the land of Egypt
> and freed us from the house of bondage;
> for the covenant which God has sealed in our flesh,
> for the Torah which God has taught us;
> for the laws which God has made known to us;
> for the life, grace, and loving kindness
> which God has bestowed upon us,
> and for the sustenance
> with which God nourishes and maintains us
> continually, in every season,
> every day, even every hour."

It had become customary for me to join the Rabbi's family for dinner before leaving to go to work, but this was the first time he had invited me to lead the prayer. "For all these blessings we thank Adonai our God with praise," I sang, making up a new tune on the spot, a happy tune that smiled as it rose toward heaven. Then I addressed the family with the final blessing of the *Birkhat*. "May God's name be praised by every living being forever, as it is written in *D'varim*: 'When you have eaten your fill, give thanks to Adonai your God for the good land which God has given you.' Blessed is Adonai for the land and its produce. May Adonai our God have mercy on His people Israel; His city Jerusalem; Zion the abode of His glory; the royal house of David, His anointed one; and the great and holy Temple that bears His name. May our God, our Father, tend and nourish us, sustain and maintain us, and speedily grant us relief from all our troubles. May Adonai make us dependent not on the alms or loans of others, but rather on His full, open, and generous hand, so that we may never be humiliated or put to shame. Amen."

"Amen," they replied, Leah's voice shy as a bird's, Talyah's warm and crackling as the hearth, and Rabbi Ezra's bold as a shofar. "I'll add one more blessing," he said, "since this is my house and I can do as I please. Blessed is Adonai, who has brought Yeshua to us, and who gave me the good sense to chase after him all the way to Nazareth." They laughed, and I laughed with them, although there had been nothing at all funny about the incident itself, except in hindsight…

After confessing to Ezra that I'd been banned from school, I all but ran the three miles back to Nazareth, whipping myself as though the armies of Pharaoh were pursuing me. I went straight to the sheepfold, but it was empty; Abba had told Saba Yoachim that I'd gone to Sepphoris, so my grandfather had led the sheep to pasture himself and was sitting with them when I arrived. Seeing the pain on my face, he wrapped me in his arms and held me for an hour or more while I sobbed. His arms were strong and frail at the same time, like my soul. He offered no advice, spoke no words to belittle what I was feeling. Instead, he murmured snatches of song over me, the same songs he sang to soothe troubled sheep; the sounds washed over me without the words really registering on my mind:

Sha'alu shalom Yerushalayim yisholayu…

Exhausted, I fell asleep in his arms.

The murmurs melted into my dreams, where they became a river, and I floated on the waters for a while without a destination. Eventually, however, the river washed me up onto the bank, where a rock pressed uncomfortably into my back; and the murmurs solidified also, becoming words once again, words that had meaning.

After the conversation I had with Zephanyah yesterday, I was ready to send him packing. I've no tolerance for liars, and less for manipulators—I won't be used by anyone. But he isn't either, is he?

No, I don't think he's capable of deception.

That's not what I was told. But then, when he came to me of his own accord—

I was awake enough now to realize that they were discussing me and that I wasn't meant to overhear this conversation, so I sat up and opened my eyes, blinking against the midday sun. "Saba?"

Immediately the two voices fell silent. And then Rabbi Ezra was standing over me, arms crossed, a frown upon his face. "What are you doing here, Yeshua?" he asked in a stern voice. "You are late for school."

At the memory, my joy welled up again, buoyed by the warm laughter and the love that so tangibly filled Ezra's house. I smiled broadly and echoed my teacher, "Blessed is Adonai, who has brought us together."

"Amen!" Talyah added emphatically. She turned to her husband, still laughing. "Didn't I tell you, you needed a *talmid*? Was I right? Was I?" When he didn't answer her, she turned to me. "You're an answer to prayer, Yeshua. Poor Ezra—he's been so desperate for someone to dig with."

"Dig?" I asked.

"You're two of a kind, that's what you are, never content until you've dug deep into the books to find what's buried there. But the children in the *bet-sefer*…"

"Hmmph," Ezra interjected. "It's not just the children. Their fathers are no better. As Isaiah said, 'This people's heart has become calloused; they hardly hear with their ears, and they have closed their eyes.' They have no curiosity, no passion at all for the things of God."

Talyah ignored his interruption. "I've seen the look on their little faces some days when he's gone digging. The poor things. They can't keep up with him, and he ends up at the bottom of a hole by himself and they're all standing up on the surface wondering where he's gone." She reached out and wrapped me in a motherly embrace. "Bless you for restoring his hope," she whispered into my ear so that no one else would hear. Then in a louder voice as she straightened up, she proclaimed, "Of course, now he stays down in that hole with you, and it's all I can do to get him to climb out again."

Rabbi Ezra laughed. "Woman, God has blessed me in you!"

"It's about time you realized that."

"I realized that twenty years ago, on our wedding night."

"Ezra!" Talyah blushed. "Please, husband, not in front of Yeshua. And Leah—"

"It's no shame for a man to love his wife," the Rabbi said. "As it is written..." He paused, looking at me expectantly. "Well, *talmid*?"

I thought fast. "'Isaac brought Rebekah into the tent of his mother Sarah, and he married Rebekah. So she became his wife, and he loved her'"

"Good!" He turned to his daughter. "Leah?"

"Yes, Father. Um..." She frowned in concentration, and then brightened. "'Yaakob lay with Rachel also, and he loved Rachel more than Leah.'"

"Hmm, not exactly auspicious for you, my dear Leah, but certainly an appropriate scripture for our discussion." He leaned over and kissed the top of her head. "Don't worry, Leah. I love your mother, and one day when you're a little older, I'll find you a good husband who will love you, too." She giggled. "And if he doesn't love you, I'll go to him and I'll beat him with my rod!" Rabbi Ezra growled like a bear and pretended to flog an invisible miscreant with an imaginary staff. I burst out laughing.

"How much older, Abba?" Leah asked with a twinkle in her voice.

"Much, much older."

"How much? Until I'm twelve?" That would be in about three years, I guessed.

"No, never at twelve!"

"Until I'm fourteen?"

"Heaven forbid I should give you away at fourteen! Your mother was fourteen, and look where that got her!" Leah squealed as Talyah clapped her hands. I got the feeling that they'd had this conversation before, many times, and that it never failed to delight them.

"Until I'm twenty-four?"

"Twenty-four? Such a baby should not wed."

"Until I'm forty-eight?"

"Hmmm…Yes, yes, I think forty-eight sounds about right."
I grinned. Rabbi Ezra was forty-eight.

"But then who would marry her?" Talyah piped in.

"Methuselah!" the three of them crowed together,
dissolving in laughter…

My own mother had been thirteen when she and Yosef were
betrothed, fourteen when her pregnancy had been discovered
and Yosef had rushed to marry her before all the town learned
of her disgrace. Disgrace. The irony was almost too much to be
borne. *Favored one, endued with God's grace!* the angel had
greeted her. But this was a secret. *Maryam, do not fear, for you
have found grace with God. Listen! You shall become pregnant
and give birth to a son, and shall call his name Yeshua, and
Adonai will give him the throne of his father David.* This was
also secret. *The Ruach HaKodesh will overshadow you, and so
the holy thing born of you shall be called the Son of God.* This,
of course, was the greatest secret of all. Yosef knew—it was he
who had shared these words with me, one year ago, as we'd
walked home from my first Passover in Jerusalem—and
Yoachim knew, and of course Mother knew. But none of us
spoke of it, not even to one another.

"Why not?" I'd asked Yosef.

"It's too dangerous," he'd answered. And then, for the first
time, he'd explained why our family had lived in Alexandria for
the first two years of my life. "Herod knew the prophecies, and
when he found out that the true king—the heir of David—had
recently been born in Bethlehem, he murdered every child in
that village—and he would have murdered you, too, if the angel
hadn't warned us to flee."

"But he's dead now. He's been dead for ten years."

"Herod Antipas lives, and you can be sure that he wants the
throne as badly as his father did. No, Yisu, what the angel told
your mother, what he told me…these things *must* remain our
secret."

"For how long?"

"As long as it takes."

I knew it wouldn't be forever. *To everything there is a season, and a time for every purpose under heaven... For God will bring every deed into judgment, including every hidden thing, whether it is good or evil.* These truths Solomon had written in the book of Ecclesiastes, and Saba had shared them with me, and I had pondered them many times during my months in the pasture. *The end of a matter is better than its beginning, and so a spirit of patience is better than a spirit of pride.* Wise Solomon, who had learned the value of patience too late in life...

"Yisu!"

Yosef stood in the doorway, beckoning. I tore my thoughts away from the past, pulled them back from the brink of the future, and entered once again into the here-and-now—where I was late for work. "Oh, I'm sorry, Abba!" Hastily I excused myself from the table, thanking Talyah for the meal. Rabbi Ezra still had his arms wrapped around his daughter, but he looked up long enough to smile at Yosef and me and nod a farewell.

Leah also glanced up at me, still giggling, and I smiled at her as I slipped out the door.

"Father," I heard her say just before the door closed, "you *will* do better than Methuselah, won't you?"

Rabbi Ezra's reply was muffled but I could still make it out. "I'll find you a king, my princess, as brave as David, as handsome as Absalom, as wise as Solomon, and as faithful as Job. But not this year!"

As I crossed the courtyard with Yosef, my last thoughts were for Leah—and for myself.

Wait for your prince, little Leah, or for Methuselah if that's what your father deems best. Wait, and learn patience, as I must also wait.

15

KATAN

Sivan 3769
(The Counting of Weeks)

I stared at Shimon Zealot, not sure how to react to his statement, waiting for him to say or do something to make his intentions clear—and at the same time, afraid that I already knew his intentions quite well. Instead of getting to the point, though, he crossed his arms over his chest and said, "What I need is a decent meal. Why don't you invite me to dinner, Katan?"

Still clutching my drill in one hand and the stone weight in the other, I stood up, but I didn't answer him right away. Invite him to dinner? Where did he think we were, the sheep pasture? I was a guest here myself, in no position to be extending invitations. But even if I'd owned half of Bethsaida, I'd not have welcomed his company. *You've gotten me in enough trouble already. Just go away,* I thought at him, hoping my unfriendly silence would be enough to discourage him and send him on his way before I earned another beating.

"Won't you at least introduce me to your friends?" he asked, smiling at Yoshiah and Andrai, who had stopped working on the net and were staring at him with curiosity. "*Shalom aleikhem,*" he greeted them. "My name is Shimon. Katan seems to have forgotten the rules of hospitality. I'm a stranger here, far from home—"

"This," I interrupted curtly, pointing to Yoshi, "is my cousin Yoshiah bar Zebdi. And the one in the net is Andrai bar Yonah." I pushed out the words, grudging every one of them, but it was obvious that he wasn't going to give up easily.

"Shimon what?" asked Andrai, shaking his hair out of his eyes as he peered up.

"Just Shimon."

Once, out in the pasture, I'd asked Shimon what his father's name was. He'd shaken his head. *I took a vow*, he'd explained grimly. *I won't speak his name until I've avenged it.*

If Andrai was curious, he kept it to himself. "Well, you're welcome to eat dinner with *us*, but it could get confusing. My brother's name is Shimon, too. That's him over there, mending the trammel with Yoshi's father." He pointed to the boat where they were working on the big net.

At the same time, Yoshiah got up and dusted himself off with a friendly smile, offering the Zealot his embrace and the kiss of peace. "*Shalom aleikha*, Shimon. Why don't we all eat together today, make a party out of it? I'll tell Father we have a guest for dinner. Is it just for dinner, or do you need a place to stay, too?"

"No, just dinner, thanks."

"Come on, then." Before I could stop him, he led Shimon to the boat, which was anchored a short distance offshore, and called out, "Father?" Uncle Zebdi looked up and said something, but I couldn't make out his words from where I was standing. The four of them talked for a while, and then Yoshiah came running back to Andrai and me with a huge smile on his face.

"Father says if we can finish the nets quickly, we don't have to go to school today, since we have a guest. Katan, you're supposed to go home as soon as you finish drilling that last weight and tell Mother to bring the stuff for dinner over to Yonah's house—we're all going to eat together there. And then go to the market and let Saba know about the change in plans."

I should talk to Uncle. I should tell him who and what this Shimon really is. But what if he already knew? Gamala was just across the water—you could see the town from here on a clear day—and most of the towns and villages around Gennesaret had joined Gamala in supporting Yudah's rebellion two years ago. My father was opposed to the Zealots, but that didn't mean Uncle shared his views. I decided to keep my mouth shut and see what happened.

Dinner started out well.

It wasn't the first time I'd eaten at Yonah's house. Yonah and Uncle Sheth were related (in a small village, almost everyone is related to someone) and so the two families often came together for more than just business. As usual, we older boys sat with the men around a large table while the women served up the food. Fish, of course, three different kinds; an assortment of vegetables; dried figs and raisins from last year; spiced olive oil; and barley bread.

Yoshiah took it upon himself to act as host to Shimon, explaining to him how everyone in the room fit into the family. "Saba Sheth, he's the oldest, he's my father's father. My father is Zebdi there. But you already knew that. Yonah bar Yehu—this is Yonah's house—he's Andrai's father, and Yehu was Saba's brother-in-law, so Andrai is my cousin since we have the same great-grandfather. Of course that makes Shimon my cousin, too, since he's Andrai's brother…"

Shimon Zealot—who was sitting beside me—listened to all of this for a while with glazed eyes, and then he turned to me and asked, "How do you fit into all of this?"

"My mother and Yoshiah's mother are sisters."

He looked relieved. I could imagine why: with the exception of myself, none of Yosef's blood was sitting at the table with him. He might actually live to see tomorrow.

Uncle Zebdi was sitting on Shimon's other side. "So," Uncle interjected, "you're Katan's friend." I winced at the word *friend*. Apparently some assumptions had been made. "From Nazareth?"

"Not originally, no sir, though we met there last autumn. I was born and raised in Gamala. But I've lived near Nazareth for the past two years." My eyebrows went up. What Shimon had just said was as good as a confession. No one in the Galil could hear the words *Gamala* and *two years* in the same breath without thinking of the tax revolts. Breathless, I waited to hear my uncle's reply.

"Let me guess," Zebdi said after a moment. "You have…hmm…some practice blowing the *shofar*."

"Only at night," Shimon replied with a smile.

It sounded like one of the Zealot passwords—they were always going on about Gideon and his band of trumpeteers and holding them up as role models. I shook my head. *Uncle is one of them?* If Father found out, I'd never see Yoshiah again as long as I lived.

I needn't have worried.

"Well, don't blow it in my house," Uncle growled. He grabbed the front of Shimon's tunic in a strong hand and shook him once, hard, to get his attention. "I want no trumpets, I want no torches, and I want no shouts of 'Gideon's sword!' Do you hear me, Zealot? You and your cause are not welcome here!" He threw Shimon up against the wall, knocking the wine cup right out of his hand. Blood-red droplets splashed in all directions, including my own—I was drenched in the stuff. Every other conversation in the room stopped.

"Zebdi!" Sheth cried. "Son, what are you doing?"

Yonah and his son Shimon were both on their feet, shocked at their partner's breach of hospitality. While the one Shimon helped the other to his feet, Yonah rounded on Zebdi. "How dare you start a brawl at my table? This man is my guest!" Yonah shouted.

Uncle Zebdi spat on the floor. "That for your guest. Do you know what this man is?" Then he pointed an accusing finger at me. "You! You dare call this man 'friend' after what he and his kind have done to your father and your grandfather? What sort of a son are you?"

I opened my mouth to protest, but Uncle shut it with a backhanded slap before I could get two words out. I tasted blood as my lip split open under the force of his blow.

"That's not fair!" Shimon Zealot cried out, leaping to my defense. "It isn't Katan who claimed me as friend, but I who claimed him."

"Is it true?" Shimon bar Yonah asked. "Are you a Zealot?" He sounded excited. Idiot.

"Zealot or not," Yonah said with a warning hand on Uncle Zebdi's shoulder, "he is a guest in my house and the laws of hospitality are clear. 'You shall not wrong a stranger or oppress him, for you were strangers in the land of Egypt. Do not mistreat or do violence to the stranger.'"

"Those laws don't apply to thieves and cutthroats," Zebdi said.

"Are you ready to try his case? Do you have witnesses?"

"Everyone knows what the Zealots are."

"This boy is not the Zealots. He is one man. He can only be tried for his own actions, Zebdi. When Sepphoris fell, how old was this boy? Be reasonable, man! If you cannot control yourself, then get out of my house. Shimon is under my protection, do you hear me?"

Zebdi drew himself to his full height, nearly striking his head against the beams of the ceiling. "Yoshiah, Yakob, Katan. Shelomith. We are leaving *now*." He scowled at Shimon one last time. "You fall on your face and thank God for the laws of hospitality, Zealot. If we hadn't broken bread together, I'd turn you in right now for the price that's probably on your head. Take my advice and get out of town before my piety wanes." For Yonah, his partner and cousin, he had one more word: "Righteous host, defending your guest at all cost. Just like Lot. How fortunate that you have no virgin daughters to bear the cost of your *righteousness*."

And then he stormed out, dragging me by the shoulder of my tunic. "You I'll deal with at home," he growled, and flung me ahead of him so hard I had to run to catch my balance. I was tempted to just keep running, all the way to Nazareth. (As bad as Father's beatings were, I had a feeling that Uncle's was going to be much worse—he was a lot bigger than Father, and had less cause to go easy on me.) I fought down the temptation, though, and gritted my teeth as I plodded the rest of the short distance to the house. If I was going to get a beating I didn't deserve for something I hadn't done, then at least I'd take it with a courage I didn't feel. There was no way—no way!—I was going to beg for mercy. My lip was throbbing and I had to spit the blood out of my mouth three or four times on the way. Never had Father—or anyone else—struck me across the face. *Don't cry, Yaakob*, I warned myself. *Don't you dare cry.*

I didn't. Not then, and not when Zebdi took his rod to me.

It was bad, but not as bad as I'd expected.

Not as bad as the last one Father had given me.

Afterward, my uncle spoke to me. "Katan."

"Yes, sir."

"Do you understand why I had to discipline you?"

Yes, sir, I started to say—the required words, the expected words—but I caught myself and gave him an honest answer instead. "No. No, sir, I don't."

Something in my tone or the expression on my face must have agreed with Zebdi, because he didn't get angry. Instead, he looked thoughtfully at me for a moment before replying. "No, I don't suppose you do. From where you stand, you probably don't think you did anything to deserve punishment. Maybe you didn't. Maybe I was wrong."

Wrong? Did I hear him correctly?

"You certainly didn't deserve *that*," he said, pointing to my split lip. "I owe you an apology for that, son. I shouldn't have lost my temper—no man deserves a slap across the face. If nothing else, you've shown me today that you *are* a man." He sighed. "Will you forgive me?"

"I—I—well, yes."

"As for the other, the spanking…Your father gave you into my care, and it's my duty to protect you from men like Shimon. You knew, didn't you, that he's a Zealot?"

"Yes, sir."

"Yet you allowed us to welcome him, you stood by and said nothing as we took him in and broke bread with him, and you exposed Yoshiah to him. You brought a viper into our tent! If you were anyone else, I might understand and even excuse such ignorance, but from Yaakob bar Yosef? I promised your father that I'd keep you safe, but even if I hadn't given him my word, I love you too much to let you act like a fool where the Zealots are concerned. Do you hear me?"

I love you too much…

"Yes, Uncle." I met his eyes, warmed by what I saw there. "I hear you."

16

YISU

Sivan 3769
(The Counting of Weeks)

Thousands of men took to the roads during the first week of Sivan, hurrying toward Jerusalem for the Feast of Shavuot as was commanded in Torah, carrying with them the first fruits of the wheat harvest. Thousands more did not. It's always been that way; when God chose Israel, he chose a fickle bride: devoted one moment and distracted the next, double-minded and disobedient as the infamous storms of Lake Gennesaret.

Yosef was one of the faithful ones who went up year after year—I couldn't remember him ever missing one of the required Gatherings—and I was eager to go with him this year, my first Shavuot as a *bar mitzvah*. Even so, I could sympathize with the men who stayed behind. My grandfathers were getting old and the long journey was painful for them, walking between ten and twenty miles in a day, sleeping on the open ground. If we had lived closer, it would have been a simple matter to attend every feast and convocation, both the required ones and those of lesser importance. For those of us living in the Galil, however, attendance at the gatherings was a great sacrifice. If someone was willing to travel through Samaria—and Yosef often did, despite the added dangers along that route—he could reach the Holy City in three days (providing his journey didn't overlap with Sabbath, of course); most pilgrims preferred to take the safer route along the eastern bank of the Jordan, though, and that journey took a minimum of five or six days—one way. Not many men can afford to leave their homes, farms, and businesses for two and three weeks at a time. Shavuot was a special problem because it came so soon after Passover. For the devout Galilean, that meant three weeks of travel in Nisan, then the month of Iyyar at home, and then two more weeks of travel in Sivan.

"Every year," Rabbi Ezra confided in me, "I ask myself if it truly matters whether or not I go up for the feast. Every year (so far, at least) I have decided that it does." He sighed deeply. "When I lived in Jericho it was simple to keep the commandment. Now it is hard. But I am not some *am-ha-aretz* ignorant of Torah; I am a teacher of the Law, and *hazzan* of a respected synagogue. I have to hold myself with diligence to the highest standard or run the risk of falling into hypocrisy."

"Hypocrisy?" I asked. It was a Greek word, but not one with which I was familiar.

He laughed. "I've only lived three years in Sepphoris, but already it has left its mark on me. Sepphoris, Ornament of the Galil! Herod's thoroughly modern, thoroughly Greek city. My Talyah was aghast when I told her we were coming here. Ah, but that's another story." He shook his head. "Blessed is the man whose shadow never darkens a theater! I count myself blessed, but I am aware of what goes on in there, nevertheless. Hypocrites are men who don a mask and take on the character of another, performing for the approval of their audience. Their outward acts do not match their inward beings."

I thought I understood. "Like a child pretending?"

He shook his head. "Without so innocent an intention. God preserve me from hypocrisy. Even if I were not *hazzan*, even if I were not *sofer*, a teacher of the Law, still I am Ezra ben Shimeon. I am a son of Abraham, Isaac, and Israel, of the tribe of Judah, and a devout Pharisee as well. This is who I am. No more, and no less. No more: I haven't the authority to change what Moses has written. No less: I haven't the ignorance to ignore what Moses has written. And so, Yeshua, I will go up to the feast once again. 'Obedience is better than sacrifice.' It always comes back to that."

"Then you are blessed, Rabbi," I observed, "because if obedience is better than sacrifice, and a sacrifice is ordained by God, then an obedient sacrifice must be the greatest good of all." A thought occurred to me, and I shared it with my teacher. "I think your Shavuot blessing is greater than mine—because I really *want* to go to the feast. So for me, it's a matter of desire rather than obedience. Certainly it's no sacrifice."

He smiled. "And to think I almost let you walk out of my life."

Our family split up this year; Mother had just announced that she was pregnant again, in no condition to make the seventy-mile journey, so she and Aunt Mimah were staying at home with the children. Abba didn't want to leave them alone longer than necessary, so he decided to take the western route through Samaria. Joining us on the road were our neighbors Netzer bar Abiyud with his sons Kaleb and Yafet, and Rabbi Ezra. I was surprised—pleased, but surprised all the same—that the rabbi had chosen to come with us. The Pharisees abhorred Samaria. As I was learning, however, Ezra was different from the other Pharisees I'd known—just as Saba Yoachim was far removed from his Sadducee upbringing. Perhaps the difference was a result of their move from Judaea to the Galil. Or perhaps their move was the result of the difference. I laughed. What did it matter? The joy came from the fact that they were here, and they were with me, and we would all be making the journey together.

On the morning of our scheduled departure, Abba sent me to Sepphoris to escort Rabbi Ezra back to Nazareth, where everyone else was gathering the things we'd need for our trip. I set out just as the sun was rising, as I did every day; the route had become so familiar to me that my own sandals had worn a narrow trail across the pasture and down the slope that led to the main road. That road was broad and well-traveled, running beside Netzer's fields for a short distance and then, about a mile north of Nazareth, cutting through farmland tenanted by Nahum bar Hamosh. Nahum was a poor man and his fields were plagued by poor soil, but he worked the land with diligence nevertheless. Every time I passed, I prayed that God would bless him.

I was more than halfway to Sepphoris when I saw a large company of men approaching from the north; some were mounted on fine horses, and even from a distance I could see sunlight glinting off the standards they carried proudly above their ranks. Roman legionaries, on their way from Sepphoris to Nazareth and then, most likely, on to Caesarea. Stepping off the road to leave it clear for them, I continued toward Sepphoris without slowing my pace, hoping they'd ignore me if I did nothing to draw attention to myself. It was a vain hope.

"You, boy!"

I turned to face the one who had called me, but said nothing. Nothing was expected.

"Carry this pack."

It was inevitable, really. There were dozens of them and only one of me, and I was heading in the opposite direction, but that mattered little. The laws of the Occupation gave any Roman the right to lay his pack on any man, Galilean or Judaean, for one thousand paces—one mile. It wasn't the first time I'd been conscripted, nor would it be the last. "Yes, sir," I said with a friendly smile, and shifted the burden from his shoulder to my own.

The smile always confused them.

Turning south once more, I followed a few paces behind the man whose pack I was carrying, keeping the smile on my face as I began to sing one of the psalms of ascent. This had become my practice, for it helped me to think of my labor as a service to my Father—who had, after all, permitted the conscription—rather than an oppression. It also amused me to observe the faces of the soldiers, who were frankly baffled by my cheerful cooperation.

I didn't have to count my paces; I knew how far I'd gone and how many psalms equaled a mile at the standard Roman marching pace, which was brisk. The thousandth pace fell on the road beside Nahum's wheat fields. I started to set down the pack and then noticed Nahum, who was bent over on the far side of the field, harvesting the early grains. Like many of the men of Nazareth, he had little faith in God's promise to keep his crop safe from marauders in his absence, and so he'd elected to stay home from the feast and send his firstfruits to the Temple in care of Netzer rather than bring them himself. But it wasn't up to me to judge Nahum's faith. I just wanted to help him.

"'You shall love your neighbor as yourself,'" I whispered.

If I stop now, here, they'll notice him and conscript him to carry this pack the rest of the way. Nahum was old and his health was as poor as his purse. *But if I just keep on, perhaps they'll leave him be. Father, if it please you, let me take his place here; blind the Romans to his presence.*

Instead of setting the pack down, I shrugged it a bit higher on my shoulder and continued marching. Another quarter mile and I'd be clear of Nahum's field. As if to mock me, the pack grew heavier, seeming to gain a pound with every few steps I took, but I didn't dare slow down. Again I began to sing, making my song a prayer for Nahum and all those who labored out of fear, all those who would miss the gathering because they lacked the faith to go.

> "I was glad when they said to me,
> 'The house of Adonai! Let's go!'
> Our feet were already standing
> at your gates, Jerusalem.
> Jerusalem, built as a city
> fostering friendship and unity.
> The tribes have gone up there,
> the tribes of Adonai,
> as a witness to Israel,
> to give thanks to the name of Adonai.
> For there the thrones of justice were set up,
> the thrones of the house of David…"

I sang through psalm after psalm as if I were on pilgrimage instead of laboring under a Roman pack. I was all the pilgrims, a mob of Israelites, hundreds of men on the march, losing myself in song, losing count of my steps as I sang with a thousand tongues, ten thousand,

> "Those who sow in tears
> will reap with cries of joy.
> He who goes out weeping
> as he carries his sack of seed
> will come home with cries of joy
> as he carries his sheaves of grain."

I didn't even realize I'd started dancing until I heard laughter. The sound snapped me back to the moment and I saw with surprise that I'd carried the Roman's pack all the way to the gate of Nazareth. The soldiers had halted their march and were watching me with a mixture of delight and contempt, and

I caught the word "moros" a few times; they thought I was an idiot. Oh well, at least they hadn't pulled Nahum from his field. *Thank you, Father.*

Without giving the soldiers any reason to believe I understood their Greek, I smiled once more at the man whose pack I bore and handed it over to him. Then I turned north again and ran up the road toward Sepphoris to fetch Rabbi Ezra.

"I'm sorry to be late, Rabbi," I apologized, panting slightly from my run. He was standing on his doorstep, obviously waiting for me. A large pack lay on the ground beside him.

"You're not late, Yeshua, though you're certainly not early," Ezra said calmly. "Did you have trouble on the road?"

"No, more delay than trouble. I was conscripted," I explained briefly with a shrug.

"Which way are the troops moving?"

"Toward Nazareth. That's why I was late—I was almost here, but then had to backtrack a ways. I didn't pass any other units, though, so our road should be clear now." I hoisted his pack to my shoulder and set out, holding the gate open for him to pass through. Then, as was appropriate for a *talmid*, I followed two or three paces behind him.

"Come up here, Yeshua. Walk by my side."

"Yes, Rabbi." I hastened to catch up.

"Is that too heavy for you?"

I laughed. "Oh, no, Rabbi, your burden is light!" Indeed it was, probably only twenty or thirty pounds, less than half the weight of a Roman kit.

"Yes, many burdens seem that way at the outset. If you change your mind after a mile or two, speak up. I can share the load."

"Thank you, Rabbi, but it's good training for me, don't you think? I would be a poor *talmid* indeed to stroll carefree while my rabbi carries a pack." Rabbi Ezra smiled approvingly. I should have shut my mouth then, but words kept forming in it so I let them out. "The student is not above his teacher! If the weight does prove to be troublesome, how much more is the weight you bear, sir? Besides, if I can't persevere under *your* pack—laid on me in love—how will I ever learn to bear up under the greater burdens of hatred and injustice?"

We walked on in silence after that, for which I was glad. My own words kept echoing in my heart. *How much more is the weight you bear?* Why had I said that? Ezra ben Shimeon was a man free of cares, it seemed, yet I sensed that he was indeed carrying a great burden though I had no idea what it might be. Perhaps this journey together would reveal it. Perhaps not. Again I found myself wondering why he'd chosen to make the pilgrimage with my family rather than the other rabbis of Sepphoris, most of whom had departed a week ago. I knew better than to ask—he had made it plain that his reasons were his own to share or keep hidden as he himself saw fit. In all matters he revealed to me only the head of the nail, requiring me to worry at it myself until the shaft was clear. Which was as it should be—he was my teacher.

And hadn't my Father done the same? No burning bush had ever blazed my path to Him, no angel had ever visited me waking or in dreams. Yet I was drawn to seek Him. The head of the nail lay all around me: God's glory painted in creation for all His creatures to see. The sky stretched brightly beautiful above me, a reflection of His beauty; the grass and the fields and the flowers lay upon the earth as a mosaic, a reflection of His craftsmanship; a cool breeze blew against my hot and sweaty brow, a reflection of His loving comfort. I drew in a deep breath of air, and the filling of my lungs reflected His intimacy. Yet all of this was but the head of the nail. The shaft lay buried deep in the scriptures, and beyond.

My Father, will I ever hear Your voice as Abraham did, as Moses did, as Elijah did? I opened my ears, but the only sounds were birdsong, a few early cicadas, and the pounding of our feet. Without intending to, I'd matched my stride so closely to Rabbi Ezra's that the slapping of our sandals on the hard-packed dirt of the roadway sounded like one man walking through a narrow canyon—left, *left*, right, *right*—a single set of footsteps with a slight echo. *Even if I pass through death-dark ravines, I will fear no disaster; for You are with me; Your rod and staff reassure me...* It was an odd thought, and I shrugged it off.

We reached Nazareth in good time. I added the rabbi's pack to the others that had been loaded onto our cart, while Abba welcomed him and introduced him to the other members of our caravan. "This is my father, Yaakob bar Matthan. My father-in-law, Yoachim bar Amram. And these are our neighbors, Netzer bar Abiyud and his sons, Kaleb and Yafet."

Since Netzer and his sons were farmers, they'd brought along several sheaves of wheat, each bound with the scarlet cord that marked them as the first stalks to ripen in their fields. In addition to the tithe of firstfruits, Torah also required each man to bring two loaves of wheat bread to the Temple for a wave offering. Of course, the length of our journey made this impractical. Bread baked at home would just spoil along the way. "Much as I like to adhere to the letter of the Law," Rabbi Ezra had told me, "I don't think stale bread is really in the spirit of an appropriate offering." For this reason, his "firstfruits" would be presented in the form of a small sack of flour, along with a monetary donation. Because Abba and I were tradesmen, not farmers, our offerings were similar.

In addition, along with my two omers of wheat flour, I was offering up the cart—the first thing of significance I had ever made without Abba's help—as a freewill offering. *Celebrate the Feast of Weeks to Adonai your God by giving a freewill offering in proportion to the blessings Adonai your God has given you,* the scripture said, and so I'd given extra care to the cart's construction, using every bit of the skill and knowledge I'd acquired over the years. It was a beautiful cart. Not content with making it merely sturdy and functional, I'd sanded and oiled it and chiseled elaborate designs along each side: stalks of wheat and barley, grapevines and pomegranates, olive branches and figs. Rabbi Ezra ran his hand along the carvings, smiling knowingly.

"'For Adonai your God is bringing you into a good land,'" he murmured. "'A land with streams and pools of water, with springs flowing in the valleys and hills...'" He looked at me, expectantly, and I joined him in reciting the rest of the scripture that had inspired the carvings: "'A land with wheat and barley, vines and fig trees, pomegranates, olive oil and honey; a land where bread will not be scarce and you will lack nothing.'" He laughed and patted me on the shoulder approvingly. Turning back to Yosef, he asked, "Is this all Yeshua's work?" Abba nodded. "Where is the ox to pull it?"

Traditionally, the ox pulling the cart that contained the firstfruits was slain as a fellowship offering, and then its fat portion was burnt on the altar using the wood of the cart as fuel. While the cart would indeed be broken up and burned, we had no ox. The plan was to buy a young bull for the sacrifice when we reached Jerusalem; there were always vendors outside the Temple who had suitable animals for sale. Abba smiled as he explained. "We're going to take turns pulling the cart ourselves, but don't worry! None of us is destined for the altar—unless the Rabbi objects to deviating from the tradition?"

"No, no," Rabbi Ezra assured him with a smile. "I'm quite satisfied to redeem *this* beast of burden with some silver." He rapped himself on the chest.

"Oh, no, Rabbi," Abba protested. "I didn't mean that *you* would pull the cart—"

"I most certainly will," he interjected. "In fact, if you will permit, I would consider it an honor to take the first turn. And Yosef—"

"Yes, Rabbi?"

"Call me Ezra, please. I am Yeshua's rabbi, not yours. You owe me no special deference; treat me like any other member of the company. Agreed?"

Abba looked surprised, and then his face relaxed into a broad smile. "Agreed." He turned to the rest of us. "All right, then, let's go!" Taking his staff in hand, he led the way down the rutted path toward the road to Jezre'el. After helping Rabbi Ezra get the cart moving, I ran to catch up with him.

17

KATAN

Sivan 3769
(The Counting of Weeks)

"**W**here are we going?" I asked for the third or fourth time. I'd been thrilled when Shimon (Andrai's brother, not that Zealot troublemaker) had requested me for his fishing partner tonight. And not just to tend a section of trammel, either—we were off on our own with the cast nets and some lines, skilled work that would require me to use every bit of knowledge they'd taught me over the past six weeks. While I held no illusion that I'd catch another monster fish, I was hoping to hold up my end, and anticipated a night of hard but rewarding work.

Shimon had set the sail to catch a breeze that gusted sporadically from the north, but then assigned me to an oar. "We're heading south along the shoreline a few miles. I have a spot in mind, but it's going to take forever to get there with this puny wind, so put your back into it, Katan." Great. I was only there to row. But the first rule of fishing was not to argue with your captain, and Shimon was the captain of this boat, so I bent to my task without complaint.

As I rowed, I caught myself wondering why I cared so much what he—or any of them—thought of me. I wasn't a fisherman; in a few days I'd be headed for home, back to my hammer and saw and plane, whether or not I did well tonight. In the back of my mind, though, a voice whispered a different possibility. Father had lots of sons besides me to carry on in his footsteps: Yisu, Yosei, one day Yehudah, and there would probably be others after him. Uncle Zebdi had only Yoshiah and Yakob. Maybe this visit could be stretched indefinitely; maybe I could stay here and become, in truth, a fisherman. The work called to me. I was good at it. It was fun…

"I said *stop*! Pay attention, Katan!"

I shipped my oars and looked around. Shimon was doing the same, frowning at the moon and counting on his fingers as if he were worried about the time. He peered at the shore, which was just a stone's throw from where we drifted. Finally satisfied, he threw out the anchor. I began to bait hooks, dropping half a dozen lines into the water before asking, "How many lines do you want?"

"None." He picked up a net and stood in the bow, peering out over the water. I started to pull in two of the lines I'd thrown out. Shimon noticed and frowned. "What, aren't you going to tend all six?"

Uncle Zebdi could fish twice that many lines at once, and I had a feeling Shimon could, too, but six was over my limit and I freely admitted it. What I didn't understand was why Shimon had chosen to anchor here. There were no signs of a large school anywhere in the shallow cove, and his net came back empty time after time. In spite of this, he didn't change his methods—in fact, he didn't seem to have his mind on fishing at all. After nearly an hour had passed without a single catch worth keeping (though I'd wasted a lot of bait on catfish), I suggested we pull up anchor and try another spot. Shimon immediately vetoed the idea.

We hung around Catfish Cove for another hour, during which time I pulled up six more catfish (or maybe they were the same ones over and over again, the stupid things), got my fingers cut to pieces by their barbels while trying to unhook them, and let out a few choice curses I was happy my father wasn't around to overhear. I'd had enough. "Shimon—"

"Keep your mouth shut, Katan, and listen," he interrupted. "Whatever happens tonight, you have to swear you won't tell anyone, especially not Zebdi." His voice was tense all of a sudden, and he grabbed my upper arm with a vise-like hold, giving me a shake.

"Okay, I promise."

"Not good enough. Swear it!" He shook me again. "Repeat what I say: May God deal with me ever so severely…"

"But, Shimon—" He shook me harder. I swallowed and repeated the words of his oath. "May God deal with me ever so severely…"

"If I tell anyone about what happens here tonight..." he hissed.

"If I tell anyone about what happens here tonight...."

"Let me be cursed along with my sons to the tenth generation..."

I stammered the words, wondering what on earth I'd gotten myself into. At the same time, there was a mystery to all of this that intrigued me. I felt my heart pounding and all of my senses seemed to grow sharper. By the time I'd finished the oath, I was ready for whatever might befall me. As long as my father never found out. Never.

Shimon pulled up the anchor and rowed closer to shore. When the keel scraped bottom, he anchored once again and leaped into the water, beckoning for me to follow him. Together we waded ashore. "What now?" I asked in a hushed voice.

"That depends," said a stranger right behind me. I jumped and turned. The man in the shadows laughed, but the sound did little to calm my nerves. It was not a friendly laugh, not at all like my father's. This laugh had an edge to it, an edge that promised to take delight in my downfall. I swallowed. "That depends," the man repeated, "on who you are."

"I'm a friend of Gideon's," Shimon said calmly, as if he'd been expecting the question.

Oh, no.

"How old are you, boy?" the stranger asked suspiciously.

"I'm not Yeter," Shimon replied. "I'm old enough to do what a grown man needs to do."

"If you say so. What about him?" He inclined his head toward me.

"He's a friend of Shimon's."

I knew without being told which *Shimon* he referred to, but my usual protest died unspoken. This was neither the time nor the place to be denying the friendship of the Zealot. For all I knew, this man was his brother. Shimon's claim of friendship might be the only thing keeping me alive.

"Then let him speak for himself," the man said, turning his iron gaze on me.

"I know Shimon," I admitted. "But I don't know Yeter."

"That doesn't surprise me," he said with a wry grin. "You're too young to know Yeter, though not too young to *be* Yeter. If Shimon vouches for you, though, who am I to argue? Come on, then, the night's wasting, and there's work to be done. Follow me." With that, he turned and vanished into the bushes. Shimon followed closely on his heels. After hesitating for a second or two, I also followed. *I'm going to kill Shimon,* I seethed, *assuming the Zealots let us both live that long!*

The olive grove to which he led us was filled with men. I tried to count them, but the shifting shadows of the trees made it difficult. A single watch fire burned low in the center of the clearing, and seated closest to it were Shimon Zealot and a much older man I'd never seen before, though he had an air of authority about him. "Any trouble, Yashar?" he asked our guide when we stepped into the clearing.

"They butchered the passwords, but since they matched Shimon's description so perfectly, I figured, what the hell, who else could they be?" Yashar laughed. "So, Shimon, are these your new recruits? Or should we just slit their throats now and have done with it?"

"Shut up, Yashar." Shimon (the Zealot, not my fishing partner) shook his head in disgust and turned to Shimon (my fishing partner, who was apparently also a Zealot) and me. "Don't let him scare you. We're glad you came."

The older man by the fire spoke up again. "That remains to be seen."

"Kabba, you promised their safety."

"Provided." Kabba stood and walked over to us. He eyed us up and down and at one point grabbed Shimon's hands, examining them critically as if he were thinking of buying a slave. While he was doing that—without any warning whatsoever—he reached out and shoved me. Hard. I stumbled backward a step or two but kept my balance and my temper. Kabba tried to push me again, but this time I was expecting it, and I dodged his blow. "Good," he said, and returned to his seat by the fire. "What are you called?" He looked at Shimon.

"Shimon bar Yo—"

"No surnames here," Kabba interrupted. "But I can't have two Shimons on this raid, so tonight you're Fisher." He turned to his men. "Can everyone remember that?"

"If I forget, all I have to do is use my nose," said Yashar.

"Raid?" Shimon—Fisher—asked, obviously as surprised as I was.

Kabba ignored him, fixing his eyes on me. "What's your name, boy?"

"Yaakob."

"No good. We have two Yaakobs already."

"I'm usually called Katan."

That got another laugh from Yashar. "Well, that's appropriate!"

I winced. *Why didn't I just let Kabba make up something for me? Did I really have to tell them I'm called "Junior"?*

"Shut up, Yashar," Kabba said curtly. "Maybe we should change *your* name while we're at it. You want to be known as 'Upright,' but 'Laughter' would suit you better. I'd name you Isaac right now, but this is no laughing matter."

"My apologies, Katan," Yashar said, and this time there was no sneer in his voice.

Kabba stood again, gesturing for all of his men to gather closer to the fire. They made a circle around "Fisher" and me, and I was finally able to count them, eleven all told. There were a few murmured comments as they gathered, but all fell silent when Kabba spoke. "You all know why we're here, why we've left our families, our homes, in some cases our very livelihoods. Most of you can go back to them in the morning; some of us never will. But all of us have one purpose in common: to see Israel restored to the freedom that God intended for His bride.

"Tonight we're welcoming Fisher and Katan into our circle. We bind them with no oaths; let every man look to his own conscience. Those who are afraid should leave. This was Gideon's instruction to his troops, which he received from *El Elyon*, and it is my instruction to you now. Let those who are afraid depart."

He paused, letting his eyes rest briefly on each man in turn. This was my chance. Was I afraid? Absolutely. My plans for tonight had included fishing, sailing, rowing, and (if I felt daring) maybe even some swimming. *Raid* was not on the list. But as I looked around the circle and saw the resolve in every face, I couldn't back down. I just couldn't. Father would not have approved of these men, but they weren't the monsters he

painted them out to be. They were just men. And at least two of
them—Shimon and Kabba—thought I had what it took to be
one of them. They were willing to trust me with their lives.
They thought of me as a *man*. Kabba's eyes met mine, asking
for my allegiance. With the briefest nod, I gave it.

Satisfied that everyone was committed, Kabba had us all sit
down. "Shimon, since you already know what I'm going to say,
go relieve Millo." Shimon slipped out. So there were really
twelve of them. I hadn't even noticed the sentry on my way in.
Kabba didn't speak right away, but sat with his head bowed,
silently praying or thinking or just waiting for Millo to arrive;
all the others sat quiet too, giving Kabba their full attention.

"It's thanks to Shimon's scouting that we have this
information," he finally said. "As many of you are aware, the
century quartered in Capernaum is receiving replacements this
week." There were a few groans and one or two muttered
curses. "Don't be so quick to complain, brothers. That's good
news for us, actually. These men don't know the area like the
veterans do." Millo arrived just then, and Kabba paused while
we made room for the sentry in our circle, repeating what he'd
just said about the replacement troops before continuing. "What
you probably don't know, because Shimon just told me an hour
ago, is that one of the new *contubernia* split up this evening—it
seems their ranking officer wanted to visit the hot springs, so
the fool sent most of his squadron on ahead of him to set up a
bivouac."

There was an outburst of muffled laughter at this bit of
information. Kabba let it go on for a minute, and then gestured
for silence. "I know we hadn't planned on any action tonight,
but an opportunity like this won't repeat itself. I assume you're
all armed?"

All I had was a small knife for slicing bait. Before I could
say anything, Yashar turned to me. "I've a gladius you can use,
Katan. It's just your size." He grinned but at least he didn't
laugh at me again. A gladius—a Roman *short* sword. Ha ha.
Yashar wasn't just making a joke, though. He unstrapped one of
the belts at his waist and handed it to me, and I felt the weight
of the sheathed sword even before I saw it. Carefully, I drew
the blade a few inches out of its scabbard, watching it gleam in
the firelight. "Don't think I'm doing you a favor," Yashar

warned. "That's a double-edged sword, that is, and its loyalty is divided."

"What do you mean?"

"That sword's tasted my blood. Damn near killed me. By rights it belongs to Kabba here, since he's the one who killed the *milites* who stuck it into me, but he didn't want it. Said I should teach it better manners. I've been doing my best since then to give it a taste for Roman blood." He slapped my shoulder. "You feed it well tonight, Katan."

I didn't answer him. The reality of my situation was just beginning to sink in.

Kabba was talking again. "So that makes fourteen of us and only eight of them. Yashar, you'll go to the springs with three men of your choosing; the rest of you will come with me to hit their camp."

Yashar smiled. "Magdalit's probably done half the job for us already! We'll just need to mop up. I'll take Avram, Sicae, and—oh, what the hell—Katan."

The dead man's eyes stared into mine, accusing.

Oh God, what am I doing here?

"Don't faint now, Yeter! We're almost finished," Yashar called out to me.

I did not kill these men. I did not kill these men. I did not kill these men. The truth was of little comfort. Regardless of who had killed them, I was helping Yashar make them disappear. My fingers fumbled with the buckle of the Roman soldier's *lorica*; the blood-soaked strap resisted my efforts to slip it free. Shuddering, I tore my gaze from the dead man's face and focused on stripping his body. At last, the buckle released and I pulled the bloody corselet over his head, adding it to the pile of armor in the middle of the clearing. Three *loricae* now, three helmets, six greaves, six boots…

It had been no better than murder.

Swords drawn, we'd crept swiftly down the path that led to the hot springs and totally surprised the three soldiers at their recreation. I don't know who had been the more taken aback: the Romans at the sudden appearance of four armed and hostile men, or me. Not in my wildest imaginings had I ever pictured the scene that had greeted us at the bottom of the path. One soldier was all but naked, the other two only partially armored, and all three were utterly engrossed in the woman they were raping. I stood with my eyes bugging out, watching passively as if in a dream, first as they violated the girl—whom they had gagged and bound as though she were somehow a threat—and then as Yashar and Sicae fell upon them and slit the throats of the nearest two before either could react. Their blood spurted, black in the faint moonlight, as the third soldier lunged toward me, desperately trying to reach the sword he'd left lying with the rest of his gear beside the path. "Katan, stop him!" Yashar shouted, but I froze, unable to strike down an unarmed man. Scant seconds before the Roman reached his weapon, Avram pushed me out of the way and finished the job, cursing.

Yashar had grit his teeth and shaken his head. "Yeter after all. Give me that gladius!" He'd snatched it out of my hand, and then given me the task of stripping the bodies. "Get everything off them, even their tunics. They have to disappear as if they never were."

I stared now into the eyes of the man I was supposed to have killed, the man who would undoubtedly have killed me had our positions been reversed. He was young, maybe nineteen or twenty. Once again, I found myself asking God how I had come to this place.

"The tunic, too, Yeter, and the loincloth." Yashar's command cut into my prayer. "Leave nothing that the beasts can't take care of for us."

"W-why do you keep calling me Yeter?"

"To remind myself why I shouldn't cut you down and bury you beside these dogs."

"Who is Yeter?" Perhaps it was his son.

"Don't you know the story?" I shook my head as I pulled off the Roman's clothing. I'd love a story right now—anything to take my mind off the task at hand. "Gideon the Judge had many sons in his lifetime, but his firstborn was Yeter. When Gideon drove out the Midianites from the land of Israel, he captured their kings, who confessed to having killed Gideon's brothers. So Gideon ordered his son Yeter to execute the two Midianite kings. But Yeter was only a boy. He was too afraid even to draw his sword. The Midianites taunted Gideon and said, 'You do it. You kill us. Let a grown man do what takes a grown man's strength.' So Gideon cut them down. It is so written in the *Sefer ha-Shofetim*, the Book of the Judges." Yashar looked at me with an expression that mixed contempt with pity. "It takes little strength to swing a sword. But I forgot that a boy is too weak to swing at more than a target. That takes a man's strength."

"He—he wasn't armed—"

"What difference does that make? Katan, the Romans kill our people, every day of every month of every year since the Occupation began. Some of them use swords and spears, some use whips and crosses, some use slavery and taxes and starvation, but all of them kill our people. *All*. Is it easy to stick a blade into a man's body, making the deliberate choice to end his life? No. But God has ordained that whosoever sheds man's blood, by man shall his blood be shed. Eye for eye, tooth for tooth, life for life. By *man* shall his blood be shed. One day, you'll be a man. In that day, I pray you find your strength."

After stripping the bodies of the three men we'd murdered—for although I hadn't raised my sword, I knew in my heart that I *had* helped to kill them—we dragged them to a remote wooded spot and left them lying naked and exposed in the undergrowth. "Aren't we even going to bury them?" I whispered.

"They'll vanish faster this way," Yashar grunted. As if in agreement, several birds began to *cawk* in the treetops. "Come on; the sun'll be rising soon and we need to be well away from this place."

"We still have their gear to deal with," Sicae reminded him.

"I haven't forgotten," Yashar replied. "Avram, you get the cart and meet us at the top of the path." Avram, who had obviously done this sort of thing before, didn't need to be told twice. Without a word, he disappeared into the shadows.

The rest of us ran back to the springs as quickly as we could in the near-total darkness that so often comes right before sunrise, our steps made quicker by the on-and-off crowing of distant roosters.

"Hurry," urged Yashar. He spread out one of the Roman mantles and began to pile gear on it, putting together a make-shift pack. As I bent to do the same, I heard anguished moaning behind me and realized that the young woman who'd been assaulted was no longer lying in the middle of the clearing. The poor thing had dragged herself to a corner, where she was pulling her tightly bound arms back and forth against a jagged rock, trying to cut through the ropes that pinned her arms awkwardly behind her; her head hung down and her dark hair covered her face, but I could tell from the sounds that she was still gagged as well as bound. I moved to help her.

"Katan!" Yashar barked. "Get back to work!"

"But the girl—"

"Leave her."

"But she's still tied up—"

"Yes, and we're all better off that way. Don't worry about Magdalit. She can take care of herself." How could he say such a thing? I knew Yashar was cruel, but I hadn't realized he was heartless. Ignoring him, I crossed to the girl's side.

She lifted her head and her eyes met mine. In the darkness, all I could really make out were the whites, which seemed to fill her eyes all the way to the pupils. She was obviously terrified. Her nostrils flared and she tried to speak through the cloth that had been stuffed into her mouth. I reached around to untie the gag.

"Idiot!"

The reprimand hit my ears at the same moment the blow struck me upside my head, and I was yanked backward by a rough hand pulling sharply at the neck of my tunic. Yashar shook me like a mother dog with a wayward pup and threw me several feet away from Magdalit. "I said, get back to work!" He kicked me in the butt, driving me still farther from the girl.

"I wasn't going to hurt her!"

"It's not her I'm worried about, you moron. That girl's got more demons in her than you have sense. Stay away from her. You have a job to finish here, and if you disobey my orders again, I'll kill you and leave your corpse for Magdalit to play with."

The girl laughed, a strangled and eerie sound through her gag, but laughter all the same.

I decided not to take my chances—with Yashar or with Magdalit. Hastily I piled weapons, armor, and clothing on another mantle, tying the four corners together and slinging the bundle across my shoulders. Sicae shouldered his, and Yashar took a quick look around before giving the order to move out. We carried the three packs up the narrow path and laid them in the hand-cart that Avram had brought. As soon as the cart was full, Avram tossed some sheaves of wheat on top, hiding the gear from casual inspection. Then he and Sicae took the cart and left.

"Where are they taking it?" I asked.

"To a place you don't need to know about. Come on, let's get you back to your boat."

"But what about Shimon—Fisher?"

"Hopefully, he'll be joining you there."

"Hopefully?"

Yashar turned to face me. The first pale light of morning filtered through the leaves of the olives and revealed his features. He looked a lot like my father, except he had more worry-lines on his forehead, and more gray in his hair. "Hopefully," he repeated. Then he laid a hand on my shoulder, gently but firmly. "Yaakob-Yeter-Katan, this is not a game we're playing. This is war, son. All we can ever do is hope.

Part Three

Burdens

For he will command his angels
concerning you to guard you in all
your ways; they will lift you up in
their hands, so that you will not
strike your foot against a stone.

—Psalm 91:11-12

18

YISU

Sivan 3769
(The Counting of Weeks)

My first Shavuot pilgrimage did not go exactly as expected. First there were the Samaritan bandits who waylaid us on the second day of our journey, demanding that we pay a "toll" for crossing their lands, and then taking nearly everything we possessed, including the clothes on our backs.

"Would you steal even my *tallit*?" Saba Yoachim asked, holding on to his prayer shawl until one of the bandits tore it from his grasp. The rest of us surrendered our garments without protest, though I flinched as the thief carelessly tossed my *tallit*, which I'd owned for less than a year, into a pile with the rest of the clothes. The sacred tassels with their blue cords spelling the name of God lay in the dirt, and he stepped heedlessly on one as he went about his business. I almost cried out at that, but Abba saw and shot me a warning look. I swallowed and kept still.

After some discussion amongst themselves, they allowed us to keep our tunics, sandals, and one water skin. "You may also keep your lives," the leader said in a magnanimous tone.

Standing between my father and my teacher, I watched in silence as the thieves hauled away the cart that carried all of the provisions for our journey as well as the offerings we'd dedicated to the Lord.

"You aren't just robbing us, you're robbing God!" Saba Yoachim shouted after them.

"Don't trouble yourself over that, graybeard," one of the Samaritans laughed over his shoulder. "We'll tithe for you""

"Yes," laughed another bandit, "God will get His fair share!"

Rabbi Ezra, who was standing closest to me, gritted his teeth and held his peace. I could almost hear his thoughts: *Do not answer a fool according to his folly.* And really, what was there to say?

Though Abba looked concerned, he followed the rabbi's example and held his tongue the whole time. Only after the thieves had moved on did he utter a word. "Let's go."

"Where?" asked Netzer.

"To the gathering, of course."

"Without an offering?" Scripture was plain on the matter: *No man should appear before Adonai empty-handed.*

Rabbi Ezra answered him. "As the prophet Samuel wrote: 'Does Adonai delight in burnt offerings and sacrifices as much as in obeying the voice of Adonai?' We are commanded to gather in Jerusalem—shall we not obey this command?" Then he smiled. "Look on the bright side, my friend: we no longer make a tempting target for bandits. The remainder of our journey should be without incident."

Indeed, the rest of the trip to the Holy City was uneventful, though unpleasant. By the time we reached the gates of Jerusalem, we were half-starved and filthy from lying on the ground in our tunics night after night. Abba's original plan, to stay in one of the synagogues, was out of the question; not only did we lack the lodging fee, but we were in desperate need of food and decent clothing. "We'll go to my sister," Saba Yoachim said, and so it was decided that we would spend Shavuot in the household of the High Priest. When we arrived at the Warren, Rabbi Ezra raised an eyebrow but otherwise handled the surprise with his usual composure. The servants at the gate, on the other hand, eyed us with suspicion and scorn— a ragged and disreputable lot of beggars we looked!—until Saba identified himself, and then they escorted us to Aunt Elisheba. She welcomed us warmly, of course, and saw to it that all of our needs were met.

We stayed only two days, and then it was time to return home. "Not through Samaria," Abba announced. "We'll take the Peraean route up to Sennabrin." Sennabrin was a sizeable town on the southern shore of Lake Gennesaret, where the waters of the lake poured out into the Jordan. A good road connected Sennabrin with Sepphoris and was frequented by pilgrims, merchants, and government officials alike. Abba's decision to take this route wasn't based on the robbery (though none of us was eager to set foot in Samaria again for quite a while) but on the fact that Uncle Zebdi had promised to meet us in Sennabrin five days after Shavuot. That promise, however, my uncle failed to keep. We waited by the shore for several hours, anxiously checking each boat that pulled in, but none belonged to Uncle Zebdi. Abba shifted back and forth between worry and anger.

"I'm sorry, Ezra, for the delay—"

"No apology is needed, Yosef. Truly."

"I was expecting to pick Katan up here," Abba explained for the second or third time. "Zebdi said he would be in Sennabrin today. I can't imagine why he isn't. But since he didn't come, we have no choice but to go to him."

"The delay will be minimal," Rabbi Ezra assured him.

"A whole extra day spent walking up to Bethsaida, and Shabbat tomorrow, and then still another day to travel home," Abba disagreed. "Three days is hardly minimal."

"If we hadn't been robbed in Samaria we could have chartered space on one of these boats and gotten to Bethsaida and back in a matter of hours," Saba Yaakob observed.

"Yes, Father, I know," Abba snapped. "And if Zebdi were more observant of Torah, he would have brought Katan to Jerusalem for Shavuot and we could have just claimed him there."

"And if Adam hadn't listened to his wife, we would all live together in paradise with no need to travel anywhere," Saba Yoachim interjected. "*Ifs* are nothing but a waste of time and an insult to God. Let's stop talking and get on the road."

Because Netzer and his sons had joined a west-bound caravan hours ago, our company on the northward route consisted of only the five of us. I hastened to grab the small satchel that held the last of our provisions; Saba Yoachim leaned on the staff that Abba had made for him along the way, but the rest of the men carried only the clothes on their backs. Although we hardly marched at a military pace, we expected to cover the fifteen or so miles to Bethsaida in about six hours. This would be placing our arrival close to sunset, leaving us little time to prepare for the Sabbath, but it could not be helped.

We ran into a slight delay at Magdala, where a Roman checkpoint had been set up across the road. Because we had so little baggage, the sentries frowned at our claim to be returning from the pilgrimage, and searched each of us for weapons. Of course we had none, so they let us go again without too much fuss.

"What do you suppose that was about?" Saba Yoachim asked afterward.

"Zealots have been active in the area, most likely," Saba Yaakob grunted, spitting on the ground.

Abba didn't say anything, but it wasn't hard to guess what he was thinking: *This better not have anything to do with Zebdi's absence.* He restrained himself, however, and simply marched on with a renewed determination in his steps, forcing the rest of us to hurry in order to keep up with him.

It was only a few miles from Magdala to Bethsaida. We arrived at Uncle Zebdi's house just as the sun kissed the western horizon and a *shofar* sounded the last call before Shabbat. The family was gathered about the table for the lighting of the Sabbath lamps. Since both door and window were propped open to admit the evening breeze, there was no need to knock; instead, Saba Yoachim called out, "Is there room at my daughter's table for five more hungry men?"

At the sound of his voice, Aunt Shelom looked up and then ran toward the open door with a squeal of delight, throwing herself into her father's outstretched arms. "Abba!"

"Shelomith." He hugged her, kissed her, and shoved her gently back into the house. "Hurry and light your lamp, girl, or we'll all sit in darkness tonight." She hurried to obey him. We entered the room and stood silently around the table, watching as the women—Shelomith and her mother-in-law—lit the lamps and welcomed the Sabbath to their home.

Katan was there; he looked up when we entered the room but said nothing. The look on my brother's face worried me. Glancing over at Abba, I saw the same expression form on his face as his relief gave way to apprehension. While Aunt Shelom and her mother-in-law spoke the Sabbath blessing— *Blessed are You, Adonai our God, King of the universe, who has sanctified us with His commandments and commanded us to kindle the light of Shabbat*—another prayer was forming in my heart: *Father, please send Your peace into this place.*

With our arrival, the now-crowded room held ten men and boys, as well as the two women. Saba Yoachim introduced Rabbi Ezra to those already at the table. "Ezra bar Shimeon, this is our host, Sheth bar Amnon; his son—who is also my son-in-law—Zebdi. And these other three are my grandsons: Yoshiah, Yakob, and you already know Yaakob-katan, of course." Uncle Sheth invited the rabbi to sit at his right hand, and motioned to everyone else that we were also to take our places at the table. Without hesitation, I made room for myself beside Katan. "Are you okay?" I whispered. He didn't answer.

"Sarah," Uncle Sheth called to his wife, "bring some more cups to the table for our guests." While the women poured our wine, Sheth said, "We'll go into town for the assembly after we've had a bite. I find it hard to truly welcome Shabbat on an empty stomach, and you all must be famished after so long on the road, am I right?"

"It is most considerate of you," my teacher acknowledged, sanctioning the breach of custom.

Uncle Sheth lifted his cup, recited *kiddush*, and then said, "Yoshiah, bring the basin around."

My cousin carried the bowl slowly around the table, careful not to slosh water on the floor as each of us washed our hands in turn. I smiled at him and poured the cup over first my right hand and then my left, saying as I did so, "Blessed are You, Adonai our God, King of the universe, who has sanctified us with His commandments and commanded us concerning the washing of hands." The words flowed like the water; repetition had not worn them down; every one of them was as heartfelt as the first time I'd spoken them, though I'd spoken them countless times each day of my life. *Blessed are You, Adonai our God, King of the universe, who has sanctified us with His commandments and commanded us...* It mattered not what followed. The washing, I knew, meant nothing in itself—the obedience was what sanctified us. Without obedience, there could be no love, and without commandments, there could be no obedience. Did Yoshiah understand this, or was he still too young? I looked at my teacher. Did Ezra understand this, or had he grown too old?

Uncle Sheth blessed and broke the bread and passed it around, and everyone took a small piece. If we'd been at home, we would have gone to the synagogue before supper. *A man does not live on bread alone,* Abba often reminded us when we complained of hunger. But now he held his peace and accepted Uncle Sheth's hospitality as Rabbi Ezra had, with grace, dipping his bread into the bowl along with the rest of us. It was plain, however, that his mind was not on the meal. He stared at Katan the whole time but said nothing. My brother refused to meet his eyes. What had happened while we were apart?

Not until Abba had emptied his first cup of wine did he bring up the subject that was probably on everyone's mind. "So, Zebdi, it seems you're all in good health. I'm glad to see it. Why then didn't you meet us as planned?"

"Later, Yosef."

"No, please, *brother*. I want to know why I'm spending Shabbat in your father's house instead of in my own. While I welcome the hospitality, I have to be honest—I begrudge the need for it. I've been away from my wife long enough." There was an edge to Abba's voice that I'd not heard before, not even when we were waylaid by the bandits.

"Well, then, you can thank your son for the delay." Uncle Zebdi's voice was gruff. "And I'll thank you to take him and keep him."

"Zebdi—" warned Sheth.

"No, Father. He brought it up—"

"It is Shabbat, and I will not have quarreling at my table, Zebdi. Yosef, you too—I speak to you as to a son. Control yourselves, please, in front of the children and our guest."

The two stifled whatever comments they'd been about to make, sitting wordlessly through the rest of the meal. Katan stared at his plate but barely touched his food. While the older men tried to make light conversation, I closed my eyes and asked my Father once again to bring peace to the situation. Ravenous as I was, my brother's welfare was more important. Whatever he'd done to anger Zebdi was sure to anger Yosef even more.

Not until an hour later, as we were walking back from the synagogue, did the subject come up again. "Katan," Abba said, "walk ahead with your aunts and take the boys to the house, please." I waited, expecting to be sent away with the rest of them, but Abba just ignored me. Katan, uncharacteristically, did as he was told without protest.

As soon as the women and children were out of earshot, Abba turned to Zebdi once more. "Now, just *what* exactly did Katan do that makes you so eager to rid yourself of him, yet at the same time forced you to keep him here despite your promise to bring him to Sennabrin?"

Uncle Zebdi had calmed down considerably since supper, and I realized that he'd had at least a day to prepare his words for this situation. "Promise me first," he said, "that you won't hurt him."

Abba, who'd had less than an hour to prepare *his* words, snapped back, "Are you telling me not to discipline my own son? Who do you think you are?"

"Discipline him, by all means. I've already taken a rod to his backside, and I've no doubt you'll want to reinforce that lesson yourself, but just promise me you won't lose your temper."

Impatient, Saba Yaakob interrupted. "What in *Sheol* did the boy do?"

"You should have told me, Yosef, that he's been hanging around the Zealots. I'd have kept him closer had I known—"

Abba exploded. "You let him run with the Zealots? Zeb, I *trusted* you!"

"I didn't *let* him. He sneaked off—"

Saba Yaakob, who was standing next to me, let out a choked sound and turned away. *Saba lost two sons in the rebellion*, I remembered Abba saying. *He watched his children die.* Abba had been there, too. I could only imagine what he was feeling right now. "He's twelve years old, Zebdi! Twelve! How could he sneak off without your notice?"

"He didn't go alone. It wasn't his idea at all, or so he claims. He says he didn't know anything about it, that he was just doing what Shimon told him to do—"

"Shimon?" Abba interrupted again, this time going so red with rage that his flush was visible in the moonlight.

"I know what you're thinking," Uncle Zebdi said. "Not *that* Shimon, not the Zealot. My fishing partner's oldest boy, his name is Shimon, too. He was captain of the boat Katan went out on that night; it was about a week ago. Apparently our Shimon had made an arrangement with your Shimon—"

"That scum is not *my* Shimon!"

"Granted. But he showed up here two weeks ago claiming friendship with Katan, and he must have convinced *our* Shimon to join him on some half-assed Zealot excursion. Shimon usually works with Yoshiah, but that night he requested Katan for a partner, and I had no reason to turn him down. How was I supposed to know what they were planning?"

"I ordered Katan to stay away from that troublemaker!"

"So did I!" Zebdi shouted. "It's not *my* fault he didn't listen!"

Rabbi Ezra had been quiet until now, but as tempers began to flare up again he stepped in. "The situation is serious, yes, but it seems to me that you are both overreacting. The boy has obviously survived the experience unscathed—physically, at any rate—so please, calm yourselves before you come to blows."

"Yes," Saba Yoachim said, his voice low and soothing as he laid one hand firmly on the shoulder of each of his sons-in-law. "You are like-minded on this issue; there is no reason for brothers to fight. What's past is past. Now you need to work together to decide what's to be done about it."

Abba nodded, regaining control of his temper. "What did they do, Zeb, and how did you learn of it?" His voice was still edged with anger, but he was no longer shouting.

Uncle Zebdi had lowered his voice as well. "The two of them were out all night and half the next day, and then they came in without a single fish to show for it. I would have written it off as a bad night's fishing, but both of the boys were obviously shaken up about something. Then I saw the blood stains on Shimon's tunic."

He paused a moment to let that sink in. Abba drew in a deep breath before asking, "Was he badly hurt?"

"Shimon? No, not a scratch. Katan was fine too. The blood—it wasn't theirs."

Saba Yoachim whispered, "God have mercy."

"The boys—well, it was obvious they'd tried to wash out their clothes, but there was too much blood. They were both covered in it, Yosef. I'm sorry. But that's not the worst of it."

Zebdi sighed deeply before continuing. "Two days later, word reached Capernaum that a whole squadron of Roman troops had gone missing on the road somewhere between Bethabara and Magdala. Yesterday, they set up roadblocks and checks on all the ports—rumor has it that some bodies were found in the woods near Hammath. You can see why I didn't want to take Katan in that direction. If they questioned him…"

"He's only twelve,"" Abba said again, his voice breaking.

"Twelve is old enough to hang for murder and sedition."

"Zebdi, please," Saba Yoachim admonished, glancing toward Saba Yaakob.

"No." Saba Yaakob spoke up at last, and everyone else fell silent at the pain on his face as he turned back to the group. His voice, however, was steady. "It's true. The Romans don't care about such details; the fact that Katan is not yet *bar mitzvah* would mean nothing to them. In their eyes, if he's old enough to wield a sword, he's old enough to bear the consequences of such a choice. Hopefully, God will be more merciful to the child." He looked at Abba. "You can't afford to be."

"I know."

But Abba didn't speak to Katan that night or during the long day that followed. I knew why. He never administered discipline on the Sabbath, out of respect for its holiness. *It gives the children one more reason to appreciate Shabbat*, he said. Perhaps, but my brother was not celebrating his reprieve—he spent the whole day in dread of the inevitable sunset and the confrontation that was sure to come with it. Though no one said a word about it, the tension between father and son spoiled the Sabbath for everyone, casting a gloom over the day like a pack of wolves circling the flock, held at bay but impossible to ignore.

Eventually, as if exhausted by the stress, the sun sank below the horizon, leeching the last bit of color from the sky and making way for the stars. Abba led Katan into a closed chamber, and they stayed there for nearly an hour. When the two finally emerged, Abba was shaking his head in frustration and Katan was favoring his backside, but they still weren't talking to each other. For the rest of the night, Abba kept Katan on a close leash—my brother wasn't even allowed to use the latrine by himself, and he had to sleep between Abba and Saba

Yaakob (who was also refusing to talk to his favorite grandson).

We rose early, made our farewells to Uncle Zebdi and his family, and then took the inland road home. Hoping to avoid the roadblocks to the south, Abba led us north and west toward Korazin. There we picked up the road to Sepphoris, which climbed steeply up through the hills for several hours before leveling off as it crossed the plain of Zebulun. Our pace was rigorous, and Saba Yoachim finally had to ask Abba to slow down. "You're wearing me out, son. We're not all as young as you. Why such a hurry?"

"I'm sorry, Father," he apologized. "I'm afraid I'm marching out my anger."

I trampled them in my anger and trod them down in my wrath, Isaiah had said. At least Abba was taking out his rage on the rocks of the road rather than on his son's flesh, but his shunning of Katan tore at my heart. I tried once to walk by my brother's side and talk to him; Abba snapped at me to get back to my place. "Leave him alone! I want him to think about the choices he's been making."

We walked on in near-total silence for another hour or so. My thoughts and prayers never strayed far from Katan, who was walking three or four paces ahead of me, his head hanging and his fists clenched as he trod doggedly onward. It was the fists that bothered me. Instead of repenting of his poor choices, my brother was seething.

19

KATAN

Sivan 3769
(The Counting of Weeks)

I wasn't talking to anyone, but that didn't stop me from listening to them. Father was marching ahead of everyone else, his back to me. He'd made it clear that was all I should expect from him—his back—until and unless I told him what he wanted to know. Every now and then he glanced over his shoulder as if to make sure I was still there, but he said nothing.

For some reason, Yisu had brought his teacher along on the trip. Rabbi Ezra even walked beside me for a moment, patting my arm in sympathy before moving on to catch up with Father. The two of them began to talk. Curious, I took a few paces at a jog and managed to close the gap between us enough to overhear their conversation.

"'Folly is bound up in the heart of a child,'" the rabbi was saying, quoting the proverb.

"Yes," Father replied, "but the 'rod of discipline' hasn't loosened his lips. I still don't know what he did, Ezra. How can I help him if he won't talk to me?"

"Is your silence helping him?"

He shook his head. "It's helping me to hold my temper so I don't beat a confession out of him, but that's all. I'm not blind, Rabbi. I can see that my son is hardening his heart with every step we take. I just don't know what else to do at the moment."

"You could let Yeshua talk to him."

"No. I don't want Katan playing on Yisu's sympathies. There's nothing admirable or praiseworthy about the Zealots, and the last thing I want is Katan trying to persuade Yisu otherwise."

The rabbi lowered his voice just a little, and I couldn't make out his words, but Father's reply was clear. "Of course I'm thinking about my brothers. Yehudah persuaded Matti that the Zealots were noble, righteous, our only hope of salvation. Then the two of them fed each other's dreams and goaded each other on until they wouldn't listen to anyone else, wouldn't listen to Father, wouldn't listen to me…"

"Yet you stayed clear of the trap."

"No, I didn't. In trying to protect them, I let myself get swept up in the movement. Don't you see? It's only by God's grace that I'm alive today. I was a fool, Ezra! I don't want—I don't want Yisu to make the same mistakes I made. I know he'd never chase off after the Zealots on his own, but he might follow Katan down that path if he thought it was the only way to keep his brother safe."

Why wasn't I surprised? All Father really cared about was that Yisu might get hurt. His precious Yisu. I'd heard enough. I slowed my steps until I was back where I'd been told to stay. I was so mad that it took me a minute to realize that Rabbi Ezra was walking beside me again. He was probably worried about my corrupting Yisu, too, was probably thinking about how to keep Yisu safe from the wicked brother. Probably scowling down at me in disapproval. I glanced over at him out of the corner of my eye, but he wasn't even looking at me. He was just walking. I put my eye back on the road and trudged on.

I kept waiting for the rabbi to fall back, but he stayed at my side, not saying a word. His persistence was starting to get to me. *What does he want?* I looked him square in the face this time, glaring, and to my surprise discovered that he was already looking at me—and smiling. "When Absalom was a young man," he said, "he got in a lot of trouble with his father for doing the right thing."

It wasn't what I'd expected from him. I let out a "Huh?" before remembering my manners. The man was, after all, a teacher. "I mean, I beg your pardon, Rabbi. I don't understand."

"I don't suppose you do. The story is not taught in *bet-sefer*, nor is it commonly read in the synagogue as *haftarah*. Still, it bears consideration. Next year you'll be old enough for *bet-midrash*, will you not?"

I nodded.

"So I'll give you a lesson early." He raised his voice. "King David had many wives, and many sons." Why was he talking

so loudly? Did he think I was deaf? Then I realized—he wanted
my father to hear this lesson, too. As understanding dawned on
me, I looked Rabbi Ezra over again. Maybe I'd misjudged him.
I listened more carefully as he continued. "Absalom was one of
David's favorites, though not his firstborn. That was Amnon,
the son of David and Ahinoam. Absalom's mother was
Maakhah of Geshur. Absalom also had a sister named Tamar,
who was very beautiful. Are you following all of this?"

"Yes, Rabbi."

"Now I have to warn you, the next part is probably the
reason the story is not standard fare for Shabbat or the holidays.
It is, however, integral to the story's lesson, and as I strongly
suspect that you have already lost much of your innocence, I
see no need to treat you like a child." The smile had fallen from
his face, but he wasn't scowling at me. His expression was one
of concern, and I could almost hear his thoughts: *Has the boy
truly committed murder?* "Well," he continued after the brief
pause, "Amnon saw Tamar and desired her, so he lured her into
his bedroom and then he raped her. You understand what that
means?"

"Y-yes, Rabbi." I didn't mean to stammer, but when he said
and then he raped her, all the awful details of that night came
flooding into my mind and I remembered Magdalit lying in the
dirt, bound and gagged, with one Roman thrusting into her as
the others waited their turn. I felt sick.

Rabbi Ezra shook his head. "The scriptures tell us that
when Amnon had taken what he wanted from Tamar, he cast
her aside. They tell us that Absalom brought her into his own
house and told her to keep quiet and not to worry about it. The
scriptures also tell us that when King David heard about all
these things, he became very angry. What the scriptures do *not*
tell us is how the king learned of the situation. What do you
think?"

I tried to focus on the lesson. "It sounds like Absalom told
the king."

He nodded. "Yes, that's my own interpretation as well,
especially considering all that followed. You see, David did
nothing to punish Amnon, and Absalom kept his anger and his
hatred for his brother secret. For two years he plotted revenge,
and then one day he invited his brothers to a party and had

Amnon killed. So Absalom was forced to flee into exile, because he had sinned."

"But Amnon broke the Law, Rabbi," I protested. "As it is written, 'Do not have sexual relations with your sister, either your father's daughter or your mother's daughter, whether she was born in the same home or elsewhere...Everyone who does any of these detestable things—such persons must be cut off from their people.' Isn't that what Absalom was doing, administering justice? Because the king should have, but didn't? How then could the king condemn him as a murderer?"

"Yes, didn't I begin by saying that Absalom got in trouble for doing the right thing?" I smiled, pleased that I'd gotten it right. Let Ezra see that Yisu wasn't the only scholar in the family. The rabbi, however, had not yet finished his lesson. "You've given me the answer I'd expect from a boy in his last year of *bet-sefer*, but you're wrong; that's not why Absalom fled. Tell me, Katan, what *was* Absalom's sin?"

I stopped smiling. If not murder, then what? "I—I don't know, Rabbi."

"Take a guess."

I had no idea what he wanted me to say, so I said nothing.

"Whose duty was it to punish Amnon's transgression of the Law?" he prompted.

"King David's, Rabbi."

"And what was Absalom's relationship to King David?"

Suddenly, I understood the lesson and knew the answer to the rabbi's question, but I had to force it past my lips. "He was his son, Rabbi."

"And what was Absalom's sin?" he pressed. He was going to make me say it. He wouldn't be satisfied until I did, wouldn't leave me alone until I'd condemned myself.

I muttered the words he was waiting to hear.

"What was that? Speak up, Katan."

I said it again. "He disobeyed the commandment to honor his father, Rabbi."

"But his father was wrong."

"That doesn't make any difference, does it?" The damning words came out just above a whisper. "The commandment doesn't make any exceptions for whether or not you agree with your father. Absalom wasn't the king; David was. It wasn't

Absalom's place to punish Amnon. He—he was setting himself up like he knew better than his father. That's disrespectful." I bit my lip. I'd said more than enough.

The rabbi decided to drive his point all the way home. "It's interesting to note that after this incident, when David was persuaded to forgive Absalom—whom he truly loved—the young man repaid his father's mercy by stealing the hearts of the people, setting himself up as king and judge over them, and going to war against his father. As if that weren't enough, Absalom even slept with his father's concubines, making a public spectacle of the act."

I felt my cheeks burning and hung my head, not wanting him to see the tears that were threatening to escape. He didn't need to explain how my own act of rebellion had dishonored Yosef. But he still wasn't finished with me. "In the end, after more than twenty years spent nursing a hatred of his father, Absalom died, and David mourned the loss of his beloved son with all his heart. So tell me, Katan, what 'right thing' did you do that is now standing between you and your father?"

His question—I hadn't seen it coming. It took me completely off guard, and I had to clamp my jaw down over the answer. *I swore never to tell.*

"Will you truly let this thing take over your life as it did Absalom's?"

I told him the only thing I could, the only thing I'd told Uncle Zebdi when he'd beaten me, the only thing I'd said to Father. "I swore I wouldn't talk about it."

"You swore?"

I repeated the oath Shimon had forced on me. "I called Adonai to witness, Rabbi. As it is written, 'If a man makes a vow to Adonai, or swears an oath to bind himself by some agreement, he shall not break his word; he shall do according to all that proceeds out of his mouth.'" He couldn't argue with scripture; surely he'd drop the issue now.

"Well, you have a dilemma, child. You've gotten yourself into a difficult situation, and now you will have to choose between dishonoring your father or being forsworn. I must point out, however, that Torah says 'if a *man* swears an oath.' You are not yet a man, Yaakob bar Yosef. Or had you forgotten that in your haste to act like one? Regardless—man or child—

you must now decide where you owe the greater respect: to your father, who commands you to speak, or to the friend before whom you swore not to speak. The first is a *mitzvah* laid upon you by God; the second a vow you have laid upon yourself. You cannot keep both; you must choose. Choose wisely." And with those words he finally left me alone.

My father made the choice for me, that very night.

By the time we reached Nazareth, I had decided to talk with him. I wouldn't give him the details of the raid—I didn't even want to think about them—but I would confess to having been with the Zealots that night. There really wasn't any reason to keep silent; Father and Uncle Zebdi had already guessed most of the truth anyway.

But then, before I had a chance to speak, he pulled out the chain.

"I'm not going to make the same mistake twice," he said, and then he fastened one end of the chain to a beam in the house, wrapped the other end around my ankle, and locked it in place. The key he hung around his neck. "This is how you'll sleep from now on, since it's obvious that you can't be trusted to stay away from the Zealots on your own. Keep your secrets! What's done is done, and it can't be changed, but I'm damned if I'll stand by and let it happen again. Until you're a man, I'm morally responsible for your actions; did you ever once stop to think of that?"

"Father—"

"No, I don't want to hear it! You're too late, Katan. Consider yourself under arrest, and thank God that *I'm* your jailer and not some Roman! You won't bear witness against yourself, and that's your right under *our* law, but don't fool yourself, boy—Rome doesn't care if you confess or not; Rome doesn't care if there are witnesses or not; *Rome doesn't care!*" With that, he stomped out of the room.

I stood there in shock. Twilight turned to dark, and still I stood there, unable to believe that my father had chained me like a dog. The iron sat cold and heavy around my ankle, not so tight as to cut the skin, but not so loose that I could slip out of it. I took one step, and the chain rattled. It was true, then. It wasn't just a nightmare; my father really had chained me to my bed for the night. I lay down.

I heard voices outside the window.

"But Yosef, what if there's a fire?" Mother was asking.

"I'll take that chance. It's safer than allowing him to run with the Zealots."

The voices went away.

Lamplight. Laughter. My brothers tumbled into the room and piled onto their pallets, Yosei and Shammai wrestling for the pillows as usual, Yehudah shouting, "But I'm not sleepy!" Only Yisu was quiet. He said nothing as he put the lamp up on its stand, but he stared at the chain stretched across his side of the bed and frowned, and then whispered, "*Baruch hu, dayan ha-emet,*" as if he'd just received terrible news. I didn't want his pity. I rolled over, putting my back to him, but it was the wrong thing to do and I realized this too late as the chain clink-clanked loudly, drawing attention to itself. Immediately, my younger brothers gathered around my bed like a swarm of gnats, buzzing with questions, fingering the chain, tugging on it.

"Cut it out!" I yelled, swatting at them.

"Get back to bed, all of you," Yisu said firmly. "We'll talk about it in the morning."

They grumbled but quieted down, and Yisu put out the lamp and lay down beside me. I felt him fidgeting as he tried to figure out what to do about the chain. I could have made it easy for him by moving to the other side of the bed, but I didn't want to, and he didn't ask me to. Instead he tried pushing the chain to one side, but it wasn't long enough to go around the pallet; his only real choice was whether to lie on top of it or underneath it. After trying both positions, he finally settled for underneath, and spent the rest of the night with my chain stretched heavily across his legs.

The next day established the new pattern for my life.

I woke with my bladder ready to burst, rolled out of bed, and ran for the door. Or tried to. The chain around my ankle, which I'd forgotten as I'd slept, caught and tripped me before I'd taken two steps. Yisu woke up at once, of course, and crawled out from under the chain. "I'll get Abba," he said.

"Hurry up, before I wet myself!" As if I wasn't already humiliated enough.

Father showed up just in time, unchained me, and then led me to the latrine, standing there while I did my business and escorting me back to the house afterward. He walked me to school as if I were five years old, and was waiting outside the synagogue when Rabbi Zephanyah dismissed class. Together we hiked the road to Sepphoris, and together we returned at the end of the workday. Just before sunset, Father led me to the latrine again, and then he chained me to the beam beside my bed.

The next morning I woke with my bladder ready to burst… Another day had begun.

"Where's your father, Katan? I need to see him right away."

I looked up from the wheel I was helping Yisu to fit on the axle of the new cart, right into the eyes of Shimon bar Yonah—Fisher. It had been four months since last I'd seen him, four months spent under house arrest because I'd listened to him. I felt an angry flush rising in my cheeks.

But he wasn't there to talk to me. "I need to see Yosef," he repeated. "It's urgent."

Yisu stood up and brushed his hands off on his apron. "I'll take you to him," he said, and without waiting for an introduction he led Shimon into the workshop. A few minutes later, my brother came out alone and crossed over to me, sadness carved onto his face and his eyes brimming with tears. "Katan," he said, and then wrapped me in a hug, holding me close. "Yoshiah is dead."

Yoshiah is dead. The words didn't make any sense. Old people died. Babies died. Soldiers died. But boys my age—well, they didn't. They just didn't.

Father broke the news first to Mother, and then to Saba Yoachim. The three of them made plans to leave at once for Capernaum. Aunt Shelomith needed them. Mother was in no condition to travel—six months pregnant—but she insisted on going. "I've managed worse," she said.

"Yes," Father replied. "I haven't forgotten." Then he turned to me. "You're coming, too." I wasn't surprised; since our return home from Bethsaida, he hadn't let me out of his sight. "The rest of the children will stay here with Mimah, and Yisu will help Father handle any business that comes in—"

"No," Saba Yoachim interrupted heavily. "The children will come with us. The whole family will go."

"Father," my mother said gently, "I don't think that's a good idea."

"Why not?"

My father answered him. "Zebdi and Shelomith just lost their firstborn. All they have left is Yakob. I don't want to show up with my whole brood. It would be insensitive."

"Yeshua, then." Saba was insistent.

"I don't—oh, all right. Yisu and Katan." Father glanced over at the two of us. "Pack quickly, you two, and then harness the ass to that new cart. We're leaving within the hour."

I was just a little kid when Savta Hannah died, so her funeral was only a blurred memory for me. Savta Sarah's death was more recent, but her *shiva* hadn't been especially memorable— just a week of quiet conversation and rest from work, much like a Sabbath that had gone on day after day. Nothing in my experience had prepared me for the situation at Yoshiah's house.

By the time we arrived, his body had already been laid in the grave, of course, but the mourning had barely begun. Aunt Shelomith sat in a corner, her face buried in her arms, sobbing loudly. With her, also wailing, were several women I knew from my visit: Zebdi's mother, Sarah, and his sister Zipporah; Yonah's wife, Zemirah, was there too, as was his daughter Nitza. When we walked in, Zemirah whispered something in Shelomith's ear and my aunt stood up awkwardly, holding out her arms to embrace Mother, and I saw that she was also expecting a child. I hadn't known until now.

Uncle Zebdi was not in the house; he was sitting out back, staring out over the lake, with his clothing torn and his hair uncombed and black streaks of dirt and tears staining his face. Sheth and Yonah were with him. No one was saying anything—it was a heavy silence, like the silence just before a storm. Or just after one.

Shimon had told us the whole story on our way here.

We were done with fishing for the day, and it was time for the boys to go to school, but Yoshi asked if he could skip class and go for a sail instead. The weather was perfect for sailing…you know how he loves to fly across the water in his boat. My father wouldn't let Andrai miss school, but Zebdi said it would be okay for Yoshi to skip this once, since the next day was Yom Teruah anyway. Yakob wanted to go along, so the two of them got in the boat and caught the wind and off they went. It was blowing out of the west, like usual, but not too hard.

Then all of a sudden the wind shifted, like it does in the winter sometime….it was coming straight out of the northeast and the whole sky got black in a matter of minutes, and we all knew it was going to be a Maneater, and Yoshi and Yakob were still out there somewhere, but there was no way anyone could go out looking for them in that storm. You have no idea, if you've never seen one…those Maneaters, they come out of the north like the kings of Assyria, destroying everything in their way. So we had to wait it out, for an hour or more.

As soon as it began to let up, we launched every boat in Bethsaida, looking for them. I was with my father when we spotted Yoshi's boat. The mast was broken off and it was half-full of water, riding really low but right-side-up. At first we didn't see anyone aboard, but when we got closer I heard Yakob crying, and there he was all scrunched up in the stern, under the seat, up to his neck in bilge water. But Yoshi was gone. Gone. I tried to get Yakob to come with me, but he wouldn't budge. He kept saying Yoshi told him to stay under the seat. I finally had to drag him out by force. The poor kid, he was half-drowned himself, and freezing.

We towed the boat home and waited to see if anyone had found Yoshiah, but every boat came back empty. The next day was Yom Teruah, but we went back out anyway—there was still a chance, some of us hoped, so we kept on searching, kept spreading the word. Then two days ago some men from Dalmanutha pulled in to Bethsaida, and they had Yoshiah's body with them; they'd found him down south of Seven Springs. I—I saw him. He had this nasty gash on his forehead, like the mast struck him or something. And the look on Zebdi's face, when they brought him in…I've never seen him like that.

I'd never seen Uncle Zebdi like this, either. In fact, I'd never seen anyone like this. It scared me, that such a rock of a man could be toppled. Everything in me screamed out at the wrongness of it all: Yoshiah dead, Zebdi silenced. What was next? Would the earth turn to water and swallow us all? Would death steal someone else who was supposed to be safe, someone like Yosei or Andrai or Yisu? Would—and this was hardest of all to think about—would *I* die? And if I did, would Father be shaken to his core? Or would he simply carry on?

Like the others sitting with Uncle Zebdi, Father didn't try to comfort him with words. I was glad, for if he had spoken, I would also have had to say something—and what was there to say? So I sat silently to one side and stared at the dirt under my feet.

"It should have been you."

The voice was quiet, rough, and accusing. I looked up to see Uncle Zebdi frowning at me. "It should have been you," he repeated. "Yoshiah's a *good* boy. Why would God take him from me? He should have taken *you*. Life for life. You. You and Shimon. You're the ones who deserved to die, not my Yoshiah. You're the ones with blood on your hands. It should have been *you*."

Yonah turned and said something to Father, but I couldn't hear it through the pounding of the blood that had rushed to my face. Then Father was beside me, speaking quietly but forcefully. "Go inside with the women. And try to stay out of the way." I didn't have to be told twice.

20

YISU

Tishri 3770

Death took me by surprise. In spite of the fact that I'd
known why we were traveling to Bethsaida to sit *shiva*
for an eleven-year-old boy who had died tragically and
unexpectedly, a boy who was well-loved by family and friends,
a boy who should have lived for many more years to be known
and loved by many more people—in spite of the fact that I'd
known all of this, Death took me completely by surprise.

As I crossed the threshold into Zebdi's house, I was
assaulted by darkness and the sounds of grief. Yoshiah had
died, but his room was not left vacant—Death had moved in to
take his rightful place among the family. He mocked me, he
did, daring me to do something about him. *Evict me if you can!*
Many have tried—all have failed. I knew I would fare no better.
Why had I come? What could I possibly say or do to make any
of this better? Never before had I felt so helpless.

My mother joined the women, my father and grandfather
the men, while I, left to myself, wandered from one sorrow to
the next, facing the enemy I was powerless to defeat. I watched
as he strangled Shelomith, his weight forcing her shoulders to
fold in upon themselves, his acrid scent wringing tears from her
eyes, his hands smothering her so that she gasped and moaned
without relief. The women who surrounded her were unable to
drive Death away with their feeble ministrations; their gentle
words and soft arms passed right through him without effect; he
danced to the music of their wailing.

I found the men gathered around Zebdi, but even their
strength was no match for Death. He had them all bound and
gagged, unable to move, unable to speak a single word against
him. Silent they sat, besieged, waiting for their enemy to
surrender. Fighting back tears, I left them to their hopeless

battle and moved on, for there was nothing to be gained by joining their ranks.

Father, why have You brought me to this place? What purpose do You have for me here? Surely not to challenge Death—the time for that might come one day, but this was not the day; that much I knew. My hands had not yet been trained for this war; I could not bend the Psalmist's bow of bronze. Still, there must be *some* reason for my presence here. Needing a place where I could be alone for a while to sort out my thoughts, I climbed up to the roof, but the sounds of mourning followed me, taunted me even here. Perhaps down by the lakeshore I would find the peace I craved.

Instead, I found Yakob.

Not far from Zebdi's house, beside a shallow cove, a small boat had been pulled up onto the shore and left untended there, lying on its side amidst the weeds and driftwood; from the splintered stump of its broken mast, I guessed it was Yoshiah's boat. I laid one hand on its hull, trying to imagine what my cousin had felt out there alone in the storm. No, not alone. "Yakob was with him," I murmured, remembering what Shimon had said. As if in reply, a muffled sob came from the back of the boat.

A few planks had been nailed across the stern to act as a seat for the steersman. Yakob was curled up under the seat with his arms wrapped around his knees, trying to hide from Death.

I looked at the three-year-old who had been forgotten by his family as he huddled, shivering, in the last place he'd seen his brother, and I realized in that moment that it wasn't just Yoshiah who had died, but everyone he'd ever touched.

"Hey, Kobi," I said softly, climbing into the boat and sitting beside him.

He looked up, tears and snot all over his face. "I didn't mean to," he whispered. "I'm sorry."

"Sorry?" I didn't understand what he was talking about.

"The rope got stuck. I was just trying to help. I'm sorry."

"You were trying to help Yoshiah?"

"He told me to stay under the seat," he whispered through his tears. "But the rope got stuck."

Bending down, I reached into his hiding place and slid my arm around his shoulders. He was trembling and cold, so I pulled him a little closer and wrapped my cloak around both of us. "Shhh. It's all right." How long had the child been out here? Had anyone even noticed that he was missing? "Why are you out here all alone, Kobi?" With one corner of my cloak, I carefully wiped his face. "There, that's better. Now you can see."

"I'm hungry," he said softly.

"I have some bread," I told him, gently pulling him the rest of the way out from under the seat. "Can you sit up?" There was still a small loaf of barley bread left over from the last meal I'd eaten on the road; I took it out of my satchel and spoke a blessing over it, and then handed it to my young cousin. He ate ravenously; he'd probably been hiding in the boat for hours. I waited while he finished the bread, but then I stood up and climbed out of the boat. "Come on, Yakob," I said, reaching a hand out to the boy. "Let's go back to the family now."

"No." He pulled away, shaking his head.

"Why not? It's cold out here, and it'll be dark soon."

"No!"

"It's okay, Kobi," I said.

"I'm n-not going back, ever!"

I squatted down until I was on the same level as Yakob. We faced each other over the side of the boat. He was about to start crying again. "Okay, then," I said, "I'll stay here with you, as long as you want."

"F-f-forever," Yakob insisted, sniffling.

"If that's what it takes," I murmured, and climbed back into the boat. I hadn't planned on spending "forever" down by the lakeshore, but I was in no hurry to return to the house, either. Trustingly, the child climbed into my lap and laid his head against my chest, yawning deeply. I began rocking him, singing lines from the psalm that had driven me out here in the first place.

> "I love you, Adonai, my strength.
> Adonai is my rock,
> my fortress and my deliverer;
> my God is my rock, in whom I take refuge.
> He is my shield and the horn of my salvation,
> my stronghold.

I call to Adonai, who is worthy of praise,
and I am saved from my enemies."

I hesitated before going on to the next verse, not wanting to
upset Yakob, but he was already sound asleep, so I kept singing
softly.

"The cords of death entangled me;
the torrents of destruction overwhelmed me.
The cords of the grave coiled around me;
the snares of death confronted me.
In my distress I called to Adonai;
I cried to my God for help.
From his temple he heard my voice;
my cry came before him, into his ears."

Lake Gennesaret stretched before me, its water reddened by
the light of the sinking sun but otherwise innocent-looking,
showing no sign of the many men it had swallowed over the
years. How had it dared to do such a thing, to consume those
who had been given dominion over it at the dawn of time?
"How the mighty have fallen," I murmured. Before his fall,
Adam could command even the wind and the waves to his
bidding, but that power—that authority—he had traded away
for a single bite of fruit. "Bad bargain, Adam," I sighed. "Death
knocked on your door, and not only did you let him in, you
handed him the keys to your house." *Would you have done any
better, Yeshua?* the waves mocked. And who could say for
sure? "But if my Father is willing," I whispered to the lake,
"one day I will take those keys back." Looking down into the
face of the sleeping child—this child who had been introduced
to Death far too soon—I finished the psalm.

"It is God who arms me with strength
and makes my way perfect.
He makes my feet like the feet of a deer;
he enables me to stand on the heights.
He trains my hands for battle;
my arms can bend a bow of bronze...
He gives his king great victories;

he shows unfailing kindness to his anointed,
to David and his descendants forever.

"One day," I whispered.

21

KATAN

Nisan 3770

I looked down over the cots and caves that made up most of the village of Bethlehem and wondered what on earth we were doing here. By now, we should have been halfway to Jericho; instead, Saba Yaakob had led us south without a word of explanation. Neither Father nor Yisu had questioned the detour, though, so I kept my mouth shut. I'd become good at that over the past year.

Father had finally ended my house arrest one month ago, the day I turned thirteen. "It's Purim," he'd said grudgingly, "and no one should be in chains on Purim. Don't betray my trust." That was it. No wishes of a happy birthday, no praise for my first *aliyah* as a *bar mitzvah*, no mention of my adulthood at all. Saba Yaakob had given me a *tallit* to wear when I went up to read from Torah—Father had either forgotten or else decided I wasn't worth one of his. Afterward, sitting on the floor of the synagogue at his feet, I'd tried not to think too hard about Yisu's first *aliyah* and how the men had made room for him on their bench that day, how Father had heaped praise on his firstborn.

My brother stood beside me now, balanced on the pinnacle of rock like one of the goats pasturing nearby. "He makes my feet like the feet of a deer," he sang with a grin. "He enables me to stand on the heights." I hung back from the edge, not as confident as Yisu that it wasn't about to crumble and give way beneath me.

Father must have shared my concern. "Yisu, get down from there."

"Yes, sir." He leaped off the crag in two bounds, still grinning as he passed me. I followed at a more cautious pace to the base of the rock where my father and grandfather were waiting. Father, resting his hand affectionately on Yisu's shoulder, gave it a gentle shake.

"Be more careful, shepherd boy."

My brother laughed. "Sorry, Abba. I didn't mean to worry you. It's just so—so—"

"Intoxicating?"

"Thrilling. Standing here. Somehow it makes it all more real."

Saba Yaakob cleared his throat loudly to get our attention. "My sons," he said. The three of us turned toward him. Something in my grandfather's voice told me to listen carefully, that this was important. He stood straight and tall, looking first at each of us and then out over the village below. "My sons, you know who you are. You know why we're here." He smiled at me warmly. "Yaakob, welcome. This is your first visit to Jesse's Rock, but I trust it will not be your last. Listen and learn. One day you will come here with your sons." His smile faltered and he closed his eyes, adding softly, "If it be God's will."

"Do you want me to say it this year, Abba?" my father asked.

"No, no. I can do it." Saba pulled himself together and continued in a firm tone, pointing at Bethlehem. "There are your roots, my sons. Those humble cots, the homes of shepherds—never forget that David was born in one of them. Never forget! It was when his sons forgot where they came from, when they let themselves grow proud and fat, that they turned away from God." I saw my father's lips moving silently, forming the same words Saba was speaking, and understood: he'd heard this same speech so many times that he'd learned it by heart, and I was expected to do the same. Yisu was also frowning in concentration; he whispered the next few words along with Saba. "They made the mistake of thinking they'd raised themselves to the palace on Mount Zion, instead of humbling themselves before the One who had set them there." Saba's voice broke toward the end, and he turned away with his head bowed.

Uncle Yehudah, Uncle Matthanyah—they didn't listen. That's why they aren't here with us today. And Saba can't stop remembering them; he can't stop grieving. I looked at my father, beginning to understand one reason, at least, for my house arrest. *You think I'm like them.* But I wasn't! If he'd just take the time to talk to me—to listen to me!—he'd know that. I stared at him, wishing he'd look back, wishing he'd *see* me; but he had his eyes fixed on his father. Saba's head was no longer bowed. He'd pulled himself up and was walking briskly, defiantly, down the path.

"He's trying to walk away from the past," Yisu murmured, "but it keeps following him around. Why does he put himself through this?"

Father answered him softly. "He honors the tradition of our fathers, even though it causes him pain. 'Never forget.' He takes that seriously, as should we all. It's too easy, in celebrating our victories, to forget our failures—to blame them on someone else instead of admitting that they're the result of our own shameful mistakes. Zerubbabel knew this. He brought Abihud to this same spot and said those same words to him, every Passover. It's been our custom ever since, our own addition to the *seder*. Take it to heart." He finally met my eyes, but his next words proved that he still wasn't looking at *me*. "My brothers didn't. The words stayed on their lips, but not in their hearts." With that warning, he turned and hurried back down the path we'd come up just a few minutes earlier. Saba was already a good distance away. After a brief hesitation, Yisu started to follow them. I caught his arm.

"Wait," I said. "Where are we going now?" He'd obviously done this last year.

"Home," he answered.

"You mean Bethlehem? Are we staying in the *khan*?" I asked.

"No, we're going home now. To Nazareth."

"You mean we came all this way for nothing?" I could hardly believe it. Five miles out of our way, and then five miles back—half a day of marching, wasted.

"Nothing?" He seemed genuinely confused. "Weren't you listening?"

"Sure, but they could have told us that in Jerusalem, Yisu. Father could have told us at home, for that matter, when he told us our lineage. Why drag us all the way out here?"

"Saba wanted us to see it. To be part of it. Doesn't it mean anything to you, that David probably stood on this very rock when he watched his sheep, when he wrote his psalms? It isn't just history, Katan; it's part of *our* story. It goes on to this day, and beyond. Don't you see?"

"Fine, then, but why leave so soon? Why not give us a chance to soak it in?"

He laughed. "I don't know. Maybe because it's more precious this way—the trip isn't about a visit to Bethlehem; it's about this one spot, this one remembrance." He threw out his arms and spun around with his head tilted back, the sun shining on his face. "The reason isn't important! The love is in the obedience! Blessed are You, Adonai our God, King of the universe, who has sanctified us with his commandments and commanded us to honor our fathers!" Laughing, he ran down the path to catch up with them.

Weird. He was still just as weird as ever.

We returned home and went back to work. Life went on as usual, with the exception that I was a free man again. Also I had graduated from *bet-sefer* and was now working full-time at my trade. It was all I'd ever expected to do with my life, all that most Galilean boys did. As a rule, only the brightest sons of rabbis, priests, lawyers, or wealthy merchants continued their education beyond *bet-sefer*; the poor and uneducated kept their sons at home to help put bread on the table and to prepare them for real life. (My brother was a rare exception to the rule.)

But I missed school, missed it terribly. The one place in the world where I was right more often than I was wrong, where I was praised more often than I was criticized…this place was no longer mine. Every morning when Yisu went to his studies with Rabbi Ezra, and Yosei and Shammai went to *bet-sefer*, and I stayed behind to patch leaky roofs and mend broken plows, I was reminded of my loss. To make matters worse, that summer Yehudah turned five and started school, too. As if all of that wasn't enough to make me sufficiently miserable, Father still didn't think I was capable of anything but the simplest jobs, so he held the skilled work aside for Yisu to do in the afternoons. My only consolation came on the Sabbath, when I was often called to the *bimah* to read scripture—an honor that was never offered to my brother. Never.

This angered Father, and he told me I wasn't to read anymore. "Zephanyah insults our whole family," he fumed. "To offer one of my sons *aliyah* while denying it to the other—does he think me blind to his insinuations?"

"But, Father—"

"No argument, Katan!"

I was stuck. Legally, I was a man and he had no right to make this decision for me, but I was also his son and it would have been dishonoring to go against his wishes. Fortunately for me, my grandfathers were in the room when Father issued his command; to my surprise, both of them spoke up for me. "Yosef, don't deprive Katan," Saba Yaakob said. "The boy's done nothing to deserve such a punishment."

"Would you make yourself guilty of Zephanyah's offense?" Saba Yoachim asked. "Forbidding your son to read from Torah in the assembly? Think carefully, Yosef, before you do such a thing. There is a Judge who will hold Zephanyah to account, but will He not also judge you?"

And so Father relented, but I could tell he did so against his will. I received no praise from him when I read, although I knew I read capably and my skill reflected well upon him as my father; in fact, I brought honor to our whole family. But he didn't see it that way, and I sensed his disappointment in me— disappointment that I hadn't seen the need, myself, to support Yisu by spitting on Rabbi Zephanyah's kindness to me.

But Sabbath came only once a week, my *aliyah* once or twice a month; the occasional encouragement I received from Rabbi Zephanyah was not enough to make up for the fact that the year was drawing to an end and my life had become a monotony. I started to take out my frustration on my work— since Father didn't value my efforts anyway, I stopped giving him any effort and just rushed through my assignments. I knew I shouldn't, but I did it anyway. Of course, that only convinced Father that he was right and I was a rotten carpenter, but I'd gone beyond caring what Father thought of me.

Toward the end of Elul, on a day so hot that I'd broken out in a rash long before noon, we ran low on nails and Father sent me into town to get some from Amnon the blacksmith. Amnon was at his forge, the sweat pouring down his back in streams. I told him what I needed. "I don't have many of that size on hand," he said, "but I can give you a few to hold you over until I can make some more—say, tomorrow?"

"That should be okay."

He stood and mopped his brow. "Katan, do you have a few minutes to do me a favor?"

"Sure." Father had said to come straight back, but he could wait.

"Work's piling up today, what with the heat. I'll need Hezron if I'm to fill your order on time. Would you run over to the synagogue and fetch him for me?"

"Sure." The smith's youngest son, Hezron, was still in *bet-sefer*; we'd been only a year apart, though, and had formed a friendship. I knew Ronni wouldn't appreciate being pulled out of class to work at the forge, but he *was* a blacksmith, after all—I didn't particularly like patching roofs on a hot summer day, either, but some things just come with the trade.

The synagogue wasn't far from Amnon's shop. I slipped in quietly and stood to one side, waiting for Rabbi Zephanyah to notice me—I didn't want to interrupt. He looked up and smiled, waving for me to come closer. "Hezron's father needs him at home, sir," I said, and then, having delivered my message, I turned to leave.

"Wait a moment, Yaakob," the rabbi said. After dismissing Hezron, he set the other students to copying something; then he took me aside. "Yaakob, is there a reason you didn't apply to continue your studies in *bet-midrash*? I expected you to do so months ago. Were you afraid, perhaps, that you wouldn't be accepted? I assure you, such a fear is unwarranted."

"My father—" I began, but he cut me off.

"I thought as much." He frowned and shook his head, pursing his lips beneath his full beard. "I will talk to him. You need to be in school; you have a gift. Surely Yosef sees that. Why else would I call you to the *bimah* so often?"

Why indeed? Father assumed it was just to humiliate Yisu. *It couldn't possibly be because your son Katan is an accomplished reader, now could it?* I kept my thoughts to myself. The rabbi's question was purely rhetorical anyway; he wasn't expecting an answer from me, or I would have told him that it would do no good for him to talk to Father; if anything, it would make the situation worse. But he probably knew that already.

Smiling, he said, "Don't worry so, Yaakob. I am no fool; I

will take care of it. Trust me."

Trust him? To do the impossible? I didn't even trust God to do that. Still, I thanked the rabbi politely before excusing myself and heading back to Amnon's shop to collect my nails.

The following week, Father was given a small job in Sepphoris, and decided he and Yisu could handle it while Saba and I took care of whatever business came into the shop. So just the two of us were there when Rabbi Zephanyah came to visit. Had the rabbi planned it that way? Or had God decided to smile on me at last? "Yaakob, my old friend," the rabbi greeted my grandfather, "let us talk." The two of them disappeared into the house for an hour or more, and then Rabbi Zephanyah left—but he smiled at me as he walked past. *Trust me.*

The only thing Saba had to say when he came back to the shop was, "Plane that board again, Katan; it's uneven." But the rabbi's smile gave me hope. I attacked the board with renewed enthusiasm; the rest of the day seemed to fly by as I did my work—with excellence, for a change. When Father got home, Saba kicked everyone else out of the shop and closed the doors. Their voices still drifted out the window, though.

"Should you be listening?" Yisu asked. "They obviously want privacy."

It was none of his business and normally I wouldn't have paid attention to him, but if Saba was saying what I hoped he was saying, I didn't want to do anything that might anger my father. All I'd managed to overhear of their conversation so far were a few words from Saba: *You can't hold a grudge forever, Yosef.* At my brother's warning, however, I left immediately, not even waiting to hear Father's reply. As I followed Yisu to the stable to tend to the donkey, my imagination began coming up with all sorts of things Father might have said. Most of them were bad news for me.

The next hour was pure torture as I waited for Father to reach a decision, but he didn't make his announcement until after supper. He spent most of that hour frowning, but that didn't mean much—Father had been frowning at me for a year now. Finally he spoke, addressing his remarks to all of the adults in the family. "We're going to be short-handed for a while. I think you all know what that means." He looked at me pointedly. "Fewer jobs, less income." He clenched his jaw. Father had decided in my favor, but once again, the decision was not what he wanted, and he resented me for it. *But I didn't say anything! I didn't ask you for this, not once!* Even so, he would blame me for this decision because I wanted it—how I wanted it!—and he knew that. "Katan is going back to school, starting tomorrow afternoon."

I'd won. Without striking a single blow, I'd won a war I hadn't even planned on fighting. I was getting what I wanted. Father had finally surrendered. Except...I didn't want his surrender; I wanted him to be on my side. I wanted him to let me go to school because *he* thought I should be there, because *he* thought I was good enough—not because he'd been pressured into it. But looking at his face, I knew: in winning *this* war, I'd lost the only war I really cared about.

22

YISU

Tammuz 3772
(Two Years Later)

The Tammuz sun was hot even though it was still low in the eastern sky. Sweat trickled down my forehead and into my eyes, and I blinked several times to clear them. Ordinarily I would have wiped them on my sleeve, but both of my arms were already working as hard as they could to steady the load that I bore across my shoulders. To my left and behind me, Roman legionaries marched, their only burden the armor and weapons they carried. I carried everything else.

I didn't know why this particular unit was marching south this morning. I didn't really care. All I knew is that they had seen me and pressed me into service. One—a man I'd never seen before, a recent transfer to this unit—had questioned the need. *We aren't even carrying full kits*, he'd said in Greek. *Leave the boy alone.*

Tyro! another had laughed. *Don't you know who this is? This is Onarion.*

Yes, said a third. *He'll feel slighted if we don't bring him along.*

They'd all laughed at that.

The leader of the unit, a man who'd made it plain over the past year that he delighted in testing me to my limits, had collected all of the water skins his men were carrying—eight in all, each holding about a gallon. Lashing his javelins together end over end to form a yoke, he'd hung the skins on it four to a side, added some other items the men were toting, and then laid the whole thing across my back.

I didn't mind the weight; I didn't mind the march; I didn't even mind the insults. What frustrated me the most was the fact that they'd interrupted me at my prayers. It had become my custom to slip away from home early in the morning to spend some time alone with my Father, and a few months ago I'd found an isolated myrtle grove southwest of my home where I could spend that time undisturbed. Today, however, this patrol had crossed my path while I was on my way to the grove. For the first time in years, I bent under a Roman pack without a smile on my face, without a song on my lips. I seriously considered dropping the load at the end of the mile.

But I didn't.

I could still remember clearly the first Roman pack I'd ever been forced to carry—I'd been ten years old, and Yosef had protested my conscription, but I'd taken the pack anyway though it weighed almost as much as I did. I hadn't carried it far; Abba had instructed me to lag behind as if the pack was too great a burden, which indeed it was. In the end, the Romans had laid it on him along with the two he already bore. The memory of Abba bent under the weight of three Roman packs, staggering ahead step by step to the end of the mile while they laughed at him—this memory gave me the strength I needed to endure the labor that had become the local garrison's favorite game.

Onarion they called me behind my back and to my face, not knowing that I understood every word of their Greek. (At least it was a step up from *moros*. Better a young jackass than an idiot.) In its own way the name was fitting, since I had indeed become their beast of burden. It had all started that day three years ago when I'd carried a Roman pack more than two miles so as to spare Nahum from conscription, the day I'd sung and danced my way clear to the gates of Nazareth under the load. My oblivion had amused the Romans; my seeming ignorance of the law that limited my service to one mile caused them first to question my intelligence and then to test it. Soon I became the subject of wagers—*five sesterci says he'll go two miles—ten says he'll carry a double load*—until my compliance became such a sure thing that there were no takers. I don't remember which of them first called me Onarion, but the name caught on quickly. After that, I could scarcely walk from one end of town to the other without being waylaid. As for my daily trips to Sepphoris…there were times when I was convinced that the legionaries were sent on mock errands for the sole purpose of finding me along the way and conscripting me. Surely they had never carried their gear back and forth between the two towns so often in the past.

They didn't do it when Yosef was with me. That would have spoiled their fun.

There was no one here to spoil their fun now, though. I was on my own. Once again I thought about setting the load down after the thousandth pace. I was tired of this game, tired of being treated like an animal, tired of carrying everyone else's burdens. *You deserve better than this, son of David,* the wind whispered in the treetops. Its voice sounded eerily familiar, and with a shudder I rejected its opinion. Instead, I prayed silently as I marched alongside the legionaries. *Father, You allowed the Patriarch Yosef to be sold into slavery for Your good purposes. Help me understand the reason for this burden in my life. Help me be faithful to You and to—*

My prayers were again interrupted, but this time by a shout of pain and surprise as the man beside me fell to the ground with an arrow shaft lodged in his throat. As I stood there in shock, gaping, the weight on my back suddenly doubled as if someone had leapt on top of me to shield me from the flying arrows. I collapsed beneath the added weight, and the water skins scattered all about me, several bursting as they struck the rocky ground. Fortunately the spot where I landed was soft; except for getting the wind knocked out of me, I was uninjured. Not so for the Roman soldiers, who were falling on all sides under the ferocity of the Zealot ambush. "Adonai—!" Horror wrapped its claws around my throat and cut off my prayer. I knew this wouldn't touch me, couldn't touch me. *A thousand may fall at your side, ten thousand at your right hand, but it won't come near you.* But the slaughter that surrounded me was terrifying, proof that the world had gone very, very wrong— that men could not be trusted, could never be trusted, not if they could do such things to one another. Reading about war was not the same as seeing it. Hearing it. Smelling it.

Hear my cry, Father, listen to my prayer. From the end of the earth, with fainting heart, I call out to You. Set me down on a rock far above where I am now. For You have been a refuge for me, a tower of strength in the face of the foe... Unable to flee, I hid myself in the psalm.

In a matter of minutes, the fighting was over. The dirt where I lay was slick with blood.

I tried to rise, to crawl away, to roll over, but the weight on my back was like a giant fist pressing me to the ground. And then, as quickly as it had come, the weight was lifted and I was able to move again. I rolled over to thank the man who had undoubtedly saved my life—but there was no one there. Before I had time to process that thought, however, one of the Zealots saw me move. Immediately he was on me, sword drawn and pointed at my chest. With a mixture of relief and dismay, I recognized him.

"Shimon," I said.

"Onarion," he sneered, and spat on me.

I don't know what sort of greeting I'd expected from him; certainly not this one. I blinked in shock but said nothing.

He turned and shouted at the other Zealots, "I thought I said no one!" His anger was palpable. "Idiots," he seethed, turning his attention back toward me. "Give me one reason I should let you live."

What had become of my friend?

"Shimon," I whispered.

"Give me one reason!" he repeated, pressing the point of his sword against my chest.

My soul waits in silence for God alone; my salvation comes from Him. There was only one good reason for Shimon to put his weapon down: God's reason. "'You shall not murder,'" I said quietly, reminding him of what he already knew, the reason he had hesitated. Let him call this massacre an act of war if he was determined to deceive himself; I was unarmed, unresisting, and he would be without excuse if he cut me down in cold blood.

"I don't have time for this." Again he spat, but at the ground. "I don't have time to deal with *you*." Abruptly he sheathed his sword. "Give me your hands." I sat up, holding my hands toward him. Roughly he grabbed them, pulled them behind me, and bound them tightly together. Then he threw a cloth over my head and tied another rope around my neck, tightly enough to hold the blindfold securely in place but not so tightly as to choke me. "Don't move," he warned. "Don't call out. If you value your life, you'll do exactly as I say, do you hear me?"

"Yes."

"Good." He gave me a rough shove, with his foot from the feel of it, and then I heard him moving among his men, encouraging them to hurry. His men. Shimon was obviously the leader of this band, despite his youth. He was only two years older than I—he was only eighteen! He had become so hard. How many men had this walking tomb swallowed?

The fabric that pressed against my face was damp and had a sharp, metallic odor that took me a moment to recognize: blood. I shuddered as I realized that Shimon had pulled this cloth off one of the men he'd just killed. *Whoever sheds the blood of man, by man shall his blood be shed, for in the image of God has God made man.* The scripture I'd memorized as a child echoed again and again in my mind. *In the image of God has God made man. In the image of God has God made man.* How far from that image man had fallen! *Oh my Father, have mercy on these men.* I wasn't even sure which men I was praying for, the Romans or the Zealots who'd slain them. None of these men were innocent of bloodshed. All of them needed mercy. All of them. *In the image of God has God made man.* All of them. *Have mercy.*

While I was still praying, Shimon returned and barked an order to his men. "Get him on his feet and let's get out of here." Unsympathetic hands grabbed my arms on either side and yanked me upright, and then I was half-led, half-dragged off the road and through the woods, stumbling blind over rocks and roots and loose soil at a breakneck pace that went on and on and on for half an hour or more. My guides were impatient, cursing me each time I nearly fell, bruising my arms with their vise-like grip, shaking me like a wayward cur.

Finally we slowed to a walk. One of the men holding me let go; the other shoved my head down so I had to stoop, and pushed me before him through a narrow, rocky passageway that brushed my shoulders on both sides. The coolness of the air and the muted echoes told me that we had entered a large cave. I felt a tugging at my neck as the rope securing my blindfold was loosened, and then the cloth was pulled away and I could see again. Shimon was seated on a large rock like a judge in court, and I stood before him with my hands bound behind me. All along the walls of the cave, rough-looking men surrounded us, some sitting, some standing, all watching intently to see what Shimon would decide.

"Our rule is simple," he said, getting right to the point. "You've seen too much. Either you join us now, take our oath, or you rejoin the Romans you were helping. Choose. Now."

"You know me, Shimon."

He nodded with a scornful expression, but at least he didn't spit on me again.

"Then you know I can't take your oath. You knew that when you spared me." My honesty was risky under the circumstances—with all of his men watching, Shimon would probably feel the need to administer "justice" quickly and brutally. He wouldn't want to pause for a debate. Nevertheless, I felt safe. My Father had plans for me, and I was sure those plans didn't include my death here and now at Shimon's hand. So with confidence I added, "We're on the same side, you know."

"You'll never convince me of that."

"Will you let me try?"

He hesitated, but only for a second. "You're a collaborator, just like your father. Everyone knows it." His hesitation spoke volumes. He was inclined to hear me out, to spare my life, but he didn't want to appear weak or indecisive.

"So bring out the witnesses against me." The Zealots had a twisted idea of right and wrong, but they professed to honor God's commandments. I'd counted on that fact earlier when I'd reminded Shimon that my death would have been murder; I counted on it now to give him an excuse to spare me in spite of their "rule." He didn't have any witnesses; we both knew it. All he had was anger. *Please, Father, let me speak to him alone. It's the only way he'll hear me.*

Shimon stood up and crossed the space between us, looking down a few inches to meet my eyes as he spoke. "One last chance, Onarion. Come aside with me. Maybe I can talk some sense into you." He grabbed my arm and headed toward the mouth of the cave.

"What are you doing, Shimon?" one of the men protested.

"Hold your peace, Yoash," he snapped back. "This jackass has some skills we could use. I don't want to throw him away just yet." He spoke with authority, and Yoash backed down.

Instead of leading me outside as I expected, Shimon turned down a side passage that led into a dark, cramped space just large enough for the two of us. A pallet filled half of the room, and there was a bundle at the foot of it: clothing and a few other items. Lighting a small lamp, Shimon sat down on the pallet and looked up at me. "All right, Yisu. Tell me. Convince me."

Over the years, I had learned a lot from Rabbi Ezra, especially when it came to the art of asking questions. *Tell me.* It was a challenge, not a request. Nothing I told him would convince him to let me go, I knew this; no, he would have to convince himself. "Why did you call me a collaborator?" I asked.

"Onarion asks this?" He laughed. "You're famous, Yisu. Maybe the Romans think you're stupid, but I know better. You carry their loads with a smile on your face, you carry two or three miles when only one is required, you endure their mocking and their insults without so much as a frown…you encourage them in their oppression, and yet you dare to ask why I call you a collaborator?"

"Yes."

"Are you trying to convince me that your service is an act of rebellion?"

"No, of course not."

"Then you admit to helping them."

"Helping them? Who benefits from my service?"

"The Romans." He sounded incredulous. "Maybe you really are stupid."

"Are you sure it's the Romans who benefit most? How so?"

"They don't have to carry their gear." It sounded lame and he knew it, but I wanted to be sure he really heard himself.

"And if I carried their gear one mile with a frown, how would that hurt them?"

He pursed his lips and flared his nostrils, huffing with frustration. "Well, at least they'd know that their conscriptions are resented."

"Are they unaware of that?"

"Stop it!" he hissed.

I resisted the temptation to smile. This was serious. "Do you have any idea what you've accomplished today, Shimon?" I asked instead. "Have you considered the effects your war will have on the people of Nazareth? Whom have *you* helped today?"

"There will be eight fewer Romans to oppress the people of Nazareth tomorrow."

"And next week?"

He didn't answer.

"What will Rome do about those eight men?" I pressed. "How many will be sent to replace them? Eight? Or eighty?" Shimon still said nothing, but I could see that he was listening. "And with what attitude will they arrive? What will be on their hearts? Mercy? Or revenge?" I'd asked enough questions. It was time to open my heart to Shimon.

"*Onarion* they call me, and Onarion I am. So what of it? Before I became Onarion, all the men of Nazareth were Onarion. Now the Romans pick on me. Just me. I'm the butt of their scorn, the object of their ridicule, but once they've taken out their resentment on me—you do know, don't you, how much they resent being posted here?—once they've taken it out on me, their mood is a little brighter. And whom does that help? Would you rather face a Roman in a foul mood or a pleasant one?

"Before I became Onarion, all the men of Nazareth were Onarion. Now I carry two or three miles instead of one; I bear the burden for two or three of my neighbors so they won't have to. And whom does that help? The Roman gear would be carried the same distance no matter who bore it, but old Nahum gets to work his fields in peace for a change. Would you rather I set the load at his doorstep every day? Would he thank me for that? Would he thank you?

"Before I became Onarion, all the men of Nazareth were Onarion. Now they are men. Judge for yourself if that makes me a Roman collaborator."

He stared at me without saying a word. His face had gone pale.

"Let me go home, Shimon. Let me be Onarion. Let me help my people."

"You've seen—"

"I told you once before, long ago, that I wouldn't turn you in. I haven't changed. I don't agree with what you're doing here—you're bringing destruction on yourself and on everyone you're trying to help—but I won't betray your trust." I knelt in the dirt beside his pallet and looked into his eyes. "Let me go home, Shimon."

Part Four

Love

You have stolen my heart, my sister,
my bride; you have stolen my heart
with one glance of your eyes,
with one jewel of your necklace.

—Song of Songs 4:9 (NIV)

23

KATAN

Tishri 3773
(The Turn of the Year)

"Where have you been?" Father glared at me suspiciously. Only Yisu was allowed to be late to work. I glanced quickly around the shop, but my brother hadn't arrived yet...of course. Father was always sharper with me when Yisu was late, as if it were my fault that we were short-handed. Saba just looked up from his bench, shook his head at me, and went back to work.

"I'm sorry, sir. I was on my way, but Chava's cart threw the axle again. I had to get a pin from Amnon and—"

"All right, all right," Father said. "Just get back to those boards you were joining." I'd been pretty sure he wouldn't question my story—old Chava always had something that needed repairs, and she would talk your ear off once she got hold of you, but Father insisted that we show the widow every courtesy, so she made for a great excuse whenever I needed one. Not that I'd lied to Father—Chava *had* stopped me on my way home, but the repair to her cart had taken just a few minutes of my time. I'd spent most of the hour at the blacksmith's shop talking with Hezron, who was now working full-time at the forge. Although, to be completely truthful, my visit with Hezron had just been an excuse to see Rivkah.

Rivkah bat Amnon was beautiful.

Oh, sure, she was only twelve, but I was only fifteen, so that wasn't really a problem. By the time I was old enough for marriage, she would be, too. I hadn't mentioned her to Father yet—the last thing I needed was for him to think I was arranging my own marriage behind his back—but I knew he'd approve of a match with Rivkah...as long as the idea was his own. There was time enough to work that out. For now, I was content to hang around Amnon's shop in hope of getting an occasional glimpse of Amnon's daughter. Not only had I seen her today, but she'd even spoken a few words to me. *L'shanah tovah, Katan.* Maybe it *would* be a good year.

With my mind comfortably distracted by thoughts of Rivkah, I settled down in one corner of the shop and got to work evening up the joint that ran down the center of my panel. Yisu walked in a few minutes later. No one asked where *he'd* been all this time, even though he should have gotten back from Sepphoris hours ago. Every morning, my brother got up with the cockcrow and disappeared off to who-knows-where for an hour or two, showing up at the house for a bite of breakfast before heading off to Sepphoris for his studies. He returned to Nazareth—usually—around the seventh hour, just as we were finishing dinner and I was heading out the door for *bet-midrash.* The last few weeks, however, he'd been arriving late; this was the third time I'd gotten home before him.

It aggravated me no end that Yisu could come and go as he pleased without consequence, while I was held accountable for every minute of my day. Although my house arrest had ended more than two years ago, and although I'd gotten in no more trouble, Father still treated me like a criminal most of the time. That's why I had to sneak around just to get a few minutes with one of my friends. Anyone else could have just asked, *Father, may I please go visit with Hezron after my work is done?* but friendship was one of the privileges that Father had taken away from me forty-three months ago. Forty-three months. (Yes, I was keeping count.) Except for two hours each afternoon, when I was allowed to go into town for *bet-midrash,* I was expected to be at home or at work. Yisu, on the other hand...

I'd assumed Yisu's freedom would end after the night last summer when he didn't come home at all—the night he'd spent, by his own admission, with Shimon the Zealot. Oh, the look on Father's face when Yisu had dragged in, covered in blood, just before dawn! We'd spent all day looking for him; he hadn't joined us for breakfast, hadn't shown up for his lessons with Ezra, hadn't come to work...no one had seen him anywhere. By suppertime, both of my parents were frantic with worry, and Father had the neighbors out searching the roads, the fields, looking everywhere until long after it got too dark to see, but with no success. We'd stayed up all night, everyone except for the youngest children, waiting and praying. And then the door had opened, and Yisu was standing there with dried blood on his face, in his hair, all over his clothes—and not a scratch on him.

I knew what that meant.

So did Father. That's why he burned Yisu's clothes, to get rid of the evidence. My brother didn't even try to deny that he'd been with the Zealots, though he said he'd been their prisoner and not their accomplice. Of course Father believed him. Even so, I'd expected Yisu to suffer *some* consequence for his involvement with Shimon—but no. If anything, my brother had been given even more freedom than before. Father never even asked where he'd been anymore, no matter how late Yisu came home.

So now, even though he was three hours later than he should have been, nothing was said, although I did get a tiny bit of satisfaction when Saba gave Yisu the same disapproving look he'd given me. One person, at least, was treating us equally. My brother offered neither an explanation nor an apology as he made his way to the bench we were sharing and picked up a stylus. "Are you almost finished with that one?" he asked, gesturing at the panel I was sanding.

"Almost."

He pulled out his pattern and some chalk. "It looks good, Katan. I like the way you matched the grain there."

"Thanks." My brother, ironically, was the only person I could count on for a compliment around here. I gave the joint one more pass with the sandstone and then handed it to Yisu, who began transferring the pattern to it while I started work on the fourth, and last, panel. We worked side-by-side in silence after that. Yisu tapped away with his chisel, following the lines of the vinework he'd chalked out, carving his design into the panel. I glued and sanded, getting the next piece of wood ready for my brother's creative genius—how *did* Solomon manage to build the Temple without Yisu there to help him?—and seething over the fact that I was never allowed to finish a piece like this myself.

I'd already made the mistake of asking Father if I could build this cabinet on my own. *Maybe if you had devoted yourself to learning your trade over the past two years instead of wasting half of every day with Zephanyah, you'd have the necessary skill,* he'd replied. Half of every day? Since when was two hours half a day? It was Yisu who spent half—more than half!—of every day in his studies, but *he* was trusted with the difficult jobs. I'd managed to keep the protest off my lips, but Father had seen it in my eyes. *Don't give me that look, Katan.*

But you're not being fair! I'd shouted, and then had winced in expectation of the slap that I'd surely earned with my disrespect. I didn't care; finally saying those five words that had been burning in my gut for so many years was worth any number of slaps. And besides, what else could Father do to me? He'd already taken away all of my privileges.

You want fair? Instead of slapping me, he'd stepped back, folded his arms across his chest, and smiled. *One more insolent word from you, Katan, and you'll graduate from* bet-midrash *tomorrow instead of next year. That would be fair. And then you can do all the wood-carving your soul desires.* The threat— so calmly delivered—had silenced me more thoroughly than any slap could have. *No? You don't want that?*

No, sir. I'm sorry for my outburst, sir.

Then get to work.

"Katan, get back to work. Stop daydreaming," Father snapped from across the room.

"Yes, sir." I turned my attention back to the panel in front of me, trying to force myself to care about the evenness of the joint, but the memory of Father's threat still had me shaken. *Next year.* Even if I behaved myself perfectly, this was my last year of school. If leaving *bet-sefer* had been hard, leaving *bet-midrash* was going to be impossible. It wasn't just that school was the only place I felt successful; it wasn't just that Rabbi was the only adult who encouraged me; it wasn't even that *bet-midrash* was my only chance to get out from under my father's thumb each day. The truth was, I had come to love my studies. I finally understood why Yisu had been so crushed when he'd lost access to the books: they contained riches far beyond my puny life in Nazareth, challenged me to reach higher, hinted at wonders I'd never even dreamed of. Wood and stone—of what value were they, cold lifeless things? So what if I learned how to build a house—wouldn't it fall down eventually? I wanted to build something important, something that would last forever—not a plow, or a bench, or even an ornate cabinet. The shacks of Nazareth, the mansions of Sepphoris, the palaces of Herod, the Temple itself—how long would any of them stand? Fifty years, a hundred, a thousand? *But the Word of our God stands forever,* the prophet Isaiah had written.

One more year, just one more year to study God's Word.

L'shanah tovah, Katan, Rivkah had said.

A good year. *Please, Lord God, make it a good one—for a change.* I bent over the wooden panel in front of me, inspecting my work with a critical eye, and then picked up the sandstone once more. God would write in His book for me this year whatever He wanted, as always, but—*this* year—I'd do my part to merit His favor.

For a change.

24

YISU

27 Kislev 3773
(The Feast of Dedication)

Leah was giggling musically. Captivated by the joyous sound, I stopped outside the door smiling. Truly I didn't mean to eavesdrop, no more than I meant to eavesdrop on the birds' morning songs or the breeze in the treetops or the splash of autumn rains. Music, all music. I'd enjoyed this particular song for four years, and I never tired of it.

"How much longer, Father? Until I'm fourteen?"

"No! Never at fourteen. Your mother was fourteen—"

"—and look where that got her!" Leah laughed again. Then she departed from the script, her voice gentle and warm. "Look where that got her. Right by the side of the best, most caring man in all of Judaea. May I be half as blessed!"

"Not if I can help it. You will be doubly blessed, at the least." There was something in his voice that hinted of a deeper meaning behind his words. Leah heard it too, or perhaps she read it in his expression.

"What are you saying, Father?" Her voice was curious, and hopeful. "Do you—do you have someone in mind?"

Now I *was* eavesdropping. The conversation had moved beyond the game into matters of a much more personal nature. Before they could say anything more, I reached out and knocked loudly on the door. "It's Yeshua," I called. Leah pulled the door open.

"Good morning, Yeshua," she said, glancing down modestly. She quickly stepped aside to let me enter, but not before I'd noticed a blush on her cheek. She knew, then, that I'd been close enough to overhear the end of their conversation. I bit my lip.

"Late again, I see."

I turned to face Rabbi Ezra, who was seated at his desk with a scroll open before him. There was no anger in his tone; he knew as well as I that it had become nearly impossible for me to make the trip to Sepphoris unencumbered. "How bad was it this time?"

"It gets easier every day, Rabbi." This was true, but only because I was growing stronger.

"Why do you tolerate it, Yeshua?" he asked. "Even under the terms of the Occupation, we have some rights. This harassment goes above and beyond their authority." Yosef would have said the same, had he known the extent of the Romans' game, the humiliations they always heaped upon "Onarion" along with their gear, the way they had deliberately targeted me for their attentions. But I had my reasons for cooperating, though they were difficult to explain. Last summer I had been forced to put those reasons into words as I'd argued with Shimon for my very life. He'd released me, but grudgingly, nor had my argument been persuasive enough to convince him to follow my example or even to lay down his sword. Though I'd survived, I still counted that day as a loss rather than a victory, but the war was hardly over yet. Since our first meeting, I'd thought of Shimon as my brother, and of myself as his keeper, and I refused—refused!—to hand my brother over to the enemy. In this war, surrender was simply not an option.

"Yeshua?" Rabbi Ezra had asked a question and was still waiting for my answer.

Rousing myself from the memory of that horrible day, I smiled at my teacher, considering my words carefully. "I don't mind it much, Rabbi, truly. It's just part of life, and not nearly as bad as a toothache. As for whether they're overstepping their authority, well, it doesn't really matter to me. They wouldn't have any authority at all unless God had given it to them, isn't it so?" He nodded thoughtfully. "God is using this to make me stronger. They mean it for evil, but—"

"God will use it for good," Leah piped in quickly. Though she was a girl, she knew as much Torah as any *bar mitzvah*. Her father had seen to that. Leah and I had shared lessons so often that we frequently finished each other's sentences—at least, where scripture was concerned. I laughed with her as she congratulated herself for her quickness. It wasn't often she beat me to the finish.

"All right, all right," Rabbi Ezra interrupted. "Leah, get back to your mother and help her with whatever it is she needs help with. Yeshua, get over here and help me copy this book; you know I need your eyes today."

"Yes, Rabbi."

"Yes, Abba." Leah smiled at me one more time before swishing out of the room.

I hadn't noticed before how tall she was getting, or how gracefully she moved. "Leah's growing up," I remarked. "She's almost as old as Rachel, isn't she?" My sister, who had turned fourteen last spring, was spending all of her time these days getting ready for her wedding. It had been nearly a year since her betrothal to Kaleb bar Netzer; Katan and I were helping him get a house ready for her, and it was close to completion. As soon as Netzer pronounced it fit, Kaleb would show up on our doorstep to claim his bride. It was a good match. Netzer's land was fruitful and Kaleb was a hard worker, so Rachel would never go hungry. More importantly, Kaleb feared God and respected his parents; he would be a kind and loving husband as well as a good father.

I bent to the task at hand and focused my attention on the book we were copying, the writings of the prophet Hosea. Rabbi Ezra didn't own this one, but he wanted a copy for his library, so he had borrowed the scroll from one of the other synagogues in town and the two of us were carefully duplicating every word recorded on the ancient parchment. It was painstaking work, and the rabbi didn't trust his eyesight where small lettering needed to be deciphered, so it was my task first to read each passage aloud to him and then to go back over it one letter at a time. "I will betroth you to me forever; I will betroth you in righteousness and justice, in love and compassion. I will betroth you in faithfulness, and you will acknowledge Adonai," I read, smiling to myself at how closely the passage paralleled what I'd just been thinking. Then I began to call out each letter, pausing while Rabbi Ezra repeated it back to me, wrote it down, and then repeated it once again before moving on to the next letter. We stopped at the end of the passage so that the rabbi could wash his hands and recite a blessing before writing the name of God. Then I counted the letters in both the copy and the original to be sure we hadn't omitted or duplicated any. Once Rabbi Ezra was satisfied that we'd been faithful to preserve the accuracy of the scroll, we started the process all over again with the next passage: "In that day I will respond, declares Adonai..." We'd been at this three days already, and were less than halfway through the book. Most students would be tired and bored with the assignment. I was in heaven.

At dinnertime, the rabbi called for a break. "Tomorrow," he said simply. I rose and made my way to the door. "Aren't you staying to eat with us?"

"No, Rabbi, Yosef needs me home early today."

"A large job?"

"Yes, but only for today."

"Ask him if he will come to dine with us tomorrow. I'd like to speak with him."

"Yes, Rabbi." Although my curiosity was roused, I minded my own business and said no more. If Rabbi Ezra wanted me to know the subject of their discussion, he'd tell me without being asked. He didn't, so I made my farewells and left.

The Romans found me halfway to Nazareth.

"Yo, Onarion!"

I sighed, and smiled as they approached.

25

KATAN

27 Kislev 3773
(The Feast of Dedication)

I waited nearly a week for the right time to approach my father. The day had gone well; I'd done nothing to displease him; he'd finally been paid by a customer who had been making excuses for three months; and Mother was smiling at him in a way that always brought a grin to his face. He ran a hand up her leg when he thought no one was watching; she was pouring his wine at the time, and she giggled and almost spilled it on him. I pretended not to notice. His mood would never get better than this—I'd ask him tonight, or never. And so I waited patiently until after the meal had been eaten, until after the Hanukkah lights had been kindled and the blessings had been spoken and the scriptures had been read and the songs had been sung, waited until all of my younger siblings had been sent to bed. Only after all of these things had been taken care of did I approach my father with the request he was sure to refuse.

"Abba, I have a favor to ask."

He glanced up at me, his expression neutral. At least he wasn't scowling.

"It's important to me, sir. It would be good for the family, too." That last was a mistake, I knew it as soon as the words left my lips. Father's brows drew closer together, not quite in a frown, but warning that one might be coming along soon. Who was I, to tell him what was good for the family? I was the last person to advise him; my opinions had less value than the dust on the floor of the shop. It had been that way for four years.

I almost backed down then. I probably should have. But I needed to give the rabbi an answer soon. I couldn't afford to wait any longer. Drawing in a deep breath to steady myself, I said, "Rabbi Zephanyah has asked me to be his *talmid*." Yisu looked up from his reading, eyes wide and warning. I ignored him. "I'd like to accept. May I have your permission, Father?"

"Absolutely not." He hadn't taken even a moment to consider.

"Please, sir, may I ask why not?" This was bold, all things considered, but I just couldn't give up so easily. I'd worked too hard for too long to just give up without even trying. "You let Yisu—"

"You aren't Yisu," he cut me off. "The one has nothing to do with the other."

"All right, then, forget Yisu." I was already in trouble; I might as well say my peace. "Let me do this for my own sake, because I've earned the honor. I've studied hard, and I'm a good student. Do you know how many people have asked Rabbi if they could sit at his feet? But *he* came to *me*, Father. In spite of everything—"

"That's enough, Yaakob!" Father shouted, rising to his feet. "It's precisely *because* of those things that I said no! How convenient for Zephanyah to overlook them—they were of his making, all of them! I will not have *my* son emulating that man!" Every eye in the room was now focused on us. "Bad enough you've had to sit under his teaching all these years. I let you go to his *bet-midrash*—against my better judgment. But *talmid*? Serving him? Following him? Becoming like him? No! Never! Get the thought out of your mind. Don't ever mention it to me again, do you hear me?"

I hung my head to hide the tears of anger and frustration that suddenly filled my eyes. "Yes, sir," I whispered, not trusting my voice to hold steady. "I hear you. I won't ask again." Father had laid down the law, as firmly as if he'd carved it in granite. I'd broken such a decree once; I'd be damned if I'd make that mistake again. One year chained to my bed was enough. Though I hated to admit it, I'd earned my house arrest and the beatings that had preceded it; by my own free will I'd violated Father's clear command and had come close to losing my life as a result. But this...this was different. This time I wasn't being punished for something I'd done, but for something *Father* had done. I didn't really think he'd chain me for nagging him about becoming Zephanyah's disciple, but I was pretty sure a stiff beating was waiting for me if I brought

the subject up again—that and months (or possibly years) more
of being treated like a leper. It wasn't fair, but there was nothing
I could do about it.

Yisu spoke up. "Abba?"

"What is it, Yisu?"

"Zephanyah isn't the only teacher available, sir. Katan *is* a
good student, and I'm sure that if you asked Rabbi Ezra—"

"No!" I interrupted. *Could it get any worse than that?* The
last thing I wanted was to study with *Yisu's* teacher. I'd rather
spend another year in chains. Yisu looked up in surprise. My
feelings must have been written all over my face, because he
shut right up. *That* suggestion was never made again. "Just
forget the whole thing! I'm done with studies."

"Good," Father said. "Then you can focus on your trade.
Starting tomorrow."

"Tomorrow? But—" I cut myself off, knowing that if I said
what was truly on my heart in that moment, Father might kill
me. *You son of a bitch! That's not what I meant and you know
it!* I still had four months until my sixteenth birthday, four more
months of school! How could he just take them away from me
like that? Simply because I'd dared to ask...?

It's not fair.

I looked over at Saba Yaakob, silently begging him to
intervene as he had in the past; he met my eyes but simply
shook his head. Saba Yoachim, too, had chosen to stay out of
this quarrel, and since I'd already made it plain that I didn't
want Yisu's help, he just bit his lip and looked back down at his
book. I was on my own.

It's not fair. No, it wasn't fair, but it was all I was going to
get. So much for *l'shanah tovah.* God didn't want me to become
a scholar, a rabbi, a scribe...all He had for me was wood and
stone. Fine, then. Wood and stone it would be. No more
"wasting half my day" like Yisu—I'd show them all which son
was the better craftsman. "Why wait until tomorrow?" I spat.
Let them eat their insults. I slammed out of the house and
stomped across the yard, grabbing up an axe when I reached the
stock pile. My first few dozen strokes were wild, fueled by
blind rage, maiming the logs rather than shaping them; but soon
I settled into a numb, unthinking rhythm—hot as the coals in a
blacksmith's furnace, hot with smoldering anger, but no longer

flaming out of control. Log after log I split along the grain, tearing them in two, ripping them in half as my dreams had been torn, as my hopes had been ripped. By midnight, I had transformed more than half of the raw stock to usable lumber.

26

Yisu

28 Kislev 3773
(The Feast of Dedication)

My brother's axe sang me to sleep and pounded through my dreams all night. With difficulty I roused myself at cockcrow, my breath fogging in the pre-dawn chill; Katan snored beside me, forming clouds of his own, so exhausted by his labors that he didn't even stir when I stumbled over him. For the briefest moment I was tempted to crawl back under the warm covers, but that would have meant sacrificing my hour in the myrtle grove, and no amount of sleep was worth losing even one minute of my morning prayer time.

Yosef had tried to take it away from me following my run-in with the Zealots. *It's just too dangerous, Yisu.* Arriving home late that night, I had told him the whole story: how I'd been conscripted on my way to the grove, how the Zealots had set up an ambush on the road southwest of Nazareth, how they'd held me captive. Yosef's immediate response had been to forbid my early morning excursions.

Abba, please. I need to pray! Don't take this from me.

You can pray anywhere, Yisu. I don't want you going off by yourself anymore.

I can pray some *prayers anywhere, but others are just too personal, Abba. Taking this time away from me—it would be like someone forbidding you to spend time alone with Mother.*

It's hardly the same.

For me, it is.

You put yourself in harm's way. You could have—you could have been killed.

I was never in any danger.

You were caught in the middle of a battle! Even if you weren't a target, people get killed in battles, Yisu! Look at you!

You're covered in blood! And you expect me to believe you
were never in any danger?
"No harm will befall you, for He will command His angels
concerning you, to guard you in all your ways. They will lift
you up—"
It's just a psalm, Yisu!
No, sir, with all respect, it's not just *a psalm; it's a promise.*
My *Father* did *send angels to protect me. When the arrows*
started flying, they knocked me down and caught me and held
me and kept me safe. Safe, Abba.

In the end, he'd relented, but reluctantly. My time in the
grove was his gift to me, and I cherished it all the more because
I knew what it cost him. I took extra care to evade southbound
troops, since the road to Caesarea saw the most Zealot activity;
for the rest of the year I managed to avoid conscription on my
way to the grove, and though twice I was pressed into service
on my way home, those units were headed into Nazareth along
well-traveled roads, and there were no further incidents.

This morning I actually made it all the way from the grove
to Sepphoris without being stopped. I could hardly believe the
miracle. "Thank You, Father!" I sang as I approached Rabbi
Ezra's gate, smiling at myself, at my delight in the smallest
thing, that I had walked four miles without harassment. *Such a*
simple thing, but one I never used to appreciate. I wonder how
many other blessings I take for granted each day. One blessing
I did not take for granted and never would: the hours each
morning I spent with my teacher in study of my Father's word. I
brushed my fingers lightly across the *mezuzah* on Rabbi Ezra's
door, whispering the words that were written there and
breathing a prayer of thanks as I kissed my fingertips. Then, as
was my custom, I called out, "It's Yeshua!" and let myself into
the house.

"Shalom, Yeshua," Talyah greeted me in the workroom,
her hands already coated with flour as she made ready to knead
the dough for the day's bread. "My, but you're early today!"
She tipped her head toward the back door as she added, "He's in
the synagogue."

The synagogue where the rabbi and I usually worked was
around the corner from his house, but the two buildings shared
a courtyard and it was quickest to cut across. Eager to get back

to Hosea, I headed outside with a little too much enthusiasm and bumped into Leah as I was crossing the threshold, causing her to spill some of the milk from the bowl she carried. "Oh!" she cried in surprise.

"Oh, Leah, I'm sorry!"

She mumbled something and looked down at her feet, which were splattered with milk. Hastily I grabbed a towel from the bench where Talyah had left it, got down on my knees, and began to wipe Leah's feet.

"Yeshua!" she protested, and pulled back. I looked up at her; she was blushing as pink as the morning's sunrise. Behind me, I heard Talyah laughing softly. Leah stepped around me, set the bowl down on the bench, and snatched the towel from my hand with a huff. Turning her back toward me, she bent down to dry her feet. Her loose hair fell forward, hiding her face, but the tips of her ears stuck out just enough for me to see that they were bright red. That she was embarrassed was obvious, though I wasn't sure why.

"Go to your studies, Yeshua," Talyah nudged with a knowing smile. I started to apologize once more, but she cut me off. "Go on, shoo." She laughed again as I scrambled to my feet and made my exit.

Leah had me confused. We'd known each other four years, and during that time we'd grown as close as any brother and sister, sharing meals and even lessons almost every day—yet all of a sudden, she was treating me like a stranger in the house. I shook my head as I crossed the courtyard, wondering what I'd done to make her distance herself from me. Whatever it was, it couldn't have been too bad, since Talyah thought the whole thing was so funny. One thing was obvious: I couldn't ask Leah flat out. If she blushed any harder, she'd burst. I thought about some of the things that got Rachel and Hannah upset, and decided that Leah was probably just being a girl. If I left her alone for a week or two, she'd settle down and things would get back to normal.

Rabbi Ezra was at his desk in the library, sharpening a pen. We went right to work, and I soon forgot all about Leah as I lost myself in the scriptures. "Come, let us return to Adonai," I read, and then paused and retraced the letters as Rabbi copied them down. We were now a third of the way through the book, which told the story of a man who had been commanded by God to love an unfaithful wife as a testimony to Israel of God's love for His faithless people. Reading so slowly, one phrase at a time, I'd been forced to meditate on each word in depth. "For He has torn, and He will heal us…" I recognized this passage: it was one of the "treasures" that Saba Yoachim had given me years ago. "He has struck, and He will bind our wounds…" I smiled. Indeed, He had bound my wounds. "After two days, He will revive us…"

Spelling it out one letter at a time—*yod, het, yod, nun, waw*—I went over and over it in my mind—*mem, yod, mem, yod, mem*—knowing the rest already: *On the third day He will raise us up, and we will live in His presence.* What did it mean? Why three days? And how did it apply to me? For I was certain that it did. Twice now this scripture had been given to me, and it resonated in my soul unlike any other. *On the third day He will raise us up, and we will live in His presence…*

"Yeshua."

The rabbi's voice snapped me out of my reverie.

He laughed softly. "Where did you go, son?"

In His presence… I shook myself. "I'm sorry, Rabbi. Where were we?"

"Let us know…" he prompted.

I found my place. "Let us know, let us strive to know Adonai…" *Oh, my Father, I want to know You.* "That He will come is as certain as morning…"

Abba joined us for dinner, as Rabbi Ezra had requested, bringing Katan and Yosei with him. "We're patching a roof across town," he explained. "I didn't want to leave the boys alone."

"Of course, of course. You're all more than welcome." Rabbi spoke a few words to each of my brothers, said *kiddush*, and then we all washed our hands and sat down to eat.

During the meal, my teacher leaned over and spoke softly to my father, too softly for me to hear; after the final blessings had been spoken, Abba told me to head over to our job site and take charge until he arrived. Filled with curiosity, I simply nodded. "Yes, sir." I gathered my brothers and set out.

It took us about two hours to finish the roof, and Abba still hadn't joined us. "Let's pack up," I told Katan. Yosei scrambled down the ladder and began to load our equipment into the handcart, and Katan picked up the scrap tiles that were lying about the roof while I met with the owner and collected our payment. Then, with no further excuse to hang around the job site, I grabbed the cart handles.

"Father said to wait for him here," Katan reminded me.

"Yes, I know. But he obviously isn't coming back any time soon. Come on." I pulled the cart into the street and headed back toward the rabbi's house with my brothers in tow. Upon arriving at his doorstep, I knocked and called out, "It's Yeshua," like always. Talyah opened the door, smiling warmly. "Is Yosef still here?" I asked.

"Oh, yes, he certainly is," she replied. "Come in, all of you."

Leaving the cart outside, we piled into the house. Talyah shooed Katan and Yosei into the courtyard with instructions to fetch some water from the cistern and wash up, but she pulled me aside when I moved to follow them. "No, Yeshua, your father wants to talk with you. He said to send you up the moment you arrived." She gestured toward the ceiling. Like many of the homes in Sepphoris, this one had a spacious upper room; in the summer, it served as sleeping quarters, since the windows could be opened to catch the breeze; in the winter, Rabbi used it as a study, and we often had our lessons there. I hastened outside and up the stairs, pausing on the landing and listening to the sounds of laughter and muffled conversation that seeped out through the cracks between the door and the jamb. Whatever Abba wanted to see me about, it was not bad news.

I rapped on the door but pushed it open without waiting for an invitation, since I was expected. Both my father and my teacher looked up as I entered, and I was hard-pressed to tell whose smile was the larger. A wine jug stood on the table between them, and judging from their mirth, they had nearly emptied it. "Yeshua!" Rabbi Ezra called out in a ringing voice, "Come, sit with us!" He poured what was left of the wine into a third cup and placed it in front of me as I took a seat at the table.

"You wanted to see me, Abba?" I asked, taking a sip of the

wine.

Yosef threw his arm around my shoulder, pulled me close, and kissed the top of my head. Then he shoved me away again, laughing. "Listen to your teacher," he said.

Rabbi Ezra sat up straighter and cleared his throat. (The two men were obviously intoxicated, though neither was falling-down drunk. At least it explained why Yosef hadn't returned to finish the roofing job.) "Talmid," my teacher said solemnly, "tell me: what was the first commandment?"

Did he think me back in *bet-sefer*? To humor him, I answered the question that any five-year-old could answer: "'I am Adonai Eloheinu, who brought you out of the land of Egypt where you were slaves; you shall have no other gods before Me.'"

"No, no, no, no, *no!*" he sputtered, waving his hand in the air as if to clear it. "The *first* commandment!"

I racked my brain, trying to guess what he meant by his question. *What is the first commandment?* No, wait—he hadn't said "is," but "was." What *was* the first commandment? "Ah!" I said, as understanding dawned on me. He didn't mean the first of the *mitzvot* given to Moses, but the first commandment ever given, the first recorded in Torah. *God blessed them: God said to them...* "'Be fruitful, multiply, fill the earth and subdue it,'" I recited. "That was the *first* commandment, Rabbi."

He beamed at me, and I knew I'd gotten it correct. Then Abba spoke up. "It's time you got around to fulfilling that one, Yisu."

Suddenly everything made sense: their celebration, Leah's embarrassment, Talyah's smile—everything. I felt my face growing warm as I realized for the first time where this conversation was heading.

"Ezra and I have been talking," Abba continued, "and we have reached an agreement—a most excellent and pleasing agreement, I might add—which needs only your consent. Have another sip of wine, Yisu, you look like you're about to fall over. As I was saying, your consent is required, of course." He laughed. "Can't very well do it without your consent!"

"Stop babbling, Yosef, you're drunk," Rabbi interjected. "Yeshua, we've agreed that you and Leah should wed. You're perfect for each other. We'll draw up the *ketubah* and make the betrothal official right after the Sabbath." He turned back to Abba. "Of course he'll consent, Yosef; why on earth wouldn't he consent? He's a smart boy."

I found my voice. "But I'm only seventeen."

"Better sooner than later!" my teacher proclaimed.

"You're old enough," Abba added. He met my eyes and laid one hand on my shoulder, pulling himself together and sounding more like the man who had raised me. "Yeshua, son—my beloved son—nothing would make me happier than to see you married to Leah. But if you have a good reason to feel otherwise…well, I won't pressure you."

How *did* I feel about Leah?

I loved her; that was not in question. I loved her as I loved my sisters, as I loved Talyah, as I loved Ezra. Leah was part of my life in the Promised Land, and had been for four years, ever since she was a little girl. Her sweet laughter, her quiet voice, her sharp wit, her knowledge of Torah…these things endeared her to me. It was easy to imagine the life we would live together, the home we would make, the conversations we would have. What was not so easy to imagine was holding her in my arms, kissing her as I'd seen Yosef kiss my mother. The issue here was not how I felt about Leah, but how I felt about her as my bride.

Leah would never be beautiful in the world's eyes—she looked too much like her father for that—but she was beautiful in mine. She moved with a grace that was as pleasant on the eyes as her voice was on the ears; her hair was fine and lustrous, flowing down her back when she sat still and blowing playfully around her face when she ran across the yard; she was taller than my mother but shorter than I, and I could see that we would fit perfectly together. That thought made me blush again.

Abba saw the blush and laughed. "I think he's willing, Ezra."

Of course I blushed harder at that, and both men laughed.

"Well, that's done then," Rabbi Ezra said. "I happen to know that Leah will also agree." He turned to me with a twinkle in his eye and added, "Anyone but Methuselah, hm? True, she's only fourteen—and look where that got her mother!—but I'm never going to find a better match for her, and I will rest easy at night knowing that she's with you,

Yeshua."

"You honor me, sir."

"You honor your father, son. You're a credit to him and to the way he's raised you." He and Yosef lifted their cups once more, and drank. I did the same. The warmth of the wine in my stomach relaxed me a little and pulled the blush out of my cheeks. I pictured myself with Leah, envisioned her in my arms, wondered what it would be like to kiss her...and didn't find the idea repulsive—on the contrary, I was drawn to the possibility. *You are all fair, my beloved...* The Song of Songs played itself in my heart as I took another swallow from my cup, growing accustomed to the thought of being married, of taking Leah to be my wife. I didn't realize I was smiling until Abba reached out and tousled my hair, laughing again.

"Not too fast, Yisu! You still have to build your house!" Of course I'd have plenty of help in that, but it would still take the better part of a year. I started drawing up the plans in my head: there was a good, level patch just to the north of the house Yosef had built for his bride—he'd chosen the location expecting to have many sons, so there was ample room for all of us to add on to the original structure—and it would be perfect for the building I had in mind. Light and airy, with plenty of room for Leah to dance, and a cistern like the one Abba had designed for Mother...

"He's gone again, Yosef."

Chuckling, Rabbi Ezra got to his feet, crossed to the window that overlooked the courtyard, and called out to the rest of the family to come up and join us. "And Talyah," he added, "bring up another jar of wine!"

"Save some for the wedding!" she hollered back.

She did bring the wine, though, along with a loaf of bread and some olives; more importantly, she brought Leah with her. While Rabbi Ezra announced the good news to everyone, Leah—my bride—stood quietly beside her mother with her head bowed modestly, but she glanced up at me once and the smile that graced her face lit a joy within me that blazed up like a Hanukkah lamp.

You are all fair, my beloved; there is no stain in you...

I couldn't wait to start work on our house.

27

Katan

Father had told me to focus on my trade, and so I did. Burying my plans for an advanced education, I threw myself into carpentry with a dedication I'd never shown before. Saba Yaakob noticed and began to praise my work rather than criticize it; even Father paid me the occasional compliment. By the end of the year, they were allowing me to serve as foreman on the smaller jobs. This was partly due to my skill, but I didn't deceive myself—mostly they gave me the work because Yisu was too busy to handle it.

Right after his betrothal to the rabbi's daughter—naturally, Yisu was too good for the daughter of a farmer or laborer or tradesman—my brother had started work on his house. (It was really just an addition to Father's house, since the two would continue to share not only the courtyard, stable, and workshop, but also one wall. Yisu had originally wanted to situate his house near the big juniper, but after Father had pointed out the cost of a free-standing structure, Yisu had decided to move a bit closer to home.) The construction took up all of his hours in the afternoons, and since his mornings were spent being a *talmid*, he had no time left to help Father with the business.

It aggravated me, that he would inherit the double share of a business that I'd put a double share of work into, but there was nothing I could do about it. Yisu was, after all, the firstborn. My name might be Yaakob, but I wasn't going to stoop to stealing Yisu's birthright. Since my elder brother had made his priorities clear—studies first, family obligations second—I decided to get the most out of the situation by making it clear to everyone that *my* first concern was the family business. Not that Father seemed to notice.

In fact, in the month of Ab, during the worst of the summer

heat, Father pulled me off the other jobs and told me to give Yisu a hand. Sweating and seething, I was forced to submit to my brother's authority as foreman *and* owner. We'd been working together for two weeks now, and most of the heavy labor requiring extra hands had been finished, but Father ordered me to keep working with Yisu until his house was finished. "I'm putting you on it because I want it done right," he said, which in itself was enough of a compliment that it eased the pain of the assignment.

The moon waned until it was the barest sliver, and then went out, taking the month of Ab with it. The next day Yisu didn't show up when he was supposed to. I knew already what that meant—the local garrison had run into him on the road and was having some fun with him. (I'd been with him a few times when this had happened, and I'd had to choose between setting my load down at the mile and leaving him to go on alone, or letting the Romans make a fool out of me too. The first two times I'd stayed with my brother, but there was no reward in it, and I didn't want to get marked as an easy target—let Yisu play "Onarion" if it suited him, but I had better things to do. So after that, I just carried the required load and left Yisu to his own devices.)

An hour went by, during which I worked on Yisu's house by myself; and then another hour, and another. This was more than a routine conscription, even more than was routine for Yisu. Just as I was about to run to Father, my brother arrived. He looked unusually haggard.

"What happened?" I asked.

"I don't want to talk about it," was his reply. And that was all he would say.

Now, I was used to Yisu keeping secrets. The older he got, it seemed, the more secrets he managed to acquire. Over the years I'd learned the futility of trying to pry them out of him, and I no longer wasted my breath on begging. Once Yisu said "I don't want to talk about it," there was nothing more to be done. But not this time. I wasn't going to let this one go by so easily.

"Oh, no you don't," I said, throwing down my tools. "I've been waiting for you all afternoon, working on *your* house *by myself* through the worst heat of the day, and all you can say is

'I don't want to talk about it'? You owe me a better explanation than *that*, brother!"

He stared at me. Then he dropped his gaze to his feet, shrugged his shoulders slightly, and said, "You're right, I do." He sighed heavily. "I was with Shimon."

"The Zealots captured you *again*?" I had a hard time believing that.

"No." He looked straight at me, his eyes locking onto mine with intensity. "No, I was with him of my own free will."

Of my own...

I couldn't help it. I laughed out loud. "Oh, this is rich." Father was going to *kill* him. "All the times you've dragged in late—you were with Shimon?"

He nodded. "I've been meeting with him at least once a month for over a year now. There. Are you satisfied?"

I didn't know what to say. I just laughed harder. Then the words came, a few at a time, squeezed out with the laughter. "And to think...*I* was the one...chained to the bed!" I was so angry that I wanted to scream, but I couldn't stop laughing. *Precious Yeshua. Perfect Yeshua.* The laughter was painful, brought tears to my eyes, punched me in the gut over and over again, but I was powerless to stop it. I pushed out some more words; they came out harsh and bitter as vomit. "You *bastard!*" Abruptly the laughter dried up. I drew in a breath like a sob. "You selfish *bastard!*" I bent down, picked up a rock, and threw it at him—hard. Without waiting to see if it hit its target, I threw another one, and then another.

The commotion brought Mother running out of the house, screaming hysterically for me to stop.And then, suddenly, Father was there too. He grabbed me from behind, yanked me around to face him, and tore the rock from my hand. Brandishing it in my face, he shouted, "Are you mad?" Then he flung the stone to the ground. "Whatever possessed you to do such a thing? Your brother could have been killed!" He gave me a hard shake and then flung me aside as he'd done to the rock. "Yisu, are you all right?" He ran to Yisu's side.

"Do you know what he's done?" I yelled. "Your precious Yisu?"

"I don't care *what* he did!" Father shouted back. "There's no excuse for this, Yaakob!"

He's joined up with the Zealots! I started to say, but I bit down on the words before they could escape. Why should I help Father? Let Yisu lie to him! Let Yisu play him for a fool! One day the truth would come out, and then he'd see which son had been obedient, which son had been loyal to him. In the meantime, let him swim in his own delusions if that's what he wanted. Maybe when his Zealot son was hanging on a cross he'd come to his senses.

28

YISU

1 Elul 3773

For a brief moment, I thought Katan was going to tell Abba about my involvement with the Zealots, but then he shut his mouth as if he'd thought better of the idea. I had no illusions that he was protecting me; whatever had silenced him, it wasn't that. Never had I seen my brother this overwrought.

None of his stones had touched me; the same hands that had shielded me from the arrows a year ago deflected all of the rocks, though one passed by my face so closely that I felt the wind of its passing. No, the only one injured was Katan, and that by his own bitterness. What had prompted me to tell him my whereabouts? But then I'd never dreamed the truth would have had such an effect on him. *You selfish bastard.* Sadly, I could understand the pain that had provoked those words. They weren't directed at me, not really, but Katan couldn't hurl them at his father without breaking God's commandment; I was a safer target for his rage.

Oh, Abba. At least you never gave me a coat of many colors. In every other way, though, Yosef had favored me over his firstborn son. Katan saw it; I saw it; Yosef, however, was blind to it, and this only added to my brother's frustration. "Yisu, are you hurt?" Abba asked again while Mother fussed over me.

"I'm fine." Katan was the one who needed care. *Father, help him, please.*

Unnoticed by everyone else, my brother pulled himself to his feet, dusted himself off, and walked away. His head was held high—too high, arrogantly high, defiantly high—and there was determination in his step as he passed the juniper that marked the edge of our land and continued on up the path.

Where was he going? Yoash and Shimon were still in the area; I certainly didn't want Katan to run into them while he was this vulnerable. If he fell under their influence in his current state... I redoubled my prayers for him.

Yosef didn't ask me what had prompted Katan's tirade, and for this I was grateful. Truly, though I was innocent of any wrongdoing, I wasn't yet ready to confide in Yosef—for the simple reason that he wasn't yet ready to hear what I had to tell him. I think, on some level, he understood this, and that's why he didn't press me for details now. When at last he'd satisfied himself that I really was uninjured, he turned to berate Katan once more and discovered instead that his son was gone. "Katan!" he shouted. "Yaakob-katan! You get yourself over here, right now! Katan!"

"He's out of earshot, Abba. He left a few minutes ago."

"Why didn't you say something?"

"Would it have helped if I did? He needs some time to calm down." *So do you.* I quoted the psalm, laying one hand gently on his arm: "'Be still before Adonai and wait patiently for him...Refrain from anger and turn from wrath; do not fret—it leads only to evil.'"

"'Do not fret,'" Abba repeated, shaking his head. "One of my sons is trying to kill the other, and I'm not supposed to fret about that?"

"He wasn't trying to kill me, Abba. You know he wasn't. And as I told you before—I'm in no danger." I smiled. "I'm not Abel, and he's definitely not Cain. Please, let it go."

"Let it go," he repeated again. Shaking his head, he picked up the tools he'd dropped and carried them into the workshop without another word. Mother lingered, however, worry lines making a tiny crease in the center of her forehead.

"Yisu," she asked, pitching her voice for me alone, "what happened? Why did Katan lose his temper like that?" Yosef had known better than to ask, but then Yosef knew a lot of things of which my mother was blissfully unaware. I hated to draw her into this.

"Emi, do you really want to know that?"

"Yes. Yes, I do."

"And what will you do with the answer once you have it?"

She looked into my eyes and let me look deeply into hers.

"I'll put it with all the other answers I hold silent in my heart, Yeshua. It can't be any worse than some of those."

How could I have misjudged my mother so? I'd mistaken her innocence for ignorance, her gentleness for weakness. This woman—this woman had spoken with an angel face-to-face when she was younger than my Leah. She had been chosen by God Himself to hold a secret greater than any other, and she had proven faithful in spite of the cost. This woman had given her life for mine, and up until this moment she had never asked a single thing of me.

"Woman," I said with wonder, "why have you hidden yourself from me so long?"

"Because—" and her voice broke just a bit before she regained control of it— "I know that if I let you get too close, I'll never be able to let you go." She reached up and brushed the hair off my forehead, something she hadn't done in years. "And I know one day I'll have to." Then she tore her eyes from mine and slipped back behind the wall that she'd erected between us over the years, a wall so slight and unobtrusive that I'd never noticed it until she'd opened a door and peeked through. That door was closed now, though, and I didn't think any amount of knocking would persuade her to open it again. "Please, Yeshua, tell me what happened between you and Yaakob."

She was my mother, and I couldn't refuse her. "He thinks I've been lying to Yosef. He thinks I've joined up with the Zealots."

"Why on earth would he think such a thing?"

"Because I told him that I've been meeting with them, regularly, for a long time now." Her eyes widened in shock but she said nothing, taking my words and hiding them in her heart alongside all the other secrets she'd been asked to carry since I came into the world. I did what I could to lighten her burden. "Yosef doesn't know this, obviously, but I haven't deceived him, Emi. He told me a year ago that he doesn't *want* to know."

It was the night I'd returned home so late, the night they'd all been waiting up for me until well into the third watch. It had taken me hours to get back to Nazareth; Shimon had led me from the cave blindfolded, marched me in circles for half an hour or more to confuse my sense of direction, and then left me alone in the woods to find my way as best I could. When I'd

234   ~   D. L. MAYNARD

finally reached home, exhausted and bloodstained, Yosef had demanded the whole story from me and I'd given it, willingly. Then he'd laid down his decrees: no more going off alone for early morning prayers (thankfully, I'd persuaded him to change his mind about that one); no more—*and that means NO more*—contact with Shimon, no matter what I'd promised him in the cave.

Abba, I will not go back on my word.

You promised me, *Yeshua, years ago, that you'd have nothing more to do with him.*

I didn't have much of a choice, Abba. He was holding a sword to my throat.

That's not what I'm talking about and you know it. How could you have been so rash as to promise—worse, to swear— *that you'd meet with him again?*

It was the only way they would let me go, sir.

An oath made under duress—

Is still an oath.

I disagree.

You have that right, sir, and I honor your opinion. I just can't be bound by it.

I will not *stand for this, Yeshua! No son of mine will ever join the Zealots! I'll chain you to your bed as I did Katan, don't think I won't!*

I haven't joined them, Abba.

You took their oath.

No, I took an *oath, but* not *their oath. I was careful to promise only what I'm willing to give. No violence, no rebellion, no assistance to them in their insurrection, none at all. "You are my brothers," I told them, "and I will never betray you by word or deed. I'll give my life for yours; I will help you in any way I can. I will use all of my knowledge, all of my skills, all of my strength to help you—"*

There! You've given them everything, Yeshua!

I gave them nothing, sir. I will *help them, but I won't lift one finger to harm them. What they want from me is harmful, and they aren't going to get it.*

I want you to stay away from them, Yisu. This is a dangerous game you're playing.

It's not a game, Abba, and I won't *stay away from them. I promised to help them. I have to keep that promise; at the very least, I have to try to help them. If they reject my help, well, that's their business. But I have to offer it, nevertheless.*

I can't stand the thought of you with those men—

Trust me.

I want to, Yisu. But you know so little of these men, and I know so much more—

Trust me. Please.

I'm your father—

And who am I?

He hadn't answered.

Who am I? I'd pressed. *If I'm the heir of David, then I'm your king. Isn't it so? And more—for didn't even King David call his heir "my Lord"? Please, Abba, don't force it to come to this. I love you as much as I love anyone on this earth; I respect you; I honor you and I have always obeyed you. Always. But I'm not a child anymore. Please don't treat me like one. Trust me.*

He'd started to cry then, wordless, broken sobs, and I'd taken him in my arms and held him as if I were the father and he the son. I knew what was on his heart; although it had been fourteen years since Yudi and Matti had died, he carried their deaths with him still, impaled on the guilt as if it were his own cross; he couldn't look at his sons without seeing his brothers; he couldn't look at his sons without becoming his father, making the same mistakes his father had made despite all his efforts to avoid them.

I can't bear it, he'd said at last. *Knowing you're with them, wondering if you're safe. I don't want to know. If you do this, I don't want to know. But Yisu—*and he'd looked up at me, pleading—*not Katan. Not Yosei, or Shammai—none of them. Promise me.*

I promise.

"I promised," I said to Mother. "I've kept Katan out of it. I didn't want him burdened the way Yosef was burdened; until today he had no idea that I was spending time with Shimon. I'm still not sure why I told him; maybe it was a bad idea, but it seemed the right choice at the time. Katan's grown a lot since Bethsaida." Shimon and Sicae had told me all about Katan's part in that affair, but I wasn't about to share those sordid

236 ~ D. L. MAYNARD

details with Mother or anyone else. "When he demanded an explanation for my absence, I thought he'd be able to handle the truth, so I gave it to him. But I was wrong, obviously, and before I could explain further, he started throwing rocks."

Mother reached up to give me a kiss. "Thank you," she whispered. "I'll keep it safe. Yosef won't hear it from me, and I'll make sure he doesn't hear it from Katan either. Don't worry about your brother—I'll handle it. You just do what you need to do." She smiled softly. "I trust you."

29

KATAN

1 Elul 3773

Four years. Four *years* I'd spent paying for my mistake, and for what? For *this*? *You selfish bastard.* Father hated me. I might as well accept the fact. Nothing I did could ever—would ever—make up for what I had done. All he saw when he looked at me—all he had been able to see for the past four years—was one of *them*. A Zealot. The enemy. Never mind that it wasn't true; never mind that I'd been dragged into that raid and sworn to secrecy against my will; never mind that I'd had nothing to do with them before or since—in Father's mind, I was one of them and always would be. And it was all Yisu's fault.

If he hadn't befriended Shimon, none of this would ever have happened.

You selfish bastard.

I spent the rest of the day in the pasture with Shammai. He let me borrow his sling, and while he amused himself picking out tunes on his *kinnor*, I totally demolished a rotten tree stump. I probably hurled two hundred stones before the sun set; what I lacked in skill, I made up for in determination. There was something intensely satisfying in the way the wood chips flew in all directions each time one of my rocks connected.

You selfish bastard.

When it started to get dark, Shammai reclaimed his sling and led the sheep to the fold. I stayed out in the pasture by myself, staring at the canopy of stars and remembering a passage from Isaiah that I'd studied with Rabbi Zephanyah in *bet-midrash* just last year:

Lift up your eyes on high
and see Who has created these things,

Who brings out their host by number;
He calls them all by name!
By the greatness of His might
and the strength of His power
not one is missing.

"Adonai Eloheinu," I whispered. And then I began to cry.

Hunger almost persuaded me to go home. I hadn't eaten anything since dinner, and that was eight hours ago, at least. (Eight hours is forever when you're sixteen.) But even more than food, I wanted an advocate, someone who would take the time to listen to *my* side of the story for a change. Someone who would see me for who I was, and accept me that way. Someone who wouldn't compare me to Yisu—or better yet, someone who would agree with me that my brother was a selfish bastard.

I wouldn't find that person at my house, but suddenly I knew where I *would* find him. By the light of the stars and the new moon's thin crescent, I made my way into Nazareth.

It was well past midnight when finally I crossed under the juniper and into our courtyard. I'd taken the long way home, circling back around through the pasture so I wouldn't be seen on the path from Nazareth; I didn't want anyone to guess where I'd been. My caution paid off. The windows of the house were all propped open to let the evening breezes in, and those on the ground floor shed flickering lamplight into the yard despite the lateness of the hour. Someone had waited up for me.

To my relief, I saw that it was Mother. (I didn't want to deal with Father, and I didn't care if I never saw Yisu again. As if either one of them would lose sleep over *me*.) She sat near the door with her head bowed, spinning yarn. "Hello, Emi," I called softly through a window. She raised her head at the sound. Her eyes met mine.

"Thank God," she murmured, and went to the door. Rather than letting me in, however, she opened the door just wide enough to slip through, took me by the elbow, and led me back out toward the juniper.

"You can tell me where you've been later," she said quietly.

"Right now I just want you to listen to me. You are *not* to tell your father anything that Yisu shared with you today, do you hear me?"

Mute with shock, all I could do was nod.

"Good. We can discuss it all another time, I promise. Right now, I have to get you to your father."

"I don't—"

"Hush. You don't know anything about what's been going on here, Katan, so just be quiet until you do. Listen to your father. Apologize to your brother. And then go to bed."

"But I'm hungry."

"Too bad. It was your choice to stomp off without supper. You left a mess behind you, Katan, and you're going to set things right before you even *think* about eating. Now, tell me what you're going to do when we get back to the house."

"Listen to Father. Apologize to Yisu. Go to bed hungry." I couldn't help adding that last bit.

"And no smart-mouthing or back-talking, young man." Mother sighed deeply. "What am I going to do with you, Katan? Please tell me you got it all out of your system before you came home."

"Yes, ma'am."

"Well, that's a relief." She wrapped her arms around me and gave me a warm hug. I leaned my head on her shoulder and closed my eyes, breathing in the scent of her hair and her homespun tunic. For just a minute I was four years old again, and she was my entire world. Then she let go. "Come on, it's time to eat the bread you baked."

"I thought you said no supper."

She laughed softly as she led me back toward the house. "Don't get your hopes up. It's just something my mother used to say all the time. 'You baked this bread, Maryam, and now you'll have to eat it.' Haven't I ever said it to you before?"

"No."

"Well, it's long overdue, then." We reached the house, but instead of going back inside, Mother shoved me up the stairs ahead of her. "Go on."

"Where are they?" I asked, realizing that she wasn't coming with me.

"Thinking rock."

"Oh." Thank God I hadn't come home that way.

"Relax, Katan. They aren't angry. Well, Yosef was, for a while, but Yisu talked him off the edge of the cliff. Go on. And remember—"

"Listen. Apologize. Go to bed."

She laughed and slipped back into the house, shutting the door behind her. I climbed the rest of the stairs in the dark, and then made my way over to the rock where my father and brother were waiting. They were talking softly but fell silent at my approach.

"It's Katan, Father," I said, hoisting myself onto the boulder. Then I shut up, as Mother had instructed.

Yisu slid over to make room for me in the middle. It was a tighter squeeze than it used to be when we were boys, but the three of us still fit on top of the limestone outcropping that overlooked our property. I sat with Father on my right and Yisu on my left, our shoulders brushing, our legs dangling over the side. It all felt very cozy, very intimate. I wasn't fooled for a minute. Father hadn't waited up here all night just to give me a hug and tell me how proud he was of me. Expecting the hammer to fall heavily and without warning, I swallowed hard and drew in a deep breath, but I kept my mouth shut.

"Yaakob." My real name. It was going to be bad. I hung my head, looking down into the valley, but only for a moment. *Lift up your eyes on high.* Sitting up straighter, I lifted my chin and fixed my gaze on the stars. *He calls them all by name!* I didn't know what that had to do with me, but I hung on to it all the same. *By the greatness of His might and the strength of His power, not one is missing.*

"Yaakob. I want you to listen to me, and I don't want to hear your excuses. There are none. Do you hear me?" I nodded. "I'll be plain: I'm disappointed in you. You've made some bad decisions in the past, but I thought you'd outgrown them. And then today...what can I say? I'm disappointed, very disappointed, Yaakob. I expected so much better from you. You're my son—*my* son, and I love you. What happened today doesn't change that. Do you hear me?" He reached over and clasped my shoulders. Gently but firmly, he turned me to face him. "Do you hear me?" he repeated, his face scant inches from mine. Then he kissed my forehead and pulled me into an embrace. "I love you, Yaakob," he whispered again.

I stiffened in his arms. It wasn't intentional; it just happened. His words...I wanted to believe them. But something had changed inside me today when he'd shaken me and tossed me aside like a filthy rag. Something had hardened, like mortar cured in the sun, and though I wanted to believe him, I couldn't.

Pulling away, I turned toward my brother. "Yisu, I apologize for stoning you. It was wrong. I won't do it again."

"I forgive you, Katan." His eyes met mine for a second but then moved past me, toward Father, and he frowned.

Father still had one hand on my shoulder. His grip had tightened for just a moment when I'd turned away; now it eased up a bit but he kept it there all the same. I shrugged once, failed to dislodge his hand, and glanced back over my shoulder in his direction without meeting his eyes. "Was there anything else, sir?"

His answer didn't come right away; when at last he spoke, his voice sounded almost as cold, almost as dead, as mine. "No. Nothing else." He took his hand off my arm.

"I'll go to bed, then."

"Yes, you do that."

Sliding down from the rock, I made my way down the stairs and fell into bed.

30

YISU

2 Elul 3773

Under the circumstances, I didn't think it fair to ask Katan to put any more labor into my house. There were still a few details that needed to be finished up before the wedding, though, so I left Sepphoris earlier than usual the next day and hurried home to work on them. I found Yosef inside the house, inspecting the ceiling with a critical eye. "You and Katan did a good job on this addition," he said when he saw me walk in. "Seems to me it's habitable as is. I'll tell you what—nine months is a respectable betrothal period, especially considering how long you and Leah have known each other. So let's call the house finished, and start inviting people to the wedding feast. Plan on bringing your bride home one week from tomorrow, Yisu."

I looked around the room. Habitable? Well, yes, but it didn't match the picture I had in my mind. "Can we make it two weeks, Abba?"

"Why the delay?"

"There are still a few things I want to add."

"Like what?"

"Nothing major, just some shelves and a window seat. Some latticework upstairs."

"Any chance you could finish them today?"

I shook my head. "No, sir, they'll probably take two or three weeks to complete."

"No good. I've a big job in Sepphoris that's going to need your skill with a chisel, starting tomorrow. It's about a week's worth of work, and not something I can delegate to anyone else. Build your shelves later, after the wedding."

I smiled. "The shelves and things aren't for me, Abba, they're for Leah. I want her to feel at home, comfortable, not living in a construction zone."

He laughed. "Enough said. I remember your mother's face when I asked her to move in here before the stairs were finished. For some strange reason, she didn't like the idea of climbing up and down a ladder with her laundry basket."

"I can finish everything if you push the wedding back to the last week of Elul. I've waited this long; three more weeks is nothing."

"It won't be 'nothing' if you delay until Rosh Hashanah, Yisu—you know we can't hold a wedding during the Days of Awe, and I doubt Leah will want to spend her bridal week in a *sukkah*. Make sure you finish those last touches of yours quickly!"

I laughed. "I'll get them done in time, sir, even if I have to drop everything else."

"Don't drop your studies, Yisu—even with this commission, you should still have an hour or two each day for Rabbi Ezra."

It wasn't as much as I was used to, but I could survive on half-rations for three weeks.

The two of us set off in the morning, the few tools we would need slung in a sack over my shoulder. Along the way I meditated on one of the scriptures Rabbi Ezra and I were studying, repeating its words in time with our footsteps, drumming them into my mind and into my heart as I pondered the meaning of each phrase:

> I am poured out like water;
> all my bones are out of joint;
> my heart has become like wax—
> it melts inside me;
> my mouth is as dry as a potsherd,
> my tongue sticks to my palate;
> You lay me down in the dust of death.
> Dogs are all around me,
> a pack of villains closes in on me;
> they have pierced my hands and feet.
> I can count every one of my bones,
> while they gaze at me and gloat...

It was a disturbing passage from a seldom-sung psalm, and I'd been wrestling with it all week. David had written this one, but it corresponded to nothing in the Book of Samuel. As usual, Rabbi was leaving me to figure it out for myself, though he had given me one hint yesterday: *Try Zechariah rather than Samuel.* This I planned to do as soon as we reached Sepphoris. In the meantime, I was committing these verses to memory.

"You lay me down in the dust of death," I said for the tenth time or so. "*You* lay me down in the dust of death. You lay *me* down in the dust of death. You lay me *down* in the dust of death. You *lay* me down in the—"

Enough, Yisu, Yosef begged. You're laying *me* down in the dust. What a depressing scripture! Must you beat it to death? You've obviously learned it."

"Memorized it, yes. Learned it? Not yet, not really, not until I can fit it into the puzzle." I smiled at him. "I'm still sanding the rough edges, trying to make it fit smoothly. But there are gaps in the joint."

"Must you sand so loudly?"

"I need to hear it, Abba. *How* you say it changes the meaning, did you notice? I want to bring out every bit of the grain—this is a beautiful piece, or it will be when it's properly oiled, but the plank is knotty and I'm having to work at it harder than usual."

"Is this what you and Ezra do all day? God bless the man for his patience!"

"Amen!" I laughed.

We walked together to the home of the man who had hired us, and Yosef showed me what I would be working on: an ornate pair of doors similar to the ones he'd crafted for the synagogue in Nazareth years ago. It would indeed take me the better part of a week to complete the carvings, even if I spent only an hour in study each day. For the rest of the morning, I labored over the design: first meeting with the owner to learn his tastes and desires, and then sketching my ideas onto papyrus, and finally transferring the drawings to the cedar panels of the doors themselves. By the time I was actually ready to pick up a chisel, Yosef was calling for a dinner break.

Hungry as I was for bread, what I most wanted was a chance to get back to my psalm. It had taken all of my self-discipline to put it out of my mind as I worked on the door panels (I didn't imagine for a moment that the owner would be pleased with the doors if I used this psalm as the theme for their design!), but as soon as I walked away from the work, the verses began clamoring for my attention again. *My mouth is as dry as a potsherd, my tongue sticks to my palate...* I couldn't even think of food with such words filling my soul. "Abba, that hour for study you spoke of yesterday, may I take it now, please?"

"Only if you promise to eat something first," he admonished, knowing my priorities all too well. "And by 'something' I don't mean just a single bite of bread, Yisu. Eat a meal. I can't have you faint with hunger on the way home."

"Yes, sir." I smiled at his mock severity.

"Go on," he laughed. "Get to your puzzle and your 'sanding.' Tell Ezra he has my thanks —*and* my sympathy."

I fairly flew across town to Rabbi's house in my eagerness, pushing his door open with one hand while I was still knocking with the other. "It's Yeshua!" I panted. Talyah and Leah were still preparing dinner, and Rabbi was with his *bet-sefer* class in the synagogue. After waving to let him know I was there, I slipped into the library and fell into the book of Zechariah.

At first I took my time, reading with my usual deliberation, but I found nothing in the early parts of the book that seemed to coincide with David's psalm. Zechariah was one of the prophets of the Exile, and he spoke of the rebuilding of Jerusalem. The word of Adonai had come to Zechariah in dreams and visions. He'd had a vision of horses, and a vision of horns, and a vision of a man with a surveyor's line...

"Try looking toward the end of the book." Rabbi had come in and was standing behind me, reading over my shoulder.

I'd been at this for more than half an hour already, and I hadn't eaten yet. Scrolling past the halfway mark, I began reading through the last few chapters of the book quickly— skimming, really—looking for something that would shed light on the psalm. My eyes flew over the pages, seeking out words such as *dust* or *dogs* or *bones*, or any of the images that David had used. Finally I saw what I was looking for. "'When that day comes,'" I read aloud, "'I will seek to destroy all nations attacking Jerusalem; and I will pour out on the house of David and on those living in Jerusalem a spirit of grace and prayer; and they will look to Me, whom they pierced.'" *They have pierced my hands and feet...* "'They will mourn for him as one mourns for an only son...'" I turned to my teacher. "Is that it, Rabbi?"

"What do you think?"

He had placed the chisel in my hand, but it was left to me to strike it where I would. "I don't know what to think," I confessed. "Give me the day. Maybe I can answer your question tomorrow."

"Tomorrow, or the next day, or never. Ask Adonai for wisdom, Yeshua. If this is something you need to understand, He will reveal it to you. If not, a thousand tomorrows won't make a difference. 'Unless Adonai builds the house—'"

"'—the builders labor in vain.' Yes, Rabbi, I know that one well!" I laughed. Yosef had raised all of his sons on that scripture.

"Then apply it also to your studies, *talmid.*"

"Yes, Rabbi."

"Come, let's go to dinner." Together we crossed the courtyard in silence.

As we sat down to the meal our wives had prepared for us, I pondered the words I'd read, and I prayed for wisdom. After the meal, as I crossed town to rejoin Yosef, I prayed for knowledge. All afternoon, with each tap of my hammer against the chisel as I shaped the cedar, I prayed for understanding. *For Yahuh gives wisdom; from His mouth come knowledge and understanding.*

My Father answered my prayers that same day.

Clearly.

Oh, my Father—was there no other way You could have shown me what I needed to know?

Yosef and I reached the outskirts of Nazareth about an hour before sunset, tired from the day's work—the good sort of tired that brings a smile to the face, makes the supper taste better, and makes the bed feel softer. I'd made decent progress on the doors, and I could tell already that it was going to be the kind of handwork I loved; the merchant who had commissioned them was wealthy but also God-fearing, and he had given me full rein to carve whatever I desired as long as I made sure that—

"Back! Back off the road!" the Romans were shouting. I didn't move fast enough. The soldier in front of me, holding his spear in two hands like a cudgel, used it to shove me forcefully aside. "Back, jackass!"

Immediately behind him, a full squadron was doing the same, clearing the way for the prisoner they were escorting. I felt an urgent tug on my arm. "Come, Yisu, let's get out of here," Yosef was saying, but at the same moment I saw the condemned man and I froze in my steps.

It was Yoash.

I'd first met Yoash the day of my captivity; he it was who'd protested Shimon's leniency the most vehemently, who'd insisted that I be bound by oath before being released. His vehemence was born of fear, but I didn't understand that at the time. Only later, after we'd gotten to know each other well, did I begin to understand the fear that drove Yoash as a farmer drives the ox that pulls his plow.

"Why are you with Shimon?" I'd asked him one day. Shimon had slipped off to relieve himself and it was the first time I'd ever been left alone with Yoash. The three of us had taken to meeting regularly, though sometimes a fourth, a ruffian who called himself Sicae, also came along. Yoash and Sicae had been with Shimon longer than the others, formed the core of the Zealots' local resistance; they followed Shimon like sheep even though both were older than he by several years. Yoash, in fact, was old enough to be my father and had two sons only a couple of years younger than I. It wouldn't have surprised me to see them here—they weren't—but their father seemed out of place among the young rebels.

"Why?" Yoash had considered the question carefully, chewing it over in his mind as was his habit. It was one of the things I liked about him—he was quick to listen and slow to speak. "I don't have much of a choice, really. There's a price on my head high enough that I can't ever go home. I can't survive by myself. Shimon's proven to be a good leader; I've been with him three years and I haven't starved."

"You trust him?"

"With my life."

"Why?" I'd asked again. While he'd thought that one over, I'd asked another. "Would you trust him with your sons?"

"No." His reply had been immediate, unconsidered, the truth he carried in his heart. Before he could analyze it, though, Shimon had returned and our conversation had moved back to familiar ground. Shimon and I had talked, sparred, bounced our words off each other as we always did, as we always had, neither getting a foothold in the other's heart—and Yoash had listened.

He'd listened, but he hadn't listened to *me*. And now he carried a beam across his back, lashed to his arms, and he carried it with difficulty; his tunic was blood-soaked; blood ran down his legs in narrow trails like the sweat of exertion that ran down his face. He carried the beam to the foot of the stake that stood sentry outside Nazareth, and there he was forced to lie down upon it in the dust of the ground. *The dust of death.*

"Merciful God," Yosef whispered behind me. Again he tugged on my arm, his fingers tight enough to bruise. "Come on, Yisu." But I couldn't move. The ground at the foot of the execution stake was barren, dry and dusty under the Elul sun, and the dust puffed up in small clouds on all sides as the Romans gathered around Yoash. *You lay me down in the dust of death. Dogs are all around me...* The dust held me transfixed, as if I were the one bound to the heavy beam, as if I were the one lying upon the ground, lying in the dust. *The dust of death.* Though Yosef begged me to leave, I couldn't.

I knew what was happening, what was about to happen—everyone there knew—but I had never witnessed a hanging. The stake guarding the road into Nazareth hadn't been used in years; its presence was warning enough to deter the sort of crimes it had been erected to punish. Like Yosef, the men of Nazareth remembered the razing of Sepphoris and shunned rebellion. The stake was a leftover from those days, one of hundreds that had been planted by the side of every road in the region. The men remembered the horror of those crosses. The men remembered...but their sons did not.

And so I watched, unable to tear myself away even though Yosef pulled and pulled at me. I watched as the Romans threw Yoash to the ground, as they stripped him naked, as they drove the nails through his hands, as he screamed and begged for mercy. I watched as they hoisted him onto the stake with such a jolt that it dislocated his shoulders; I watched as they nailed his feet to the post. I watched as they heaped their scorn upon him, laughing at his agony and quarreling over his possessions. I watched as the psalm I had labored over all week suddenly came to life before my eyes—if this horror could be called life.

Finally the dust settled as the sentries took up their positions around the cross.

"Yisu." Yosef spoke softly, but his voice cut through the paralysis that held me. I began to shiver, though the air was still brutally hot. This time, when Yosef pulled me away, I was able to go with him.

But part of me stayed behind, nailed to the cross with Yoash.

31

KATAN

3 Elul 3773

F ather staggered into the workshop, all but carrying Yisu.
Both of them were pale and sweating. "What happened?"
Saba Yaakob asked.

"There was a hanging," Father said.

"Adonai, have mercy." Saba paled and leaned against the
workbench. "Who?"

"No one we know, praise be to God. Some Zealot from the
hills."

Yisu spoke up. "Yoash."

"What?" Saba asked.

"Yoash. His name is Yoash." Yisu's voice was strained,
hoarse.

"You know this man?" Saba asked.

Yisu nodded, but he didn't say anything else. No one did.

*Yoash. I didn't know him. Or maybe I did. The name
sounded familiar.* If he was part of Shimon's band, he might
have been on the raid that night. He might have sat beside me
in the circle; I might have looked into his eyes, clasped his
hand. And now he was hanging on a Roman cross. *It could
have been me. That's what Father was so afraid of, why he was
so angry. It could have been me.* I looked over at Father, but his
eyes were glued on Yisu.

It could have been me. Only once before had I felt this way.
Only once before had death come this close and taken someone
who could have been me, when Yoshiah had drowned; Uncle
Zebdi had kept saying that it *should* have been me…

It could have been me.

Father finally tore his eyes off Yisu long enough to look at
the rest of us. "Katan, Yosei. You too, Yehudah. Stay away
from town. Don't go anywhere near the road. You boys stay

close to home for the rest of the week, do you hear me? That goes for Shammai too, as soon as he gets back from the pasture."

"I'll go tell Yoachim," my grandfather said heavily. "And Yemimah." My Aunt Mimah had lost her husband in the uprising. It wouldn't do for her to head into town and happen upon a hanging.

"Where's Maryam?" Father asked.

"Inside with the girls."

"Tell her to make do with whatever food we have on hand. No trips to town this week, by anyone, for any reason."

"Agreed," Saba said, and left the room. Through the open door, I could hear him breaking the news to those in the house.

Yisu suddenly slid down the wall as if his legs had given out. He drew his knees up to his chest and buried his face in them, wrapping his arms around himself and rocking back and forth. He was saying something over and over again, but the word was muffled by his tunic; it sounded like "dust."

Father knelt beside him. "Yosei, go get some wine."

"Yes, sir."

My little brother ran out and came back within the minute, a cup and a jar in his hands. Father poured some of the wine into the cup and held it out to Yisu, who was still rocking and mumbling, "Dust, dust, dust..."

"Yisu, drink this," Father commanded.

Yisu raised his head but kept his hands clasped around his knees, so Father held the cup to his mouth as if he were a baby, and kept it there until my brother had swallowed everything in it. But just as quickly as it had gone down, the wine came back up. Oblivious to the mess in his lap, Yisu buried his head once more, though now he was rocking silently instead of chanting "dust." Father got a rag and cleaned up as much of the vomit as he could.

It was starting to get dark in the room. Night was falling. In the next room, Mother put out some food for the children—no one else had much of an appetite. Father tried to get Yisu up, but he had pulled into himself and refused to budge. "Katan, help me get your brother to bed."

I didn't think even the two of us could carry Yisu up the stairs, not in his present state, but I was willing to try. I crouched down beside him and laid a hand on his shoulder. "Yisu, put your arm around my neck," I said. I didn't expect a response, so I wasn't disappointed when he ignored me. I grabbed his arm and tried to lift it into position myself, but Yisu had clenched his fingers so tightly that I couldn't pry them loose, at least not without hurting him. "Father—"

But Father had already come to the same conclusion. "Never mind. Go fetch some bedding and bring it in here. He can sleep in the shop tonight. And bring down a clean tunic for him, too." As I was leaving the room, I could hear Father talking to Yisu. "Please don't shut me out, son. Let me help…"

Father must have gotten through to him because, when I returned, Yisu's soiled clothing was lying in a heap beside him. My brother was still curled up in a ball, still rocking himself, but he relaxed enough to let Father put the clean tunic on him and wrap a blanket around him. I spread out the rest of the bedding, piling sawdust beneath it for a cushion. Yisu ignored it.

I stood there a while, watching him rock. Then I gave it up for a lost effort and went to get myself some supper.

32

YISU

3 Elul 3773

From all sides, darkness was closing in on me. *You lay me down in the dust of death.* I sank down, into the darkness, into the dust. *Dogs are all around me, a pack of villains closes in on me; they pierced my hands and feet; I can count every one of my bones, while they gaze at me and gloat; they divide my garments among themselves; for my clothing they throw dice...* Voices murmured in my ear, but they were faint and far away. *But you, Adonai, don't stay far away! My strength, come quickly to help me! Rescue me...* Hands pulled at me and let me go again. *Save me from the lion's mouth!* And then, one voice got through, Abba's voice: "Let me help."

For just a moment, all was quiet. I lifted my head, opened my eyes, met his. "Let me help you," he said again.

"Save me," I whispered. For I had seen. I knew.

Yosef tended to my body, but he couldn't save me. He couldn't save me.

I closed my eyes again, turning to the only one who could. *Father!* But there was no answer. There was never an answer. *Don't stay far from me, for trouble is near, and there is no one to help!* There was no one to help. No one to save me. *My God! By day I call to You, but You don't answer; likewise at night, but I get no relief.* I was alone, naked and cold and alone in the darkness, and there was no relief. *My God, my God, why have You abandoned me?*

And then, hands reached out to me and touched me gently, wrapping me in soft folds of homespun wool. No longer was I naked; no longer was I cold. Life seeped back into me, life and hope. I was not alone. "Thank you," I whispered. *You have answered me...* I looked up.

A single lamp flickered in one corner, throwing light in waves across the room, painting a strange picture of shadows and half-shadows that danced upon the walls and ceiling and made it hard, at first, to realize that I was still in the workshop. A bed had been laid out beside me, but it was empty. Yosef sat leaning against the wall, his head tipped back and his eyes shut in sleep. All was silent.

I knew what I had to do.

Standing up, I stepped over the empty bed and headed toward the door. It was bolted, and as I pulled back on the latch, Yosef woke up. "Where are you going?" His voice was remarkably calm under the circumstances.

"You know."

"Don't do it, Yisu."

"I have to."

"There's nothing you can do for him. Nothing."

"I can sit with him. I can let him know he's not alone."

"He won't even know you're there."

"He'll know."

"He won't." There was a world of pain in Yosef's voice. "You don't understand, Yeshua. I thought the same, when my brothers died. I went—I went and sat with Matti, all night. He—it was—" He sighed, swallowed hard, and shook his head. "I don't want you to go through that."

"I have to."

Yosef rose to his feet and crossed slowly to the door. Reaching past me, he drew back the latch and pushed the door open. "Be careful."

Be careful. I knew what he meant, what he hadn't needed to say. Yoash was one of the Zealots, and there was always the chance that they'd try to rescue him. The Romans would have a guard up; they'd be on edge, waiting for an attack.

I also knew that no attack would come. Shimon was a fool, but he wasn't a suicidal fool, nor was he the kind of man to lay down his life to save another. His "patriotism" wasn't altruistic but vengeful; he cared less for the freedom of Israel than for his own need to inflict pain. He might talk about brotherhood and loyalty, but in the end he was loyal only to himself, and he had no brothers.

I walked slowly toward the execution site but made no attempt at stealth. I wanted the guards to see me coming. *Be careful.* I wanted them to recognize me. There was a danger inherent in what I was doing—anyone who cared enough about Yoash to come and sit with him ran the risk of being considered guilty of Yoash's crime, insurrection against Rome. Guilt by association. I wanted—no, I *needed* them to recognize me.

They had no torches blazing—such would have served only to light up their position for enemy archers while blinding them to attackers lurking in the darkness beyond. For dark it was: the moon was still but the faintest sliver; the only light came from the stars. They heard my approach before they saw me, and went on the alert. I was prepared for this, and started singing softly, not the ascent psalms I usually sang along the road during my conscriptions—my heart was too heavy for that—but a lament from the Exile:

> "By the rivers of Babylon
> we sat down and wept
> as we remembered Zion.
> We had hung up our lyres
> on the willows that were there,
> when those who had taken us captive
> asked us to sing them a song..."

As I sang, I kept walking toward them at the same deliberate pace, holding my hands out from my sides to show that I carried no weapons. When I'd gotten within a spear's throw of them, one of the soldiers laughed and called out to the others in Greek, "Relax, it's just Onarion."

"Belay that!" their squadron leader barked. "He could be a diversion. Keep alert."

They kept their weapons at the ready, but otherwise made no threatening moves toward me, so I kept approaching until I was just a few feet from the cross. Only two of them were even watching me; the rest had their senses trained out into the darkness, looking and listening for any sign of pending attack.

My senses were focused on Yoash.

I could smell his agony.

I hadn't expected that. I'd prepared myself for the sight of him, for the sound of his screams, his moans, his cries of pain and fear; but I hadn't realized that the smell of him would be so potent that I could *taste* his pain and fear as if I were drinking it. My reflex was to push the cup away, to hold my breath, to turn and run—anything, anything to keep myself separate. With determination, I fought against the reflex. Inhaling deeply, I sat myself down in the dust at the edge of the road and fixed my gaze on Yoash.

The darkness shielded my eyes from the worst of it. For that I was grateful, intensely grateful. I didn't want to see what had been done to this man. *Eyes and ears, Shimon,* I had once said. My words came back to taunt me now. *Eyes...at least they can be shut. But ears...there are things it's best not to listen to.* Nevertheless, I listened. I didn't want to, but I needed to. To do otherwise was to shut Yoash out, and I couldn't do that. So I forced my eyes to remain open, staring into the same darkness that Yoash stared into; forced my ears to hear what his were forced to hear; breathed in the same fetid air that he breathed; tasted it as he must be tasting it; and tried to imagine his pain, the pain that I was not yet ready to embrace.

I stayed with him, sharing in his suffering as much as I was able.

I didn't want to, but I needed to.

For Yahuh gives wisdom; from His mouth come knowledge and understanding.

I needed to know. I needed to understand.

Most of his cries were wordless, unreasoned, involuntary—physical expressions of physical pain, bursting out in surprise. These I understood already; they flew from my own mouth each time I struck my thumb with a hammer. To do so repeatedly, however, without respite, again and again and again, hour upon hour upon hour upon hour...

Sometimes, I knew, men hung for three days before dying.

Father... I couldn't bring myself to finish that prayer. Not yet.

Silence tried to fill the moments between these startled cries of agony, but it was invaded by other sounds, softer sounds. If wood could feel pain, these were the sounds it would make as it was sanded. I had made these sounds when I was ill with fever and unable to breathe, when every inch of my body burned and my stomach twisted and my head throbbed; I had made these sounds when Abner was done beating me, when my ribs were bruised and broken and every breath was a torment, when even light itself was unbearable; I had made these sounds, these mewling, moaning, gasping sounds. I understood them, too. A man can endure constant, unrelenting pain for only so long.

The sounds of pain were themselves painful. I listened a long time—five minutes would have seemed long, but I think it was much longer than that—and then the sentries began to sing their own song, a harsh accompaniment to Yoash's anguished cries, and I was forced to listen to that as well.

"Shut up!" one of them hollered.

Another laughed. "Not bloody likely!"

"It's driving me mad!"

"This your first time?"

"Yes." There was a sound of wood striking wood as he slammed the butt of his spear against the pale of the cross. "I said, shut up, you! Yelling about it isn't going to make it go any faster, you cut-cock son-of-a-bitch!"

Again the laughter, this time from three or four of them.

And from the cross, an answer: "Damn you! Damn all of you!" And a howl of pain.

More laughter.

"I'm laying my wager on two days—he's a fighter, this one!"

"Nah, he'll go down tomorrow."

"How much will you back that?"

"A quadrans."

"You cheap bastard! Make it a sesterce at least!"

"A quadrans. Even odds."

"Cheap bastard. You're on."

"Anyone willing to take three days?"

"Not for a lousy quadrans!" More laughter.

"What are you offering?"

"Three-to-one on a sesterce."

"I'm in."

"Me, too."

"I'll lay four-to-one that he goes down before sunrise!"

"No chance. I'll take that one, for a denarius!"

258 ~ D. L. MAYNARD

"Accepted!" Whistles and hoots filled the darkness.

"You can't cover it!"

"I can—here's the purse!"

"No cheating!"

"Yeah—you keep your stinking hands off him!"

"And your *pilum*, too!"

"What, none of this?" There was another anguished howl from Yoash, followed by a stream of barely coherent curses. "Or this?" The curses cut off in a choked scream.

"Bet's off!"

"Cheater!"

"You do that again, and you'll take his place, do you hear me?" It was the squadron commander, and he wasn't laughing. Abruptly the guards' banter ceased. "Get back to your positions, now, all of you!"

"Yes, sir!"

"Sir!"

Again, silence except for Yoash, who was whimpering breathlessly a sound I'd *never* made and *couldn't* understand. Too quietly to be overheard by his commander, the soldier nearest to me smirked, "Couldn't do *that* again even if I wanted to, you cut-cock son-of-a-bitch!" He smothered a laugh. My stomach heaved. A single, muffled sob escaped my lips before I could force it back down.

He heard. "What are you doing here still, Jackass?"

I didn't answer.

He repeated his question in stilted Aramaic.

"This man is my brother," I answered in the same tongue.

He grunted at that, but left me alone.

Yoash no longer cried out. His agony held no more surprises, only pain.

Father... Even after all that had happened, I could not finish the prayer.

Another hour passed. My senses had grown so attuned to Yoash that I was no longer aware of anything else, anyone else. My world began and ended at the cross. Each breath I drew cost effort, brought pain; I couldn't breathe until Yoash breathed— or perhaps he couldn't breathe until I breathed. I forced myself to breathe, for his sake, just in case. My lungs were cramped from the position in which I was seated, but I couldn't move.

My arms and legs ached, but I couldn't move. I had to pee—my
bladder felt ready to burst—but I couldn't move. I couldn't. My
discomfort was a pale shadow of his agony; to give in to it
would be a mockery. Sleep tugged at me, promising relief, but I
refused to give in to it either. "You're not alone, brother," I
said, pushing the words out with effort, praying Yoash would
hear me. "You're not alone."

Another hour passed, and a new sound encroached on my
senses. Footsteps, approaching from the south. Solitary. The
guards snapped to attention, barked orders, shouted a warning.
A familiar voice called back: "Yisu, are you there?"

The sound cut through my bonds, released me to leap to my
feet. "That's my father," I said to the nearest sentry, who was
already aiming his *pilum*, arm cocked back, ready to throw.

"What? Damn it, Onarion, get out of the way!"

I didn't have time to waste on Aramaic—I couldn't risk him
misunderstanding me. I switched to Greek. "That's my father!
He's not here to cause trouble. He's looking for me."

The sentry jerked his head around to face me, eyes wide
with surprise. Not once in the seven years since my first
conscription had I ever given any indication that I knew Greek.
His surprise was fleeting, though; he was far too good a soldier
to be taken off guard for long. He didn't stand down, but he
held back his throw long enough to see that I had told him the
truth. Reversing his grip on the pilum, he took a defensive
stance, still alert to the possibility of attack. Yosef approached
slowly with his hands open, as I had done earlier.

"I'm not armed," he said in Greek. "I'm not a Zealot. I don't
even know that man—I just want my son." He looked at me. In
Aramaic, he said, "Why didn't you come back? I've been
worried sick about you. I thought—"

The Roman was frowning, unable to follow the
conversation. "Use Greek, Father," I said, taking my own
advice. I had nothing to hide. "I'm sorry to have worried you. I
thought you understood: I'm going to stay with Yoash. As
long—as long as it takes."

He stared into my eyes, gauging the level of my
determination, reading the depth of my pain. "All right," he
sighed at last. "I'll sit with you."

"You don't have to do that." I knew—now—what it was

costing him just to be here.

"Yes," he said. "Yes, I do." Then he looked up at Yoash for the first time. "I don't know this man, but he's a son of Abraham. No son of Abraham should die like this. Certainly not alone." He looked back at me. "You shouldn't have to do this alone, either. Forgive me."

"Always."

Together, we sat down in the dust and the darkness.

"Abba?"

"Yes, Yisu?"

The prayer I hadn't prayed had never left my heart. It was weighing down my soul, growing heavier with each hour that passed. "Is it wrong—would it be a sin—to ask God to take a man's life?"

Yosef understood. He looked away from me, gathering words for his answer, considering them carefully before presenting them to me. "I think, under the circumstances, it would be all right. His life is already over. All you'd really be doing is asking God to end his suffering."

These were the words I'd needed. *Father, end his suffering. Please.*

Please.

I bowed my head, closed my eyes, and tried to shut out the suffering I could no longer bear.

Leah pours the wine as I gather my sons in my lap, Yudi on my right knee and Matti on my left. "Let me hear your lessons," I say to them.

Yudi goes first, his missing front teeth causing him to lisp the words slightly; I'd had the same problem at his age. "'Though mistreated, he was submissive—he did not open his mouth. Like a lamb led to be slaughtered, he did not open his mouth. After forcible arrest and sentencing, he was taken away; and who can speak of his descendants? For he was cut off from the land of the living for the crimes of my people.'"

"Well done, Yudi."

"My turn, Abba, my turn!" Matti crows. He is the younger but only by a few minutes, and he is always trying to prove his worth. He has nothing to prove, and I tell him so every day—

his worth is immeasurable—but he tries nonetheless. Sitting straight, he recites his assigned portion of Isaiah: "'Although he had done no violence and there was no deceit in his mouth, yet it pleased Adonai to crush him, to see if he would present himself as a guilt offering. At his hand Adonai's desire will be accomplished; after this ordeal he will see satisfaction. By his knowing pain and sacrifice, my righteous servant makes many righteous; it is for their sin that he suffers.'"

I kiss the top of his head and squeeze his shoulder. My sons are a delight; I cannot imagine life without them. My daughters also, though they are too young for this sort of interaction, bring joy to my heart. I send the boys to the other side of the table to eat their supper and take Mari into my lap, singing a song with her while Leah nurses little Dinah.

Outside, I hear a distant rumbling, like thunder far off.

The sound fills me with dread, though I don't know why. I feel that I should know, that I do know, but I can't remember what the sound means no matter how hard I try. A small voice deep inside tells me that, if I were awake, I would know, but the voice falls silent before it can tell me any more than that, and I dismiss it as a figment of my imagination. Perhaps the thunder was also in my mind, for no one else seems to have heard it.

And then I hear it again, much closer this time, and I want to call out a warning but I don't know what to say, so I say nothing.

The third time I hear the thunder, it is upon us.

The ground beneath us begins to shake, and the walls of the house buck and sway. The children run to me, screaming with terror, and I hide them beneath my arms. "Come!" I shout over the noise of the earthquake. "We need to get out of here!" Leah joins me, and the two of us lead the children toward the door. The room has grown, keeps growing as cracks appear in the floor, and the door seems impossibly far away.

Over my head, the weight of the building also grows; it is massive, floor upon floor upon floor, stacked to heaven like the Tower of Babel; every room packed with people, thousands of people, millions of people. Though I cannot see them, I can feel them, feel their presence, feel their terror. When this building collapses, they will all be crushed.

Yosef appears at my side and shouts into my ear: "Yeshua!

The center post!"
The post that supports the ceiling is beginning to buckle. I let go of Leah, pushing the children toward her. "Go!" I tell her. "Take the children and get out, now!"
"I won't leave you!" she cries.
"Go!"
I race to the falling post and catch it before it can give way. Pushing against it with all my might, I wrestle it back into place. But it threatens to slip out of my grasp again. I brace myself against the beam of the ceiling, leaning my back against the post, reinforcing it with my own body as I hold onto the beam with both hands. Somehow I am tall enough; somehow I am strong enough.
"Hold on, Yeshua!" my father calls. "The alarm's been sounded; everyone's evacuating the building! Just hold it up a little longer!"
The weight of the structure is unfathomable, but somehow I am able to stand beneath it. The task takes every bit of my strength. I begin to sweat, huge drops of sweat that coat every inch of my body, wet my palms, and cause my hands to slip on the beam. "Abba! Help me!"
"Hold on!" My father grabs his tool bag, pulls out his hammer and a handful of long, iron, framing nails. He grabs my right hand before it can slip off the beam and quickly drives one of the nails through my flesh and into the wood. The pain is incredible, but the nail holds my hand firmly to the beam. "Just a little longer, Yeshua!"
"Abba, it hurts," I breathe.
"I know, son. I'm so sorry. There's no other way." He is weeping.
My left hand begins to slip.
"Abba."
He drives in another nail.
The building is crushing me. I fight to keep my footing.
"Just a little longer, Yeshua." He nails my feet to the floor.
"It hurts," I whisper. "Abba."
I don't know if everyone has gotten out. My bones are melting like wax; I can't stand up much longer, nails or no nails. I am not made of wood or stone—I am a man. Only a man. "Get out, now," I warn Yosef. He kisses me, turns, and

runs.

But I am not alone.

Leah has stayed behind, with all of my children.

"Get out, Leah!" I gasp. "Go!"

"I won't leave you."

"Go!"

"I won't leave you."

My strength gives out at last, and the building falls, crushing all of us.

I opened my eyes.

Daylight.

My head rested in Yosef's lap. He was awake.

"Yoash?" I asked.

"Gone."

"Thank God," I whispered.

I knew what I had to do next.

It wasn't going to be easy.

But it was necessary.

33

YISU

4 Elul 3773

It was no kindness to drag this out. Every day I waited would make it more painful for everyone involved, and I didn't want to hurt anyone. I needed to be sure, though; I couldn't rush into this without being sure, absolutely sure, that it was the right thing to do. And so I told Yosef that I needed to be alone for the rest of the day, and I set out for Sepphoris.

My plan was simple: I would fast and pray and sequester myself in the library, reading the books I hadn't yet managed to memorize, listening for my Father's voice—and I would stay there until I was sure. *Trust in Yahuh with all your heart; lean not on your own understanding but in all your ways acknowledge Him, and He will level your path.*

No one waylaid me on the road. The legionaries had better things to do—Onarion was free to go on his way undisturbed, for today at least. It was the smallest of the gifts Yoash had given me this day, this freedom to walk an empty road, this freedom he'd bought with his blood. Gladly would I have exchanged the burden I was carrying for something as light as a Roman pack, but that was not possible. This gift could be accepted or rejected, but it could not be returned to the giver.

I didn't go to the door of the house; I didn't want to see Leah or Talyah. If I could have avoided Ezra as well, I would have; I had no desire to explain my need, only to assuage it. I went around the corner to the synagogue, let myself in, and crossed the assembly hall; my footsteps echoed in the empty room. The door to the library was latched but not locked, which told me that the rabbi was already at work within. *Father, please...*

I didn't know what to ask. I only knew what I wanted—a way out of this. I was fairly certain that I was meant to walk through this valley, however, not around it. To ask to be spared—I just couldn't do it.

I pulled the door open and stepped through. Rabbi Ezra stood beside one of the cabinets, a scroll in his hand. He turned in surprise. "Yeshua! You're very early this morning. Are you ready to give me the answer, then?" *The answer? What answer?* My confusion must have been written on my face. He raised his eyebrows slightly and said, "You told me to give you one day, and then you would let me know whether or not you'd discovered the key to the psalm. Have you forgotten? It's not like you, to give up on a difficult scripture."

The key to the psalm. The key to the psalm. Had it really been only one day since I'd read Zechariah? Yes, I'd forgotten my assignment. I had the answer, though. Yoash had unlocked it for me. "I understand it now, Rabbi." *I wish I didn't, but I won't give up on it. Difficult? Yes, but not impossible. Not impossible. Oh, Father...*

"Wonderful! Share your understanding with me, *talmid*."

No, please, not yet. Not ever. I opened my mouth, but nothing came out.

He finally saw me. "Sit down, Yeshua, right now, before you fall down."

"Yes, Rabbi."

He sat beside me at the desk, studying my face as if it were a scroll. When he spoke, it was not as my rabbi, but as my father-in-law. "Why did you come here this morning, Yeshua? What do you need from me, son?"

Relief washed over me. This I could answer without falling apart. "I need time, sir. Time and privacy. Please…may I use the library for the rest of the day? Alone?"

He considered my request and then nodded slowly. "I'm not going to ask why. If you wanted me to know, you'd have told me already, am I right?"

What could I say? I wanted to be able to share this burden, but I didn't really want to lay it on anyone I loved. So, no, I didn't want him to know; to say otherwise would be a lie. He was hurt, though; hurt that I didn't trust him enough to share this with him. *It will hurt worse when I do.* The thought was small comfort.

He rose to his feet and laid a hand on my shoulder. "It's all right, son. Take all the time you need. Lock the door; no one will disturb you." As he was leaving, he asked, "Are you sure I can't help you with this, Yeshua?"

"You already have, Rabbi, but I could use your prayers."

"You have them, son."

The books lay open before me, spread all around me, crying out to me in the voice of my Father, answering the question on my heart—and breaking my heart in the process.

Then God caused a deep sleep to fall upon Adam; and while he was sleeping, He took one of his ribs and closed up the place from which He took it with flesh. The rib which Adonai God had taken from Adam, He made a woman, and He brought her to the man. The man said, "At last! This is bone of my bone and flesh of my flesh; she is to be called Woman because she was taken out of Man." This is why a man is to leave his father and mother and be joined to his wife, and they are to be one flesh. So wrote Moses in the Book of Beginnings. I had known this since I was just a child; this was the reason I had come here today, seeking wisdom.

There were still so many books I had not studied, and though I had read through every book in the rabbi's library at least once, I didn't yet know them well enough to harvest their wisdom on my own. I needed my teacher, but I couldn't involve him, not yet. I had to do this on my own. And so I'd pulled down scroll after scroll, seeking, praying, skimming through them in search of the words that would bring understanding, the words that would "level" my path.

In the Book of Malachi I found this:

Here is something else you do: you cover Yahuh's altar with tears, with weeping and with sighing, because He no longer looks at the offering or receives your gift with favor. Nevertheless, you ask, "Why is this?" Because Yahuh is witness between you and the wife of your youth that you have broken faith with her, though she is your companion, your wife by covenant. And hasn't He made them one flesh in order to have spiritual kin? For what the one flesh seeks is a seed from God. Therefore take heed to your spirit, and don't break faith with the wife of your youth. "For I hate divorce," says Yahuh the God of Israel.

These words brought me no comfort; they added to my burden rather than lightening it, cast larger stones onto my already-rocky path. In my dream, Leah had refused to leave my side... and she had been crushed along with me. She *would* be crushed with me. I knew that now. I wanted to spare her this—I *needed* to spare her this. But I couldn't break faith with her—I couldn't go against my Father's clear command. I couldn't put my wife aside. "Oh, Leah!" I cried. "What have I done?"

Moses allowed divorce.This I also knew, had known for years. Ezra's copy of *D'varim* lay open before me: *Suppose a man marries a woman and consummates the marriage but later finds her displeasing, because he has found her offensive in some respect. He writes her a divorce document, gives it to her, and sends her away from his house.* But Leah had done nothing wrong, nothing displeasing, nothing offensive. To write her a bill of divorce would disgrace her, cast doubt on her virtue. Yosef had done this to Maryam—though he later tore up the bill—and Zephanyah, who knew of Yosef's plan to divorce her, had never believed in her innocence; he had persecuted her, and me, ever since. I couldn't do that to Leah. I couldn't do it to Ezra. A daughter so disgraced would never attract a husband of worth, and Ezra loved his daughter too much to give her to the sort of man who wouldn't care. I loved Leah too much to send her into the bed of such a man.

"Oh, Father, show me the way out of this. Surely You wouldn't have allowed this if there were no way out! Please, Father, Adonai, *Elo'i*—my lord and my God!—show me the way out of this!"

I began scrolling backward through *D'varim*, my eyes skimming over the words I'd committed to memory years ago, the words I'd read over and over and over since first I could read. Wherever I saw the word "wife" or "marriage" I paused. *If a man marries a woman, has sexual relations with her and then, having come to dislike her, brings false charges against her and defames her character...evidence of the girl's virginity...she will remain his wife...forbidden from divorcing her...* This wasn't of any help. Leah's virginity was not in question and I had no plans to bear false witness against her. I skimmed on. *When you go out to war among your enemies...see among the prisoners a woman...want her as your wife...she will stay there in your house...after which you may go in to have sexual relations with her and be her husband and she will be your wife...if later you lose interest in her...you humiliated her...* This was also of no help. Leah was not a foreign slave girl. I skimmed on. *Is there a man here who is betrothed to a woman, but hasn't married her yet? He should go back home; otherwise he may die fighting, and another man will marry her....*

How could I have been so blind?

Quickly I went back over all the other verses I had just read. *Suppose a man marries a woman and consummates the marriage... If a man marries a woman, has sexual relations with her... you may go in to have sexual relations with her and be her husband and she will be your wife... Is there a man here who is betrothed to a woman, but hasn't married her yet?*

Leah and I weren't married yet. We hadn't had "sexual relations." Not yet.

Don't break faith with the wife of your youth.

There was no faith to break. She wasn't my wife.

I was so used to the customs of my culture that I had forgotten the words of my Father. We regarded the betrothal as binding; we took the promise for the act; only a bill of divorce could break a betrothal...but this was our custom. Our custom. It was not God's Law.

I'd thought of Leah as "my wife" for almost a year now, but she wasn't.

Not yet.

"Not yet," I whispered, as relief washed over me.

Not ever.

Not ever.

"Not ever," I whispered, letting her go.

My heart broke then, and I wept.

It was dark by the time I got home. Yosef was sitting on a bench outside the shop, watching the path for my approach. As I passed beneath the juniper, he rose and headed quickly toward me. "Did you find what you were looking for?" he asked with concern.

"Yes, sir."

"Don't shut me out, Yisu." His voice was pained.

"No, sir—Abba. I won't." Of all the impossibly difficult things I was going to have to do this week, I dreaded this one the most. I'd wrestled with this all the way home. Yosef had a right to know. He'd invested his entire life in me. He had a right to know. *How can I possibly tell him?* "We need to talk. Now would be best."

"Here?" he asked, gesturing toward the bench.

"No. This—this needs to be private.'""

"The thinking rock, then."

"No, sir. Totally private."

He frowned in confusion and lowered his voice. "Yeshua, the thinking rock is the most private place I know—that's where I brought you to tell you your heritage—"

"And Katan overheard our entire conversation, remember?"

"I'd forgotten about that." He sighed. "Where, then, son? Did you have a place in mind?"

"High Point."

"One moment." He walked over to the house just long enough to let Mother know that I was home safe and that we'd be out again for a while, together. Then we followed the sheep path as it wound south and east into the pasture, hiking nearly a mile before climbing to the top of the highest overlook. The path was steep and treacherous in the dark, but the location was impossible to sneak up on; we would see any intruders long before they were close enough to overhear a word of our conversation.

I'd thought long and hard about what to say. *Father, please give him ears to hear.*

Before I uttered a word, though, I wrapped my arms around him and held on tightly, burying my face against his shoulder as if I were a small boy again. He hugged me back, and the warmth and strength of his arms gave me the courage I needed to continue. I breathed in deeply, losing myself for just a moment in the scent of homespun and wood resin that was so much a part of him. "Oh, Abba, I love you so much," I whispered. "If only it could stay like this forever." I didn't want to let go, but the things I had to say needed to be said man to man. Much as I'd like to, I couldn't hide any longer.

Sitting up straight, I released him.

"Go ahead," he said. "Whatever it is, you know I love you."

I nodded, pushing back the tears I couldn't afford just yet. "There are three things. Three things I have to do." I'd start with the easiest—easiest for me to say, easiest for him to hear. "First, I won't be able to work on the doors this week or the next, because I have to go to Korazin."

"Why? What's in Korazin?"

"A widow and two boys who don't know yet that Yoash is never coming home. A father who's lost his only son. I'm going to tell them, and sit *shiva* with them."

"Can't someone else—"

"There is no one else, Abba. I'm sorry to leave you with the doors, but I have to do this."

"I'll come with you."

I'd expected him to offer. "No, sir. Thank you, but no. It would be too dangerous."

"If it's that dangerous, I won't let you go alone."

"It's not dangerous for me. I've told you that, again and again. I'm protected. But it could be dangerous for you, and I'm not willing to risk your safety. It's best I do this alone." *Hear me.* We'd had this conversation before, a year ago. *Trust me.*

He remembered, and nodded grudgingly. "All right."

One down.

"You said three things."

"Yes, sir." This would be harder. These two were so closely intertwined that there was no way to fully explain the one without going into the other, and I wasn't ready to do that yet. "I promise I'll explain everything to you later, everything I've learned, the reason I have to do these things. Right now, though, I'm just going to tell you what they are." *Do you hear me, Abba? Try to understand.* "Please hear me out."

"All right. I'm listening."

Again I pushed away the tears. "I can't marry Leah. I'm going to write up a bill of divorce and hand it to her tomor—"

I hadn't really expected him to remain silent. "You—you're *what*? Yisu! What has she done? Why are you—"

"She hasn't done anything. This isn't about Leah. It's about me. I promise, I'll explain everything to you if you'll just be patient—"

"Don't lecture me about patience, young man! It was impatience that prompted me to divorce your mother, and look where that rash decision landed us! And now you're going to do the same thing—"

"Be still!"

Yosef cut off his tirade in mid-sentence, his eyes wide with shock. I didn't mean for the command to come out so forcefully; I had warned him that this day would come, but I didn't mean for it to come so soon. I'd never raised my voice to Yosef before, not once. It shook me as much as it did him. "I'm sorry, Abba, but you said you would hear me out. This is hard enough...this is hard enough, without...without..."

"Without my interruptions. I'm sorry, Yeshua. Please forgive *my* impatience."

"Always."

Yosef's lips turned up in a soft, brief smile; then he closed his eyes tight and clenched his jaw as if he were in pain. He swallowed, exhaled sharply, and finally looked up at me. "All right. You're going to Korazin. You're divorcing Leah." He pursed his lips, but only for a moment. "What's the third thing?"

"I have to tell you something I don't want to tell you." I fell silent.

"Is that the third thing?" Yosef asked after a full minute had gone by.

"No, actually that's the fourth thing."

"You said there were three."

I smiled wistfully. "I counted wrong. Like the proverb: 'There are six things Adonai hates, seven that are detestable to Him...' I counted wrong. There are three things I have to do, four things that must be done by me."

The humor helped a little, but not enough. "What's the third thing?" he nudged gently.

"I have to tell Ezra who I am." I'd made the decision as I was leaving the synagogue. It felt good—it felt *right*. Yosef knew who I was, but he was ignorant of the prophecies. He was a blind guide; following his lead, I had almost fallen into a pit.

"No! I forb—" He caught himself, reined himself in with tremendous effort. This reversal of our roles was difficult for him, but he was making a wholehearted effort. *Trust me.* "All right, then. All right. Those are the things you have to do. Go to Korazin, divorce Leah, confide in Ezra, and tell me something you don't want to tell me." With his elbows resting on his knees, he laced his fingers together, leaned over with head bowed, and rapped his doubled fist nervously against his forehead three or four times, rocking slightly and breathing deeply. "Is there anything else, or do I get the explanation now?"

"That's the fourth thing, the thing I don't want to tell you." *Really, it's the first thing, since I have to do it before all of the others. Oh God, give me the words. Give me the strength.* I'd wrestled with this more than all the others—did I really want to lay this burden on Yosef's shoulders? But I couldn't leave him in the dark, not when I was about to reveal everything to Ezra. I reminded myself that Yosef had a right to know this.

I wanted to throw myself into his arms again, but his posture didn't invite intimacy—it was obvious that he knew this was going to hurt, and he was preparing himself for the blow. To strip him of his armor now would be unkind. So I steeled myself and said, "I need to tell you why I was so upset last night."

He didn't look up, but kept rapping his clenched hands against his head.

"Watching Yoash..." This was going to be even harder than I'd thought. As horrific as the experience had been, putting it into words was...was... How could such a thing be discussed, as if it were just part of life, like a sheep-shearing or a tax-collection or a sunset? "Watching Yoash die was awful. I don't have to tell you that. I know it was hard for you, too, because of your brothers. When you sat with Yoash, you were thinking about Matti, right? Living it all over again?"

"Yes." It came out as a whisper, and I knew he was hearing me.

"And that made it even harder, right?"

"Yes."

It was time to get to the point. "When I sat with Yoash, I was thinking about someone else, too. I was thinking about me."

"I don't understand."

He needed to. I couldn't afford to be ambiguous, discreet, tactful. "I was thinking about myself, Abba. Hanging on a Roman cross."

Yosef looked up. "That's normal, Yisu. I've imagined mys—"

"I'm not talking about imagination. I'm not talking about empathy, either. I'm talking about the fulfillment of prophecy. You know who I am, but do you have any idea what I'm supposed to do? Yesterday I saw my destiny. I saw my death."

"What are you talking about? You're David's heir. You're the Messiah!" He'd never said it flat out like that before. "You're not destined to hang—"

"With all respect, sir, but you don't know what you're talking about. Yes, I'm David's heir. David himself is the one who prophesied how the Messiah would die. I've been studying that prophecy all week, don't you see? 'You lay me down in the dust of death.' And there are so many others. Isaiah prophesied *why* the Messiah would die. I've studied that one, too: 'He was wounded for our transgressions; he was crushed for our iniquities.' And Zechariah, he prophesied what would happen next: 'They will look to me whom they pierced; they will mourn him as an only son.' Oh, Yosef, *do* you know who I am? Apart from the prophecies, *can* you know who I am?"

He stared at me, saying nothing. Then he began to shake his head. "No. No. *No!*" Leaping to his feet, he grabbed me and held me in a tight, frantic embrace. "No! You're wrong, Yisu. Wrong!"

"I wish I were! Do you think I *want* to die like that? Do you think for one minute that I would tell you this unless I was *certain* I was right?" The tears I'd been pushing away all night burned my eyes; the effort of holding them in choked off my voice and I whispered, "I've known for over a year, Abba, for over a year that I'm going to have to die for my people. I just didn't know how, not until last night, because I'd never seen a hanging, do you hear me? I didn't know. But I know now. And because I know, there are things I have to do. Yoash was a friend of mine, but even if he'd been a total stranger, I would owe him a great debt. His death—it opened my eyes. His suffering helped me understand who I am and what I have to prepare for. The least I can do is offer comfort to his family.

"And Ezra—don't you see? I *have* to tell him. He knows the prophecies so much better than I do; he can help me avoid mistakes like—like getting betrothed to Leah." *Oh, Leah. I still have to face you with this...* I couldn't hold back the tears any longer. They soaked into Yosef's tunic as I clung to him. "You see why I can't marry her, don't you? I can't give her children—if I do, they'll be destroyed along with me—the prophecies are clear. So how can I be a husband to her? And how can I marry her knowing—knowing!—that we'll have a few years at best, and those years will end like *this*?" I pointed toward the distant road, where Yoash's corpse was still hanging, would still be hanging until there was nothing left but bones. "It would tear her apart! How can I do that to her, knowing? How can I do that to *any* woman?"

"You can't," he whispered.

"No, I can't."

"Oh, God," he sobbed. "This can't be happening. This can't be real. Not you, Yisu. Not you. This can't be real. I'm sleeping, and I'm trapped in a nightmare."

Trapped. Oh, Father, is there no way out?

And He answered, bringing to my mind the words I'd read that morning, the words He'd spoken to His prophet Malachi: *Surely the day is coming. But for you who revere My name, the sun of righteousness will rise with healing in his wings.*

"We're all trapped in a nightmare, Abba," I said. "But the day is coming."

34

KATAN

5 Elul 3773

Father had been pretty clear: *No trips to town this week, by anyone, for any reason.* I should have known it wouldn't apply to Yisu. *You boys stay close to home.* Right. I hadn't seen my older brother in two days. The rest of us were cooped up in the shop, working on all the tedious chores we normally saved for bad-weather days, because all of our large commissions this week were either in Nazareth or Sepphoris. The only other project "close to home" was Yisu's addition, which was all but finished. He had been planning to put in some more shelves, though, and I decided I'd rather spend my time doing that than sanding and oiling drill bits.

So, leaving my little brothers to help Saba Yaakob sort nails and sharpen chisels, I took myself over to Yisu's and got to work. He'd sketched out his plans, and the lumber was leaning against one of the walls in the downstairs room. It needed to be cut to size. Picking up my saw, I started to remove about a span from the end of one plank and was nearly halfway through when I hit a knot. "Balaam's ass!" I cursed. I pushed down harder on the blade, trying to force it, and it stuck. "*Qalown!*" (That one would have gotten me in trouble if there'd been anyone around to hear it.) "Come on, Katan," I badgered myself. "You can do better than that!" I shimmied the blade up and down, pulled back on it, and managed to get one or two teeth free; then the cursed thing stuck again. "Balaam's ASS!" I grabbed the saw handle with both hands, braced my foot against the plank, and pulled hard. The blade broke free all at once, knocking me off balance and sending me to the floor with another loud curse. As I sprawled there on my aching butt with the saw in my hand, I couldn't help but notice that it was missing half its teeth—I'd pulled hard enough that last time to snap them clean off. "Great. Just great," I muttered, and topped it off with a curse that would have brought Father's rod down across my back had he been in the room.

I'd already ruined two saws this year, and Father had warned me that if it happened again I'd be in big trouble. He hadn't said *what* the trouble would be, but I wasn't in the mood to find out. Quickly I ran through my options. I had some money saved against the day Father agreed to my betrothal; it didn't look like that would be any time soon, though—I could use some of the money to repair or replace the saw blade. I was still best friends with Hezron, the blacksmith's son; he would probably do the work for a reasonable price, and quickly, too. All I had to do was slip into town unnoticed, get the blade fixed, and get home again before I was missed.

I hadn't seen Father since breakfast; he'd barely eaten a thing, and then he'd gone back up to his room with a curt, "Get to work and don't disturb me." Saba was running the shop. I knew he wouldn't be stopping in to check on my progress, though, not with Yosei and Yehudah to supervise. The plan was workable.

Wrapping the broken saw in my mantle, I tucked it under one arm and slipped out of the house, across the yard, and up the path as quickly and quietly as I could. I was pretty sure no one had seen me; if they had, I hoped I was moving fast enough that they'd think I had a latrine emergency. Then I hightailed it down the road toward town.

I was about two-thirds of the way there when a breeze blowing out of the west hit me in the face with a rotten odor that grew stronger and stronger the closer I got to town. Along with the stink was a harsh noise—it took me a minute to realize what it was: dozens of cawking birds. By the time I was close enough to see the execution stake, the stench of rotting flesh and the raucous clamor of the birds had prepared me for the worst. Or so I thought. Pulling the neck of my tunic up over my mouth and nose and trying to breathe in as little as possible, I looked up at the man hanging from the cross, wondering if he was the same Yoash who'd been on that raid with me four years ago. I couldn't tell; even if he'd been my own brother, I wouldn't have recognized him. I could barely tell he was human. Gagging, I turned away.

Trying to get the image of him out of my mind—*this is why Father didn't want us coming to town*—I hurried down the road toward Hezron's shop. *Please be home.* He was. "Father isn't letting me go anywhere," he confided. "Not since—you know." He tilted his head in the direction of the town gate. "I'm surprised Yosef sent you out."

"He didn't." Handing him the saw blade, I explained my predicament.

"Sure, I can fix it for you," he said, and named a price that I could afford. "Be done in a day or two, tops."

"I need more like an hour or two, Ronni. It's the skin off my back if my father needs this saw tomorrow and it's missing."

He grinned. "I've been *there* once or twice myself. Okay, I'll put a rush on it, but don't blame *me* if it breaks again."

"As long as it doesn't break in *my* hand, I don't care."

"You owe me big for this, Katan."

"Don't I ever! Thanks, Ronni." Hezron's father, Amnon, walked in at that moment. He and my father did business regularly; I sure didn't want him to know what I was up to. Neither did Hezron. While my friend slid the broken blade discretely out of sight, I made polite conversation with Amnon.

"Hello, sir, glad to see you're well."

"And why shouldn't I be? Though I wasn't expecting to see you here today, Katan."

"I had some errands, sir."

"Yes, life does go on, doesn't it?" His expression brightened somewhat. "You certainly are growing. Be getting yourself a bride soon, I'll wager."

"I'm only sixteen, sir."

"Lots of men get married at sixteen, or betrothed at any rate!"

"Yes, sir."

"Your father got anyone in mind for you?"

"Not yet, sir." Where was he going with this? Was it possible he'd finally begun to see me as a man? That he was considering me as a match for Rivkah? I drew myself up straighter and tried to look responsible. "But my brother Yisu is getting married at the end of the month, you know, and maybe after that Father will start making plans for me."

"And have *you* got anyone in mind?"

"Um, well..." This was awkward. I couldn't just come out and tell him I'd been mooning over his daughter all year. Behind him, Hezron snorted—trying not to laugh, I guess.

Amnon smiled knowingly. "I thought as much." He slapped my shoulder. "We'll talk. After the new year. I've had my eye on you, Katan—you're a good worker, from all accounts. And I've always liked Yosef; a decent man, whatever some people might say. Still, I'm glad he's decided to marry his sons off at a young age. He waited too long, himself, and that's never wise. 'Better to marry than to burn,' as they say." He chuckled again. "Rivkah's back in the garden, if you want to say hello."

"Yes, sir. Thank you, sir." I left the shop, trying not to appear too eager, and made my way around the house to the vegetable garden. Rivkah and her mother were pulling weeds. My offer to help was welcomed with enthusiasm, and I was soon on my hands and knees in the hot sun, surrounded by cucumbers. I passed an hour there, coming face to face with Rivkah at the end of each row while her mother kept a watchful eye on both of us. Hot and thirsty, we found a ripe melon and ate it together, shortly after which Amnon appeared and sent me on my way.

Hezron wasn't done with the saw yet, so I decided to head over to the synagogue and pay my respects to Rabbi Zephanyah. He was with his *bet-sefer* class, but the boys were busy copying their letters onto wax tablets, so he told the older ones to help the younger and then took a moment to come aside to greet me.

"I'm surprised to see you today, Yaakob," he said after we'd done with the formalities. "I should think Yosef would keep his son closer to home, all things considered." He shook his head, eyes downcast. "A bad business, that. A very bad business. May God be merciful."

Old habits are hard to break. "'Adonai your God is a merciful God; He will not fail you, destroy you, or forget the covenant with your ancestors, which He swore to them'" I recited as if he'd called on me in school.

Rabbi smiled sadly. "I miss you," he said simply.

Those three words reached deep inside of me, grabbed my guts, and twisted. *I miss you.* It felt so good that it hurt, and I had to fight back against the urge to cry. I had missed school, had missed the freedom and feeling of accomplishment it gave me, had missed my studies and they knowledge they brought me...but Zephanyah had missed *me*.

I bowed my head so he wouldn't see my tears. Trying to keep my voice light, I said, "You see me in the assembly every week, Rabbi."

"Once a week is not enough."

"Once a week is more than enough where my father is concerned, sir." I didn't need to explain any further. We both knew what Yosef's reaction would be if he knew that I'd been here two nights ago.

"Well, I will see you on Shabbat, then," he sighed. "You are long overdue for *aliyah*. Shall I call upon you to read this week?"

If it were up to Father, I would never be called to the *bimah*. By his logic, if Yisu wasn't called up, then I shouldn't be called up either. But I couldn't say that flat out. For three years now, my father had grudgingly allowed me to read, but only because Yisu kept insisting that he didn't mind. Father minded, though. Given the events of the past forty-eight hours and how angry he already was with me, I didn't want to do anything else to upset him. "Now wouldn't be the best time, Rabbi," I said, choosing my words carefully.

Though I kept my reasons to myself, Rabbi Zephanyah knew all too well what was prompting my reticence. "Yosef has got to accept the fact that you are entitled to certain privileges and your brother is not," he huffed. "Certainly you must honor your father's wishes, Yaakob, but you are of an age where honoring him and obeying him are not synonymous."

"I don't understand. The commandment—"

"The *mitzvah* to honor your father was given to ensure that God's Law would be passed down from generation to generation. But when a man's father commands him to do what is contrary to God's Law, he must not obey. The Sages are clear on this, as you would know by now if you had been permitted to study with me. The duty of studying Torah supersedes that of honoring parents. You are one of the best readers in town, and one of the best students I've ever taught. It is not fair that you should be denied *aliyah*, nor is it right that you should be denied the chance to study the Scriptures as my *talmid*."

"Father has forbidden me even to mention that subject again, Rabbi."

"Then do not. To argue with him would be dishonoring. However, to neglect your studies would be *wrong*. A young man who persists in wrongdoing brings no honor to his father."

"With respect, Rabbi, but you tie my hands and ask me to juggle."

He laughed and patted me on the shoulder. "Wait in the library until I've dismissed the children, Yaakob. Perhaps I can loosen those knots for you."

I sat in the library, my thoughts reeling. No, Father's treatment of me wasn't fair and it wasn't right, but he was still my father. I'd never forgotten Rabbi Ezra's lesson about Absalom; every time over the past four years that I'd been tempted to curse Yosef, I'd remembered Absalom and swallowed my anger. *But what if Ezra was wrong?* Crossing to the shelves where the scrolls were stored, I found the Book of Samuel and brought it to the table. While I waited for Rabbi Zephanyah to return, I began rereading the story of Absalom in light of what he had just told me.

"The *mitzvah kibud av v'em*—the commandment to honor your father and mother—has been called the most difficult of all the *mitzvot* to obey." The rabbi spoke softly. I looked up from my reading. "I am glad to see you spending your time profitably, Yaakob. It is no more than I would expect of you. The fact that Yosef fails to appreciate your diligence and talent shows that he is a fool."

"Rabbi—" Was I to sit silent while my father was insulted so blatantly?

"Hear me out, Yaakob. I do not make such an accusation lightly, nor would I make it publicly, but it is the truth nonetheless. Yosef has been blessed with a firstborn son to make any man proud, but he has blinded himself and cast you aside in favor of Maryam's bastard. That is the action of a fool."

I gasped, unable to believe what I was hearing. "Rabbi—"

He shook his head. "The truth must be spoken at least once. Or should a lie be permitted to ruin your life, too? Yosef is a fool. 'Like snow in summer or rain at harvest time, so honor for a fool is out of place. Like one who ties his stone to the sling is he who gives honor to a fool.' Do not trouble yourself over this any longer, Yaakob. You are not a child. Pay Yosef the honor due a father publicly and to his face, but do not allow his folly to stand between you and what we both know to be right. I have told you repeatedly that I will accept you—and gladly —as my *talmid*. Aside from Yosef's disapproval, is there any reason that you continue to decline my invitation?"

"N-no, Rabbi."

"Then I expect you to meet with me for one hour every day."

"Against my father's wishes?"

"Without your father's knowledge. Surely you can free up one hour without needing his permission. Or does he still watch over your every move day and night?" I shook my head. "He forbade you to mention studying with me, you say. So obey him—do not mention it."

"You're telling me to sneak out."

He pursed his lips, considering. Then he smiled and nodded. "Yes, I suppose that is exactly what I'm telling you to do."

For four years, Father had treated me like a criminal because he'd been afraid I was going to sneak out to join the Zealots. Now, finally, for the first time, I was preparing to sneak out—to join a rabbi for Torah study. At the irony of it, I laughed aloud. "All right, Rabbi, I'll do it. I'll do it."

He embraced me. We spoke for a little while longer, setting up the time for our clandestine studies, and then he had to get to his *bet-midrash* students and I needed to check on that saw and get my butt home. Fortunately, this time Hezron was finished and Amnon was nowhere in sight; I slipped my friend the price we'd agreed on and reclaimed my saw. "Thanks again, Ronni. You're my savior."

"Remember, you owe me."

"You can be best man at my wedding!" Bundling the saw blade up in my mantle once again, I turned to head for home and found myself face to face with the last person on earth I wanted to see.

"Yaakob."

"Father." I was so dead. Forget best man...Hezron could be one of my pallbearers instead.

35

Yisu

5 Elul 3773

Yosef said he'd talk to Katan. It was up to me to convince Rabbi Ezra. But first, there were two things I still had to do.

I hadn't gone back to the house after my talk with Yosef. We'd sat together on High Point until the roosters began to crow, and then Yosef had gone home and I'd spent the last hour before dawn in prayer. As soon as the sun had risen high enough to light my path I headed north, bypassing the road altogether, not wanting to go anywhere near the place where Yoash was still hanging—would still be hanging days from now, until there was nothing left to hang and his bones fell to the ground to be gnawed by dogs.

Instead, I clambered up and down the sheep trails, trying not to think about what lay behind me or what lay ahead of me, but only what surrounded me at the moment. Faint and far off, Shammai's voice ululated across the hills, calling his sheep to follow. *Yahuh is my shepherd; I lack nothing. He has me lie down in grassy pastures, He leads me by quiet water, He restores my soul.* I breathed deeply, concentrating on the feel of the sun on my back, the rocks beneath my feet, even the strain of my leg muscles as they pushed me uphill—these things anchored me in the moment and reminded me that I was alive.

Alive.

I was also exhausted. How long had it been since I'd last slept, really slept? The days were starting to blur together, the joints sanded over by sleeplessness, forming one large panel on which was painted a scene of misery. First my frustrating conversation with Shimon and Yoash, then being stoned by my brother, another long talk with Yosef as I persuaded him to be merciful to Katan, a few hours respite spent in study of

Zechariah followed immediately by Yoash's execution and my sudden understanding of all I'd have to do, hours digging through the scriptures, begging my Father for help, breaking Yosef's heart with the truth I'd kept secret so long and then sitting with him all night while he wept and clung to me, and now this grueling trek to Sepphoris to face Ezra... I was exhausted.

What little sleep I'd gotten over the last three days was riddled with nightmares, and I knew that if I lay down now, before finishing these two tasks, I'd find no rest. Sleep, perhaps, but no rest. *He makes me lie down in grassy pastures, He leads me by quiet water...* I wasn't there yet. *He guides me in right paths for the sake of His own name.* I had to keep following the path my Father had laid out for me. *Even if I pass through death-dark ravines, I will fear no disaster; for You are with me; Your rod and staff reassure me.* Wherever He led.

I couldn't handle the sheep trails much longer, though, not in my current state. Deciding I was far enough from Nazareth to risk the road, I bore west until my path intersected the highway, and then I turned north again along the broad, well-traveled route. It was much easier going; the few people I passed said hello but then continued on their way without disturbing my thoughts; the only Roman I encountered was a messenger on horseback, intent on his mission and galloping past me without so much as a glance. This was Shimon's legacy, the fruit of his labors—no longer were the legionaries content to vent their petty frustrations on Onarion; now they had purpose and were hunting in earnest, and their prey they would hang like trophies wherever their hunt was successful. "Oh, Shimon, why wouldn't you listen to me?" I murmured. Four years I'd spent soothing the Romans with my lullabies, but he just *had* to blow Gideon's trumpet in their ears and rouse them. I feared that Yoash was just the first of many who would hang this month.

I didn't like where my thoughts were wandering, so I pulled them back onto the path. *You prepare a table for me even as my enemies watch; You anoint my head with oil from an overflowing cup. Goodness and grace will pursue me every day of my life.* Even today. Even today. "Father," I whispered, though no one was around to overhear my prayer, "give me strength." I still had so much to do before I could claim the promise that concluded David's psalm: *And I will live in the house of Yahuh for the length of my days.*

I held that promise in front of me the rest of the way to Sepphoris. The hour was early enough that I should find Ezra still at home, so I went straight to his door, knocked, called out my name, and entered. I knew it would be unlocked, that he was expecting me, for I'd promised him yesterday that I would return early this morning to explain my odd behavior. The family was still at the table, finishing breakfast, and Talyah asked if I'd like to join them.

The smell of the food was tempting, but I didn't want any distractions. Ezra understood and declined the invitation for me. "Come, Yeshua, let's go over to the study." Together we walked to the synagogue and entered through the private door that led to Ezra's library. "Sit down, son." I did, still without having said a word. He stood over me for a moment, reading my face like a book, and then he pulled his stool around to sit in front of me. When we were eye-to-eye, he spoke again. "Have you slept at all since yesterday?"

"No, sir."

"I thought not. I haven't seen you look this haggard since the day you became my *talmid*, Yisu. What's going on? Are you ready to tell me?"

I couldn't remember him ever calling me *Yisu* before. It was an invitation to intimacy, I knew; he was speaking not as my Rabbi, not even as my father-in-law, but as my friend. There was concern in his voice, in his eyes, in his posture as he leaned toward me. More than concern, there was love. Such love. It tied my tongue in knots. Everything I had planned to say to him dried up, and all I could do was stare at him mutely.

"Yisu?"

I didn't want our relationship to change.

"Yisu?"

In a single night, I'd watched Yosef go from being my father to being my subject; our relationship would never be the same again after the things I had shared with him, the demands I had been forced to make. I knew the same thing would happen here, now; that the words I was about to speak would transform Ezra from Rabbi to *talmid* whether I wanted them to or not. If he chose not to believe me, then our relationship was over. If he believed, then our relationship was forever changed. It was inevitable.

I didn't want our relationship to change.

But it must.

"Rabbi," I said, cherishing the word on my lips as I never had before, cherishing the freedom it gave me—to call another *Teacher*, *Master*, to allow another to take authority over me, to bear my burden for me—ah! such freedom! I said it again, savoring the word and all it meant, even as I laid it on the altar. "Rabbi. *Rabbani*."

He'd opened the door for me when he'd mentioned the day our relationship had begun. I drew in a deep breath and started there. "The day you asked me to be your *talmid* was one of the happiest of my life, but also one of the most difficult because of the secret I was carrying."

I paused, considering my next words carefully, but Ezra misunderstood my hesitation and tried to help. "The fact that Zephanyah had expelled you, believing you to be *mamzer*."

"That, too."

He blinked, startled, and swallowed whatever he had been about to say.

"I told you, sir, that he had good reason for his belief."

"You also told me that he was in error." His tone was guarded. "I chose to believe you, Yeshua, to believe your claims over his. Was I wrong to do so?"

"No, sir. Your faith was not misplaced. But there was more, something I didn't tell you at the time, something my f—Yosef forbade me to discuss with you."

My hesitation did not escape his notice, nor did my choice of words. His eyes narrowed. "Are you telling me that Yosef is not your father?"

"The words are yours. I've always considered him my father, and always will, since God saw fit to give me into his care and since he claims me as his own. But no, in the way you mean, Yosef is not my father." It was the first time these words had ever left my mouth. I didn't like the taste of them; they were bitter as vomit. They felt like a lie.

"Who is? Do you know?"

I nodded, but said nothing. Instead, I rose from the bench and crossed to the shelves where the scrolls of the Neviyim were kept. I pulled out Isaiah, laid it on the table, and began unrolling it. Keeping my voice steady, I read:

"Listen here, house of David!
Is trying people's patience
such a small thing for you that you
must try the patience of my God as well?
Therefore Adonai Himself
will give you people a sign:
the virgin will become pregnant, bear a son,
and name him Immanuel."

Leaving the scroll open on the table, I fell silent, but I watched Ezra's face while I waited for his response. He was frowning, not in displeasure but in concentration, and I knew he would understand why I'd read this scripture; his next words proved me right. "You are claiming this for yourself? A prophecy nearly seven hundred years old, a sign fulfilled long before the Exile?"

He'd chosen to attack my scholarship rather than my claim. In like vein I answered him. "Fulfilled? By whom, sir?"

"By Isaiah's son." He pointed to the next page of the scroll.

"With respect, sir, but his name was Maher-shalal-hash-baz, not Immanuel," I challenged, as though this were simply a test. "The two names aren't even close in meaning. And his mother was Isaiah's wife, not a virgin."

"The word is *almah*. Virginity is not specified," he countered.

"Where in the scriptures does *almah* ever refer to a married woman, sir? And if it did, how would that be a sign from God, a married woman giving birth?"

"It matters not! You are taking out of context a sign promised to King Ahaz by the prophet Isaiah, a sign that Damascus and Samaria would fall and be abandoned, which indeed happened when the Assyrians conquered them more than six hundred years ago! What has such a thing to do with *you*?" When I didn't answer, he said, "You're not seriously claiming that your mother was a virgin while she carried you?"

I shook my head. "My claim would be meaningless—I wasn't even born yet; how can I make a claim to be a witness to my mother's condition, virgin or not?"

"Then why—"

"Because there are other witnesses, sir, who do make that claim. Reliable witnesses."

"Who?" It was a challenge, laden with disbelief.

"My mother—"

He cut me off. "No doubt. But hardly reliable under the circumstances."

"And Yosef, sir."

He grunted. "And his testimony is based on what?"

"You may ask him yourself, sir. Although he didn't want me to share this with you, I've convinced him that it's necessary, and he's willing to answer any questions you might have."

He sputtered with impatience. "So I'm to take you at your word in the meantime—I'm to accept your outrageous claim— your *audacious* claim—your blasphemous claim, some might add—simply because you wave Isaiah in my face and smile at me? What do you take me for, Yeshua? A credulous fool?

This was going well, all things considered. Zephanyah would have struck me across the face by now. "No, sir, certainly not. I apologize if I've given you that impression. I realize how outrageous this sounds, and I'm sure that, in your position, I'd be tempted to feel the same way." He sniffed and leaned back with his arms folded across his chest, mollified somewhat but not satisfied. "I don't want to speak for Yosef, sir, but I can share with you what he told me."

"Do so."

Abba could give him the details tomorrow, or whenever they spoke; that they *would* speak, I had no doubt whatsoever. For now, I would stick to the barest facts. "He and Maryam were betrothed late in the summer, and because of her youth, it was agreed that he would wait at least a year before taking her home as his wife. Just after Shavuot, though, her parents discovered that she was pregnant. They accused Yosef, but Maryam swore he hadn't touched her, that no man had touched her. Of course, they didn't believe her."

"Naturally."

"Yosef went to Zephanyah and had him write up a bill of divorce."

I paused, giving Ezra time to fully consider that fact before moving on to the next one; it was strong evidence that Yosef truly was *not* my father. "Only a handful of people know about his intention to divorce my mother, since he never went through with it."

"Zephanyah being one of those people."

"Yes, he was the only one outside the immediate family."

"It certainly explains his attitude toward you." He pursed his lips. "So, why didn't Yosef divorce your mother? What happened to change his mind? I assume that is the 'evidence' to which you've referred?"

"Yes, sir." *Father, give me the right words. Open his ears to hear.* "He had a dream." I proceeded to describe the dream as Yosef had related it to me. Ezra listened quietly and without interrupting, though he sat up straighter when I got to the part where the angel addressed Yosef as *son of David.* "And then he said, 'Do not be afraid to take Maryam home as your wife, for that which is conceived in her is of the Holy Spirit. And she will bring forth a son, and you shall call his name Yeshua, for it is he who will save his people from their sins, though they are many.' So Yosef went home, and he burned the bill of divorce, and he married my mother. But he didn't sleep with her until after I was born."

Ezra stared into my eyes without replying. For a full minute, the room was totally silent. Then he dropped his gaze, wincing and rubbing his temples. He drew in a long breath and let it out again in a short burst. In a voice clenched as tightly as his furrowed brow, he said, "Is that all?"

I nodded, and then realized he couldn't see me with his eyes scrunched shut. "Yes, sir."

"A dream." He sighed again, less forcefully this time, and stood up, pacing the length of the room as he continued to massage his temples. "A dream so compelling that he would rearrange his entire life as a result. Poor Yosef. 'The heart is deceitful above all things.' Such pain. He must have loved your mother beyond reason, to go to such lengths to convince himself of her innocence—"

"Begging your pardon, sir, but Yosef's dream was not the only evidence. It's true, he loved Emi very much and the dream gave him an excuse to believe her, but he admitted to me that he didn't *really* believe her until—well, until I was born. That's when the other witnesses began to come forward. These people were total strangers to us and to each other, but they all said the same thing: this child is the king we've been waiting for." My face grew warm. Let others say such things about me, but it felt awkward and inappropriate to be saying them about myself, even if they were true. "Torah says to let every matter be established by two witnesses; Yosef's dream was confirmed by all sorts of people, more than a dozen of them. Shepherds from Bethlehem, astronomers from Persia, an old man named Shimeon in Jerusalem—"

"Shimeon?"

"Yes, sir, that was his name." I opened my mouth to tell him about the unusual events surrounding my dedication at the Temple, but before I could say another word he went pale and sat down, shaking like an old man.

"Father," he whispered.

"Sir?" It was my turn to be confused.

"My father," he said again, and he looked at me with a new question in his eyes. "He told me, years ago—seventeen years ago—he told me he'd seen the Messiah."

Ezra ben Shimeon. All at once, I made the connection. "Your father's name was Shimeon."

"Yes."

It made such perfect sense. Ezra was a Judaean. He'd moved to Sepphoris from Jericho just a few years before we met. "Your father," I said, sure that I was right, "he was the *same* Shimeon, wasn't he? The one who prophesied to Maryam in the Temple." At the irony, the divine irony, I began to laugh aloud. *Oh, my Father, how intricately the threads are interwoven in this coat of many colors You are making for me!* Then I looked at my teacher and the laughter faded. He was pale, so pale I thought he might faint. "Are you all right?" I asked, laying a hand on his shoulder.

He shook his head. "All right? No, I am all wrong. I've been all wrong for years. Oh, Father, forgive me!" Again he buried his face in his hands. I pulled up a stool and sat facing him, our knees just inches apart. Leaning forward, I listened as he opened his heart to me, though he did not look up and his voice was so soft that I had to strain to make out the words, as if he were having a conversation with himself and I just happened to be overhearing it. His words, however, were clearly intended for my ears. "My father, like Yosef, had a dream that shaped his entire existence. That cursed dream hung over my head, ruling his life and mine. I never believed it; and when he came home from the Temple that day, I dismissed his ravings as the delusions of an old man, nothing more. 'I have seen the Messiah!' he said over and over again. 'Just as Adonai promised! I saw him, I heard him, I held him in my arms!' He kept going on and on about the child..." His voice trailed off and he sat with his head down and his face hidden.

I continued the story for him, the one I'd been planning to tell him. "The child had been brought to the Temple for his redemption because he was his mother's firstborn. Shimeon approached the family and asked to hold the baby." Ezra was nodding. "He told them that the child was destined to cause the fall and rise of many in Israel, that he would be a sign spoken against, but that he would bring light to the Gentiles and glory to Israel. Shimeon thanked God and said, 'Your servant can now depart in peace, for I have seen with my own eyes—'"

"'Your *yeshu'ah*,'" Ezra finished with me.

Yeshu'ah. *Salvation.* A play on my name. Except for the emphasis on the last syllable, it *was* my name. Shimeon had had no way of knowing this when he'd spoken; my parents had taken it as one more sign that the old man was truly a prophet.

Ezra finally looked up, and there were tears in his eyes. "You. It was you."

I nodded.

He drew in a deep, shuddering breath and then sat up straight. "On his deathbed, my father asked me to follow his dream—his dream that I hated, his dream that I never believed—and out of guilt, perhaps, I swore to him that I would. That's why I'm here, in Sepphoris. Because of his dream. His stupid, demanding dream."

"What was it? May I ask?"

He laughed ruefully. "On the night before my *brit milah*, just one week after my birth, my father dreamed of the coming Messiah; but in his dream the Messiah was not a king but a baby, and the baby was lying in a sheepfold, of all places! The baby was crying and no one was there to help it, he said. And then he saw a young man, and somehow he knew it was me. In his dream I walked over to the baby and picked it up and fed it. Then I handed it to my father and said, 'Shimeon ben Asaph, your ears will hear what many have desired to hear, and your eyes will see Adonai's *yeshu'ah*. And you shall name your son Ezra, for he will be a Help to me. He will build my Temple; though it be destroyed, yet shall it be raised up, and therein you will find your Help, among the humble of Zebulun and Naphtali.' Then, Father said, I turned into a dove and flew north with the sun shining off my feathers, which were sheathed in silver and gold." Again Ezra laughed, a wrenching sound filled with remorse. "You can see why I considered the dream foolish; not one bit of it made any sense at all. But Father took it very seriously. The next day, at my *brit milah*, although he'd already been calling me Hananyah for a week, he announced that my name was Ezra.

"He spent the rest of his life trying to interpret that dream. He told it to me so many times that it is forever engraved on my memory, and he made decisions for me based on the words of the dream. According to the dream, for example, I was supposed to build God's Temple, so my father went to the book of Ezra and studied it carefully. You know it says Ezra was a priest and a scribe of Torah—well, my father couldn't change my lineage, so the priesthood was not an option, but he did make sure I'd become a scribe and a teacher of the Law."

He stood up and walked over to the cabinet that held the books, running his hand lightly across them. "One day, perhaps, I'll walk you through all of the scriptures my father used to justify the decisions he made as a result of that dream, but not today. Suffice it to say that he believed the dream was calling me to the land of Zebulun and Naphtali—the Galil—and specifically to Sepphoris."

"The dove with gold and silver feathers," I concluded. Since Herod Antipas had decided to renovate his capital, Sepphoris (called "the Bird" for the way it perched atop its hill) had become widely known as the Ornament of the Galil.

"Exactly." He returned to the table, stood beside me. "For years he begged me to move to Sepphoris, especially after he saw the baby in the Temple, but always I refused. When the city was razed to the ground two years later, he began to doubt his interpretation, but then when Herod started to rebuild it, he grew more insistent than ever. And so, as he lay dying, I finally agreed to his request—it was my last chance to honor my father. He died happy, believing that his dream had come true."

He smiled then, the first real smile I'd seen on his face since our conversation began, and looked down at me. As he did so, his gaze fell upon the scroll that lay still open to Isaiah's prophecy; and then, as the full implications of our conversation began to sink in, his smile faltered and he whispered, "His dream *was* true. My father's dream was *true*. Adonai, have mercy on me. All this time...here with me, breaking bread with me, sitting at my feet, calling me Rabbi...you..." His voice trailed off uncertainly. Then, bowing his head, he backed slowly away from the table with his eyes downcast and his hands up as if to show me that he was unarmed.

I wasn't at all surprised—I'd known this moment would come sooner or later—but I'd hoped for more time with him first. I tried to hang on to our relationship for a little while longer. "Rabbi—"

"You," he repeated. "It was you. It *is* you."

"Rabbi—"

He shook his head, a nervous gesture, more like a shudder than a denial. "Audacity. To think for a moment that I could... God forgive my audacity." His head was still bowed, his eyes still cast down, his hands still begging me to keep a distance between us. "'Who has measured the Spirit of Adonai? Who has been His counselor, instructing Him?'"

I finished the quote from Isaiah, letting my tone soften its meaning, making it a plea rather than a chastisement: "'Whom did He consult, to gain understanding? Who taught Him how to judge, taught Him what He needed to know, showed Him how to discern?' Please, Rabbi, don't pull away from me. Don't abandon me."

"Abandon you? *You*, my Lord? You don't need me—"

"Yes, I do. Rabbi—"

He groaned, as if the word caused him pain. I didn't want to cause him pain.

"Ezra," I said. It was awkward in my mouth, but only for a moment. "Ez'ri." *My help.* "You're well named. You've been my help when no one else would help me, and I still have so much to learn. I need your help, Ez'ri." Rising from my stool, I closed the distance between us and took his trembling hands in mine, interlacing my fingers with his before he could pull away again. "I'm only seventeen, and I'm not prepared for the task ahead of me. I barely understand it. You were put here for a purpose, you said so yourself: 'He will build my Temple.'"

He looked up, searching my face, gathering himself together, trying to make all of the pieces fit—trying to fit himself into the puzzle he'd spent his life studying. "'But who is able to build Him a temple, since heaven and the heaven of heavens cannot contain Him?'" he murmured, and I knew from his tone that he was quoting a scripture, though I didn't know which one—there was still so much I didn't know. "'Who am *I* then, that I should build Him a temple?' And yet, Solomon did so."

"Solomon built *a* temple," I corrected, "but he didn't build *the* Temple, Rabbi. For when David brought the ark of the covenant into Jerusalem, didn't the prophet Nathan come to him and say that Adonai would build a house for David, and not the other way around? I'm the Temple, Ez'ri, the Temple God is building with His own hands, as He promised David so long ago—and He has appointed you to help." *Please, I don't want to lose you.*

"But don't you see? Already *you* are teaching *me*. You've been teaching me for the last four years. How then can you call me Rabbi? I should call *you* Rabbi."

"'To everything there is a season, a time for every purpose under heaven.'" The words were from the book of Ecclesiastes—he'd taught them to me himself. "Yosef is also wrestling with this, Rabbi, and he has been for nearly eighteen years. As have I. But I truly believe, in *this* season, it's for you to lead and for me to follow. One day that will change, but that day is not here yet."

Ezra frowned. "Do you *command* me to be your Rabbi?" he scolded. "Why can't you see that I'm right about this? Please, my Lord, listen to me—"

The absurdity of his remark overcame both of us at once. I started laughing first, but Ezra joined me almost immediately. "Audacity, indeed! Shall I tell you what to do? Or shall you tell me? If you have your way—as you should!—then you are my *talmid* and cannot tell me what to do!"

"And if you have your way, then I am your Lord and must tell you what to do! And I command you to let me be your *talmid* still! So I have no right to command you—"

"So I need not obey you, which means I need not command you—"

"And I need not obey you—"

We both dissolved in much-needed laughter, having totally confused ourselves. I suddenly remembered our very first conversation. "It's the paradox of humility all over again! The first is last, and the last is first. The king is the servant, and the slave—"

"The slave is Emperor!" Ezra laughed, catching on quickly.

But another idea had occurred to me, a much more practical idea, and as soon as we'd both quieted down again, I proposed my compromise. "Will you continue to teach me, Ez'ri, not as my Rabbi—since you find that idea 'audacious'—but as my friend? Side by side, pulling the plow with me? Please?"

He nodded thoughtfully. "The paradox of humility. Agreed. This I can live with. Not easily, not comfortably...even side by side. You are still—"

"I'm still the same person I always was. I haven't changed."

"No, that's not true." Ezra fixed his gaze on me, looking at me as he had when first I'd arrived this morning. "You have changed. Something happened to you this week, something that prompted you to tell me this secret. Something that is weighing heavily on you. Whatever it is, it's changed you, Yeshua. Will you tell me? As your friend? As you promised yesterday?"

Yesterday.

Everything the laughter had pushed away returned in a flood.

"The psalm," I said. "Zechariah." I was drowning in the flood; each word came with effort; each word was a cry for help. "I saw—" *My God, why have You abandoned me?* "I saw a man hang, Ez'ri. Oh, Rabbi." *Help.* "I watched a man hang and I realized—I realized—"

I couldn't say anything else.

I didn't have to. He knew better than I did what was coming. "God have mercy," Ezra whispered, and folded me in his embrace.

36

YISU

5 Elul 3773

wo down. Ezra held me close for a long while, saying nothing, just comforting me with his presence and understanding. Side by side. Focusing on his pain, I had managed for a time to forget my own; now, in comforting me, he found the same release. To everything there is a season. The dry heat of summer gives way to the soft rains of autumn. But the year turns, and eventually summer comes again. I'd indulged my own sorrow long enough. I had accomplished two of my tasks, had broken the hearts of the two men who loved me most, who knew me best. It was time to face my third task. I had another heart to break.

It was time to face Leah.

I'd already spent a whole day in prayer about this, but I turned to my Father one more time before leaving the shelter of Ezra's arms. *Thank You for showing me what I need to do. You're so faithful, so patient with me. You've given me so much; help me give this one thing back to You. I know You wouldn't take it away from me without a good purpose—please help me set down my own desires so I can better understand Yours, Father. Help me see the good in this. Help me...* Pushing back the tears that were once again threatening to overwhelm me, I slipped out of Ezra's embrace and stood to my feet. What had Isaiah said? *I set my face like a flint.* I mustered every ounce of self-control in my possession and forced my emotions to submit to my will in this matter, hardening my face and my heart against cowardice. There was no easy way to do this. However, although the situation was only partly of my own making, I was the one, ultimately, who had made every choice that led up to this moment; the responsibility for it rested squarely on my shoulders, and I had to deal with it.

My teacher—my father—my friend—was looking up at me with concern. He read the resolve in my face. "What is it, Yisu? Is there more—?"

"Yes." If I waited long enough, he would see it for himself, but every hour that passed would make it harder, make it worse. I crossed to the shelf where he kept his writing supplies and helped myself to a piece of papyrus, a pen, and some ink. Setting them on the desk, I said, "I would have done this myself, yesterday; I started to, but I don't know the right words. I'm sorry, sir, but I do need your help with this." I sat down and picked up the pen. "I'll write it out, but you'll have to dictate the wording. It's important that this be done right; it has to be legal."

"What are you talking about, Yisu?""

"A bill of divorce."

"Why do you—" He cut himself off, answering his own unfinished question. "Leah. Merciful God. I betrothed my daughter to you."

"Yes, but I wouldn't have agreed to it if I had understood the prophecies."

"I wouldn't have offered if I had known who you are."

"At least we're in agreement about that."

"What was Yosef thinking, to allow such a thing?"

"He didn't know any better, Rabbi. He never studied past *bet-sefer*."

"Oh." He considered that. "Does he know now—?"

I nodded. "I was up all night consoling him."

"I'm sorry."

Flint. Again I pushed my grief aside, but it was getting harder and harder to do; I was so tired. "Please, sir, I need to write this bill." *Before I fall apart.*

"Yes." Without further comment, he dictated the words that would set Leah free. I wrote them as neatly as I could, but my hand was unsteady and some of the words were barely legible. "It's good enough," Ezra said, looking over my shoulder at the finished document.

"No," I corrected softly. "There's nothing good about it."

"It's the best thing you can do under the circumstances, Yeshua."

"That doesn't make it good."

"No," he agreed. "You're right. It isn't good." He laid a hand on my shoulder. "Come, let's go in and break the news to Leah. Together."

I didn't reach for the papyrus, but left it on the table. "There's one more thing that has to be resolved first, sir."

In the end, I decided to talk to Leah alone.

Oddly enough, it was the first time we'd ever been alone. This was something both Yosef and Maryam had been adamant about. *I know you won't do anything inappropriate, Yisu, but it's best not to give people a reason to gossip,* Mother had said.

Yosef had been a bit more blunt. *I don't care how strong you think you are—you don't need to be putting yourself in a situation where you might be tempted. You're seventeen, and you're human. You don't need to be alone with that girl until your wedding night. Anything you* should *be saying to her, you can say around her parents—and anything you can't say around her parents, you don't need to be saying to* her. *Trust me, son, you don't want to put her through what your mother went through. Women can be vicious.*

Nevertheless, I needed to talk to Leah alone.

She was out in the courtyard, working at her loom. Ezra nodded in her direction and then went into the house to break the news to Talyah in his own way. He left the door open behind him, so technically we were still being supervised, but I knew Ezra would give us the privacy I'd requested.

Leah looked up from her weaving as I approached, but her hands continued working. "Hello, Yisu," she said with a smile. "Are you staying for dinner? We missed you yesterday." Her eyes fell on the rolled up papyrus in my fist. "What's that? Nothing important, I hope—you're crumpling it." She reached out and grabbed it from me, opening it and smoothing it out by pressing it flat across her lap and rubbing it with her hand. "What does it say? Is it a scripture you're studying?" She bent over and began to read it aloud.

"'On the fifth day of the week, the fourth day of the month of Elul in the year 3773 from the creation of the world according to the calendar reckoning we are accustomed to count here, in the city Sepphoris, which is situated near wells of water, I, Yeshua bar Yosef, who today am present in the city Sepphoris, do willingly consent, being under no restraint, to release, to set free and put aside you, my betrothed wife Leah bath Ezra...'"

She looked up, her brow lifted in confusion. "What is this, Yisu? Is this a joke?"

"No," I said, willing my voice to hold steady. It disobeyed, cracking on the word.

She went back to the document. "'My betrothed wife Leah bath Ezra, who is today in the city Sepphoris, who has been my betrothed wife from before. Thus do I set free, release you, and put you aside, in order that you may have permission and the authority over your self to go and marry any man you may desire. No person may hinder you from this day onward, and you are permitted to every man. This shall be for you from me a bill of dismissal, a letter of release, and a document of freedom, in accordance with the Torah of Moses.'"

Then she turned her eyes on me, and they were large, dark, and full of pain. "Why, Yisu? What have I done to so displease you?"

"Nothing. You've done nothing wrong, Leah."

"Then why?" She almost breathed the word, so faint and sweet was her voice, like a sigh of the breeze or a distant dove. *Music, all music.*

Flint. "I can't tell you that. Your father knows my reasons and he agrees with them."

The pain in her eyes faded then, and was replaced by anger. "You're divorcing me and you won't even tell me why?" *Even raised in anger, her voice sings. Music.*

Flint. Joshua used flint knives to circumcise the Israelite army before attacking Jericho. *Hard and sharp. The sharpest knife causes the least pain.* "That's right. Please don't ask again."

She gasped as if I'd struck her.

"One more thing." *Flint.* "In a few minutes, your father is going to call you inside to tell you that he's already made another match for you. I want you to know that I approve of the match, Leah. Accept it. Rejoice in it. For your sake and for mine."

"Who is it?"

"Yaakob bar Yosef."

"Yaakob—? You mean *Katan*? Your *brother*?" *Flint.* "Yes."

"No!" she said, stamping her foot. "Absolutely not! The Law forbids it! 'You shall not uncover the nakedness of your brother's wife; it is your brother's nakedness.'"

"You're not my wife." *Hard and sharp.* "You never were." She'd raised a valid objection, but it was one I'd already studied and I was prepared for her. "How could Katan uncover my nakedness when you've never even seen me naked? Don't be absurd."

"But the Law—"

"The same Law also states that if you *were* my wife, and if I died without giving you children, my brother would *have* to marry you."

"Now who's being absurd? You're not dead, Yisu!"

Yes I am, woman, you just don't know it yet. "You're missing the point, Leah. There's no shame in marrying two brothers, as long as you aren't uncovering one before the other. The law is intended to prevent comparison and jealousy. That's why it also says a man can't lie with a woman and her daughter, or a woman and her granddaughter, or two sisters—the jealousy tears apart their relationship, turns them into rivals and sets them one against the other."

"But that's exactly why I can't marry Katan—"

"That's exactly why you *can* marry him. Since you've never been intimate with me, you'll have no basis for comparison."

"But won't you be jealous of him anyway? That he'll have me and you won't?"

It will be a great temptation, my sister. "No." *Cut swiftly. Cut deep.* "It was my idea to give you to him."

Shoving her loom roughly aside, she leapt to her feet, rage blazing from her eyes. For a moment I thought she was going to strike me—indeed, I would have welcomed it. But instead, she turned and ran out of the courtyard, slamming the door shut behind her. *Three down.*

I left through the synagogue so I wouldn't have to face her again. There was no flint left in me. All I had was bruised and bleeding flesh. I dragged it back to Nazareth, crawled into bed, and fell at last into a deep and dreamless sleep.

37

KATAN

5 Elul 3773

Father marched me back home without speaking a single word to me. This gave me plenty of time to imagine what he was going to do to me once we got there. Not only had I broken the saw, but I'd tried to cover up my crime, which was a much more serious offense; and then on top of all that, I'd defied a direct order to stay away from Nazareth. At the very least, I could expect to go without food for the rest of the day—except, of course, the "food for thought" Father would deliver with his rod.

Instead of the rod, however, I got the Rock—the Thinking Rock. Climbing up to my usual place, I gritted my teeth, prepared to hear a lecture on responsibility and obedience, or perhaps another tirade against the evil influence of the Zealots. Either one of them I could have delivered myself by now, so often had I heard them. I was careful not to roll my eyes, though. I didn't want to give Father added incentive to use the rod.

He sat next to me. "Be glad I've had a chance to cool off, Yaakob."

"Yes, sir."

"I don't at all appreciate the fact that I had to go into town today to find you. You have no idea—no idea—how much that's upset me."

"Yes, sir. I'm very sorry, sir."

"I wish I could be sure of that." He sighed. "Your disobedience couldn't have come at a worse time. But never mind that right now. I was looking for you for a reason."

"Yes, sir." My response was automatic—he'd paused, so I'd filled in the gap with the mandatory phrase. It took me a second to realize that he'd deviated from the usual lecture. "Sir?"

"I need your help, Katan. No—let me start over. I need your help, *Yaakob*. You're not a child anymore, and that's good, because this situation is something only a man can fix."

And he was coming to *me*? Instead of Yisu? I sat up straighter. "Yes, sir. How can I help you?"

"By doing as I ask." His eyes locked onto mine. "You're not going to like it, but I'm asking you to put aside your likes and dislikes for once, and do what's best for the whole family, for everyone involved—yourself included. I'm asking you to be a man. Can you do that?"

"I'll try, sir."

"I'm not asking you to *try*, Yaakob. I want you to *do* it. It's not a matter of ability. It's a simple matter of obedience. Can you—will you—obey me for the good of the family?"

"Won't you tell me first what I'm agreeing to do?"

He pursed his lips, clenched his jaw, and huffed in frustration. I could almost hear his thoughts: *I don't have to explain myself to Yisu. Yisu would obey without question. Why can't you be more like Yisu?*

In my mind, I answered him: *I'm not Yisu. Why can't you accept me as I am?* But only in my mind. I knew better than to say it aloud. Instead, I said, "All right. I'll obey you." Did I really have a choice?

"Good." He smiled at me, but it was strained; forced rather than heartfelt. "As I was saying, you're not a child anymore. You're sixteen, and that's old enough to read from Torah in the assembly, old enough to practice a trade—and old enough to marry. It's that last one I want to talk to you about. I've decided that it's time for you to marry."

Was this why Amnon had brought up the subject earlier? Had he and my father already spoken about Rivkah and me? I smiled back at Father—grinned, really. "Yes, sir. You can count on my obedience."

"I'm still in the process of arranging the match, but I'm pretty sure she and her father will agree, so I'll tell you now. I want you to marry Leah bath Ezra."

Leah bath Ezra? "But she's Yisu's bride!" I protested.

"No, she's not. Not any more. Yisu divorced her today."

"He did *what*? Why?"

Ignoring my question, Father continued, "I expect your full

cooperation, Yaakob. We'll meet with Ezra tomorrow to draw up the contract, and you'll need to bring something of value as your gift to Leah—you have some savings put aside for your betrothal, am I right?"

"Wait a minute! Aren't you even going to tell me why?"

"No, I'm not. It's your brother's busin—"

"No!" I interrupted, leaping to my feet. "It's *my* business! I am so *sick* of all your secrets, Father, you and Yisu, all the time talking about things no one else is allowed to know. Why? Because he's the firstborn, because he's David's heir? And what am I?" I bit my tongue before Zephanyah's accusation could come flying out. "What if something happened to Yisu, did you ever stop to think of that? Then I'd be next in line. I have a *right* to know what's going on!"

"Don't you take that tone with me!"

"Why did Yisu divorce Leah? What's wrong with her? What did she do that makes her not good enough for Yisu anymore? If you're going to foist her off on me, then I have a right to know!"

"There's no *foisting* going on! Leah's a good girl, and she'll make you an excellent wife. Can't you just leave it at that?"

I threw my hands up in frustration. "You say you're going to treat me like a man, but *no* man would take her under these conditions!" That was the truth and he knew it. "Whose father are you, anyway? Mine? or hers? It's not *my* fault Yisu divorced her. Why should I have to clean up his mess? I don't even *like* Leah!"

"What's not to like? She's sweet, smart, hardworking—"

"And skinny, and her nose is too big, and her ears stick out, and she's as tall as I am! Plus, she's always giggling." *Not to mention the fact that she's in love with Yisu.*

"She's a good girl, and she deserves a good husband."

"That's not my problem."

"Yes. It is." Father stood up and walked over to me, his expression stern. "I started this conversation by reminding you that you have an obligation to your family, that the good of the family is more important than your petty likes and dislikes. Her ears stick out? Listen to yourself! This girl's entire life is at stake, and it's within your power to help her. She's *family*, Yaakob. Leah has been like a sister to you—don't you care about her at all? Do you expect me to just throw her away? I can't! I won't! For nearly a year, I've thought of her as one of my daughters, and that isn't going to change, not if I have any say at all in the matter! I told you, I want your obedience. You talk about rights? I have a *right* to your obedience. It's not like I'm asking you to do something hard—I'm not asking you to sacrifice anything! You don't know what sacrifice is! You have no idea—"

He winced as if in pain and fell silent, breathing hard, with one hand pressed to his stomach. "Abba, are you all right?"

He nodded. After a minute or so had gone by without either of us speaking a word, he looked up at me and quietly said, "I want you to marry Leah. No more argument."

In the same tone of voice, I replied, "On one condition. You tell me why Yisu divorced her. I'll marry her regardless of the reason, but I do have a right to know who I'm taking into my bed."

"Won't you just trust me when I say that it's nothing that need concern you?"

"Give me this one thing. Please."

He sighed. "All right. Leah didn't do anything wrong. Yisu didn't find any fault with her. It has nothing to do with Leah at all. Your brother just...he believes...well, that God has a special calling on his life that would make marriage—any marriage—extremely difficult. He's decided he's never going to get married."

"You're kidding me, right?"

"No, I'm extremely serious."

I studied his face. "You believe that? About a calling from God?"

"What I believe doesn't matter."

I took that for a *no*. I didn't believe it either. "Fine then. I'll sweep up after Yisu. I'll spend the rest of my life finishing what he started—so *he* can do what he wants with *his* life. That's all that really matters, isn't it, Father?" I turned and walked away.

"Where do you think you're going?" Father called after me.

"To finish *my* house!" I shouted back. "So I'll have a place to put *my* bride!"

And that damned saw better not break again.

304 ~ D. L. MAYNARD

"You are hereby my wife, consecrated to me in accordance with the laws of Moses and of Israel." I handed Leah the coin that sealed our betrothal. She accepted it, but she didn't look any happier than I was. *And behold, there was Leah.* I couldn't get the scripture out of my mind; I'd been repeating it to myself over and over during the entire ceremony. *And behold, there was Leah.* The thing that made the joke perfect was the fact that my name was Yaakob. Considering the joke was on me, though, I didn't much appreciate it. Or maybe the joke was on Leah, since she was the one who'd been expecting to marry the other sibling. Maybe she was thinking *And behold, there was Yaakob.*

Either way, there we were—trapped in a two-thousand-year-old story from the book of Genesis. Only, instead of weak eyes, my Leah had big ears. *Behold!* I smothered a laugh, biting the inside of my cheek hard enough that it hurt. She noticed anyway, and pursed her lips, turning her face away from me disapprovingly. That just made it worse, since now I was standing eye-to-ear with her. Even though my lips were clamped tightly shut, one high-pitched giggle escaped before I could stop it, earning me an angry glare from Father. Quickly I tore my gaze off Leah and focused instead on memorizing the pattern of Ezra's floor tiles.

Once the formalities of the *kiddushin* were out of the way, our fathers got down to more practical business. Ezra, my father-in-law (*that* was going to take some getting used to!), invited us to sit with him in a shaded corner of his courtyard while the women prepared a meal. "Now," Ezra said, "as to the contract..." He pulled out a papyrus scroll and spread it out for father to see; I looked over his shoulder, curious about the terms they'd worked out for my life. "Technically, the bride-price Yeshua agreed to pay is still due, since—as we both know—Leah committed no act of indecency to merit the divorce. However, I'm not going to hold you to that, given the circumstances." My father was nodding, and it was obvious that the two of them knew something I didn't know; but it was also pretty obvious they weren't about to include me, so I didn't say anything. "Let's just keep the same terms for Yaakob, agreed?"

""Yes, certainly," Father said.

"As to the period of the betrothal, I should think another year—"

"No, sir," I interrupted. They both looked at me as if astonished that I'd dare to speak up regarding my own marriage contract. But I'd been thinking about this all day and had reached a decision, and I wasn't going to let them sway me from it. "I already know Leah, and she already knows me. Waiting another year is pointless. Let's just get this over with, shall we?"

"But you need time to prepare a home—" Ezra said.

"It's already built, sir." I turned to Father. "I put as much labor into that addition as Yisu did—maybe even more. I'm claiming it for my own. You owe me that much, at least. *He* owes me." Grudgingly, Father nodded. "Fine. Then there's no reason to drag out the betrothal. You were planning a wedding feast at the end of the month anyway. Let's just go through with it as planned." As far as I could see, there was only one advantage to me in this wedding—as Amnon had put it, *better to marry than to burn*—and I wasn't going to wait a whole year to consummate the marriage that had been forced upon me.

"Rushing this is a bad idea," Father warned. "The change in bridegrooms is going to give people enough reason to gossip as it is. Rabbi Ezra is already preparing the arguments you're going to need to convince the elders that your children are legitimate; why add fuel to the fire, Katan? You know what I went through with Yisu—"

"I don't care what you went through, Father! This situation is nothing like yours. For one thing, Leah isn't pregnant. She's not going to start swelling up like a ripe melon two months after I bring her home. And—unless you've all been lying to me—Rabbi Ezra will have proof of her virtue to wave under the nose of anyone who dares to question it. I'll see to that myself on our wedding night."

Both of them stared at me, aghast at my blatant disrespect. I didn't care. This whole thing was their idea, not mine, and I'd had enough. For a second I thought Father was going to backhand me across the mouth, but he didn't, although his hand was raised and trembling with the effort he was using to hold himself back. Oddly enough it was Ezra who came to my rescue. He laid a hand on Father's arm. "No, Yosef, we've already asked more of him than we've a right to. Give him this. It's only fair. I'll handle the accusations."

Then he turned to me. "Just be good to my little girl, Yaakob. None of this is her fault. Please don't punish her for what we've done to you."

"Is that what you think of me?"

"No. If I thought that, I never would have consented to this." He looked into my eyes and then smiled softly, content with whatever he saw there. "Yeshua assured me that you would treat Leah well. I think he was right."

Of course he was right. Yeshua is always right. Didn't you know that? I bit down on the words before they could fly out of my mouth. Ezra was just trying to help. This wasn't his fault any more than it was Leah's, any more than it was mine. It was Yisu's fault, but Yisu wasn't here. Having torn down the building because it stood in his way, he'd simply walked off.

And Father had let him.

38

YISU

6 Elul 3773

Three down, one to go. I'd left home well before dawn, not wanting to be around while Katan got ready for his *kiddushin*. Even if it was my idea, I didn't think I could handle witnessing it—not yet. By the time the wedding rolled around I'd be fine, but right now the wounds were too fresh, the temptation to covet too strong to be resisted—I needed to flee from it. The trek to Korazin would give me something else to focus my thoughts on.

I made the journey in two stages. Heading east on the road to Sennabrin, I walked as fast as my legs would carry me, racing the sun toward the Sabbath. I reached the town an hour or two past noon—it was a good road, and no one had bothered me along the way—and made my way to the shore of Lake Gennesaret, looking for someone who'd ferry me to Capernaum for a price I could afford to pay. My Father was smiling on me; not only did I find a fisherman bound for Bethsaida, but he knew my uncle and offered to let me ride for free. And so it was that I showed up on Zebdi's doorstep as the *shofar* was sounding the second warning.

My uncle was surprised to see me, but he welcomed me in and gave me a seat of honor at his table after Aunt Shelomith provided me with water for washing and a clean set of clothes for the Sabbath. It had been nearly four years since last I'd been in his house, when I'd come with my parents for Yoshiah's funeral. Something had happened between Yosef and Zebdi during that visit (though what, I had no idea), and relations between the two families had been strained ever since. We still saw one another periodically, but not often, which explained the mistake I made when my young cousin first ran into the room. Though he'd grown quite a bit since the last time I'd seen him, I immediately recognized the seven-year-old by his mop of tangled, sun-bleached curls. "*Shabbat Shalom*, Kobi."

The boy came to a sudden stop and glared at me. "Don't call me that!" he yelled. "Don't you ever call me that!"

"Yakob!" Zebdi scolded. "Apologize to your cousin this instant! I won't have you talking to a guest that way, boy!"

"I-I'm s-sorry," the child stammered. His face was pale and his hands were trembling.

"That's better. Now sit down and be quiet."

"Yes, sir," he whispered.

Before I had the chance to ask Zebdi what had caused Yakob's outburst, another little boy came careening into the room, bumping into me in his haste to get to the table on time. "Whoa!" I laughed, catching him before he could fall over. From the size of him, he was about three or four years old; even if he hadn't looked just like Yoshiah I would have known him by his age. "*Shabbat Shalom*, Yuannan."

"Who're you?" he asked.

Zebdi answered."Welcome your cousin Yisu, Yuani." Though he was correcting his son, fondness had replaced the harshness in his voice.

"*Shalom*, Yishu," Yuani said.

I smiled at the boy, who had been born just three months after his brother's death, and who apparently didn't share Yakob's aversion to affectionate nicknames. "Do you always come thundering into a room like that, Yuani?" I asked. "Or was that in my honor?"

He laughed, a sweet sound that reminded me of Leah.

I turned to his brother. "And what of you, Yakob? Do you like to race also?"

He glanced at his father before answering, as if to get permission, and I remembered too late that Zebdi had told him to be quiet. Zebdi nodded impatiently, and the boy spoke. "Yes. I beat Haggai last week, too."

"Is he a fishing partner, or a classmate?"

"Both. But he's two years older than me. Last week, when we were—"

"Enough, Yakob," Zebdi interrupted. "Time for prayers."

Aunt Shelomith had come back into the room (much more sedately than her boys) carrying some lamps, which she set out on the table in preparation for sundown. Lighting them, she spoke the words that ushered in the Sabbath: "Blessed are You Adonai our God, who has sanctified us with the commandments and who has commanded us to kindle the lights of Shabbat."

I began to sing the Sabbath psalm, as my family did every week immediately after the lamp-lighting. "It is good to praise Adonai, and make music to Your name, El-Elyon!" No one else was singing, though little Yuani had started to clap more or less in time with the music. I paused. "Don't you sing that song here, Uncle?"

"No, but you're welcome to teach it to us. Can it wait until after we eat?"

"Certainly, sir."

He said *kiddush* and then we ate, after which we went to the synagogue. Returning home, we sang for nearly an hour, and then Shelomith put the children to bed and I was finally able to ask what had so upset Yakob. "You called him Kobi," Zebdi explained. "That was Yoshiah's nickname for him; no one else used it very often, and now he won't let anyone use it at all."

Recalling how hard Yakob had taken Yoshiah's death, I fell silent. The child had clung to me during the entire week of *shiva*, over and over again telling me that he was sorry and it was all his fault, although how a three-year-old child could have been responsible for the drowning death of an eleven-year-old was beyond me. Katan had told me that the two brothers were very close, that little Kobi had followed Yoshiah around everywhere, and that Yoshiah had welcomed his company. I thought about Yakob's pale face and trembling fists. Apparently this was a wound that would require more than time to fully heal.

I stayed through the Sabbath and the night that followed, playing with the children and resting from the ordeal of my week. Yuani was fascinated by my flute, so I let him blow into it and taught him a few basic fingerings; even though the instrument was too big for his chubby little hands, he was able to produce a tune of sorts. When I left the next morning, I gave him the flute as a present. "Take good care of it," I charged him. "Next time I see you, you can play a song for me, okay?" I blew one last tune, the first few lines of the Shepherd's psalm. "Goodbye, Adam," I murmured, and then I handed the flute back to my little cousin.

I made my farewells to the rest of the family and set out on the last leg of my trip. The road connecting Capernaum to Korazin was a lot like the one between Nazareth and Sepphoris, four or five miles long and uphill all the way, but it was less traveled and not as good; the hike took most of the morning. I didn't mind. I needed the time to prepare myself for the encounter with Yoash's family.

Korazin, though I'd never been there before, felt familiar. I wondered briefly if all the villages of the Galil were basically the same. Of course there was no gate *per se*, since there was no wall around the cluster of simple homes, but there was one building near the outskirts of the town that closely resembled the structure that served as the "gate" in Nazareth, and I found several of the village elders gathered there, as I'd expected.

"Can you direct me to the home of Amos, the potter?"

One of them pointed me in the general direction and rattled off a string of turns and landmarks I should watch for. Thanking him, I made my way through the crooked alleys that served as streets, appreciating anew the planning that had gone into the rebuilding of Sepphoris.

Eventually I wandered down the right alley; the large oven and potter's wheels that filled the cramped yard were impossible to miss, as were the three men at work there. All wore aprons coated with clay, and little besides—not surprising given the heat of the day and the heat of their furnace. One of the younger men was adding fuel to the fire; his brother was fanning the flames to make them even hotter. Both were drenched with sweat. *I'll never again complain about a summer roofing job.* The third man was standing as far from the oven as possible, calling out instructions.

I approached him. "Sir, are you Amos?"

"Yes."

"May I have a word with you, privately?" I kept my voice low, not wanting the boys to overhear. "I bear news of your son Yoash."

He frowned, expecting the news to be bad, no doubt. Gesturing toward the adjacent house, he led me through a low doorway into the comparative coolness of the interior. The room was empty except for a few furnishings. "Your wife and daughter-in-law?" I asked.

"Gone to do the laundry. We're alone. What do you have to tell me?"

"My name is Yeshua bar Yosef. I've come from Nazareth. I'm sorry to bear sad news, sir, but your son is dead."

He nodded slowly. "I had a feeling. It's been so long since we heard from him. I didn't expect your news would be good. Wait a moment, will you? I want the boys to hear the rest of what you have to say."

"It might be best if I told you first—"

"No, no, the worse it is, the more they need to hear it. You'll understand after you've had a chance to talk with them. It *is* bad, isn't it?"

I nodded.

He stuck his head out the door and shouted. "Micah! Yudah! Leave the kiln and get in here. Now!" He turned back to me. "Please, take a seat. Um—what was your name again?"

"Yeshua."

"I'm sorry, Yeshua. I'm not much of a host."

"Please, sir, don't apologize. I'm not much of a guest." This was going to be even harder than I'd feared. *Father...*

The boys entered the room just then, still dripping sweat. Except for the pattern of clay streaks on their faces and aprons, they were identical. Yoash had boasted about them, often. *They look alike, but they're different as day and night. Micah's the older by five minutes, and the better potter, but Yudah's smarter. He was talking in complete sentences by the time he was two—not those baby babblings, either, but real sentences. Always taking things apart to see how they work. Micah, now he could throw a pot that would survive the kiln by the time he was five! He made one with a narrow neck one day, a real beauty, and Yudah wanted to know what was inside. Micah told him it was full of honey cakes. Yudah tried to look inside—this was when they were five—but the neck was too narrow, so Yudah, he poked a straw down inside. "There's nothing in here, Toma!" he yelled—they always call each other Toma—but Micah insisted there were honey cakes inside. "They're just so soft your straw went right through, Toma. They're just as soft as air," Micah told him. So Yudah smashed the jar. "See! I knew it! Nothing inside, you liar." Like I said, he's smart. No fooling that one.*

I looked at the twins, trying to guess which was Micah and

which was Yudah, not that it really made a difference to my mission. Their grandfather introduced them quickly and without making a distinction; briefly I wondered if he even knew which was which. They each grabbed a dipper of water from a bucket by the door and drank deeply before sitting down.

Again I gave my name, and again I said, "I've come with bad news. Your father is dead."

They were silent for only a moment. Then one of them asked, "How do you know?"

This was probably Yudah.

"I was there," I answered. "I saw him die."

"Are you sure it was our father? It could have been someone else. Another Yoash."

I shook my head. "No, I'm sorry. He told me about you and your brother, many times."

"If you were there, why is it he's dead and you're not?"

"Yes," said the other twin. "How did he die?"

I didn't want to tell them.

"Tell us what you witnessed, Yeshua," Amos said. "That is what you came for, isn't it?"

Why did I come? I'd wanted to comfort his family, not horrify them. But Amos had used the word *witness*. I was a witness. I had to tell them the truth; I couldn't bear false witness. "He was executed for rebellion against Rome." Amos, at least, would know what that meant.

"Oh, God," he said. Then he started to cry.

I wouldn't say another word about Yoash's death in front of the boys, not unless Amos ordered me to. Mercifully, he did not. It was bad enough watching him go through this, imagining the reaction of my own grandfather when his sons had been executed, imagining Yosef's pain when I— *No. Not yet. Let tomorrow worry about tomorrow; I have enough real pain to deal with right now, without borrowing pain from an imagined future. Father, why did You lead me here? What is it You want me to do?*

"My father—" one of the twins was saying, the one I thought was Micah. "You say he was executed for rebellion—is he—was he one of the freedom fighters?"

"That's what they call themselves. The Zealots. Yes, he was with them."

"What do you mean, 'what they call themselves'? Aren't they fighting to free us from Rome? To end the injustice of the Occupation?" Micah was indignant.

"You're not one of them, are you?" Yudah asked suspiciously. "How do you know my father? What were you to him, anyway?"

Instead of answering, I asked him a question. "How old are you?"

"We're fifteen. What's that to you?"

Shimon's age when we met. He was fifteen the first time he murdered a man, driven to avenge his father's execution. I understood, now, what I was here to accomplish. Comfort? Perhaps. But more important than that, I was here for their *yeshu'ah.* These boys needed to be saved from themselves. They'd already set foot on a path that would lead right to their father's side. Like wayward sheep, they needed someone to chase after them and bring them back into the fold. Amos had already given me permission. *The worse it is, the more they need to hear it. You'll understand after you've had a chance to talk with them.*

Amos didn't need to hear it, though. He'd already heard all he could bear.

"Come with me, Toma," I said to both of them.

"Where?"

"We're going for a walk."

"Why?"

"So I can answer all of your questions."

Amos heard, looked up, and nodded. "Do what you can," he whispered.

An hour later, they finally ran out of questions. Each one they'd asked was worse than the one before, and I listened to myself in horror as I recounted every gruesome detail of Yoash's hanging, some of it again and again, reliving it all for his sons. And they...

They were angry.

"Where were his friends? The others in his band?"

"Hiding."

"Why didn't they come to set him free?"

"They didn't want to hang with him."

"Cowards!" Yudah pronounced his judgment with

vehemence.

"You think it cowardice to avoid torture and certain death?"

"Yes!"

"I would have tried, at least. If I'd been there," Micah said.

"You would have failed."

"At least I would have shown some courage."

"It's not courage to throw your life away for no good reason, Micah."

"Like you know what courage is!" Yudah shouted. "You just sat there, Yeshua, and did nothing."

"Would it have helped your father if I'd charged at the Romans with a sword, Yudah? Even if I'd killed three or four of them, I couldn't have saved Yoash. I simply would have given Rome one more victim to hang beside him."

"At least you would have died fighting."

"Fighting for what? To give the Romans yet another reason to hate the Galileans?"

"No, to show them that the Galileans won't accept injustice!" Yudah was now doing all of the talking for the pair. His twin had relinquished the lead to him as soon as the conversation turned into a debate and was now sitting back, listening to every word and watching to see who would emerge victorious before committing himself to either side. Although I was answering Yudah's questions, I was really speaking to both of them.

"And what will that accomplish?"

"An end to the injustice."

"Has it worked so far? Have the Romans become more just since the rebellion began?"

"All right then, if we can't end the injustice, we'll fight to avenge the injustice."

These boys had been poisoned by the same rhetoric that had destroyed Shimon. It hadn't come from their grandfather, that much I knew, nor from their father—Yoash had confided in me that he was horrified at the thought that his sons might one day join Shimon. But someone had convinced them that violence held the solution to our nation's problems; judging from their insistence, they'd heard it from more than one person. Yosef had told us often enough that the area around Lake Gennesaret was rife with zealotry, that Sepphoris and its villages were an exception to the general attitude of the Galil, but I hadn't understood what he meant until now.

"There's nothing to be gained by vengeance, Toma. If you rely on the sword, then that's all you have, and all it can bring you in the end is death. It can never bring life. Rely on God instead, the creator of life. Hasn't He promised to exact revenge on His enemies? Don't you think He can do a better job of that than you?"

"You're just afraid to die. I'm not, not for a good cause."

This was the first thing he'd said that gave me some hope for him. "You're right, Toma. A man should be willing to die for a good cause. If life can be purchased, death's not too high a price. But a cause that doesn't lead to life isn't a good cause."

"You're just saying that because you're afraid to hang. You're a coward."

"No, I'm not. Am I afraid to hang? Absolutely. Anyone who's witnessed a hanging and *isn't* afraid to hang—that man isn't brave, he's just a fool. I don't think I'm a fool. I hope you're not one either. Your father didn't think you were a fool—just the opposite. He was always telling me how smart you are, how you're nobody's fool. Was he wrong?"

"You watched my father die and did nothing to help him."

"There was nothing to be gained by my death."

"The words of a coward."

I closed my eyes for a second, asking my Father to spare this boy. Then I said, slowly and deliberately, considering every word carefully before I let it pass my lips, "If ever there is anything to gain by hanging, then I pray I will have the courage to hang. If even one life can be saved that way, then I'll trade mine for it. But there is no merit, Yudah, in your throwing away your life to avenge the dead. Instead, live. Deny death the victory by living. Honor your father by living up to his opinion of you. That's not cowardice—it's wisdom."

I couldn't tell from the expression on his face whether he'd heard me or not, but I'd said all I could. I walked the boys home and went inside to sit with Amos. The women were with him, crying, their baskets of laundry forgotten beside the door. Stacking the baskets one atop the other, I carried the wet clothes up to the roof and spread them out to dry in the sun. Later, I put together a simple meal from the food on hand and set it before the family. I didn't say anything as I served them— some griefs cannot be lightened by words.

I stayed with them a week, sitting *shiva* and seeing to their needs as best I could.

And then, having done what I'd come to do, I left.

39

KATAN

27 Elul 3773

Elul lasted forever. But then—all at once, it seemed—the moon waned to its last quarter and it was time to claim my bride.

Although Yisu had asked me to serve as his groomsman, I knew better than to return the favor. I'd promised Hezron, and though I'd done so fully expecting his sister to be sharing the *chuppah* with me, I still wanted him for my best man, and he was willing (dare I say eager?) to fulfill the duties of that role.

Mother had spent the last week going through my house, adding womanly touches here and there. She'd taken the change of plans pretty calmly, all things considered. "If I could have my way, there'd be two of Leah," she'd said to me, "so you and your brother could each marry one of her. She's the bride I'd have chosen for you, Yaakob, from the very beginning, because you deserve the best. I know you're not seeing it that way right now—who could blame you?—but you really are getting the best end of this arrangement." She'd smiled mischievously and added, "Leah's not doing too badly, either."

The thing I loved best about Mother—she didn't add a comment about poor Yisu.

Poor Yisu.

There was one other person I could trust not to sympathize with poor Yisu—Rabbi Zephanyah; and after what Ezra had said about the legitimacy of my children, I made a point of consulting him on the issue. I showed him Ezra's argument, neatly written out, claiming that my union with Leah was not forbidden under Torah even though she had been Yisu's wife, on the grounds that the marriage was not only unconsummated, but that consummation had not even been attempted—that Yisu had never brought Leah "into his house," had never "uncovered her nakedness," and therefore it was as if their marriage had never been. To tell the truth, I didn't expect Rabbi to go along with Ezra's interpretation, but he did.

"Leah is much better off with you, Yaakob," he said. "Her children by Yeshua *would* have been *mamzerim*—to the tenth generation!—but I have no objection to her marriage to you. Be fruitful and multiply in good conscience!"

Father also gave me some advice about multiplying, but he got us both drunk first.

"I dreaded the day my father would have this talk with me," he said after our third cup of wine, "but not half so much as I've dreaded having it with you. Here, have another cup—it helps the advice go down better."

"Yes, sir. What did you want to talk to me about? Or rather, what did you *not* want to talk about? To me."

"You know Torah commands you to be fruitful and multiply, right?"

"Yes, sir!"

"And you know how that works, right?"

"Yes, sir. That is, I think so." I chugged down the rest of my cup and poured another. "I watched a few times to make sure."

"You did *what?*"

Oops. I probably shouldn't have told him about that. I mean, look what happened to Ham, and all he did was peek at his father passed out butt-naked drunk. "Please don't curse my children, Abbi. I promise I won't do it again."

"You watched *me?* With your *mother?*"

Oops. "Um, no sir, I watched, um, the sheep. You know, up in Saba's pasture."

"Hm. Well, don't do it that way."

"No sir. I won't."

"You're supposed to make your wife *happy.* You have to, well, cuddle with her. Kiss her. Tell her she's beautiful."

"Not like the sheep. Yes, sir."

"You have to be gentle with her. And don't rush her."

"Don't crush her?" I had worried about that, just a little. After all, lying on top of her like that—maybe that's what made Mother cry out. Although Leah wasn't as small as Mother, so maybe it wouldn't be a problem.

"No, don't crush her either."

"So if she starts moaning or anything, I need to get off of her?"

"No, of course not."

"No? But you said don't crush her."

"That's not what moaning means. Moaning—well, that's a good thing. That means she's happy." He poured some more wine for both of us. "I've done some moaning myself."

"Yeah, I know."

He frowned at me. At least, I think it was a frown.

"So, is that all I need to know?"

"No. I'm supposed to tell you about the first time."

"The first time what?"

"The first time you, um, lie with your wife."

"With her or on top of her?"

"It's the same thing."

"But don't crush her. Even if she moans. 'Cause that means she's happy." Another thought occurred to me. "What about crying out? Is that a happy sound, too?"

"Yes, but not the first time. If she cries out the first time, you're probably hurting her."

"What do you mean?" This was all getting too confusing. Maybe I shouldn't have had that fifth cup of wine. Or was it six? I took another drink just in case.

"I'll tell you the truth, Katan, I don't really know. But that's what my father told me. So be gentle but don't worry, there's supposed to be some blood the first time—that's how you know she's a virgin."

Yuck. Did he really have to bring that up? I already knew that. "No more, Abba. I know enough now."

"You sure?"

"Absolutely. Make her happy, not like the sheep, don't crush her, and moaning's good."

"Good. Sounds like you're all set."

We poured another cup of wine to celebrate.

Rachel and Hannah went to Sepphoris the day before the wedding to spend the night with Leah, whom I hadn't seen in a week. Technically, she wasn't supposed to know when I was coming, but the arrival of my sisters—Rachel, to give her some last-minute advice (hopefully better than what I'd gotten from my father) and Hannah to serve as one of her bridesmaids—

probably gave her a pretty good idea that I was on my way. My brother-in-law Kaleb, who'd gone through all of this earlier in the year, also gave me some wedding advice of a much more practical nature than Father's, and since Rachel seemed happy, I decided to take Kaleb's advice seriously even though some of it struck me as a bit farfetched. I mean, blow in her ear?

I thought about that, and all the other advice I'd received over the past two weeks, as I lay alone in my new bed that night. (I'd moved into my house right after my betrothal because I wanted to establish ownership; besides, it felt weird to keep sharing a pallet with Yisu after everything that had happened.) The one thing that kept coming up was Leah's happiness. Even the scriptures commanded it: *If a man has recently married, he must not be sent to war or have any other duty laid on him. For one year he is to be free to stay at home and bring happiness to the wife he has married.* I didn't see how I could. Leah had made it pretty clear during our betrothal *kiddushin* that she was far from happy to be marrying me. She wanted Yisu, and—as I'd been saying for the past sixteen years—I was not Yisu. Unless I miraculously changed into Yisu before sunrise, I was not going to be able to bring happiness to my wife.

Still, I would try. Maybe Kaleb was right and all I needed to do was blow in her ear.

Eventually, I fell asleep.

I woke up late the next morning when the sun hit me in the face. Leaning out the window, I saw my brothers busy at work setting up some trestle tables in the courtyard to hold the food for the feast that would follow the wedding. Yisu emerged from the shop, carrying a stack of planks over one shoulder. *I guess that means I didn't turn into Yisu while I was sleeping.* Leah would just have to adjust.

I threw on some clothes and ran downstairs and across the yard to the oven where Mother and Mimah were baking. Judging from the stack of *challah* cooling on the table, they'd already been at work for hours. "Smells delicious! Can I have some?"

"Absolutely not!" Mimah scolded. "You know you're supposed to fast today, Katan!"

"Just one bite?" My stomach was already growling.

"No. Now shoo."

"Go up to the rock and do some thinking," Mother suggested.

It would be more fun to help with the wedding preparations, but as the groom I was supposed to spend the day contemplating the sanctity and purpose of marriage, or something to that effect. I sighed. I'd done nothing but contemplate this marriage for the past two weeks, but I headed for the stairs like the dutiful son my father yearned for and my mother believed me to be. As I was climbing the stairs, Yisu asked, "Katan, where's your *tallit*? I need it for the *chuppah*." He waved at the framework he was erecting in the center of the yard. Without pausing, I told him where to find my prayer shawl. "Thanks!" he called after me.

He seemed awfully cheerful for a man whose bride was marrying someone else today. Had he ever cared about her at all? If our places had been reversed, I wouldn't have been building his wedding canopy; I'd have been building a gallows to hang him on. Then again, if our places had been reversed, I wouldn't have divorced Leah. Or if I did, I wouldn't have allowed her to marry Yisu. But Yisu—he hadn't just allowed this wedding, he'd encouraged it; in fact, according to Ezra, Yisu had vouched for me! *My brother is an idiot,* I concluded.

I climbed up onto the rock, standing perched on the very edge while I looked out over the pasture and the lands surrounding it, listening to the laughter and chatter drifting up from the yard below and savoring the aroma of fresh-baked *challah*. Off to my left, I could just make out Netzer's farm, where my sister Rachel lived with Kaleb—in happiness. Their house blocked my view of their courtyard, but I knew Kaleb was probably out there with Hezron and my other friends, getting an oxcart ready for the trip to Sepphoris. They would come pick me up on the way—no walking for the bridegroom; today I was king! I didn't know exactly when they'd come; sometime after noon, I guessed. Father would make that decision, sending us to fetch Leah as soon as everything had been gotten ready to his satisfaction.

Before that I'd need to wash and get dressed in my wedding clothes. Really they were Yisu's wedding clothes, but he'd lost his claim to them the day he divorced Leah, and now they were mine, just like everything else. Yisu's house, Yisu's clothes, Yisu's bride...poor Yisu.

My brother is an idiot.
But enough of that—I was supposed to be contemplating the purpose and sanctity of marriage. *In the beginning...* God had created Adam in His image. He'd then pronounced that it wasn't good for Adam to be alone, so he'd taken a rib from Adam's side and made a woman from it, to be a help to Adam. *And Adam said, "This is now flesh of my flesh and bone of my bone, and she shall be called* Ishah *because she was taken out of* Ish." *Therefore shall a man leave his father and his mother and cleave unto his wife and they shall be one flesh. And they were both naked, Adam and Ishah, but they felt no shame.* What was to contemplate? Every schoolboy knew that. Marriage was sanctified by God Himself; it wasn't just something people had thought up on their own. As for its purpose, that was equally clear: God didn't want anyone to have to face life alone. (Oh, and there was also that command to be fruitful and multiply.)

The scriptures gave many examples of marriage—most of them examples of what *not* to do. King Solomon with his hundreds of pagan wives, for instance. Or King David's adulterous affair with Bathsheba. The scriptural marriage nearest and dearest to my own heart, the one I'd been contemplating for two weeks now, was that of my namesake, the patriarch Yaakob, who'd asked for Rachel but slept with Leah, and ended up married to both of them. The sisters had spent the rest of their lives competing for his attention. (Of course, that was before God laid down the Law: *Nor shall you take a woman as a rival to her sister, to uncover her nakedness while the other is alive.*) I'd often wondered just how drunk Yaakob was, to have slept with the wrong sister and not realized it till morning. *Then came morning. And behold, there was Leah.*

Well, that wasn't going to be a problem for me. Nowadays, it was customary to hold the wedding feast *after* the groom went in to his bride, not beforehand; plus we made both the bride and groom fast all day, so neither of them would be drunk; *and* we looked under the bride's veil before bedding her, just to be extra sure we were getting the right woman. So *this* Yaakob was going to get his Leah, all right, as planned. No surprises. Not tonight. And no Rachel to fret over, no rival for my affection. No sister coming between us. Just a brother...

I pushed the thought away. *Later. When I'm good and*

drunk. I'll worry about it then.
The sanctity of marriage. The purpose of marriage.
Right.
I stretched out on the rock the way I'd done as a boy, lying on my back with my arms folded beneath my head, looking up at the sky and thinking about nothing in particular. It was a holiday for me, everyone else busy working while I enjoyed my own private Sabbath. I watched the sun climb higher in the sky until it stood directly overhead and the heat was blistering. *Better to marry than to burn.* Then it started to go down again.

I should have brought my kinnor. I could have played some tunes to pass the time. I liked the idea, so I ran back down to the house—*my* house, though it was full of women at the moment, making the bedchamber fit for a bride—and grabbed my harp. After climbing back to the rock, I sat strumming snatches of familiar songs for a while, and then began to make a new song.

The tune was simple, the chording easy, but the notes came together in a way I'd never heard before and wasn't sure I liked. Still, this was the song my fingers had decided to play, and I let it flow from me, repeating the notes until words started to form in my mind to accompany them, and then I sang:

> "How long, Adonai, how long shall I strive in vain?
> How long until Your arm is bared before me?
> Victory eludes me; I box at the wind
> And the wind laughs in my face.
> How long, Adonai, how long shall I strive in vain?
> How long shall Your arm be hidden from me?"

It wasn't exactly a wedding song, but it expressed my frustration perfectly.

> "You place a choice before me,
> and command me to choose:
> An empty box or a hollow gourd.
> How long, Adonai, how long shall I strive in vain?
> How long until I see your salvation—"

No, this wasn't a word I wanted to hear right now. The last thing I wanted to see was *yeshu'ah.* I grimaced. Setting the kinnor aside, I sat back and watched the shadows lengthen in front of me as the sun made its descent.

"Katan!" My father's voice drifted up from the courtyard.

"Yes, sir!" I shouted.

"Come down and get dressed!"

It was time.

I stood under the *chuppah,* watching Leah move in and out of the lamplight as she circled me. Night had fallen, but it wasn't dark: countless stars shone above us as a reminder of God's promise to Abraham: *Look up at the heavens and count the stars—if indeed you can count them...So shall your offspring be.* Leah moved with a quiet grace I hadn't noticed before; in fact, she'd been quiet during the entire ride from Sepphoris, even though her bridesmaids giggled and chattered among themselves the whole way, flirting with my groomsmen in a way that was only acceptable during a wedding procession.

After she'd circled me seven times, Leah took her place by my side under the *chuppah* Yisu had built for us. The wings of my *tallit* stretched over our heads like a tent, a tangible illustration of my commitment to take her into my home and under my wing from this time forward. To further demonstrate my commitment, Father read the *ketubah,* our marriage contract, for all to hear. Then Ezra pronounced the first of the seven blessings over us.

"Blessed are You, Adonai Eloheinu, King of the universe, Who has created everything for His glory." He drank from the cup of wine he held, and then passed it to Father for the next blessing.

"Blessed are You, Adonai Eloheinu, King of the universe, Who fashioned the man." He also drank and passed the cup to Saba Yaakob.

"Blessed are You, Adonai Eloheinu, King of the universe, Who fashioned the man in His image, in the image of His likeness, and who prepared for him from Himself a building for eternity."

Saba Yoachim spoke next. "Bring intense joy and exultation to the barren one through the ingathering of her children amidst her in gladness. Blessed are You, Adonai, Who gladdens Zion through her children." After drinking, he passed on the cup.

"Gladden the beloved companions as You gladdened Your creature in Gan Eden from aforetime. Blessed are You, Adonai Eloheinu, King of the universe, Who gladdens groom and bride." The speaker was Rabbi Zephanyah, and the fact that he had come to my wedding despite all of the animosity between him and my father over the years gladdened me greatly, as did the fact that he had been invited to pronounce one of the blessings. He smiled at me before drinking deeply and passing the cup to another honored guest, Shofet Abiyud.

"Blessed are You, Adonai Eloheinu, King of the universe, Who created joy and gladness, groom and bride, mirth, glad song, pleasure, delight, love, brotherhood, peace, and companionship. Adonai, our God, let there soon be heard in the cities of Judah and the streets of Jerusalem the sound of joy and the sound of gladness, the voice of the groom and the voice of the bride, the sound of the grooms' jubilance from their canopies and of the youths from their song-filled feasts. Blessed are You Who gladdens the groom with the bride." He drank.

Stepping forward to take the cup from Abiyud's hand, my brother Yisu spoke the last of the blessings.

Yisu?

"Blessed are You, Adonai Eloheinu, King of the universe, Creator of the fruit of the vine." Yisu looked at me, then at Leah, and then at me again, smiled, and added his own words to the blessing: "May your union be fruitful." Then he drank and handed the cup to me.

I took it from him without a word, trying to hide my shock and anger. Of course he'd had to come to my wedding; it would have added to the scandal if he hadn't. But I hadn't asked him to serve as a groomsman and I certainly wasn't expecting him to be the one to hand me the bridal cup. *Your selfish decisions robbed me of my choices, put my life on a whole different path—and now you act as if you did me a favor? You bless me?* I stood there holding the cup and stared at him until the smile fell off his face. Then I turned to my bride. As I'd done at our betrothal, I held the wine to Leah's lips; she lifted her veil just enough to accept the drink but not enough for me to see her face. She took a single sip, and I drained what was left.

As if I'd given a signal, there was an immediate rush of activity as my groomsmen pulled me in one direction and

Leah's bridesmaids pulled her in another. Yisu got left behind somewhere in the chaos, so I didn't have to deal with him anymore, for which I was intensely grateful. Hezron was saying something to me, but I missed half of it before I focused enough to realize it was important. "What, Ronni? Tell me again."

"After you've bedded your wife, you need to take the sheet off your bed—not the big sheet, the little one, you'll see when you get there—you need to take it off, fold it up, and give it to me. It's important. Don't forget. We can't start the feasting until you do." Hezron would give the sheet to Ezra and he'd hold on to it in case I ever decided to dispute Leah's virginity. It would also serve as proof that we'd actually consummated the marriage.

"Don't worry," I assured him, "I won't forget."

Looking over his shoulder, I could see the girls with their lamps climbing the stairway that led to my bedchamber. Leah was somewhere among them. They'd need a few more minutes to get her ready for me. I could use a few more minutes myself. "Ronni, can you get me some wine? I'm a nervous wreck all of a sudden."

"What, and get you too drunk to do your duty?"

Kaleb intervened. "Here, Katan, I already poured you a cup when no one was looking."

"Thanks, Kaleb." I downed the whole thing in one swig.

"Careful, man! You haven't eaten all day, remember?"

Someone started to play a lively tune on the flute; a moment later another pipe joined in, and then a drummer, and soon the courtyard was filled with music, singing, and clapping. "That's intended to give you some privacy, Katan!" Kaleb laughed. "Make all the noise you want—no one will be able to hear you over that din."

"Come on," Hezron urged. "Let's get him up there so the girls can come down and join the fun."

"Not so fast, boys." It was my father, walking over to our little huddle and laying a hand on my shoulder. "How are you feeling, Katan?"

"I think he's *up* to the challenge," Kaleb offered.

"Yeah, how *hard* can it be?" Hezron added with a grin.

My other friends all threw in the jokes they'd saved up just for this occasion. I didn't find them nearly as funny as the jokes we'd told at Kaleb's wedding. "All right, boys," Father finally interrupted. "Give me a minute alone with my son, and then you can escort him to his bride." They moved the huddle a few feet away and continued to amuse themselves with bawdy comments while Father leaned close to me and smiled. "I just wanted to tell you, Yaakob, how blessed I feel tonight—I feel blessed in you, son. I know this wasn't your plan, but you've made the right choice and I know God will bless you for it. Leah will bless you for it, too. I wish—" His eyes filled with tears. *Oh please don't mention poor Yisu.* "I wish you both all the happiness you so richly deserve." He kissed me. "I love you, Yaakob. I'm sorry I had to put you through this. Will—will you forgive me?"

Maybe it was just the wine on an empty stomach, but, for the first time in four years, I believed he really did care about me, and the automatic *yes, sir* that normally fell from my lips without thought or feeling was replaced by the words I'd wanted to say—and mean—for so long. "I love you too, Abba." Awkwardly I hugged him.

"Minute's up!" Kaleb crowed, and suddenly I was surrounded by my friends and they swept me away from my father and across the courtyard to the house where my bride was waiting.

40

YISU

I'd meant to bless my brother, but all I'd done was hurt him again. I watched as his friends gathered around him, laughing and teasing. I wanted to join them, but I knew Katan wouldn't welcome my company, so I stayed where I was, under the *chuppah* I'd built, alone.

Father, keep me as the apple of Your eye; hide me under the shadow of Your wings.

No one is meant to stand alone under a wedding canopy. I stepped back a few feet, looking up at Katan's prayer shawl, and my eyes caught the parade of lamps on the far side of the courtyard just as they began climbing the stairs to my—my brother's bedroom. *I can't do this anymore. Please. It's too much.*

It was easy to slip away unnoticed as the music started and people began to dance. The myrtle grove wasn't too far away, but it was far enough. The sounds of celebration faded into the distance. Yosef would miss me once the feast began, but he'd understand. I couldn't be alone tonight. I needed my Father.

I sank into His embrace and opened the books He'd written on my heart, taking them out and scrolling through them in search of comfort. But all I found were reminders of the work I had yet to do. "Oh, my Father. Oh, my Father." All other words forsook me, and I curled into a ball, sobbing these three words again and again, until I fell asleep.

I sit in the main room of my house, and Leah and the children are there. I know this place—I know what is coming. When the ground begins to shake, I know what must be done. "Go!" I tell Leah.

"No!" she says. "I won't leave you."

And then my brother is at my side. "Get her out of here!" I beg. He nods. Grabbing Leah by the hand, he drags her from the building, and the children follow him as I brace myself against the buckling column that supports the structure and raise my hands to hold the beam in place...

I woke in pain as the building collapsed, but the horror of the dream had gone.

Leah was safe.

41

KATAN

28 Elul 3773

The last girl left, giggling all the way down the stairs as I shut and bolted the door behind her. Ignoring the sounds of celebration outside, I turned toward the bed. The single lamp that remained in the room cast enough of a glow that I could see Leah, but she was shrouded in mystery, her face still hidden beneath her veil as she sat in the middle of the bed wearing nothing but a shift. I took a few steps toward her and she pulled a blanket up to cover herself more.

I didn't stop, but crossed the room and sat on the edge of the bed. Leaning over, I lifted the veil from her face, folding it back over her hair and looking long and hard at her features. Yes, it was Leah, but in the soft light of the lamp she almost looked pretty. I pulled the veil away from her and dropped it on the floor, but I made no further move.

"Aren't you going to kiss me?" she whispered.

"No," I answered her. "Not until we're alone."

She looked around the room, puzzled. "Is someone else here?"

"Yes."

"Who? I don't see anyone."

"I do. Yisu. He's in the room with us, and I'm damned if I'm going to lie with you while he's looking over my shoulder." I needed to get this off my chest. "We're both thinking about him, so we might as well talk about him." I tried to look her in the eyes, but her head was bowed. "Look, Leah, I understand, really I do. You've spent the last eight or nine months thinking of yourself as Yisu's bride, and just two weeks trying to get used to the idea that you're mine. I know I'm not the husband you want. But I'm the one you have. And I won't pretend—I won't lie to you. Marrying you wasn't my idea either. I'm not happy about having my life dictated by Yisu's choices. But you're the wife I have, and I'm going to do the best I can by you. But I'm not Yisu, and I won't share you with him. I can't kiss you—or anything else—if I think you're seeing his face while you're in my arms. I can't, and I won't."

Still without looking up, she asked, "Why did you agree to marry me?"

"I know what I should say—that I think you're beautiful, that I've been wanting you for years. But it's not true. The only reason I married you is because—well, because what Yisu did to you was *wrong* and I couldn't just let your life be ruined, not when there was something I could do to help. I'm sorry, Leah, but that's the truth. I don't love you; I don't know if I ever will."

"Is that what you think?" She lifted her head to look at me, and there were tears in her eyes. "You really only married me to help me? Not because you wanted me?"

I hated to hurt her, but I wasn't going to lie. "Yes."

"So you married me for me, not for you. You gave up what you wanted to give me what I needed. Yaakob, if that isn't love, then I don't know what is." She smiled softly. "I don't know another woman whose husband loves her like that. Not a single one." She leaned toward me, dropping the blanket. "I don't want Yisu. He doesn't love me. You do. You're the only one I want. If Yisu's in this room, it's because you brought him here. Not me."

I'd never noticed how pretty her smile was. "Not me either. I don't want him here!"

"Then we're alone." She leaned over the rest of the way, closing the gap between us, and kissed me.

"Ronni!"

I leaned out the window and tossed the sheet to him. Then I went back to my wife. Let them feast without me—who needs food, anyway? Hours later I fell asleep. My last coherent thought as I wrapped my arms around my happy, uncrushed bride was, *My brother is an idiot.*

And when I woke the next morning, behold—there was Leah.

Part Five

Sacrifices

The word of Yahuh came to me:
"Son of Man, why should wood from
a grapevine be better than some other
kind of wood, than some branch that
one might find among the trees of the
forest? Its wood can't be used to
make anything, not even a pin on
which to hang a pot. So now it is
thrown into the fire as fuel…"

—Ezekiel 15:1-4 (NIV)

42

KATAN

17 Adar Alef 3775
(Two Years Later)

As I walked through the door, Eli began to wave his arms and shriek with delight. "Buh-buh-buh-buh-buh!" I picked him up and tossed him a few times, mindful of the ceiling beams.

"Yaakob! Be careful!" Leah protested. "Ooh, I hate it when you do that!"

I just laughed. Emi used to say the same thing when Father tossed Shimeon, and before that, Sarah; and before that, Yehudah; and presumably all of us when we were babies. None of us had died from it. I gave Eli one more good toss, missing the beam by at least two inches, and then set him down on the floor with a tickle or two. "Buh-buh-buh-buh!" he begged.

"Nope, not today, son." I lowered my voice in a conspiratorial whisper. "Abba has to wait until Ema's out of the room."

"Muh-muh-muh."

"That's right, Ema spoils all the fun."

"Yaakob!" Leah's hands were buried in the dough she was kneading, so I felt safe walking up behind her, wrapping my arms around her, and nibbling on her ear. She giggled and tried to get away, but I was relentless. "That tickles!" she squealed.

"What about this?" I breathed gently on her ear, and then down her neck, lifting her hair out of the way as I nuzzled the top of her shoulder where it peeked out from her tunic, which had been pulled awry by my wandering hands. Hers were still trapped in the dough, so I took a few more liberties. "Does this tickle? How about this?" Her giggling had turned to little moans, so I knew she was happy. I was feeling pretty happy myself, but I was in the mood to get happier. "I'll be right back," I whispered. Sweeping Eli off the floor again, I headed for the door.

"Where are you going?"

"Eli's going to visit with his Aunt Hannah for a while."

"I think I'll finish the kneading later."

"Good idea," I called back over my shoulder, and went in search of my sister.

One benefit of belonging to a large family is that there are always people around to help; our home was always bustling, always crowded, always bursting with life. Hannah was Eli's favorite playmate (besides me, of course), and she never minded watching him for an hour or two when I wanted time alone with Leah, but this afternoon I couldn't find her anywhere.

"Oh, she's with Rachel," Sarah told me. "Emi's there too. And Aunt Mimah."

"Is it time?"

"I don't know. Mimah's gone to check."

There weren't many women in Nazareth who knew more about childbirth than my aunt—who'd learned much of what she knew by helping deliver six of my siblings—and she was valued as a midwife not only in our family but in the community as well. According to Mimah, Rachel was due to deliver twins any day now. Certainly the term "bursting with life" described my sister—if she got any bigger, she wouldn't be able to fit through a door. Mimah had spent a lot of time at Netzer's farm over the past eight months, though I suspected she had reasons other than Rachel's pregnancy for her many visits. (Netzer's wife had died last year, and Mimah, though too old to be having children of her own, was not too old to enjoy Netzer's company. According to Kaleb, the enjoyment was mutual.) Hannah had also been spending a lot of time there, some of it with Rachel, but most of it bossing Yisu around as he worked with Yafet to build Hannah a house. I refused to have any part of it. Hannah was born bossy, but since her betrothal to Netzer's youngest son, she'd become impossible.

With both Mother and Hannah away, Sarah was the only one available to watch Eli, but I figured she could handle the responsibility on her own for a little while. I'd watched Yehudah when *I* was eight. It was easy. "Just don't let him stick anything small into his mouth," I reminded her.

"I know how to watch a *baby*, Katan," she said, rolling her eyes at me as she set him on her hip and took him into the house. Knowing how overprotective Leah could be, I decided not to mention Hannah's absence until after I'd made my wife *very* happy. Not having come from a large family herself, there were some things Leah just didn't understand.

I raced back to my house, eager to finish what I'd started. Leah had thrown a towel over the dough, shuttered the windows, and unrolled our bed (it was still too cold to sleep upstairs); she was sitting in the middle of it with her back toward me and her hair pulled to one side, exposing the shoulder I'd bared earlier. "*Ishi*," she murmured invitingly. *My husband.*

"*Ishati*," I answered. *My wife.* Bolting the door, I took up right where I'd left off.

"Well, *Ishati*," I said when we were both spent, "have I brought you happiness?"

"Yes, *Ishi*," she answered with a smile, "you have fulfilled the *mitzvah*."

This had become our joke, pretending that we came together only because we were pious. It was almost too good to be true, that God had commanded such a thing as this. "Blessed are You, Adonai Eloheinu, King of the universe, Who has sanctified us by His commandments and Who has commanded that a husband should bring happiness to his wife," I intoned solemnly.

"Blessed are You, Adonai Eloheinu, Creator of all things, Who has commanded that a man and his wife shall become one flesh," Leah sang sweetly. "Blessed are You, Adonai, a King to be praised in adoration!" We stood up together, embraced one last time, and then tugged our clothes into position. "Back to work," Leah chirped. She folded the bed into a corner and opened the window to let in the light, and then returned to her bread.

"I'll go get Eli," I said.

As I reached for the door latch, someone began to knock hard on the other side. Quickly I pulled the door open, worried that Sarah had come looking for me, but it was Hannah standing there. "Leah, it's Rachel's time. Do you want to help?"

"Of course." She threw the towel over the bread again, and I remembered that Rachel had held Leah's hand as she labored with Eli. "Yaakob, my husband, if you want bread in the morning, you'll have to finish that dough yourself. Get Sarah to help you." She looked at Hannah, frowning in confusion. "Where's Eli?"

"Why are you asking me? I've been with Rachel all day."

"Yaakob!"

"He's with Sarah. Don't look at me like that; Sarah knows how to watch a baby."

"I'll get him, Leah," Hannah offered. "He'll have to come with us, anyway, since we'll probably be there all night. I'll bring Sarah, too. She's too young to be in the room during the worst part of it, but she can stay close by and keep an eye on Eli for you until you need to nurse him. Katan, you tell Father the women will all be with Rachel tonight."

Bossy, bossy, bossy. "Sure. Why don't you send Kaleb up to sit with us? Netzer and Yafet, too. Tell them to bring their instruments; we'll have some music while we wait." *Oh, well, at least I got a chance to make Leah happy before she left.*

It was going to be a long night. Two or three times every hour, one of us ran over to the farm to check on Rachel's progress; the last report we'd gotten from Mimah said that Rachel was having a difficult time of it and would likely be laboring until dawn. Mimah didn't seem worried, though.

Just before sunset we'd eaten together, all the men of Kaleb's family and ours, and then we'd spent some time in prayer; as Saba Yoachim pointed out, "We have a *minyan* gathered here, so we might as well make use of it." Counting heads, I saw that he wasn't exaggerating. Even with Shammai and Yosei out in the pasture, we had ten adult men and two boys.

After the prayers, we pulled out our musical instruments and made joyful noises well into the night. As the sun fell behind the horizon, so did the temperature. A couple hours before midnight I grabbed up a pile of blankets, tucking one around Shimeon (who had fallen asleep about an hour ago) and wrapping two more around myself before heading toward the door.

"Where are you going?" Father asked. Yehudah had just brought a report from Mimah ten minutes ago.

"I'm going to relieve Yosei and bring Shammai some extra

blankets." Even though it was Yosei's turn to help guard the sheepfold, I'd decided to give my little brother a break; after all, with Leah and Eli away, the only thing I had to go home to was a cold bed.

Yisu stood up. "Let's give Shammai a chance to warm up, too. I'll come with you." He threw a blanket over his shoulders and picked up a loaf of bread and a jar that was still half full of spiced wine. Side by side, we headed out to the fold at the eastern edge of the pasture. It was cold going, and our breath formed clouds as we walked; I pulled a blanket up over my head and saw that Yisu had already done the same. "Spring's coming late this year," he remarked.

"Pregnant sister, pregnant mother, pregnant year," I replied. Leah was the only married woman in the family who wasn't pregnant right now, but she was still nursing. In fact, she'd not resumed her cycle yet, which didn't bother me in the least— except for the forty days following Eli's birth, it was over a year since she'd been *niddah*, so I'd been able to make her happy whenever I wanted instead of only two or three weeks each month. I smiled at the thought, and kept that smile on my face all the way up to the sheepfold.

Shammai had a small fire going just outside the cave, and a pile of twigs that should keep it burning for a few hours at least. Yisu stuck the wine jar into the coals to heat it up and then told our brothers to go home. (In truth, Shammai was our uncle, but he'd been raised alongside Yosei as one of our brothers.) They didn't wait to be told twice, but ran down the path in their haste to get out of the cold night. That left just Yisu and me to huddle beside the fire at the entrance to the cave where Saba kept his sheep at night. It was probably a lot warmer in there, with over a hundred woolly bodies pressed together in the tight space, but it would be impossible to see marauders approaching if we both sat inside. I knew that if it got much colder, we would take turns standing watch. In the meantime, the two of us sat with our backs to the flame and our eyes trained on the hillsides, passing the warm drink back and forth and listening to the sounds of the crackling fire and the somnolent sheep. All else was silent.

The silence—like the women and the year—was pregnant, begging to be broken, but I really had nothing to say to Yisu. The way he'd jumped up to come out here with me, I'd expected him to deliver a lecture on something or other, but he was quiet, too. I stood it as long as I could, fidgeting and tapping my fingers, and finally started to hum one of the songs we'd been singing earlier.

"Did you bring your *kinnor*?" Yisu asked.

"No." It was too hard to pick out a tune with half-frozen fingers. "Your flute?"

"No."

I went back to humming. Yisu sang along, but softly, as if to himself. "O Adonai, what is man that You care for him, the son of man that You think of him?" About halfway through, his voice trailed off.

I continued to hum until I reached the end. Yisu was staring at his hands, unmoving. It wasn't like him to sit silent through a song of praise. "Are you all right?" He didn't answer. "Yisu? Are you all right?"

He jerked as if I'd startled him awake. "What?"

"You'd better not be falling asleep on me. Are you all right?" I asked for the third time.

"Yes, yes, I'm fine." He got up and put some more branches on the fire. "Do you ever wonder about that? I mean, really wonder?"

"Wonder about what?" He'd gone off in his own little world, and I had no idea what he was talking about. "About whether you're all right? Yeah, I wonder about that all the time." I was only half joking.

He laughed. "I guess I had that coming. No, I meant did you ever wonder why God cares about us at all?"

"No, not really. Scripture makes it clear: He puts up with us because of His promises to Abraham and David. How many times does He say, 'Nevertheless, for the sake of my servant David,' or words to that effect?"

"Yes, but why did He promise David anything? And why did He reach out to Abraham in the first place? Why did He spare Noah? For that matter, why did He create Adam? Don't you ever wonder?"

"Nope." *This is what happens when a man decides not to marry.* "Don't you have anything more important to think about?"

"More important? No, I don't think so. The God who created the universe cares about me, listens to my prayers.

Why? Who am I? What am I?"

"You're a son of Abraham, same as all the rest of us. Let it go, Yisu. What's the point of asking questions that have no answers? Here—take some advice from the wisest man who ever lived: 'Much dreaming and many words are meaningless; therefore fear God.'" Rabbi Zephanyah and I had been working our way through the writings of Solomon all winter. "What more do you really need to know?"

Yisu shook his head, but fell silent once more.

I watched for another hour, but the cold was starting to get to me. We'd run out of the hot wine long since, and there was no other way to get warm all the way through. When I faced the fire, my back froze; when I turned my back to the fire, my face froze. Yisu saw me shaking. "Go inside for a while," he suggested. "I'll keep watch while you thaw."

"Th-th-thanks," I managed to get out. I crawled in amongst the sheep, who were packed in the cave but not uncomfortably so—it was cozy rather than cramped, and almost before I knew it, I was asleep.

I awoke some time later to the sound of voices outside. One was Yisu's. The other two were vaguely familiar, but I couldn't place them immediately.

"Would you be forsworn, then?" one was asking. He sounded shocked.

"God forbid such a thing," Yisu answered. "You know me better than that."

"I thought I did."

"You promised your help," the third voice accused. "I've seen none."

"Then you've had your eyes closed," Yisu replied. "I've helped often and in more ways than you know, Sicae. Certainly by my silence. But there's a time for silence and a time to cry out, and I won't be silent forever."

"Is that a threat?" *Sicae*. His was a name I wasn't likely to forget, though I didn't know the man well. He was one of Shimon's band and had been with me on the raid; his real name was a mystery, but he called himself "the Dagger"—in Latin, so the Romans would understand who was killing them, he'd boasted. Of all the men I'd met that night, Sicae scared me the most.

"The word is yours." Was my brother *possessed*? It

sounded like he was deliberately provoking Sicae. "If by 'threat' you mean a promise I intend to break, then no, it's not a threat. I keep my promises. If you mean a danger, then yes, I suppose my crying out could pose a danger of sorts." I recognized Yisu's tone of voice—he was playing the rabbi, trying to have an intellectual debate. *You moron!* Sicae wasn't the sort of man one debated with. "But you're crossing a line, breaking your own promises, and I won't stand silently by while you get yourselves and others killed. As you said, I promised to help. When a ram tries to lead the flock into a pit, he needs to be stopped. The shepherd who refuses to act is no shepherd at all; he's a wolf, and the blood of the entire flock is on his head. Far be it from me to become a wolf."

"Do you call *me* 'wolf,' then?" asked the one who'd spoken first.

"Do *I* call you 'wolf'? What does it matter, Shimon? Ask instead what *God* is calling you. Examine your heart. Examine the fruit of your actions." So, Yisu was still meeting with Shimon. Why didn't that surprise me? He sounded pretty frustrated, though. "How many times have we had this discussion? How many more of your men will hang before you admit your folly? Yoash, Gershom, Netanyahu, Eleazar..." His voice broke. "When will you stop this madness, brother? Can you really not see where it's leading you? Must I see *you* on a cross, too?"

"I can't believe you would betray me like this, Yisu."

"It's not a betrayal. If it were, would I have told you ahead of time? But it's written, 'Rescue those being led away to death; hold back those staggering toward slaughter.' I won't stand by and pretend ignorance; I won't be responsible for your slaughter. I won't."

"You talk about 'won't'?" Sicae said. "This is betrayal, and *I* won't put up with it. I'm warning you now, *brother*," and he laced the word with sarcasm and scorn, "that if you do this, you will pay. Eye for eye, tooth for tooth, life for life. Consider that a threat, or if you prefer, a promise I have every intention of keeping."

Yisu didn't answer.

From where I lay, I couldn't see the men, just a faint glow from the fire; however, when a moving shadow blocked out the glow for a second or two, I realized that at least one of them had gotten up. *Adonai Elohim, spare my brother's life*, I prayed, almost certain that Sicae was about to slit Yisu's throat. As quietly as I could, I got to my feet and crept toward the mouth of the cave. Surprise was the only thing that would give me even a chance of taking them; they were trained fighters and probably armed, whereas I had nothing but a staff. Most likely, both of us would be killed, but as Yisu had pointed out, I couldn't just lie there and let them murder my brother without lifting a finger to help him.

Before I charged, though, Shimon spoke. "Put away your dagger, Sicae—you've made your point. I hope you heard it, Yisu. Don't do this thing. You've spoken your mind, delivered your warning. Let that be enough. You're innocent of our blood...*if* you keep your mouth shut. Do you hear me? Honor your oath; hold your peace; keep your mouth shut or you *will* bear the responsibility not only for my slaughter, but many others' as well. Come on, Sicae, we're leaving now."

I remained hidden inside the sheepfold for several minutes after they left, positive that if they knew I'd been listening, they'd kill both of us on the spot; I wanted them well away before I revealed myself. Then, from the cave's mouth, I said softly, "So what is it you're planning to do that's worth your life?"

Yisu, who had his back to the fire and to me, jumped slightly at the sound of my voice, but he didn't turn around. "I hope you're still in the shadows," he said quietly.

"Unlike you, I'm not trying to get myself killed."

"Believe it or not, neither am I."

"Then you should choose your friends more wisely, brother."

"Would it help? 'Even my close friend, whom I trusted, he who shared my bread, has lifted up his heel against me.'"

Was he going to play the rabbi with *me*, too? I countered, "David also wrote, 'His speech is smooth as butter, yet war is in his heart; his words are more soothing than oil, yet they are drawn swords.' It's not like you didn't know who Shimon is or what he stands for. Did you really think he wouldn't turn against you?" I shook my head, even though he couldn't see me. "How can you be so smart about some things and such an idiot about others, Yisu?" Without waiting for a reply, I repeated my earlier question. "So what did you do to upset them?"

"It's too complicated to explain. This has been building for over a year."

"Have you told Father yet?"

"No."

I thought about the little sermon he'd preached to the Zealots. "It's gone on long enough, brother, this double life of yours, and my silence about it. No more. You tell Father or I will. I don't care what Mother said; I'm not going to stand by while you throw yourself off a cliff—that *is* what you said to Shimon, am I right?"

"The gist of it."

"So...?" He said nothing, kept his back to me. "Are you going to tell Father what's going on, or am I?"

"Did Mother explain to you—"

"Yes, she did. Like I said, I don't care. She's a woman. She doesn't understand what men like Sicae are capable of. *You* don't understand what he's capable of."

"And you do?"

"I've seen it. Trust me. You don't want to."

"No, I don't. That's why...never mind. I promised Father I wouldn't drag you into it."

"Then why did you plan to meet with them tonight, with me here?"

"I didn't. They just showed up."

"You expect me to believe that?"

"It's the truth, whether or not you believe it." He came back to the fire and sat down.

"What did they want?"

"It's nothing you need to concern yourself about."

"You're really not going to tell me, are you?"

"No, I'm not. And you aren't going to tell Father."

It was cold by the mouth of the cave, too far from the fire and away from the sheep. "Do you think it's safe for me to come out yet?"

"I don't know. Let's do this instead: I'll come in there, and then you can come out by the fire. That way, if they are watching, they won't see two of us. Besides, it's my turn to warm up; you've been asleep for hours."

"Fair enough." We made the switch, and I put some more fuel on the fire, standing as close as I dared to the flames until I was no longer chilled through. "So, Yisu," I continued our conversation after a few minutes had passed, "why are you so sure I won't tell Father?"

There was no answer. Peering into the cave, I saw that he'd already fallen asleep.

43

YISU

17 Adar Alef 3775

I*f you falter in times of trouble, how small is your strength!
Rescue those being led away to death; hold back those
staggering toward slaughter. If you say, "But we knew
nothing about this," does not He who weighs the heart perceive
it? Does not He who guards your life know it? Will He not
repay each person according to what he has done?*
The words of the proverb kept pounding at me, lending
strength to my conviction.
*I promised them that I'd help them. I swore that I'd never
betray them.* This was not betrayal. If they went through with
their plan, many lives would be lost—Roman lives and the lives
of the Zealots, and undoubtedly many innocent lives as well.
Yosef and I had had several long talks over the past year about
the rebellion of Yudah bar Hezekiah and the horrific toll it had
taken on the people of Sepphoris. Shimon was not as powerful
or influential as Yudah had been—not yet, at any rate—but his
goals were the same. Armed, he could pose as great a threat.
Yudah's raid on the armory had resulted in the destruction of
the city and its inhabitants; Shimon could not be allowed to do
the same.

Katan thought Yosef needed to know that trouble was
brewing, but there was nothing Yosef could do about it; I was
loath to add to the burden he already carried. At the same time,
I was hesitant to do this thing without first receiving counsel
from someone I could trust. For years, Yosef had been that
someone. He knew me better than anyone else and, unlike Ezra,
he also knew what the Zealots were capable of. He'd managed
to live in relative peace under the Roman Occupation for forty-
three years—and God had placed me in his care. If I was going
to seek advice from anyone, Yosef was the logical choice.

I sought him out the next morning.

"Abba, can we talk?"

Katan looked over at me and nodded encouragingly.

Yosef took one look at me and put his tools down, expecting this to be long and private. "Where?"

"The upper room is fine, sir." I watched him relax. Some of the things I'd shared with him over the past two years... I didn't want ever to drag him out to High Point again; the thinking rock was bad enough. But it was so hard to find any privacy at home, and so many of the things I needed to discuss with him were intensely private. Today, however, with all the women still tending to Rachel, the house was fairly empty, and even if we were overheard, nothing I had to say to him was profoundly secret; it was just routinely secret.

I perched in the window, sitting casually with one leg dangling in and the other out; my position allowed me to keep an eye on the yard below and the stairway up to the roof, although the only one likely to eavesdrop was Katan. More importantly, my nonchalance helped Yosef to further relax. "What do you need, son?" He managed to ask the question without wincing.

"I'm trying to make a decision, and it's turning out to be harder than I expected. I need your advice."

"You know it's always yours for the asking."

"Yes, sir, but this decision involves some things I haven't shared with you before—things you asked me not to share with you." He would know, of course, what I meant. "If you still want me to keep them to myself, I will. I just didn't want to make that assumption without asking. Once before you told me I should never shut you out. So the door's open, Abba, if you want to come in. I'll understand if you don't."

Even this might have been too much. I watched his face.

He dropped his eyes, but only for a second. Then he raised his head and looked me square in the face. Remorse was etched into every line of his features. "I'm sorry. I am so sorry." He stared at me for a long moment before continuing. "I shut *you* out, Yisu. That was—that was wrong of me. I put my needs above yours—I abandoned you. Please, may I have your forgiveness?"

I smiled and answered him in his own words. "You know it's always yours for the asking."

He was too caught up in self-reproach to hear me. "I couldn't bear the thought of you with those men, so I left you all alone with them. How could I have been so selfish, so stupid?" He shook his head. "I'm your father. I'm supposed to protect you—not the other way around. And now you're afraid to come to me...afraid of hurting me. Give me another chance."

I nodded. This time, though I used no words, he heard.

"What do you need, son?" he asked again.

"Remember what I told you when the Zealots let me go, that I swore I'd help them and never betray them?" He nodded, somber but not distressed, listening with an open heart. *Thank You, Father. I've missed him so.* "I don't know how to do both of those things any more." Suddenly the weight I'd been carrying around seemed so heavy. "They're planning something, something terrible. Shimon told me about it, wanting my help. I refused to do what he asked, but now he wants me to forget I ever heard his plans. Abba, if I keep silent, lots of people are going to die. If I don't keep silent, the burden is put back on Shimon—he can abandon his plan or go through with it anyway. If he chooses to go through with it—which he probably will, knowing Shimon—then there's a strong chance that he'll die, along with most of the men who follow him, the ones who've trusted me to keep my oath."

"You have to keep your oath, Yisu. That's why—" He stopped.

"Please say what's on your heart, Abba. 'That's why—'?"

"That's why I was so upset when you told me what you'd promised. I knew this day would come." The *I-told-you-so* didn't sting, coming from Yosef. "Is there any choice here that doesn't lead to death?"

"One. If I warn the Romans of Shimon's plan, *and* if he abandons his intentions, then no one will get hurt."

"Then that would be my advice. You're certain that your silence would prove fatal?"

I nodded. "His plan is sound. If he attacks, he'll succeed. But if he succeeds, it will be only a matter of time before he drags the entire region into rebellion. It will be Yudah bar Hezekiah all over again. Hundreds, maybe thousands, will die. Including Shimon, in the end."

"What aren't you telling me?"

He was so perceptive. "I told Shimon that I was going to

the Romans."

"Oh, Yisu."

"Otherwise they would simply have turned his ambush back on him. That *would* be a betrayal, Father, to send Shimon unaware into a trap. I won't have his execution on my head."

"No, no, you couldn't do that. I understand. But now..."

I sighed. "He's threatened to kill me if I talk."

"Naturally. I'm surprised he hasn't done it already." Yosef shook his head at his own words. "I can't believe I just said that. Adonai! The man has threatened your life!"

"I'm not in any danger."

"You keep saying that—"

"Because it's true. It won't always be that way, but for now, it's true. I'm protected."

"What else aren't you telling me?"

You know me so well. "I'm curious—how do you know there's more?"

"Because, based on what you've told me so far, your decision is obvious. You don't need my help making it. Since you came to me wanting advice, I can only assume there's more to it than what you've already shared." He smiled wistfully. "Unless you really didn't want my advice at all; unless you just wanted to talk."

You know me so well. "I love you, Abba."

"And I, you."

"But, yes, there is more. I'm concerned that Shimon will take his revenge on my family if he can't touch me."

"Oh." He pursed his lips.

"What should I do?" I whispered.

"Whatever you have to do to avoid another bloodbath in the region. You know that."

"I know." I looked into his eyes and asked the question that burned inside, the one I'd wanted to ask so many times over the past few years, the one I'd asked my Father over and over without hearing His answer. "Why doesn't knowing help, Abba? Why is it that even the *right* thing feels wrong?"

He didn't even have to pause to think it over. "Because the world is broken, son." He crossed over to the window and stood beside me, looking out over the hillside toward Jezre'el.

"Yisu..."

"Yes, sir?"

"Whatever you decide. Whatever happens, son, I want you to know. I trust you."

What Abba had said agreed with what my Father was telling me through His word and agreed also with the leanings of my heart. Yosef would be praying for me today, even as he was praying for my sister Rachel, who had labored throughout the night and was laboring even now to bring life into the world. *I set before you today life and death...choose life, that you may live...* I had sworn to help them, these men who were following Shimon headfirst into the valley of death like sheep without a shepherd. *If you make a vow to Yahuh your God, do not be slow to pay it, for Yahuh your God will certainly demand it of you and you will be guilty of sin.* Any further delay on my part would result in death.

And so I took Onarion for a walk.

Things had been a little different between Onarion and his taskmasters since they'd discovered that he understood their Greek. They no longer spoke so freely around him. However, they still laid their burdens on him with regularity and with a savage glee, as if to pay him back for the years of silence. I was sure they'd find me on the road to Sepphoris.

I was not disappointed.

"Yo, Onarion!"

"Yes, sir." I spoke to them in the language they were most comfortable with, as I'd done for a year now. It gave them one more reason to like me, as the farmer likes the ox that plows the straightest row, or as the shepherdess likes the ewe that comes quickly when called to be milked; their young ass had learned a new trick that made him more useful—they didn't have to strain out their Aramaic to order him around. I smiled and took the load without complaint, as always, adding a blessing in both Hebrew and Greek: *"Yisah Adonai panav aleikha v'yasem l'kha shalom.* May the Lord lift up His countenance upon you and give you His peace."

I'd used the Hebrew because I knew this man—Demetrius, he was called—and that he actually had a heart to learn more about the people among whom he had been ordered to live. I had no illusions that he was my friend, but neither was he my enemy. *One day, he will have to decide,* a small voice whispered deep in my soul. *They all will.* Sensing the truth in this, I took care to plant seeds of friendship wherever and whenever I could. *Choose life that you may live.*

I marched with them for a mile before speaking. "Sir?"

Demetrius looked at me in surprise. It was the first time I'd ever initiated conversation. "What is it?" He omitted the epithet, for which I was grateful. There were other officers who would have been much more difficult to approach—the fact that Demetrius was the one who had conscripted me this day was a sign of my Father's blessing, a sign that I had heard Him correctly.

"Sir, with respect, it would be best if you didn't look at me while I'm speaking," I said with my eyes fixed firmly on the ground in front of my feet. There was a chance—a good chance—that Shimon had men watching me today. That's why I hadn't simply gone to the garrison. There was nothing unusual in my walking to Sepphoris, nor in my being conscripted, nor in my carrying the load past the mile marker with a smile on my face. Today I did not want to be seen doing anything unusual. This was not deception; this was wisdom. Trusting that Demetrius had taken my rather strange advice, I continued. "There is rumor, sir, that the Zealots in the area are planning an ambush."

"Why would you tell me such a thing?"

"You know me. My heart is for peace."

"I didn't think you were a traitor. You disappoint me, Onarion."

"I'm not a traitor, sir. To allow the Zealots to bring Rome's fury down upon the heads of my people would be treachery. I'm simply letting you know what I've heard so that bloodshed can be avoided. Yours *and* theirs." Without waiting for his approval, I said what I'd come to say. "I heard there's a shipment of weapons coming in to Sepphoris soon. I also heard that the route this shipment will take is known to the Zealots, and that they plan to have those weapons for themselves."

"And how did you hear all this, Onarion?"

"To tell you that *would* be treachery, sir. As I said, I'm not a traitor."

"You know I could force you to tell me."

"Yes, sir. I know." Again I breathed a prayer of thanks that this was Demetrius.

He was silent.

I was silent.

"Yisu."

I smiled, but I kept my head down. "Yes, sir."

"I'll do what I can."

"Thank you, sir."

Arriving in Sepphoris, I made my way immediately to the synagogue and into the library at the back of the building. Ezra and I were beginning a new book today. The timing could not have been better. I needed something to take my mind off Shimon's threats; I'd done all I could do, and worrying about it now would just be a waste of my energy. *It's in Your hands, Father.* I knew from past experience, however, that worry is a determined guest who will not leave simply because you bid him to go. I needed to drive him out by giving his room to a more welcome tenant. Ezra's book—the words of the prophet Ezekiel—were indeed welcome.

"Has it arrived?" I asked eagerly.

He looked up from the table and gestured expansively. "Come and see!"

"'In the thirtieth year, in the fourth month on the fifth day, while I was among the exiles by the Kebar River, the heavens were opened and I saw visions of God,'" I read. This was exactly what I needed today. "And this copy is yours to keep?"

"Yes, you can study it as often as you want, Yeshua."

I'd been longing for Ezekiel for years now. As a rule, only a few passages from the end of the book were read in the synagogue during assemblies, so most of what the prophet had written was completely unknown to me. This opening passage, now, this was familiar to me: it was usually read as the *haftarah* on Shavuot, but everything that followed it would be a new revelation. In my excitement, I didn't know whom to thank first—my lips said, "Thank you, Ez'ri," while my heart cried, *Thank You, Father!* and to both I said, "This is a priceless gift."

"Well, do you want to stand here talking about it, or do you want to read it?"

He didn't have to invite me twice. Grinning, I sat down at the table and read through the Shavuot passage without a pause. Then I stopped to draw a deep breath. "Do you remember, Rabbi, the first time you had me read for you?" It had been a similar passage to this one, another vision of God's throne.

"Yes. I gave you Daniel as a test; I knew you would never have heard it, and I wanted to see if you could read or if you simply had a good memory."

"'His throne was flaming with fire, and its wheels were all ablaze,'" I quoted now from memory. "It was the same vision, though told in less detail." And then, of course, had come the part about the *one like a son of man*, the part that had shaken me till I could scarcely breathe, as I'd recognized myself in the words of the prophecy.

"Do you want to read on now, or refresh yourself first?"

"Read, if it's all right with you."

"There's nothing I enjoy more than listening to you read, Yeshua. I consider it one of the great blessings of my life, that you should read to me." He gestured at the book, impatiently. "So read."

I turned back to the scroll. *Father, open my ears, that I may hear Your voice in the words of Your prophet Ezekiel.* Then I read, "'This was how the appearance of the glory of Adonai looked. When I saw it, I fell on my face, and I heard the voice of someone speaking. He said to me, Son of man, stand up! I want to speak with you!'"

I stopped. Time itself stopped.

I had asked to hear my Father's voice; as the words rolled from my mouth, they took on life: they *spoke* to me. Directly to me. I had to obey them. *Son of man, stand up!* I leapt to my feet so suddenly that the stool I'd been sitting on crashed to the floor, but I hardly noticed. My attention was riveted on the words that lay before me, the words begging to be breathed to life. I answered their silent prayer and gave them voice. "'As He spoke to me, *ru'ach* entered me and put me on my feet, and I heard Him who was speaking to me. He said, Son of man, I am sending you to the people of Israel, that nation of rebels who have rebelled against Me—they and their ancestors have been transgressing against Me to this very day. Because they are defiant, hardhearted children, I am sending you, and you are to tell them, Here is what Adonai Elohim says. Whether they listen or not, this rebellious house will still know that a prophet has been among them…'"

I kept reading; the words kept pouring out of me like a river, like a flood, sweeping me along on their current, speaking to me, to me, only and always to *me*, telling me what I would have to say, telling me what I would have to do. *But the house of Israel will not be willing to listen to you, because they aren't willing to listen to Me; since all the house of Israel are obstinate and hardhearted. However, I am making you as obstinate and defiant as they are; yes, I am making your resoluteness harder than flint, as hard as a diamond. So don't be afraid of them...*

On and on I read. Seven times He called me. *Son of man... son of man... son of man...* Each time, He told me what I was going to have to do. Each time, He warned me that they wouldn't listen. Each time, he exhorted me not to fear them.

And then He called me an eighth time, and His tone changed. *As for you, son of man...* I read His instructions to build a model of Jerusalem and lay siege to it without really understanding, until I came to His next command. *You are to lie on your left side, and have it bear the guilt of the house of Israel—for as many days as you lie on your side, you shall bear their guilt. For I am assigning you one day for each year of their guilt; thus you are to bear the guilt of the house of Israel for 390 days. Then, when you have finished that, you are to lie on your right side and bear the guilt of the house of Judah for forty days...*

You shall bear their guilt... you shall bear their guilt...

"'I will tie you down with ropes, and you are not to turn from one side to the other...'"

You shall bear their guilt...

"'The bread you eat is to be baked before their eyes, using human dung as fuel...'"

You shall bear their guilt...

"'I will do things to you that I have never done before, and I will never do such things again...'"

You shall bear their guilt...

"'For as I live, says Adonai Elohim, because you defiled my sanctuary with all your detestable things and disgusting practices, therefore I swear that I will cut you off—my eye will not spare, I will have no pity...'"

My eye will not spare, I will have no pity.

You shall bear their guilt.

I will have no pity.

I understood. For the first time, I truly understood.

I stopped reading.

I stepped back from the table.

I started to shake.

"No pity," I whispered.

"Yeshua, what is it?" Ezra asked.

"No pity," I said again. "Why didn't you tell me?"

"I don't understand, Yisu."

"He's so angry. So angry. I never knew. So much anger. So—*much.*" *Oh, God, how will I bear it?* "All the years He's spared them. All the years He had pity. All the years. Stored up. For me. For me. No pity. No pity for me."

I'd mistakenly thought hanging was the worst of it. I'd spent a year getting used to the idea that, one day, I was going to hang. But this was worse. This was far worse.

"Defiled. Detestable. Disgusting. 'I will turn my face away; then they will profane my secret place; robbers will enter and profane it.' Profaned."

"The Temple?"

"*I* am the Temple! Profaned! Defiled! All their disgusting practices, brought upon me, brought *into* me. And then He will pour out His fury on me, He will spend His anger on me. Weren't you listening? Didn't you hear?"

"He was speaking to Ezekiel—"

"No. He was speaking to me. To me."

"How can you know—"

"Because He spared Ezekiel. He relented. Cow dung instead of human dung, so Ezekiel wouldn't be defiled. He spared Ezekiel. He had pity on Ezekiel. But not on me. Weren't you listening?"

"I *was* listening, Yeshua. The doom He pronounced was on Israel—"

"'You shall bear the guilt of the house of Israel. You shall bear the guilt of the house of Judah.' Not Ezekiel—*me.*" Suddenly all my words dried up. I couldn't speak. I could barely even breathe. The trembling started again, and this time it wouldn't stop. I heard sounds coming out of my mouth—harsh, choking cries—not cries of sorrow—not cries of pain—

I didn't know this feeling. I'd never had this feeling before. I couldn't stand up under it. Shaking and crying out, I fell on my face, and then I knew. *Fear.* This was fear.

The fear of Yahuh is the beginning of wisdom.

Never in all my life had I feared God.

I had loved Him; I had respected Him, reverenced Him, humbled myself before Him, stood in awe of Him, worshiped Him, adored Him—but I had never, until this moment, feared Him.

Lord God, have mercy on me.

He wouldn't.

The certainty of that was terrifying. This was no blind fear, no unreasoning fear. I could see all too well what was coming; I had every reason to be afraid, for I knew the scriptures: *Your wrath lies heavily upon me; You have overwhelmed me with all Your waves. Who knows the power of Your anger? For Your wrath is as great as the fear that is due You. You alone are to be feared. Who can stand against You when You are angry?* Year upon year of justice delayed, judgment postponed, wrath stored up—hundreds of years, thousands—all waiting to be unleashed, all waiting to be poured out... upon me.

But first... first...

"Oh, God," I whispered.

"Yeshua."

The still, small voice cut through the waves of fear that wracked my body and my soul. Not my Father's voice. Ezra's. "Yeshua," he said again, and laid a hand on my shoulder. The touch brought me back to myself, and I stopped struggling against the fear. It was an opponent I was unprepared to face, and so I did what I'd done when Abner had beaten me, when I'd realized there was nothing I could do to save myself from his assault: I went limp, surrendering to the inevitable. I let the waves wash over me, accepting the fear for what it was and placing myself fully in my Father's hands. After a while, the fear lost its grip on my flesh and the trembling subsided. I lay quiet. The cold stone of the floor pressed against my face uncomfortably; since there was nothing to be gained from lying there, I sat up. I was still afraid—still so very afraid—but the fear no longer had control of me.

"Ezekiel," I murmured, beginning to understand. "God will strengthen."

Ezra crouched beside me, his brow furrowed with concern. His hand still rested on my shoulder. "What?" he asked softly.

"The prophet's name. Ezekiel. There's a reason *this* prophet was chosen to give me this message, and not another." *God will strengthen.* It was the meaning of his name. I wasn't strong enough to withstand the fear...not yet. "I have to read the rest. No matter how bad it gets, I need to read it all." My Father would use this book to strengthen me, to prepare me.

I got up from the floor and returned to the table, where the book still lay open to the words *because you defiled my sanctuary with all your detestable things and disgusting practices,* but I couldn't get the words off the page and into my mouth. I stood there staring at the scroll *the time has come, the day is near* with my jaw clenched *there is panic, not joy, upon the mountains* and cold fingers of fear running up and down my spine *I am about to pour out my wrath on you* and digging into my bowels *and spend my anger against you* and I couldn't move, couldn't speak, couldn't turn away until Ezra leaned over me and rolled the parchment closed.

"Not today," he said. He took the scroll away without another word and locked it in the cabinet. Then, pursing his lips thoughtfully, he unlocked the door again and pulled a smaller book off one of the shelves. This he brought over to the table. "*I* am going to read to *you*, Yeshua. Sit down." Opening the book to the middle, he squinted to bring the words into focus and read, "'Then he showed me Yeshua the high priest standing before the Angel of Adonai, and Satan standing at his right hand to oppose him.'" *Yeshua the high priest...* The words caught and held me as Ezra continued. "'And Adonai said to Satan, Adonai rebuke you, Satan! Adonai who has chosen Jerusalem rebuke you! Is this not a brand plucked from the fire? Now Yeshua was clothed with filthy garments, and was standing before the Angel. Then He answered and spoke to those who stood before Him, saying, Take away the filthy garments from him. And to him He said, See, I have removed your iniquity from you, and I will clothe you with rich robes. And I said, Let them put a clean turban on his head. So they put a clean turban on his head, and they put the clothes on him.'"

I let the words soak into me. *I have removed your iniquity from you.* A promise of hope. A reminder of love.

"'The angel of Adonai gave this charge to Yeshua: This is what Adonai Almighty says: If you will walk in my ways and keep my requirements, then you will govern my house and have charge of my courts, and I will give you a place among these standing here. Listen, O high priest Yeshua and your associates seated before you, who are men symbolic of things to come: I am going to bring my servant, the Branch...'"

The words carried with them a warmth—no, the words themselves *were* a warmth—that melted away the fear in my soul and restored my voice to me. "What book is this, Rabbi?" I asked softly, interrupting his reading.

"Zechariah."

This book... I'd read it before, years ago, but quickly—far too quickly—in my single-minded search for the key to David's psalm: *they will look to Me, whom they pierced.* "May I hear it again, please?" Closing my eyes, I shut out everything except the words of the prophecy.

Ezra started over, and I heard in his voice my Father's love, my Father's concern for me, my Father's assurance that all would be well in the end. When Ezra reached the end of the passage and stopped, I felt a chill as if someone had stripped me of my cloak. "Is there no more?"

"Indeed," he said, "a bit further on." He found his place in the scroll and continued. "'Take the silver and gold and make a crown, and set it on the head of the high priest, Yeshua ben Yehozadak. Tell him this is what Adonai Almighty says: Here is the man whose name is the Branch, and he will branch out from his place and build the temple of Adonai. It is he who will build the temple of Adonai, and he will be clothed with majesty and will sit and rule on his throne. And he will be a priest on his throne. And there will be harmony between the two.'" He paused. "Again?" With my eyes shut, I nodded.

As he read through it a second time, I began to feel like myself once more.

Yeshua ben Yehozadak.

The man had live—and died—four hundred years ago. He was a figure from our history lessons, high priest during the time of the Temple's rebuilding, when Zerubbabel was governor of Jerusalem under Cyrus king of Persia. But as I listened to the words of Zechariah's prophecy, I realized that he was much more than an historical figure. *Listen, O high priest Yeshua and your associates seated before you, who are men symbolic of things to come...*

He was me.

"Again, please, Ez'ri."

Yeshua ben Yehozadak. Yeshua, son of Yehozadak. Yehozadak—like so many of our names, like my own name,

Yeshua—was a blending of the sacred and unuttered name of God and one of His attributes. My name, in its most basic form, was simply *Yahuh salvation.* Ordinarily it was taken to mean "God is salvation," which was a simple declaration of faith. But it could also mean "God's salvation," which would be a proclamation that I was the means of that salvation; or, boldest of all, it could mean "God of salvation." Yehozadak—that meant *Yahuh righteous.* Like Yeshua, it could be taken several ways. "God is righteous," or "God makes righteous," or "God, made righteous" were three of the possible nuances.

What I heard now as Ezra read through the passage for the third time was this: "Take the silver and gold and make a crown, and set it on the head of the high priest, God's salvation, son of God, made righteous." As that began to sink into my soul, one of Saba Yoachim's treasures rose up in my heart to meet it.

> Come, let us return to Yahuh;
> for He has torn, and He will heal us;
> He has struck, and He will bind our wounds.
> After two days, He will revive us;
> on the third day, He will raise us up;
> and we will live in His presence.

Together the promises wrapped their arms around me and whispered words of comfort.

44

KATAN

13 Adar Bet 3775
(Purim)

We played and danced in the courtyard until it just got too cold for the musicians, and then we all moved inside. Kaleb and Yafet dragged the furniture to the corners, clearing as much open space as possible so the dancing could continue; those of us with instruments squeezed in along the edges as best we could. I was actually sitting in the workshop, as were Father and Yisu, but the door that joined the two rooms was propped wide open so our music could be heard in the main room of the house. Yehudah and Shimeon beat a rhythm on their drums; the women and girls took turns passing around three tambourines; everyone else either sang, danced, or did both. Everyone was loud, everyone was happy, and (except for the youngest children) everyone was at least a little bit drunk. That's what Purim is about, after all.

Rachel wasn't as outwardly jubilant as the rest of us, but then, she was still recovering from her ordeal last month. *Two beautiful boys in payment for two days' hard labor*, Mimah had remarked afterward. My sister had barely survived the birth, and Leah had to help her nurse the infants, but with Mimah's care Rachel had gotten back on her feet sooner than any of us had dared to hope. She sat now with Abshalom in her lap while Hannah held Abiram, listening to the music and singing softly.

The older men also sat out most of the dancing, though not all of it. Shofet Abiyud and my grandfathers, all of them nearing seventy, still got up and led several of the slower dances. But they laughed when we began the "Roni" and refused to compete with the younger folks. "We already know that your fingers are faster than our feet, boys!" Abiyud had called as he took his place on the bench. Yisu and I began to race each other as well as the dancers, and Father had to drop out after eight or nine verses—I wasn't counting. The last dancer gave up shortly after that, and then it was just Yehudah, Yisu, and I. Yehudah abandoned his complex rhythm and started pounding a simple *thump-thump-thump*, faster and faster. I glanced up at Yisu once, for just a second; his eyes were shut in concentration as his fingers flew over the holes in his flute. I fixed my eyes on the strings of my *kinnor*, leaving out the flourishes (as Yisu had dropped his trills) and sticking to the barest line of the melody. But then I made the fatal mistake of actually thinking about the music, and I missed a phrase, lost my place, and tumbled all over myself trying to repair the damage. For a moment I thought I'd handed the victory to my brother; at the very same instant, however, he played a discordant note that wasn't even in the song and his eyebrows shot up in surprise; like me, he tried to recover, but it was too late, and the rest of the song died a loud and painful death as Yisu began to laugh into his flute.

"A tie! A tie!" Everyone started shouting, laughing, and clapping, and someone handed each of us a cup of wine. Yehudah tried to protest, claiming that he was the true winner, but the elders were unanimous in their verdict that he'd forfeited the contest when he'd dropped his rhythm. I grinned at my little brother as I drained my cup to the dregs.

"I think I've had enough," Yisu commented, and passed his cup to Yosei, who had stayed in the dance longer than anyone else and was sweating hard from the effort. "You look like you need this more than I do!"

"Thanks!" Yosei drank deeply from the cup and then turned to me. "I'm going to sit out for a while. If you want to dance, I could take a turn on the *kinnor*."

That sounded like fun. "Sure." I handed over my instrument and joined the dancers for the next three or four songs, but it was late and people were starting to get tired. Sarah and Shimeon had both fallen asleep, Sarah across Aunt Mimah's lap and Shimeon curled up in Mother's; and Eli was drowsing at Leah's breast. The wine was catching up with me, too, and I was ready to say goodnight to Purim and head off to bed. Others had reached the same point, and soon we were all nodding and yawning.

"I think that's enough for tonight," Saba Yaakob finally

announced. Abiyud and Netzer made their farewells and started for the door, but Saba stopped them. "It's a long walk for this time of night, and you're none too steady on your feet, my friends. Why don't you all stay? We have room and to spare." So it was agreed that all of our guests would accept our hospitality at least until morning. We did have to do some rearranging of sleeping quarters; the main room of my father's house wasn't big enough for all of his boys *and* our guests, so Yisu, Yosei, Yehudah, and Shimeon carried their bedding into the woodshop and settled there for the remainder of the night. Ezra and Talyah were staying with Leah and me, of course, and everyone else crowded into the remaining spaces with good cheer.

I'd planned on making Leah happy before going to sleep, but she informed me that she most definitely would *not* be happy, not with her parents sleeping in the same room, so I doused the lamps and called it a night.

I woke sometime before dawn to the sound of shouting and the smell of smoke.

I ran to the window, but it faced toward the pasture, away from the rest of the house, and I could see nothing but flickering shadows. *Flickering?* The light dancing among the shadows wasn't the cold silver of the moon, but the warm gold of firelight. Alarmed, I roused everyone else in the room. "Fire!" I shouted, all but pushing them out the door. Leah clutched Eli in her arms, first down the steps, followed by her parents and then me. "Wait out past the stable!" I told them, and then ran around to the front of the house, pounding on the door. Kaleb opened it, blinking the sleep from his eyes; as soon as he saw me standing there, he realized what was happening.

"Rachel! Yafet! Get up!" Kaleb took one of his infant sons in his arms and handed the other to his brother while I helped my sister get up and out. I sent them all to join my family and rushed over to my father's house to make sure everyone there had already made it safely outside. Two people were scrambling down the stairs: my parents. Hannah and Sarah were already in the courtyard with Aunt Mimah. Off to one side I saw Shammai bent over Saba Yoachim, who was coughing but seemed otherwise unharmed. Netzer called for help from one of the windows on the ground floor of the main building. I ran to the window.

"The door is blocked! Help me get my father out!" He boosted Abiyud to the sill, and I steadied the old man as he climbed through, coughing from the smoke, which was everywhere. As soon as he was safely outside, I grabbed Netzer and pulled him out. Only then did his words fully register on my awareness: *The door is blocked.* Leaving him, I raced around to the far side of the building. "Yaakob—" he called after me, but I didn't hear anything else he said.

Flames were leaping from the workshop windows, smoke pouring out in thick clouds.

Merciful God. I thought of all the oils and resins we kept in there, along with the scrap wood. And then I remembered: my brothers were all sleeping in the shop.

45

YISU

13 Adar Bet 377
(Purim)

M y fingers fly across my flute, singing a song otherwise impossible, each sound taking flight in a shower of sparks that fill the void of the sky with light. The light continues to sing, each spark crackling in a chorus like the rushing of many waters, and rain begins to fall from the heavens, but it is a hot rain, a fiery rain, like the rain that fell on Sodom, a thick choking hot rain that muffles the music, suffocating my song with each breath I take. The stars falling from the sky all around me beat the ground ith a harsh patter that seems to speak: Arise! Arise! Arise! Adonai, you must arise!

"Get up, Yisu! Yisu!"

The voices yanked me out of sleep and thrust me straight into hell.

All around me, as in my dream, flaming embers were falling from the ceiling, landing in the sawdust, starting new fires everywhere they landed. Shimeon was screaming—in pain or from fright, I couldn't tell—and Yehudah was shaking me and shouting my name, frantically. I sat up and immediately wished I hadn't; a pall of thick smoke hung just above the floor, burning my eyes and choking me. *Father!* Rolling over onto my hands and knees, I kept my face close to the ground where there were still a few pockets of breathable air and called out, "Shimeon! Where are you?" *Help me, Father!* My littlest brother didn't answer, but he kept screaming and I followed the sound, crawling as fast as I could through the inferno until I reached his side.

His tunic had caught fire and was blazing up toward his face as he slapped wildly at the flames, shrieking. I threw myself on top of him, knocking him flat and smothering the flames just as they reached his hair. At the same moment, a section of shelving broke free of the wall and crashed just inches from us, blocking the door that led into the house and cutting off our closest escape.

"Yisu! Yosei! Shimeon!" a voice was shouting over the roar of the fire. "Yehudah! Yisu!"

"Here!" I called, but my cry was cut short by a spasm of coughing; the smoke was getting worse. I'd never make it to the front door in time, but there was a window not too far away. Throwing Shimeon over my shoulder, I lurched to my feet and ran to the window. Katan was just outside, and Yehudah was already with him—*thank You, Father*—and I pushed Shimeon through to them, drew in a quick breath of cleaner air, and turned back once more into the shop, searching for Yosei.

He'd been sleeping under one of the workbenches, sleeping soundly, exhausted by the dancing and lethargic from the wine; perhaps he was still there. Dropping to the floor again, I crawled over to where I'd last seen him, only vaguely aware of the voices that were still calling out his name and mine. I didn't call out—it was hard even to breathe, let alone speak. I found him where I expected; he was still unburnt but I couldn't rouse him no matter how much I shook him. *Yahuh, give me strength, please. Let me get him safely out of here.* Yosei was only fourteen, but he was almost as big as I was. Crouched under the table, I couldn't get him across my shoulder, so I dragged him out by his arms and then, bent nearly double, I backed toward the door, pulling him as quickly as I could through the flaming debris that fell from the ceiling beams, and praying with every step that the roof would hold until we were clear of the building. Just as I reached the threshold there was a loud groaning, cracking, tearing sound and the center beam folded in half, collapsing under the weight of the building above it. I felt several strong hands grabbing me from behind and pulling me and my brother out from under the doorframe scant seconds before it, too, fell in. As I knelt in the courtyard, gasping for air, my eyes fell on the lintel I'd carved as a child; it lay in the dirt, flames licking the words of the *Shema*, erasing them from the wood but not from my heart: *Hear, O Israel! Yahuh our God, Yahuh is One.*

At that same instant, I heard a muffled cry from within the

building that cut off almost before it began, and Yosef screamed "No!" and let go of me and ran toward the house as it slumped to one side and then dissolved into a pile of smoking rubble, burying whoever it was that was trapped within, whoever had cried out in pain and surprise.

Coughing, I swept my eyes over those standing in the yard, wondering who was missing, who would always be missing— but I didn't have to wonder for long. "Father!" Yosef cried. And then Leah began screaming the same thing, over and over, while Katan held her back from the edge of the ruin.

46

KATAN

13 Adar Bet 3775
(Purim)

I'd been so busy helping everyone else get out of the house that I hadn't even noticed when Ezra went back in. "But why?" I asked. I'd left him safe at the northern end of the courtyard, safe with Leah and Talyah and Eli. "Why didn't he stay with you?"

Leah was crying too hard to answer, and Talyah was in shock. "Netzer," she whispered, and then she, too, began to sob hysterically. Mimah held her.

"Netzer?" I turned to him. "What happened?"

For nearly an hour following the collapse of the house, we'd all sat in a stunned silence broken only by the sounds of coughing and weeping. Netzer had taken control of the situation, leading all of us over the ridge to his house. It had been a slow procession. Saba Yoachim coughed the whole way, and Father carried Shimeon in his arms, careful not to jostle him too much—my little brother had severe burns on the left side of his face and neck, and half of his hair had burned away. The hair would grow back eventually, but the scars he would undoubtedly bear for the rest of his life; though one day, God willing, his beard would hide the worst of it (assuming he ever would be able to grow a beard on that side of his face). Yosei couldn't walk at all, but had to be carried on a makeshift litter. At least he'd regained consciousness. Astonishingly, Yisu was unscathed.

"What happened?" I asked again. "Why were they in the building?"

"I tried to tell you," Netzer said. His tone wasn't accusing, but his words were. "After you pulled me from the window, I tried to tell you that Yaakob was still inside, but you ran off."

Merciful God. I'd thought he was talking to *me* when he'd said "Yaakob."

"When the fire started, when we smelled the smoke, the first thing he said was, 'The boys are sleeping in there!' Then he pulled the door open and rushed into the shop, but before I could follow him, something fell over and blocked the way. The flames were too intense—I couldn't get in and he couldn't get back out. That's when Father and I escaped through the window. I tried to tell you, but I guess you didn't hear me."

Abiyud spoke up. "Ezra came over to make sure we were all right. I told him we were fine, but Yaakob had gone in after Yisu and the boys. When he heard that, he climbed through the window. I could hear him in there, calling their names. I don't know if he managed to get through the door into the shop; we couldn't. It was just too hot."

Netzer added, "We kept waiting for him to come back to the window, but then..."

Then the house had collapsed.

"Oh, God, forgive me," I said. "It's my fault. If I hadn't run off, if I'd listened..."

"No," Yisu said softly. "It was my fault." Every eye in the room turned to Yisu, but he was looking only at Yosef. "I'm sorry, Abba."

"The fire—"

"He warned me. Eye for eye, tooth for tooth, life for life."

"The fire was deliberate?" Father drew in a deep breath and let it out slowly.

Eye for eye... Years ago, a Zealot who called himself Yashar had used those same words to justify murder. More recently, I'd heard them from Sicae. The memory of that night washed over me, unbidden and unwelcome: *I'm warning you now, brother, that if you do this, you will pay. Eye for eye, tooth for tooth, life for life. Consider that a threat...* What had Yisu done? Horrified, I looked over at my brother, who sat staring at Father with tear-filled eyes. Sicae hadn't been the only one to threaten him last month. What had Shimon said? *Keep your mouth shut or you will bear the responsibility not only for my slaughter, but many others' as well.*

Was this what he had meant?

Keep your mouth shut...

"Yisu," I whispered, not wanting to believe it, "what did

you do? What did you say?" I shook my head as he locked eyes with me. "Please. *Please* tell me you weren't stupid enough to provoke Sicae. Please tell me you had enough sense to know how *fatal* that would be!" All the times I'd called my brother an idiot, I'd never really believed it to be true, but this... this...

"Yes," he whispered.

"Yes, *what?*" I all but shouted. "Yes, you had sense? Or yes, you were *stupid* enough to defy Shimon?" Enough was enough! No more! Taking a deep breath, trying hard to keep some sort of self-control, trying not to look at Shimeon's maimed face, not to think about Saba lying crushed beneath the house, about Ezra lying dead in my place—dead because he had tried to save *Yisu*—I turned to my father. "Abba, you have a right to know what Yisu's been up to for the past three years—"

Father interrupted me. "I know, Katan." His voice trembled as he spoke. "I know." With his eyes on Yisu, he continued, "This is as much my fault as yours. We both knew the risk. Don't take this on yourself, Yeshua. You didn't do this. Their blood is *not* on your head, whatever Shimon may have told you. If this is his doing—God have mercy on him if it is, because *I* won't—if this *is* his doing, then he's the one who'll have to pay for it, not you. Not *you*, do you hear me?"

Yisu said nothing, for which I was grateful. If he'd spoken just then, I probably would have hit him. *Father knew?* Not only knew, but *condoned* Yisu's choice? I clenched my hand into a fist, so tight that it hurt—if Yosef weren't my father, I might have hit *him* in that moment. Whatever mistakes I'd made in the past paled in comparison to this. Never, *never* had I endangered the family. Never. *You hung my sin around my neck, nailed it to me like a sign for all the world to see.* And what had I really done? Watched—just *watched*—while Sicae and the others killed a few Roman soldiers, and then helped them clean up the evidence. But Yisu...

I couldn't even finish the thought. I didn't want Yisu's blood on *my* head.

Turning my back on him, I wrapped my arms around Leah, giving her what comfort I could. She sobbed softly against my chest; no one else made a sound. After a long while, Leah's crying subsided and she grew heavier in my arms, and I realized that she'd fallen asleep. In fact, almost everyone in the room had given in to exhaustion; some slept stretched out on the floor, while others dozed restlessly as they slumped against the walls. Looking around, I saw that only Yisu and I were fully awake. He stood in the corner opposite me with his head tipped back slightly and his lips moving as if he were having a conversation with the ceiling beams, though he spoke so softly I couldn't hear what he was saying. I didn't need to. I knew he was praying—Yisu was always praying about something. The lamplight flickered and leapt up for a moment, falling on his face, and I caught the word "forgive" as it formed on his lips. Was he praying for himself, hoping to avoid the consequences of his stupidity? Or was he actually asking God to forgive Shimon and Sicae? My stomach knotted at the thought.

"Forgive?" I hissed. "God *forbid* this night's work be forgiven!"

He dropped his gaze from the ceiling and met my eyes. I didn't wait for his answer. Leaning over, I blew out the lamp and shut out the sight of him, and waited for sleep to take me.

47

YISU

Nisan 3775

You meant evil against me, but God meant it for good. I couldn't see it. I couldn't see the good in any of this, try as hard as I might.

"For My thoughts are not your thoughts, neither are your ways My ways," declares Yahuh. "As the heavens are higher than the earth, so are My ways higher than your ways and My thoughts than your thoughts."

I missed my teacher. I missed my friend.

"Ez'ri," I whispered to no one, for no one was there to hear. "Could even you have helped me to understand all of this?" The books sat on the shelves, silent. Though I'd always thought of them as Ezra's books, in truth they belonged to the synagogue. A new *hazzan* had already been chosen from the congregation, and now these books were his. As if to demonstrate how much higher God's ways were than mine, how very unknowable His thoughts were, my Father had seen fit to allow one of Zephanyah's friends to take over Ezra's position. The books that had shown me who I was and what I must do, the books that had spoken to me in my Father's voice for the past six years, these books were now forbidden to me. I laid one hand longingly on the scroll that contained the book of Ezekiel—the book I'd not had a chance to finish—and it whispered *take me with you*, but I resisted the temptation and left the room for the last time. "'Yahuh has given, and Yahuh has taken away; blessed be the name of Yahuh,'" I murmured.

"Yisu, are you done in there yet?" Katan was impatient, on edge.

"Yes." I rejoined him in the courtyard, where he had finished disassembling the loom. "I was just saying goodbye," I explained, picking up a box of Talyah's things. "Is this the last one?"

"Yes. Put it on the cart so we can get out of here." He put the loom over his shoulder and followed me through the house and out to the street where Yosei was waiting with the cart. I set my box carefully in with the rest of Talyah's possessions and then, as Katan was strapping down the loom, I went back to the door of the house. "What are you doing?" my brother asked.

I pulled out a small tool and began prying out the nails that held the *mezuzah* to the doorpost. "This is Ezra's," I said. "I'm not leaving it behind." I would attach it to the doorpost of our new workshop—when we got around to building one. We had to build a house first. Katan had taken charge of that project and was already working on the architectural plans; Yosef should have been the one to do so, but he had focused his energy instead on rebuilding the business. *We have to eat,* he'd said, *and that means paying jobs come first. Katan knows how to build a house. Yisu will work with me; everyone else will help Katan.* Originally he'd planned for me to design the house, but then I'd reminded him that it would all go to Katan one day, so Yosef had given Katan complete say and total authority in the matter. *Just make sure you take your mother's wishes into account,* he'd added.

Netzer bar Abiyud had put all of his resources at our disposal, and had himself taken charge of the workforce that combed through the debris to recover the bodies of Ezra and Yaakob. This was perhaps the greatest blessing of all those we'd received over the past two weeks, that Netzer and his sons would spare Yosef from such a burden. At the funeral, Yosef had of course spoken the blessing for his father; Katan had spoken for Ezra, since the rabbi had no son of his own flesh to honor him.

It was as Katan was speaking the blessing that I understood for the first time what I had been sensing from him since the night of the fire.

You have no place here.

He hadn't spoken those words, not once, not with his lips; every line of his face, every nuance of his posture, every tone of his voice, however, pushed me away. He tolerated my presence the same way the men of Nazareth tolerated the presence of the Romans—he did me no violence by word or deed, but he extended me no warmth. *You have no place here.*

"You know what," I said, digging a nail from Ezra's doorpost, "you two go on without me. I've got a few things I need to take care of before I go home."

"Like what?" Katan made a derisive sound halfway between a laugh and a grunt. "Do I even want to know?" When I didn't answer him, he spat on the ground in my direction.

"Katan!" Yosei protested. "He saved my life—"

"He shouldn't have had to."

"Don't worry," I told Katan. "It's nothing you need to be concerned about."

"Yeah. That's what you said last time." Katan stepped between the cart handles and heaved the load onto the street, and then stomped off without another word.

Yosei stood still for a minute or so before shaking his head and shrugging apologetically. "I'm sorry, Yisu. Don't take it to heart. He'll get over it—he always does."

"Perhaps." I smiled sadly. "Go on, catch up with him. Tell Father I won't be long."

"All right." He turned and jogged after Katan.

I watched them go.

When they were out of sight, I turned back to Ezra's door and worked at the rest of the nails until I'd gotten them all free and the *mezuzah* rested firmly in my hand. I stared at it for a moment. Without really planning to, I reached up and knocked on the door. "It's Yeshua," I called out. The tears came then, and I surrendered to the grief.

The myrtle trees wove a basket over my head and all around me, their gray branches just beginning to bloom with soft, newly-budded leaves as the old ones finally let go of life and fell to the ground. Beneath my feet, last year's leaves were slowly turning into soil—a rich, fertile soil already sprouting with early flowers. I sank to the ground, pressing my face into the loam, breathing in its earthy fragrance and listening for God's voice. I so needed to hear it.

When I'd told Katan not to worry, that there was nothing he needed to be concerned about, I'd been speaking the truth— though there was no way I could convince him of that. My brother's involvement in this situation would help no one; nothing he could possibly do would make things better. There was only one man who could make a difference right now, and it was to him I needed to speak. However, I didn't know where he was or how to find him.

Shimon had always sought me out, never the other way around. The only time I'd been to his hideout, three years ago, I'd been blindfolded. Was he even in the same place now? It was unlikely. "Father, You know exactly where he is," I whispered into the fallen leaves. "If You want me to confront him, please bring him to me."

I remained in the grove, quietly listening, for a while longer. All I heard were insects, an occasional bird, and the sound of the branches rubbing together in the breeze. That was all I ever heard in the grove, all I'd ever heard anywhere, but I listened anyway. *One day, Father. One day You'll speak to me the way You spoke to Moses, to Samuel, to Elijah. One day. When You do, I'll be listening.*

Sighing, I rose to my feet. Though I would gladly have lingered in the grove all day, I'd promised Yosef that I wouldn't be long. We had several jobs to finish before Passover, which didn't leave either of us much time for other pursuits. "Thank You," I said, leaving the rest of the prayer to unfold in my heart as I walked home. *Enter His gates with praise; enter His courts with thanksgiving. Give thanks to Yahuh, for He is good; His mercy endures forever. Though He slay me, yet will I praise Him. This is the day Yahuh has made; I will rejoice and be glad in it!* The bits of scripture danced rapidly through my mind, but the last one leapt and spun and refused to leave, clamoring for me to give it voice. "I will rejoice," I said aloud, but once was not enough to silence the clamor. "I will rejoice. I *will* rejoice. I will *rejoice. I* will rejoice." *I don't think I can, Father.* How ironic, that of all the things He was asking me to do, this should prove to be the hardest! I started to laugh at myself—a self-deprecating laugh at first, to be sure—but the mere act of laughing birthed more laughter, genuine laughter, and I felt my spirits begin to lift. "I will rejoice!" I shouted defiantly. "I will rejoice!"

"No doubt."

Startled, I jumped.

Shimon stood just a few feet off the path, watching me with an expression of disdain.

"Only you," he commented, shaking his head.

Seldom had my prayers been answered this quickly, or this

definitely. I couldn't help it—I laughed again. *Father, even if I never hear Your voice with my ears, I know You always hear me. Thank You for listening.*

"Is there something wrong with you, Yisu? I know you don't give a damn about us—you proved that—but I'd have thought you cared at least a little bit for your own family. Guess I was wrong, huh?"

My laughter dried up as if he'd slapped me across the face. "About a lot of things, but not that. Please, Shimon, tell me the truth. Did you set that fire?"

"No."

"Did you give the order?"

"No," he said, but his face told me the rest.

"You know who did it."

He nodded.

"Sicae?"

"What did you expect, Yisu? You betrayed us to the Romans. The *Romans.*"

"Then come after *me.* Not my five-year-old brother. Not my grandfather. *Me*, Shimon."

"When we attacked, they were ready for us.We barely escaped. We lost five men." He named them, one by one; all were well known to me. I grieved in silence for the waste of life.

"Why did you do it?" Shimon demanded.

"I warned you to abandon your plan."

"Yeah? And I warned *you* to keep your mouth shut! I thought I knew you! I *trusted* you! I never dreamed you'd actually go through with it, actually break your oath and sell your brothers to Rome! Damn it, Yisu, do you think I *wanted* your family dead?"

"Did you know what Sicae was planning?"

He met my eyes without flinching. "Yes."

He'd answered his own question.

"When will it stop, Shimon?"

"When the oppression ends."

"How can it end, when the oppressed have become the oppressors?" I shook my head. "I love you, brother. Everything I've done, everything I've said, has been born out of my love for you. Even now. Even after this. I've been praying for you, and I'll keep praying, that God will open your eyes and soften your heart to understand that this is not the way to honor your father's memory. One day…one day you'll understand."

"I should have killed you three years ago." His hand gripped the hilt of his sword.

"Here I am." I spread my arms out wide, hands open and empty.

He drew the sword. I didn't move. "Damn you, Onarion!" he yelled, flinging his blade to the ground. "Go home!"

I didn't budge. "My family?" I had to hear it from his mouth.

"There won't be any more attacks. I swear it. Now go."

I went.

We would not meet again for many years.

48

KATAN

Tammuz 3775

It would take us years to rebuild what we had lost in the Purim fire: in short, everything. Home, food, tools, clothes—everything but Saba Yoachim's sheep and the land beneath our feet had been devoured by the flames or buried in the rubble. Some things might be restored one day, but they'd always carry the mark of that awful night. Other things, of course, we'd never get back: my grandfather, Leah's father. After a while, I got used to the absences, but I couldn't get used to the broken things. Each time I saw one I was reminded of the tragedy we'd suffered.

Shimeon's face, for example: it had healed, but the left side of his mouth was always pulled up in a sardonic half-smile now. The worst of the scarring would probably be hidden by his hair when it grew longer—it had finally started to grow back—but for now, every time he turned to face me I suffered the same shock, the same horrified surprise. He saw it in my face no matter how hard I tried to hide it, and soon he stopped coming around me.

Father was also scarred, though not physically. The fire, and all that followed in its aftermath, had scorched his joy and twisted his infrequent laughter into an expression of pain. That was the hardest thing for me to get used to. My father's laughter had always been such fun to listen to: loud and joyful and unrestrained. Whenever he'd laughed, the sound had filled the room and made it a brighter place, like music. No longer.

Part of it, I'm sure, was simple grief and exhaustion. Not only had Father lost a parent, but he'd also lost his most experienced business partner at a time when every skilled worker was desperately needed. He gave me the task of rebuilding our house, and Yosei and Yehudah dropped out of school for a while to help me. Yisu tried to take Saba's place, but even so, Father had to work twice as hard as before, taking in all the paying the jobs he could get. There had been a time when our workshop was filled with song and story, but that time was before the fire. Even our family devotions were sacrificed; though we still recited a verse or two after supper each night, we no longer read from the scriptures or played music—our only book had burned up in the fire along with all of our musical instruments. We still had our voices, of course; our hands hadn't forgotten how to clap, nor had our feet forgotten how to dance, but we were all just too tired to stay up late singing and dancing. Our only rest came on the Sabbath.

Even so, I'm convinced that with time, Father's joy would have returned. A person can grieve for just so long. As the scripture says, *Sorrow may last for a night, but joy comes in the morning.*

The real deathblow to Father's joy came a few months after the fire.

Though I'd already put a roof on the ground floor of the house, it was far from finished. The boys (including Yisu) had been sleeping in it for a week or two, just to give Netzer's family some room to breathe, but it was crude quarters to say the least. Certainly it was no place for Mother to be having her baby, though Father had commented that it was better than the stable. She and all the other women were at Rachel's house for the occasion.

Yehudah had gone to *bet-sefer* with Shimeon today; I wouldn't need him again for a few weeks, and Father didn't want him to fall too far behind in his studies. Yosei, on the other hand, had pronounced himself permanently done with higher education, and Father hadn't argued with him. My plans for today were to work inside the house, but Father needed a place to dry some panels, so Yosei and I worked on framing the second story while Father and Yisu varnished.

The sun was hot and the aqueduct hadn't been repaired yet, so I climbed up the ladder to get a drink from the cistern at the top of the escarpment. Yehudah and Shimeon were racing down the path toward me, shouting something I couldn't make out.

"Whoa! Slow down! What's wrong?" I asked, taking in

their expressions.

"A hanging!" Yehudah panted. "There's been a hanging!" Shimeon just cried.

"Father!" I called over the edge of the cliff. He came out of the house, squinting up at me. "There's been another hanging!"

He immediately scrambled up the sheep trail, with Yisu right behind him. "Stay here," he told the boys. Yisu was already running up the path, probably anxious to know which one of his friends had been taken. Father ran after him.

"Stay with Yosei," I told my brothers, and took off after Father.

Yehudah's report had been incomplete. There hadn't been *a* hanging, but *four*. The lone execution stake that had stood outside Nazareth for as long as I could remember had been joined by three more. Each of the crosses bore the tortured body of a Zealot; in between their cries of pain they heaped curses upon their executioners, evidence that they hadn't been hanging long. Above each man was nailed a crudely-lettered sign: insurrection. There were no names.

I recognized only one of the men; Father noticed my reaction and rightly guessed the cause of it. "Which one is Sicae?" he asked me.

"Abba—" Yisu began.

Father cut him off, still talking to me. "Which one, Katan?"

I pointed him out. Father got as close as the guards would allow and spat on the Zealot. Then he laughed. I'd never heard a laugh like that one come out of my father's mouth before— hard, bitter, mocking, rejoicing in someone's pain; I never wanted to hear that laugh again. "You son of a bitch," he said. "I hope you live for days. Days!" He turned to the guards and spoke in Greek. "You keep this one alive as long as you can."

Sicae was staring at Yisu. "Traitorous. Dog."

Yisu's eyes were full of tears.

"Come on, boys," Father said, turning to leave. He started back the way we'd come.

Yisu didn't follow.

"Yisu, now."

"No."

No? My jaw dropped and I stared at my brother in shock. Had he just defied Father?

"No son of Abraham should die alone. You said so

yourself. These men, regardless of what they've done, are also sons of Abraham." He sat down.

Father stood still for a moment, trembling with suppressed rage. Then he whirled on his heel and, without so much as a glance in my direction, stomped off toward home.

Something broke in my father that day, as if his joy had been nailed to the cross along with Sicae. He went about his business quietly, looking more and more like his father—and less and less like himself—with each day that passed.

Outwardly, as our life slowly returned to something that could be considered normal, he seemed to heal. He smiled on occasion, usually when he was playing with his youngest child, the little girl who'd been born late in the day of the hangings, whom he'd named Rebekah. Around the time she began to walk, he even made himself another flute, and soon the nights were filled with music as before the fire.

But his laugh—his rolling, joyous laugh—never returned.

.

Part Six

Mercy

I remember my affliction and my wandering, the bitterness and the gall. I well remember them, and my soul is downcast within me. Yet this I call to mind and therefore I have hope: Because of the LORD's great love we are not consumed, for His compassions never fail. They are new every morning...

—Lamentations 3:19-23 (NIV)

49

YISU

Tishri 3778
(Two Years Later)

The sun set. A new day began. *And there was evening, and there was morning—the first day.* How many "first days" had come and gone since that very first one? Thousands upon thousands, I knew, and every week since the dawn of creation the cycle had started over again: light, air, water and earth, things that rooted deep into the soil and the sun that drew them upward, creatures that swam and flew and ran and crawled and stumbled through life as best they could until exhaustion forced them to rest.

The sun rose. I opened my eyes to its light, drew in a deep breath; made my way to the latrine and watered the ground; stood barefoot in the grass with the sun warming the back of my neck as the early birds sang and a lizard snapped up a fly that was too sluggish to evade death. The whole of creation was re-created in the first few minutes of every new morning, or so it seemed to me in that moment.

Instead of returning home, I ran the mile to my myrtle close, beginning my prayers as I went. Time, it seemed, was one of the things that had burned up in the fire; if I was to complete all of the tasks waiting for me each day, I could waste not a single breath of time. My hour alone with my Father, however, I would not sacrifice. It did not belong to me. It was His. Never mind the fact that my ears were still too small to hear His voice; I knew He was listening to mine, and so I poured my heart out to Him with the rising of every sun. Because time was precious, I spent none of it on empty words, beautiful though they might be; let the traditional blessings fall from my lips when others were around to share in them—*Shema Yisrael! Adonai Eloheinu, Adonai echad!*—and ring silently in my heart when silence was needed—*Baruch ata Yahuh Eloheinu, melech ha-olam*—but in our alone time I spoke only those words too private for anyone else to hear. Painful words, torn and bleeding, like my heart.

"How long, Father? How long?"

How long, Yahuh? the psalmist had asked again and again. *Will You be angry forever?* It was not my Father's anger, however, that had been tearing me apart for so long now. It was Yosef's. "Will he ever be able to forgive? Soften his heart, Father! Please!" The hatred that had consumed Yosef, that had smothered his joy and turned his face away from me, had grown from the seed of a single word I'd spoken two years ago: *No.*

Watching Sicae hang was the hardest thing I had ever done.

Never before had I witnessed a mass execution. Not *one* of my friends hung dying, but *four* of them, brothers all, men I'd sworn to protect—men I'd been forced to abandon. This was hard. Harder still were the curses they had rained down upon me as they'd died. *Traitor. Liar. Dog.*

God rot you in Sheol, Sicae had gasped toward the end. And the end—it had been slow in coming. Only one of the men had died quickly, breathing his last ten hours later, during the first watch of the night; two had died the next day after enduring hours in the searing heat of the Tammuz sun. Sicae, however, had refused to surrender to death—and I had refused to leave him. Three days and nights I'd sat at his feet, fasting from food, fasting from water, praying for him and for myself as I'd wrestled against the hardest thing of all—the overwhelming temptation to hate him.

My hatred, I knew, was something Sicae deserved, something he had earned. But it was not something I could afford to spend on him. I hated what he had done, hated it with a passion that burned inside me more intensely than the flames that had devoured my home. I hated the death he had brought with him, hated the lie that had twisted him, hated the hatred that drove him. These things I hated, and I sensed that such hatred was right. *God forbid this night's work be forgiven!* my brother had said, and I agreed with him. Such actions should never be forgiven, never be condoned. *Vengeance is mine, says Yahuh; I will repay.* Repay, Father! my soul had cried out then, filled with righteous hatred of the murders that had been committed in the name of God. I'd raised my eyes and gazed upon the men who had committed these acts that I hated, ready to hate them as well—and I'd paused. These murderers, were they not still *men*, created in the image of God? How then could I hate them? And looking up at the man who called himself Sicae, I'd known that to hate him was to hate God, in whose image he had been made. I couldn't do it.

Hatred, however, has a life of its own, I discovered during those three days. Once born, hatred needs a target, demands release. It will not simply die. The hatred born in me that day had fought against death as tenaciously as Sicae. I'd struggled to kill it, but without success—the more I'd denied the hatred within me, the larger it had grown. Victory, I'd finally come to realize, lay not in denying the hatred but in fixing it upon its proper object: the lie that had driven these men to commit murder. However, it had been hard—almost impossible—to focus my hatred on something I couldn't see and to keep it there despite provocation. With each of Sicae's curses, the temptation to hate him had risen up again. Only after fighting this same battle over and over had I seen my mistake: hatred, like mildew, grows best in an empty house. Not hating Sicae was not enough. I couldn't be neutral in my feelings for him. Somehow, somehow, I had to love him.

Again I'd looked up at Sicae, trying with all my might to love him. *In the image of God has God made man.* The scripture that had been sufficient to deflect my hate was unable to awaken my love, for God's image had become so twisted in this man that it was no longer lovable. "Please, Father, help me to see him," I'd whispered. Shimon I'd understood, Yoash I'd understood, but Sicae had always been a closed book to me. He hadn't joined the Zealots out of hope or need or pain or fear, but out of a desire to inflict suffering. I couldn't understand that, try as I might. "Help me to see this man as he was when You created him." *For You created my inmost being; You knit me together in my mother's womb.* By the time we'd met, Sicae had already been warped, but he hadn't always been that way, surely; once he had been a boy, and before that, a baby. "A baby," I'd whispered again, and had smiled through the tears that were already starting to form in my eyes. A baby I could love. And so, sitting in the dust at the foot of Sicae's cross, I had pictured the baby that he once was—had pictured the baby, not lying in his mother's arms, but nailed to that cross.

I'd vomited at the thought, so vivid had been the image it invoked, and as I'd lain sobbing, doubled over with grief for the one I loved, my hatred had at last fixed itself firmly where it belonged: on the forces of evil that had brought my beloved to this place. "Forgive him, Father," I had begged. "Punish me, punish me in his stead; let Your wrath fall on me; only let this man be new again as once he was, as You created him. Forgive him, Father, please."

"Please forgive him, Father," I prayed now as I ran toward the myrtle grove, but this prayer was not for Sicae. I prayed for Yosef, a man I'd never had trouble loving. "Oh, Father, soften his heart. Make him new. Restore his joy. Please." *Please.*

For months following the hanging, Yosef had barely spoken to me. My soft but unyielding *no*, my refusal to leave Sicae's side, had angered him beyond reason. He saw my love for Sicae as betrayal, and my one attempt to explain had only increased the stress between us. *To everything there is a season, and a time for every purpose under heaven,* Solomon had written, *a time to tear and a time to mend, a time to be silent and a time to speak.* And so I respected Yosef's pain and waited in torn silence for the time of mending. I had been waiting for more than two years. *How long, Yahuh?*

Last week, the *shofarot* had sounded the start of a new year. In two days' time, we would observe Yom Kippur. Every year since the fire I had gone to Yosef on Rosh Hashanah and asked for his forgiveness. Every year he had casually replied, "There's nothing to forgive, Yisu." Three times now those words had fallen from his lips, but not once had they come from his heart. Saliva, that's all they were. *The life is in the blood.* Saliva can mask thirst, but it can never quench it. My Abba was dying of thirst and was oblivious to the fact, and until he would talk to me there was nothing I could do to help him. Except pray.

Reaching the grove, I crept in amongst the myrtles and inhaled deeply of their soothing fragrance. Unlike many of the trees in the area, the myrtles had not changed their green for gold, and never would. Next week, their branches would be cut and tied into *lulovim* to be waved throughout the land in celebration of Sukkoth, and the myrtles would dance before God, side-by-side with the willows, citrons, and palms. "The trees of the field will clap their hands," I sang, improvising a tune to accompany the passage from Isaiah. "You shall go out in joy and be led forth in peace, the mountains and hills will burst into song before you, and all the trees of the field will clap their hands." The simple act of worship revived me, and I gave myself over to it fully; just as the *lulov* was woven from the four sacred plants, I wove my prayers for Yosef together with scripture, song, and dance. I became the *lulov*. Waving myself before God, I worshiped my Father with total abandon, losing all sense of time and place, until finally my body collapsed in sheer exhaustion and I lay panting on the ground, spent.

"I thought I'd find you here."

Yosef was sitting on a stump at the edge of the small clearing, waiting. How long he'd been there, I had no idea. I sat up, brushing a few leaves from my hair as I searched for the right words. They wouldn't come. Yosef stared at me for a moment, his expression unreadable, and then filled the silence with words of his own. "In your Father's house, about your Father's business. That's what you said to me when you were twelve: 'Didn't you know I'd be here?' When I couldn't find you. When you were missing. When I didn't know where you were and all I could think was, dear God, how could I have been so careless with Your son? Please, *please* let him be all right. And that's all you said. 'Didn't you know I'd be here?'"

I couldn't say even that much now, but my words weren't needed. Yosef was talking, talking to me, talking to me at last. All I had to do was listen.

"When you didn't show up this morning, I felt that same panic. *Please, please let him be all right.* I made the same stupid mistake, looking for you all over town before I figured out that you'd be here. Do you have any idea how hard this place is to find? How many myrtles there are between Yaffa and Nazareth?"

For the first time, I noticed that the shadows in the grove were all pointing the wrong way. I'd been here for hours. Hours. "I'm so sorry, Abba—"

"No!" He cut me off, his anger finally asserting itself in this small way, making its existence known. "Don't apologize! Why should you? You haven't done anything wrong." Was it fear, or merely habit, that drove Yosef again and again to deny his anger toward me? "The panic was of my own making. *Please let him be all right.* How many times have you told me not to worry about you, that you're safe? How many disasters have you survived unscathed? It's not your fault that I don't trust you. You've proven yourself trustworthy." Having buried his true feelings once more, Yosef stood up to leave. "Don't apologize, Yisu. There's nothing to forgive."

I couldn't let him go, not like this. Not with a mouth full of insincere saliva. "That's not true."

He ignored me, started walking back the way he'd come.

"There's plenty to forgive, Abba," I said to his back. "You just don't want to admit it." He froze in his steps. "I know I've hurt you. I'm sorry for that. Why is it that I can admit the truth but you can't? Are you so afraid of me, Abba?"

Even as the words left my mouth, I knew I had spoken truly. Yosef turned to face me, but slowly. His eyes had filled with tears. "Who am I, to forgive you for anything? How can I pass judgment on you like that, to say that what you did was wrong and needs forgiveness?" He shook his head. "The fault is mine."

"Who are you," I countered gently, "to pass judgment on yourself? That's why God commands us to forgive. In the end, every act comes under God's judgment, whether it is good or evil. When we forgive, we simply acknowledge that truth—we leave the judgment in God's hands. To withhold forgiveness is to pass a judgment only God has the right to pass. In failing to forgive me, you judge yourself guilty."

Yosef was silent, and his head was bowed. I couldn't see his eyes. "I am guilty," he said softly.

"That's for God to judge, not you." I walked over to him and took his hand, kneeling at his feet. "I'm sorry I hurt you, Abba. Will you forgive me for that?"

"You didn't set out to hurt me. You didn't do anything wrong."

His stubbornness was monumental. "There you go again, only this time you're not just judging my actions but my motives as well! Don't you see? Forgiving me is the *opposite* of judging me! You don't have to decide whether or not my actions are worthy of forgiveness before you can forgive me; you don't have to decide whether or not you're worthy to forgive me; you just have to forgive me and trust God to work out the rest!" I tried again, speaking slowly. "I'm sorry I hurt you. Will you forgive me?"

He smiled. "You don't have to talk to me like I'm two years old, Yisu. I get it. I forgive you."

"Do you forgive me for talking down to you, too?" I teased.

"Yes, even for that."

"Do you forgive me for scaring you by not showing up to work this morning?"

"Yes."

"And that day in the Temple when I was twelve, for not being more sensitive to your feelings?"

"Yes, that too."

"And for messing up your work so many times, like when I was three and smashed all your tiles to make a mosaic?"

"Come on, Yisu, don't be ridiculous. Of course I forgive you for that. You were a baby!"

"That's judgmental, Abba. In my favor, but still judgmental. What if I ruin your work tomorrow, will you forgive me then?"

He laughed. "Yes, don't worry, I'll forgive you." Yosef was finally relaxing, allowing me to guide him along the path of healing. I decided to risk something a bit more difficult.

"Do you forgive me for neglecting my trade for so many years, for spending so much time with Ezra instead of with you?"

He met my eyes. "Is that how you see it?"

"It doesn't matter how I see it, Abba. Do you forgive me?"

"Yes."

It was time. So far, I hadn't led Yosef anywhere he hadn't already been on his own; he had already forgiven all of these things long ago—he had judged them and found them to be worthy of forgiveness. The path was about to become steep, treacherous, run counter to his judgment. "Do you forgive me for becoming friends with Shimon when I was thirteen?"

He hesitated. "Yes. I forgive you."

"For getting involved with the Zealots?" I looked him in the eyes. "Don't lie to me."

"I—" He stopped, swallowed, drew in a deep breath. "Okay. That one—that one's hard, but yes, I forgive you."

"And do you forgive me for my part in causing the fire? For Saba's death? For—"

He cut me off. "I forgive you, Yisu. Enough. Please stop."

"No." His eyes had filled with tears again, but I pressed on.

To do otherwise was to leave him stranded on the face of the cliff. "Do you forgive me for staying with Sicae when they hanged him?"

He didn't answer.

"Abba, do you forgive me for staying with him, for treating him with the same respect I gave all the others? Do you forgive me for forgiving Sicae?" The tears were running down his cheeks. I reached up to wipe them away. He pulled back sharply.

"I don't understand that," he whispered fiercely. "I don't understand how you could betray your family like that, how you could betray *me*, choose that—that *scum*—over your family..."

He was in such pain. "This is between me and my Father," I said as gently as possible, though nothing could soften a truth this hard. "There was no betrayal, no choosing one over the other. My relationship with Sicae has nothing to do with my love for *you*, Abba, or my love for Saba and Ezra and Shimeon—"

"I don't know you!" he shouted, his anger bursting free at last. "I don't know who you are! How can you forgive what that man did to us?"

"I don't!" I said. "What he did was wrong—it will always be wrong! I *hate* what he did!" For a brief moment, I gave full vent to my own anger, letting it pour through me unfettered for Yosef to see. Then I reined it in again. "I don't forgive what he did, but I forgive him for having done it."

"It's the same thing."

"No, it's not the same. A man is more than the sum of his actions." I held out my arms. "Please, Abba, didn't Sicae do enough damage to our family three years ago? Must you let him come between us, too? Abba—can you only love me if I hate him?"

He stared at me, struck dumb by the enormity of the truth contained in my question. Eyes wide with dismay, he took a step back. Silence filled the grove.

I did nothing to break that silence. My words had not fallen on deaf ears; that I could plainly see—there was no need to repeat them, no need to add to them. Patiently I waited, watching as Yosef wrestled with the feelings he had been suppressing for more than two years. He had carried this burden without looking at it, as if his blindness would make it lighter, would make it disappear. My question, however, had pulled the load off his back and thrown it at his feet; he had no choice now but to examine it. Indeed, the only decision remaining to him was whether or not he would pick it up again now that he knew what it was.

"I... I..."

He broke then, wrapping his arms around me and sobbing, "I love you, Yeshua."

"Do you forgive me for not hating Sicae?" I pressed.

"Yes," he whispered. "I forgive you."

I held him close. It was enough for now, the most he was able to give. I couldn't ask him to forgive Sicae, not yet. He wasn't ready for that. But there was one more thing he needed to forgive *me* for, one more thing that had been festering inside him for years. "Abba," I whispered as I held him, "do you forgive me for telling you that one day I'll hang? Do you forgive me for laying that burden on you? Can you—will you be able to forgive me for dying?"

For a long while, I wasn't sure he'd heard me. Then, gradually, his tears subsided and he straightened, meeting my eyes. "I don't know," he confessed. "How can you ask such a thing of me? How could a merciful God ask such a thing of any man? That I stand by and do nothing as you—as you—" He shook his head. "Do I forgive you for telling me? Yes, I do. Will I forgive you for deliberately walking down a road that leads to your own hanging? I don't know, Yeshua. Perhaps I'll be able to forgive you for that. But forgive myself? Forgive God? I don't know."

He got to his feet and walked off.

50

KATAN

9 Elul 3778

Three years after the fire, toward the end of winter, we got a big job in Sepphoris, one that would take all of us to complete; only Shimeon was excused—at eight years old, he wasn't up to really hard physical labor, and Father didn't want to pull him out of school for no good reason. For several months we worked to complete the building's foundation and erect the walls. By late summer it was time to lay the beams for the roof.

These beams weren't the ones we usually worked with; it was a large building and the beams were correspondingly large: imports from the Lebanon. Even with three sets of tackle, it took all five of us to lift each timber, two men on the ground and everyone else on the roof. We'd already gotten one of the things in place, but Father wanted to lay two more before we broke for dinner. It was blistering hot, and we'd all stripped down to the barest that modesty would allow. I was running the crew on the roof, where the heat was the worst. "Let's get this over with quickly!" I called down to Yisu, who was working with Father on the ground.

"Right!" he shouted back. He set the ropes in place, one around the middle of the log and one more at either end, hooked the tackles to them, and then gave the signal for us to take up the slack.

We had three pulley blocks set up on a scaffold overhanging the roof; Yehudah, who'd just turned thirteen, was manning the center rope, while Yosei and I took the ends. "Brace," I said.

"On four!" Father's voice rang out from below. "One—two—three—"

"Haul!" I called out. We all heaved on the ropes, taking

most of the weight while Father and Yisu got the thing off the ground and guided it up the side of the building. As soon as it got too high for them to reach, all of the weight was on us, but the pulleys made it doable. Once the beam reached the edge of the roof, it was a simple matter of rolling it into place. Then we all took a few minutes to recover our strength before tackling the third strut.

"Look at my hands," Yehudah complained. I checked them out—they were raw and blistered from the rope.

"You're holding it wrong," Yosei told him. "You need to wrap the rope around your waist and take it under your arms, like this."

"Like this?"

"No, you idiot, you do it like that and you'll fall off the roof if someone drops the log. Like *this*, moron."

"Father hears you talking to him like that and *you'll* be the one who falls off the roof," I warned Yosei. Crossing to the corner where we had a bucket of clean water, I poured a dipperful over my head and swigged down another while my brothers worked on Yehudah's technique. "Before we raise the last beam," I suggested, "you'll want to wrap a rag around each hand so you don't make those burns worse." That's what I always did from the start, having learned the hard way (like Yehudah was doing now).

"Are you boys ready up there?" Father called.

"Almost, sir!" I hollered down. Yosei helped Yehudah with his bandages, and then we took our places. I called, "Set!" to let Father know we were in position.

"Set," Yisu echoed from below.

"Brace!" Yehudah had his rope wrapped as Yosei had instructed.

"On four! One—two—three—"

"Haul!" I called, and put my back into it, pulling the rope hand-over-hand a span at a time. One span, two spans— suddenly the rope jerked in my hand and the weight nearly pulled me off my feet—someone had dropped the strut. Yehudah moved just a bit and Yosei was not at all affected, so I knew it was Father's end that had crashed.

"Abba!" Yisu shouted a second later, and Yosei jerked forward. Yisu must have dropped his end, too.

I instructed my brothers to lower the beam quickly, and

then ran to the edge of the roof.

My father lay on the ground. The beam hadn't landed on him, but he wasn't moving.

51

YISU

9 Elul 3778

We really should have had four men on the ground crew, but Yosef was reluctant to spend the money needed to hire labor. He'd insisted that the two of us could handle it. *The only hard part is the first lift. After that, the top crew is doing all the work. I can't justify paying two men a day's wages for—what?—ten minutes' labor?*

The first two beams went up with no trouble, and I had to admit that Yosef knew his trade better than I did. He grinned and slapped me on the back. "Get some water. It's hotter than Gehenna out here today." While he got himself a drink and sat down to cool off in the meager patch of shade cast by the building, I rolled the third log into position and fastened the ropes around it, passing them under the log through the shallow trenches I'd dug for that purpose earlier in the day. After securely tying all three knots, I helped myself to some water.

"Ready?" Yosef asked. I nodded. "Are you boys ready up there?"

"Almost, sir!" Katan's voice drifted down.

I got into position at one end of the beam, squatting so I'd be lifting with my legs and not my back; Yosef got into the same position at the opposite end.

"Set," came the signal from above.

I looked at Yosef; he nodded. "Set," I called back.

"On four!" Yosef shouted. "One—two—three—up!"

I pushed myself up, feeling the rope tighten as my brothers took their share of the weight. The strut was still unbelievably heavy, and would be until I got myself positioned under it. Bending my knees again, I inhaled deeply and got ready for the second lift; the tricky part here was shifting from an underhanded grip to an overhand one. After that, I'd be pushing instead of pulling. I nodded at Yosef to let him know I was ready—we didn't waste valuable breath on words here—and he nodded back, grimacing slightly. There was no countdown to the second lift; I simply watched Yosef and moved on his signal. It came, and I exhaled sharply and hoisted the beam up and over my head in one smooth motion.

A split second later, the beam lurched forward and I almost lost my grip on it as my end jerked sharply upward. I knew what that meant—someone's hold had slipped, either Yosef's or Katan's, possibly both. I looked over at Yosef. He was doubled over, gasping; as his end of the beam crashed to the ground beside him, he staggered a few paces and then collapsed.

"Abba!" I shouted.

Dropping my end of the strut, I ran to him.

He lay on his left side with his forehead pressed into the dirt; his legs were drawn up, his breathing labored; his left hand was balled into a fist, and his right hand was clenched around the upper part of his left arm.

"Abba," I said again. I knelt beside him and rolled him over so that his head was in my lap instead of the dirt. His face was pale and streaked with sweat.

"Hurts," he gasped.

Oh, God. Father. Please.

He gasped again, his whole body tensing from the pain.

"Abba, don't leave me," I whispered, taking him into my arms as best I could and holding on to him, as if I could keep him with me that way. *Father, please. Please don't take him.*

Suddenly Yosef relaxed, and he smiled at me. "God is merciful," he said.

And then he died.

52

KATAN

9 Elul 3778

I flew down the ladder and to Father's side, but I was too late. He was gone. Just like that.

Yisu held him tightly. "No," he said. "No." He bent over Father, pressing his ear to Father's chest. I held my breath. Yisu didn't move for a long time. Then he turned his head to look at Father's face. "No," Yisu said again, a hint of anger staining his voice. "No more. This has to stop. No more." He sat up, reached over to touch Father's forehead gently, smoothing a stray piece of hair, and then pulled his eyes closed. His hand lingered there, as if in a caress. "Oh, Abba."

Something snapped in me. Kneeling opposite Yisu, I laid my own hand on Father's chest. "Get out of my way," I said. "Get your hands off my father." As the words took shape, I realized I'd been wanting to say them for years. *My* father. Not Yisu's. Mine. I spoke the words and I saw the truth of them reflected in Yisu's eyes. Vindicated by his silent agreement, I said them again. "Get your hands off my father."

He swallowed and backed off.

Yosei and Yehudah ran over at that moment and fell to the ground beside me, wailing.

Drawn by the commotion, people from the neighborhood began to gather. One offered his house to us and helped us move Father's body out of the hot sun; another offered us a wagon to carry Father home to Nazareth. Yisu stood quietly by during all of this, allowing me to fulfill my duty as Yosef's firstborn son.

One thing he insisted upon for himself, and I didn't argue. It was his by right.

While we waited for the oxcart to be made ready, Yisu ran home to prepare Mother for our arrival.

53

YISU

9 Elul 3778

Stopping only long enough to throw on my tunic, I ran down the highway at the fastest pace I could manage. The more time Mother had before the arrival of the funeral cart, the better.

Perhaps, after I told her, I would be able to cry.

Then again, perhaps I wouldn't. Perhaps I'd shed so many tears over the last decade that I had none left. Perhaps it would take Moses, striking me with his staff, to get the waters to flow again.

What a thought.

I ran faster, but only for a moment. It was still brutally hot, and I'd forgotten to bring a water skin. I slowed to a jog, and then to a brisk walk. Still a mile to go. Nahum's field stretched out before me, a few stalks of wheat still standing here and there for the poor to glean. *By the sweat of your brow you will eat your food, until you return to the ground, since from it you were taken; for dust you are, and to dust you will return.* I wiped the sweat out of my eyes with my sleeve, only then realizing that I hadn't yet torn my tunic. I reached up to do so, but stopped myself. I didn't want Mother to see me in mourning before I'd had a chance to tell her what had happened.

I heard voices on the road ahead of me and looked up.

"Yo, Onarion!"

Oh, no, Father, please not now, not today. They were headed toward Sepphoris.

I kept walking, eyes down, as if I hadn't heard. They surrounded me, laughing, walking with me for a few paces. Then they closed ranks and pushed me back, forcing me to stop. "What's the hurry, Onarion?"

I longed for Demetrius, but he'd been transferred some time ago. Raising my eyes, I met the gaze of the soldier who'd spoken last. The smile fell off his face. "Damn, Yisu, what happened? You look like hell."

"My father," I said. "He—" The rest stuck in my throat, refusing to be spoken. Speaking these words, I knew in that moment, would make them true in a way I could no longer ignore, and I was not yet ready to embrace this truth. Even to acknowledge it was almost more than I could bear. Acknowledge it, however, I must. Swallowing, I pushed the words past my lips, hating the taste of them. "He just—died." *It's true. Oh, God, it's true. How can it be true?* "I'm on my way home, to tell my mother. Please—"

"You don't have to say another word. Go. Nobody's going to bother you." They'd all fallen silent.

I started walking again.

"Wait!" he called after me. "Did you just come from Sepphoris?"

"Yes."

"Where's your water?"

"I don't have any."

"In this heat?" He pulled a skin out of his gear and tossed it to me. "Here."

I unstopped it and drank, then offered it back to him.

"Keep it," he said. Before I could thank him, he waved me on. "Now go."

Five years ago I'd been astonished to learn that my mother was strong. I'd seen her strength again in the aftermath of the fire. "Father," I whispered, "let her be strong now." Pushing open the door, I called out, "Emi, it's Yisu."

I'd run across Sarah out in the yard and sent her to fetch Leah, Rachel, and Hannah, without telling her why. At the same time, I'd thanked God for the tears that hadn't come yet, for my voice that wasn't shaking and my eyes that weren't red.

"Ssh. Rebekah's napping." Mother looked up from her sewing with a smile. "You're home early. Is it just you, or everyone?"

"Just me," I said. "The others are on their way." I crossed the room, leaned over, and embraced her tightly. Burying my face in her hair, I whispered, "I love you, Emi."

"I love you, too." Her voice was soft. "What's wrong, Yisu-yuladi?" *Yisu, my child.*

"Emi. I have bad news." She stiffened in my arms, bracing herself for the worst. "While we were working, Abba collapsed." I pulled back just enough to meet her eyes. There was no kind way to say what I must say next, no painless way to ease her into the awful truth. Words could mask the truth, but they could not change it. The fewer the words, the better. "He didn't make it, Emi." *Say it.* "He's dead."

"Yosef...?" Her lower lip started to quiver.

I reached up, grabbed the neck of my tunic, and pulled at it until it ripped down the front with a harsh, tearing sound like— like—

We say a heart breaks, but really it's nothing so neat as that. Hearts don't break; they shred.

Epilogue

10 Elul 3778

P*ut my tears in Your bottle; are they not in Your book? When I cry to You, my enemies will fall back; I know You are for me. Put my tears in Your bottle...* Yisu kisses the top of Sarah's head, wipes his eyes, and faces the grave. In a loud, clear voice he begins to recite the words of the *kaddish,* the mourning prayer. *"Yitgadal ve'yitkadesh, Shmei rabbah..." May His name be magnified and made holy...*

Katan turns at the sound of these words, these words that are supposed to come from the firstborn son of the deceased, and he glares at his brother. Yisu sees but is not deterred. Without pause he continues to praise God, fighting against death in the only way he knows. "May the great Name of God be exalted and sanctified, throughout the world, which He has created according to His will..."

Death is the enemy. Death is the thief that comes to rend hearts and tear loved ones apart. Death is the army camped outside the gate, besieging the earth, standing between men and their God. Irresistible, indefensible, undefeated...

No more. This has to stop.

His recitation turns into a song, shaky at first but growing in strength until it fills the narrow valley. "May there be abundant peace from Heaven, and life, upon us and upon all Israel. He who makes peace in His high holy places, may He bring peace upon us, and upon all Israel."

To win that peace, he will take this battle into death's camp itself.

Your will be done, Father.

He looks at the torn faces of his loved ones, at his brother's rigid, angry stance.

This has to stop.

He sets his face like a flint, resolute.

This will *stop.*

I promise.

Map of Eretz Israel
First Century A.D.

Showing principal locations and travel routes mentioned in the novel.

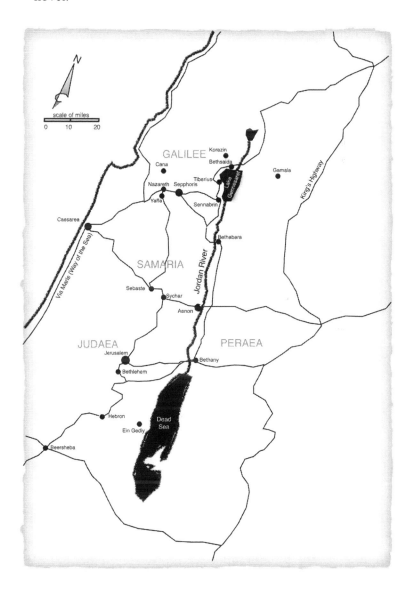

Glossary of Hebrew and Aramaic Terms

Note: Terms which appear only once in the novel along with their translations are not included here.

Abba – Daddy

Adonai – Lord (often used in place of YHWH, the name of God revealed to Moses, which is usually translated Lord in English Bibles)

Adonai-Tzeva'ot – Lord of Hosts

aliyah – the privilege of reading from Torah in the synagogue; traditionally, the hazzan selects the men who are to receive this privilege each week

am-ha-aretz – illiterate peasant; one uneducated and/or unobservant of Torah

bar – son of (Aramaic)

bar mitzvah – a young man who has reached the age of accountability, traditionally thirteen (literally "son of the commandment")

Baruch atah Adonai Eloheinu, melech ha-olam – traditional beginning of most blessings (literally "Blessed are You, Lord our God, King of the universe")

Baruch hu, dayan ha-emet – "Blessed is He, the righteous Judge"; a blessing spoken at funerals

bat, bath – daughter of

ben – son of (Hebrew)

bet-sefer – elementary school, for boys ages 5-12 (literally "house of the book")

bet-midrash – secondary school, for the top students graduating bet-sefer; in ancient times, this was usually boys ages 13-16 (literally "house of study")

bimah – the podium in the synagogue where men stand to read from Torah

brit milah – circumcision ceremony

challah – a fancy bread often served on Sabbath and holidays

chuppah – wedding canopy

contubernium (*plural* contubernia) – (Latin) the basic unit of a Roman legion, a squadron of eight men living together in one tent; ten contubernia form a century

denarius (*plural* denarii) – (Latin) a coin equal to one day's wages for a working man

Doda – Aunt
Dodi – Uncle
D'varim – Deuteronomy (literally "Words," taken from the first line of the book: "These are the words...")
eikhah – lament
El-Elyon – God Most High
Elohim – God
Elo'i – my God
Ema – Mom, Mommy (variant **Emi** – my Mommy)
Erev Sukkoth – the day before Sukkoth (literally "Sukkoth Eve"); 14 Tishri
Gehenna – hell; the valley outside Jerusalem where refuse was burned
haftarah – a scripture reading from one of the Prophets, usually following a reading from Torah
HaShem – a term used in place of "God" (literally "the Name")
Hallel – a group of psalms (113-118) traditionally sung at Passover
hazzan – the worship leader in a synagogue
ish – man, husband
ishah – woman, wife (variant ishati, my wife)
Katan – Junior (literally "lesser")
ketubah – marriage contract; also used to refer to the bride price
khan – a caravan shelter, providing travelers with lodgings for a small fee; although commonly translated "inn," the khan was the most basic of accommodations, usually just a single large room sheltering both people and their pack animals
kiddush – the mealtime blessing
kiddushin – the betrothal ceremony
kinnor – a small harp
kohein (*plural* kohanim) – priest
L'shanah tovah tikatevu – "May a good year be inscribed for you." Traditional greeting on Rosh HaShanah (often abbreviated to L'shanah tovah, "a good year")
lulov (*plural* lulovim) – the branches of four plants (myrtle, palm, willow, and citron) woven together and used in celebration of Sukkoth (*see* Leviticus 23:40)
mamzer – bastard; specifically, a child born from a forbidden union (including incest and adultery); a child of unknown

parentage might also be considered mamzer (*see* Deuteronomy 23:2)

maskil – a type of song found in the Book of Psalms, usually serious or introspective in tone

megillah (*plural* megillot) – scroll; "*the* megillah" usually refers to the Book of Esther

Messiah – a savior king promised in many ancient prophecies (literally "Anointed One")

mezuzah – scripture attached to doorposts, usually in an ornate box (*see* Deuteronomy 6:9)

milites – (Latin) foot soldier

mitzvah (*plural* mitzvot) – commandment

moros – (Greek) idiot

niddah – menstruating; Torah forbids sexual relations with a woman during this period

omer – a measure of grain; "counting the omer" refers to the practice of counting off the days and weeks between Passover and Pentecost (*see* Leviticus 23:15-21)

onarion – (Greek) a young male donkey

Pesach – also called Passover; an annual remembrance of the exodus of the Jews from Egypt; 14 Nisan (*see* Exodus 13:3-10)

Pharisee – a member of a strict religious sect that believed in the inerrancy of Scripture, the Resurrection, the existence of angels, and the Oral Traditions; most rabbis were Pharisees

Purim – an annual celebration of the deliverance of the Jews from the Persians; 13 Adar (*see* Esther 8:11-17)

quadrans – (Latin) the least valuable Roman coin, worth 1/16 of a sesterce (1/64 of a denarius)

rabbi (*plural* rabbim) – a teacher (literally "my master") (variant Rabbani, my teacher)

Rosh HaShanah – the start of the Jewish new year (literally "the head of the year"); also called Yom Teruah; 1 Tishri (*see* Leviticus 23:23-25)

ru'ach – breath, spirit

ru'ach ha-Elohim – breath of God

Ru'ach haKodesh – Holy Spirit

Saba – Grandpa

Sadducee – a member of a religious sect that rejected certain teachings of the Pharisees (such as the Resurrection and the Oral Traditions); most Sadducees were high-ranking priests and elders in Jerusalem

Savta – Grandma

Sefer ha-Shofetim – the Book of Judges

sesterce (*plural* sesterci) – (Latin) a silver or bronze coin worth ¼ of a denarius

Sha'alu shalom Yerushalayim yisholayu – "Pray for the peace of Jerusalem, may they be secure"

Shabbat – the Sabbath; the seventh day of the week, on which no work is permitted (*see* Exodus 20:8-11)

Shabbat Shalom – a traditional Sabbath greeting (literally "Sabbath peace")

shalom aleikha (*plural* shalom aleikhem) – traditional greeting (literally "peace to you")

Shavuot – the Feast of Weeks; may refer specifically to the last day (Pentecost) or the entire seven-week period of counting the omer (*see* Leviticus 23:15-21)

Sheol – hell, the grave

shiva – a seven-day period of intense mourning following the death of a family member

shofar (*plural* shofarot) – trumpet

shofet (*plural* shofetim) – judge; a court of law was usually comprised of three shofetim but a single judge could rule on lesser matters of arbitration; also used to refer to the Book of Judges

sofer – scribe; one educated in matters of Law

sukkah (*plural* sukkoth) – a booth made of temporary materials; during Sukkoth, people eat and sleep in these booths (*see* Leviticus 23:42)

Sukkot *or* Sukkoth – the Feast of Tabernacles; 15-22 Tishri (*see* Leviticus 23:33-36)

tallit – a prayer shawl, fringed and with tassels (*see* Numbers 15:37-40)

talmid (*plural* talmidim) – disciple; more than just a student, a talmid would attach himself to one rabbi with the intention of becoming exactly like that rabbi through a combination of service and study

Tanakh – the entire Jewish Bible; the word *Tanakh* is an acronym for *Torah* (the Law), *Neviyim* (the Prophets), and *Ketuvim* (the Writings)

tefillah – prayer

tefillin – small leather boxes containing verses from Torah, which observant Jewish men tie on their arms and foreheads during prayer services (*see* Deuteronomy 6:8)

teruah – trumpet blast

teshuvah – repentance, turning away from sin and toward God

Toma – twin

Torah – the Law; refers to the first five books of the Bible and/or the commandments that are written in these books (Genesis, Exodus, Leviticus, Numbers, Deuteronomy)

tzedakah – charity

tzitzit – the tassel on each corner of a prayer shawl; the knots are tied in such a way as to spell the name of God (*see* Numbers 15:37-40)

Yahuh – one possible pronunciation of the revealed name of God (YHWH); since the Jews ordinarily substitute "Adonai" for God's name when reading or praying, the actual pronunciation was lost hundreds of years ago

Yamim Noraim – the Days of Awe; a period of ten days beginning with Rosh HaShanah and ending with Yom Kippur

yeshu'ah – salvation

Yom Kippur – the Day of Atonement; 10 Tishri (*see* Leviticus 23:26-32)

Yom Teruah – the Day of Trumpets; another name for Rosh HaShanah; 1 Tishri (*see* Leviticus 23:23-25)

yom tov – a greeting; when capitalized, refers to a holiday (literally "good day")

Zealots – revolutionaries who fought for Jewish independence from Rome

About the Author

D. L. Maynard lives on Florida's Space Coast, where she spends as much time as possible enjoying nature. She worked out most of the dialogue for *Brothers* while soaking up sun at the beach and hiking through the woods. In between novelizing, she attends Asbury Theological Seminary, leads kayak tours on the Merritt Island National Wildlife Refuge, teaches middle school English, and serves as ministry coordinator for LifePointe Ministries.

If you enjoyed **Brothers**
be sure to check out the other books
in the Immanu'El series:

The Carpenter
Yosef doesn't really believe in God, but his unbelief is shaken when God chooses him for the most important parenting job in history.

The Voice
Yochanan knows that he's special: an angel announced his miraculous birth and ordained him for greatness. So why does God seem determined to crush him?

Beloved Disciple
Yuannan is a fisherman and the son of fishermen, but he dreams of a destiny far beyond the shores of Lake Gennesaret. Then a radical teacher enters his life, and his dream turns into a nightmare.

Immanu'El is a series of novels told from the perspective of those who walked with Jesus along the dirt roads of Galilee two thousand years ago. To keep abreast of new books and see what goes on in the mind of the writer between those marathon novelizing sessions, visit my blog "DeeTween the Lines" at http://DLMaynardNovels.blogspot.com.

Made in the USA
San Bernardino, CA
11 January 2014